# MUSINGS

## *of the*

# MUSES

An Anthology Edited by
Heather and S.D. Vassallo

# MUSINGS
## *of the*
# MUSES

Brigids Gate™
PRESS

Edited by Heather Vassallo and S.D. Vassallo.

Cover illustration and design by Elizabeth Leggett.
www.archwayportico.com

First Edition: April 2022

ISBN (paperback): 978-1-957537-03-0
ISBN (Kindle ebook): 978-1-957537-02-3
Library of Congress Control Number: 2022936167

BRIGIDS GATE PRESS
Bucyrus, Kansas
www.brigidsgatepress.com

Printed in the United States of America

*This anthology is dedicated to all the women who have been told they are:*

*Too loud.*
*Unladylike.*
*Not a "real woman."*
*Unnatural.*
*Monstrous.*
*Selfish.*
*Too aggressive.*
*Too sexual.*
*Frigid.*
*Unworthy.*
*Unlovable.*

*You are enough. Exactly as you are.*

*Sing on, sisters, sing on.*

Content warnings are provided at the end of this book.

# Contents

# ACKNOWLEDGEMENTS

Thank you to the following:

Elle Turpitt for her careful and thoughtful proofreading.

Tracy Fahey, for the powerful introduction she wrote for this anthology.

The Gang—Kim, Max, Laurie, Cindy, and Steph—for all their support and encouragement. You guys rock!

Eric J. Guignard, whose advice and tips were invaluable.

The authors who submitted stories and poems to this anthology.

To all of you, the readers, who grabbed a copy of this book.

And thanks to C.J., wherever your journeys have taken you.

# FOREWORD

## BY HEATHER VASSALLO

In the old stories, the ones told by old men with long beards around the roaring fires, they speak of a woman on the run, escaping the unwanted advances of a man, only to die, and the hero's failed attempt to rescue her. But listen to the whispers on the wind, long after the embers have been banked and the old men, full of wine, sleep the sleep of well-sated beasts. The wind brings the voices of women. Their murmurs slice through the night. If you listen you can hear them. Thousands of years of prayers whispered over sick children. Lullabies crooned long after most have slipped into the land of Morpheus. The giggles of girls as they romp through the meadows and play in the sun speckled forests. The moans of women bringing life into the world. The spells breathed into stews and weaves. The sighs of passion well spent. The mournful tears of widows as they bury their partner's armor. If you listen closely enough, the not so silent cries of suffering, of pain so great it cannot be contained within the stories of men. In these whispers you will hear the truth. And rediscover what you've always secretly known.

Heather V.
Kansas
March 2022

# INTRODUCTION

## BY TRACY FAHEY

'For women, the boundaries of acceptability are strict and they are many. We must be seductive but pure, quiet but not aloof, fragile but industrious, and always, always small. We must not be too successful, too ambitious, too independent, too self-centered—and when we can't manage all the contradictory restrictions, we are turned into grotesques. Women have been monsters, and monsters have been women, in centuries worth of stories, because stories are a way to encode these expectations and pass them on'

(Jess Zimmerman (2021) Women And Other Monsters; Building A New Mythology)

*Musings of the Muses* is a formidable book; an epic, sprawling collection of sixty-five stories and poems that rewrite the Greek myths, lending the female figures of these stories new and powerful voices. Like Greek temple plinths in their original state; the results are brightly coloured, vivid, striking. This collection is a treasury of work, assembled by Heather and S.D. Vassallo. Rich and intriguing, these revisionist takes on the Greek myths are also *important*. They re-inscribe women at the heart and center of stories. They are fierce and unapologetic. They right old wrongs.

They are important, because folklore is important. Because myths are important.

One of the great writers on folklore, Alan Dundes in his *Folklore Matters* (1989) refers to ideas of folklore as a *living entity*. Folklore is something that bonds us together—it's a series of shared cultural memories that enshrine rites, stories and rituals which hold a special and specific meaning for a community of origin, preserved through collective memory. It is bound up in rites, observances, re-enactments and retellings. Most pertinently here, folklore tells us about the world around us, our place in it, and warns us about the consequences of transgressing the borders.

Myths are a vital part of this folklore. They form an overarching master-narrative of a community of belief. The Greek myths represent a hierarchy of power, topped by Zeus, the chief Greek deity; father of the gods, ruler of Olympus and all beyond it, Zeus embodies many of the negative qualities of the male figures in Greek mythology; murderous, rapacious, cruel. The patriarchal standpoint of the Greek myths stripped female figures of their agency, rendering them mute or passive. Complicit in this were those who wrote down these myths, a succession of male writers; Hesiod and Homer, and later, the Roman poets Ovid and Virgil. But the myths they wrote of were older than they, deriving from an oral culture that would have reflected a different reality to how these writers interpreted it.

In his ground-breaking work, *The White Goddess* of 1948, Robert Graves' central thesis on reclaiming this reality is explained by Gevel Lindop in the editorial preface;

> The book's argument is that in late prehistoric times, throughout Europe and the Middle East, matriarchal cultures, worshipping a supreme Goddess and recognizing male gods only as her son, consort or sacrificial victim, were subordinated by aggressive proponents of patriarchy who deposed women from their positions of authority, elevated the Goddess's male consorts into positions of divine supremacy and reconstructed myths and rituals to conceal what had taken place.

*The White Goddess* is a revolutionary book. Graves wanted to re-inscribe women as powerful figures; to write them back into mythology as emblems of the Divine Feminine. He goes back further than the earliest written sources to behold the Triple Goddess, and the original matriarchal cultures that enshrined images of powerful women. His research reveals women at the heart of—not only stories—but at the heart of power itself. Within this matriarchal culture, women held sovereignty. They shaped the landscape, they chose kings.

Over the last ten years, we've witnessed different feminist revisions of the Greek myths that continue this tradition established by Graves, and an examination of their central female characters. Margaret Atwood's *The Penelopiad* (2005) re-wrote the idea of the hero's journey from a female perspective. Madelaine Miller's astonishing *Circe* (2018) gave us an entirely new vantage point on the famous witch of the Odyssey.

And *Musings of the Muses* performs the same function. It opens myriad apertures into the Greek myths and allows us—the readers—to re-experience them from the previously non-dominant viewpoints of the female characters. And it does so in many different ways.

This intelligent and thought-provoking collection challenges our very conception of the term 'muse'; playing with a set of meanings. It is about 'musing'—a deep reflection and reconsideration. It's about 'muses,' both as poets and goddesses, but this collection resists the familiar patriarchal construction of the term (woman as passive inspiration), but instead widens out the familiar world of the Greek myths to repopulate this set of folkloric stories with unforgettable, angry, courageous, fearless women.

Why is this important?

It's a necessary act.

As a child, I loved the Greek and Roman myths. Every type of myth, to be honest. I read the children's versions of the Irish sagas, the *Táin Bó Cuailgne*, *An Toraíocht Diarmaid Agus Gráinne*. From further afield, I read the *Ramayana* and Graves' *Myths of the Norsemen*. But in reading many of these, my unconscious child-brain amassed the idea that the hero was essentially *male*; that the hero's journey was fundamentally about a superhuman man forging his way in the world. Women were side characters at best; at worst they were teachable moments about the perils of life. They were silenced, assaulted, murdered.

And that's why, when I opened *Musing Of The Muses*, my heart soared. Here were the women I'd only half-glimpsed in Greek myths, now vividly recreated and revoiced. The book divides into sections; *Monsters, Mortals, Goddesses*, each one brimming with fascinating sub-sections; stories explored in a variety of forms—short fiction, poems of all types, even short plays.

Opening with Hailey Piper's 'One Thousand Nights for Beloved Medusa', a transfixing rewriting of Medusa that encapsulates rage and pain and love ('Only through that darkness has she come to know there is no monster here, but a woman in pain who for the most part wanted to be left alone.') and closing with a *lagniappe*, a little bonus—'As Long as There's One' by M.M. Schreier) that takes the world of Greek myths into the portal of Welsh mythology, this is a vast collection that can be dipped into, savored, or simply read, as I did, cover-to-cover.

*Musings of the Muses* is best read with a side-order of Greek myths, or a reliable dictionary of mythology, simply to appreciate how long and hard these authors have thought about alternative ways to tell familiar stories. This band of predominantly female and female-identifying writers (though I was also glad to see male writers joining the chorus celebrating the women of the stories) have thought long and hard about the original tales before carefully recrafting them in many different guises. I'd love to write something on each, but alas!—an introduction is an introduction, not a set of story notes—so what follows is an overview, a signpost to some of the compelling themes and treatments in this collection.

Some of these pieces are relatively straight but hauntingly beautiful retellings, like 'Songbird' by Romy Tara Wenzel—'I part my lips and sing up the bones of our grief,' Wenzel writes of the Sirens. 'We reflect a triangle over the still water, a white hot arrow burning with love. Love, the other side of grief. Combined, they form a new musical key, a key that will cast sailors to their doom, that will wreck ships, that will send mortals into madness. This is the voice of grief, and I swear to defend it with my life.'

Sometimes the twists are entirely unexpected, as in the two revisionist takes on the story of Orpheus and Eurydice; which both subvert the notion of 'rescue'—'Possession' by Elle Turpitt, and 'And Eurydice' by Louis Evans ('Once there was a poet, and his woman. This poet went down into the underworld to reclaim his stolen property. And he never, ever, returned. And the woman? Well. Hers is another story.')

There is a sinister poetry that runs through this epic volume, through the prose as well as the poetry. But given that the original Greek myths most often exist in verse, a special mention for the poets whose work is collected here. It was a special thrill to see works by prose writers like Stephanie Ellis and Alyson Faye (how talented are this duo?). There's also a succession of beautiful moments in poems; Alison Jennings's 'Sapphic Fragments' ('Again love, the limb-loosener, rattles me/ As a wind in the mountains/assaults an oak'), Kate Meyer-Currey's 'Move Through Darkness (Hecate Speaks) ( 'I hold dominion over darkness:/my supplicants are witches and /ghosts; the message-bearers/between living and dead') and Mari Ness's 'Ursa Major' (You breathe in starlight /as you dance, claws/ sharpened on the moon./You won't give him this.')

There's a darkness in this writing, born of the responsibility of setting injustice to rights. But there's also some flashes of fun. 'Beauty is in the Bearer of the Apple' by Erin Sweet Al-Mehairi reimagines Olympus, Kardashian-style. 'Respectfully Yours, Bridezilla' by T.L. Beeding, a defense of Hera, brilliantly uses the modern concept of a 'bridezilla' to mount a forthright defense of the beleaguered wife's reactions to Zeus' many infidelities.

There are also many dialogues that sparkle on the page; from the fascinating 'Helen/Hermione' by Rose Biggin, to 'Lover's Quarrel' by Georgia Cook on Charybdis and Scylla. ('Is there no worse fate? What else is love contained but sorrow? Love compounded, love forced under the pressure of a thousand lifetimes. What else is love in isolation? Bubbling and burning, spilling over the edges. What else is love, left to rise like snatching fingers to the storm-grey skies?')

Of particular interest (and sadly, of particular relevance, as I type this in

February of 2022) is the compelling 'Izzy and Anti: A Tragedy in Texts' by Deborah Markus, an epic told in text form:

'oh they'll be patrolling
in helicopters

                                                    wait WHAT

it's already started
hasn't made the news yet but
you'll see it soon enough
they're shooting us like they're
hunting wolves'

*Musings of the Muses* also utilizes unusual vantage points in the stories, as in 'Three Fathers' by Gordon Grice, a tale of Medea that poignantly foreshadows her later, terrible sacrifice. "'I saw myself floating across with the ferry man," she said, and her voice became languorous. "He had a black horse aboard. He fondled its ears and whispered to it. I could almost hear what he said. And lying with me, nestled beneath each arm was a child—our children, Jason, sons we have yet to meet. They slept uneasily, tossing in their dreams, murmuring about the wrongs I'd done. The coins fell from their little eyes. I kept trying to find the coins. I kept trying to make everything right."'

For me, some of the most haunting parts of this book lay in re-imaginings of the stories that were set in either the present, or a strange netherworld. A stand-out here is 'Laborers Wanted' by S.J. Townend; an uncanny and unsettling tale of a Lamia factory that manufactures 'reborns'. The result is a confident and successful translation of ancient myth into modern day magical realism.

So how to best describe this collection? I'll borrow from a quote from a tale of Arachne ('Requiescat' by M. Regan) describing the work of the Cursed. 'There is a pattern to her work, and it is obscene, grotesque. It is complicated and beautiful.'

These works in *Musings of the Muses* are harrowing, strange. They are a Greek chorus peopled by tragic and relatable women. Reading it is like the ultimate unboxing of Pandora's Box; here are all the misfortunes, but also, fluttering inside, Hope. For these accounts are also heroes' journeys into dark and fearful lands, where the women emerge bloody and triumphant.

They are complicated.
And they are beautiful.


*A post-script:*

A final note. The collection ends with a tantalizing glimpse into another realm of Celtic mythology as the old goddesses repudiate Greek God colonizers. My hope is that this story is prescient and that Brigid's Gate continues to act as a true gateway to the rich world of revisionist tales, tackling more and more mythologies, reinterpreting them in ways that celebrate the women within.

# PRELUDE

# THE OFFERING

## BY CALLIE S. BLACKSTONE

You have journeyed all this way, miles
and miles and years and years
to embody this moment.

The statue is crumbling. Her visage
is a mere mockery of what she once
was. Now, she is neglected—
the base of the thing is cracked,
water has softened it over the years.

You wonder how she is still standing.
You suffocate on the smells of the place,
the neglect, the mold, the debris.
No sun or living creature has been here
for a long time.

You ask her permission,
you approach with reverence,
you keep your gaze lowered.

You place your hands on the statue
and breathe in. Words come out
spontaneously, out of control, your
prayers line this place. You plead,
you grovel, your words drum up energy
that expands in the room.

The bowl on the altar is like everything here—
it is cracked. You kneel before it, honor her,
honor the fact that she was once
something more than cracked stone,
cracked glass.

You pour the water in the bowl,
water that has been blessed

by the cycles of the moon.

You leave offerings at her feet,
poetry that was written in her honor
thousands of years ago, incense,
flowers. Food items that are native
to her land, food items that are expensive
in your own land. Bottles of mead,
tins of caviar. *Please please*

*please.* You have the audacity
to gaze into her eyes
for several moments, waiting
for something, some kind of response.
Movement. Any kind of answer.

You get up and slowly
begin to leave. You turn,
you walk,

you hear something behind you.
But you know the stories of the old
days too well. It is not wise to turn and look
on something ancient that lives underground.

The sound grows, your steps grow quicker,
you jolt up the stairs, filled with terror.
You are blinded by sunlight.
The taste of *please* lines your mouth
for weeks months years

# MONSTERS

# MEDUSA

# ONE THOUSAND NIGHTS FOR BELOVED MEDUSA

## BY HAILEY PIPER

A scream splits the night.

Meropi has never heard anything like it all in the nights she's wandered the gorgon sisters' temple. Past sunset is the only time she can walk safely without her blindfold, but the illusion of safety dies with that scream. She runs through the temple's pitch-black maze, toward the sound of men's cheers, but she arrives too late.

Darkness gives way to Medusa's bedchamber torches, their firelight reflecting on blood-slick stone and reptilian scales. Her body lies cold and abandoned, her silk robe and bedsheets stained crimson. And her head—where is it?

Meropi covers her mouth against a shriek and retreats into the dark halls. A maze of forking twists and turns fills the temple. It's easy to get so lost that she isn't sure where or when she'll find torchlight again.

Just when she thinks she's reached the other gorgons' chambers to tell them what's happened, the temple drives her toward the invading men, to minutes earlier when they were still creeping toward Medusa's bed. The darkness goads Meropi into thinking she'll stop them this time if she raises her dagger. Murder will prevent murder.

She's too late; she'll always be too late. Another scream splits the night, men cheer, and blood slickens the temple's stone floor. Medusa is dead again.

Meropi lowers her dagger and flinches back into the halls.

Their darkness has been familiar ever since she arrived many months ago. Hard earth battered her feet when she first crossed the winding garden toward the temple, an unseemly ruin of marble pillars and crude edifices carved into the face of a toothy mountain. Statues of warriors stood frozen between olive trees and patches of yellow grass, their expressions immortalized in disgust and terror.

They should have warned Meropi to turn back, but a crimson rag flailed in the wind, tied around the end of one statue's sword. She took it for an invitation.

"Wear the blindfold and enter," a voice said, crackling from the temple's dark mouth.

"Why?" Meropi asked, but she tied the rag around her eyes as instructed.

"Long ago, I was Athena's priestess, before that predator Poseidon laid eyes on me," the voice said. "Proud Athena cursed me that I might become a gorgon, my skin turned to scales, my hair to snakes, my eyes and ugliness turning men to stone. Yet cover your eyes, and you'll be safe to enter."

The foolish goddess of wisdom couldn't have guessed that her "curse" had instead blessed Medusa with sisters and protection.

All for naught. Athena has realized her mistake and sent the mighty Perseus to undo it.

At the next scream—has that been three or thirteen now?—Meropi lingers just outside torchlight, where she watches the hero and his men. He has no poet among his group, never thinks to bring one. The only present tongue loquacious enough to boast about him is his own.

"Behold, the hero Perseus!" he declares, and Meropi shuts her eyes against the snake-haired head he thrusts into the air. "The chosen son of Zeus, with my blessed sword, sneaking helm, polished shield, and winged sandals, I have conquered the beastly Medusa!"

The men cheer again; it's all they're good for. It's the only reason he brings them, but their presence shows him for what he really is. Only a coward would carry so many divine gifts and yet still need an entourage to help him murder a sleeping woman.

The clamor rouses Medusa's sisters, but they have no better luck stopping the murder than Meropi.

She drifts back into darkness and follows further screams. Sometimes she catches Perseus before he flees. Once, she even kills him. Neither sharp dagger nor petrifying glare will bring Medusa back from the dead.

Only the temple's dark maze resurrects her, and only to kill her again. No labyrinth in Crete could ever be so unknowable and unforgiving.

Sometimes, there is no scream. Instead, Meropi hears a man's voice with an odd accent. When she peers at him from around a corner, she finds him wearing strange clothes and a band around his forehead, where a light shines across his audience. He is a storyteller, and these families listen. Some have gray hair and hold rectangles full of strange writing; others are children, their faces focused on glowing stones.

"This temple has a fascinating history," the storyteller says. "According to legend, the heroic demi-god Perseus sought out the monster Medusa here. After a great battle, he lopped off the monster's head and escaped before her fellow gorgons could catch him."

The storyteller never mentions Meropi, and why should he? What has she ever done? She's a forgettable wanderer who by chance stumbled past wastelands and beasts to the gorgons' isolated temple.

Once, one of the children looks up from their glowing stone, locks eyes with Meropi, and points at her dark corner.

"Someone's there," the child says.

Meropi slips back into the temple halls before any others glance her way.

"These ancient ruins are full of ghosts," the storyteller says, laughing at the child. "No one ever knows what will come out of the dark." And then his story carries on. Always the same ending, where brave Perseus battles the monstrous Medusa to her death.

But if Medusa has always been a monster, why not let Meropi see Athena's handiwork and turn to stone? Why offer the rag to shield Meropi's eyes? Why bandage her travel-worn feet and feed her needy stomach?

"The gods demand a host aids every visitor," Meropi said then. "But you're the first to help me in fifty-six days; I've counted. You must be quite pious."

"I do nothing for the gods," Medusa said. "But I've been a lone woman who wandered wastelands until she found this sanctuary. It can be your sanctuary, too. Those men outside found no such succor."

"I saw their statutes. You're an incredible sculptor."

That made Medusa laugh, a raucous thunder through the temple, as if she hadn't laughed in ages.

She was wrong; the temple was not Meropi's sanctuary. It became her home. She learned to walk its halls without seeing, and Medusa helped her to memorize the inner twists and turns and the statues' placement in the garden. Whenever warriors or heroes stormed the temple grounds, new statues grew in their place.

Medusa once offered to move them. "To simplify your strolling," she said.

Meropi laughed then. "I'm blindfolded, not helpless."

She has spent most waking hours here laughing, she realizes, more than in her entire life before. If any god has sense at all, it is Aphrodite for leading Meropi to this sanctified place.

But now there is no laughter, only a thousandth scream that splits the night. Men cheer, boast, and then flee Medusa's furious sisters. Nothing changes.

This time when they're gone again, Meropi kneels beside Medusa's body and kisses her scaly hands, chest, and neck. Her lips taste acrid gorgon blood. It's her last sensation of love before she wanders back into the dark temple to do it all again, trapped in the hands of some god of time whose name she doesn't know.

The night replays over and over, an uncreative storyteller who only knows the same bitter ending.

Still tasting her lover's blood, Meropi stumbles into torchlight again, but this time there's no scream, no murder, no Perseus. Instead, on the far side of the room stands another Meropi. She's a near identical copy, worn ragged from staggering through this endless night. How long has it been, six hours or six hundred?

The only difference between them is that the other Meropi can't see her double and not because of any red rag wrapped around her head. Wet stains run down her cheeks from two darkened eyes. It's as if the sight of Medusa's body will, after enough repeats, drive Meropi to cut sight itself from her head.

"Medusa?" this other Meropi asks. She can't know that her double stands across the room. For her, torchlight and darkness are one.

A chill runs through Meropi's skin, and she turns to flee from her wounded mirror. Her cheeks are wet, but not from blood. She isn't sure how much more of this she can take. What will she find when she sees the flicker of torches again? Storyteller, mirror image, or Perseus? If the temple's darkness is likewise a storyteller, its light knows only tales of terror and pain.

The story of time has become lost in this darkness, Meropi realizes, just like herself. Every retelling brings death, yes, but no one ever knows what will come out of the dark, do they? That torchlight is the trouble, always deciding how the darkness ends, bringing Medusa's death into merciless light.

And if there is no light?

When Meropi first arrived, she wrapped her eyes in Medusa's blindfold without pause. Only through that darkness has she come to know there is no monster here, but a woman in pain who for the most part wanted to be left alone. And she has come to adore that woman. Love is blind, some say, but the gods did not arrange a blind woman to find the temple. Meropi found this place. She chose darkness.

She looks down at her dagger, its blade dry with a hero's blood from one turn or another. Eons ago, and yet all in the same night. So long as she can find torchlight to tell the story's tragic finish, then the world is not dark enough for happiness.

She turns the dagger, aims its point at her eyes, and chooses darkness again.

Her screams are new to the temple.

When that work is done, the maze looks no different, but now she thinks she understands it better. Darkness is all it has known. She stumbles at first and then finds her stride.

A scream splits the night, but this time when Meropi gets too close, she doesn't have to see what follows. Soon she hears whispers and footsteps at the moment before they'll crescendo into a death scream. She can't tell where they are; there is no torchlight anymore. The maze looks no different than a murder in a bedchamber.

Now she hears Perseus whisper orders to his men, as if they've first arrived. And then she hears them wonder if this is the right temple. Her dagger bled him once when she could see him, but that was then, and now she's not confident she can stop him alone. The darkness will help her. She's wandered it so long that it's becoming her friend.

The storyteller's voice beckons her around another corner. "This temple has a fascinating history. According to legend, the heroic demi-god Perseus sought out the monster Medusa here. However, the night he came to slay the beast, his men abandoned him, and—"

Meropi takes another turn, and the voice fades. This story has been told and retold, but Perseus always wins. No matter its new twists, she doesn't want to hear it again. She has to find what will come out of the darkness herself.

Someone stands in front of her. They don't speak, but their breath is harsh and tired. This might be the moment she met herself, now on the far side of the room with darkened eyes, but no one ever knows what will come out of the dark. It could be anyone.

"Medusa?" she asks, hopeful.

"No," says a familiar voice. "You stand in the presence of the hero Perseus."

He has no poet among his group, could never convince one to join them, but now he seems to have no group at all. The storyteller must have been right; the hero's men have abandoned him.

"Do you know where to find the monster here?" Perseus asks.

"I've wandered these halls for what feels like forever," Meropi says, her voice sullen. "I always seem to find a monster."

"If you'll lead me to it, the gods will smile on you." Perseus sucks in breath as if to puff out his chest. "I am the son of kingly Zeus, blessed by wise Athena, aided by—"

Meropi shushes him and leads away. He follows, still boasting, but now in whispers. He never asks about his men or wonders aloud why blood paints Meropi's cheeks beneath darkened eyes. His sole interest is himself.

A desperate piece of Meropi's heart wishes they might stumble upon him as a boy here in the temple halls. She would like to speak to that child and tell him the truth about monsters and gods. He should never have come to the temple at all.

But she and Perseus are alike in that they've stepped inside these halls as outsiders, and there is no dissuading either of them from finding the temple, at least not from the inside. The maze has ensured their fates have crossed and cannot uncross.

She guides him down its twists and turns. While there are moments when she clutches her dagger and would like nothing more than to drive it through his proud heart, that will only stop him once. She must stop him forever, within every corner of the maze. Its darkness is her friend now. She only has to feed it.

When she feels Perseus is striding with brisk steps, she presses herself against cold stone and lets him pass her by. He walks several paces, still boasting in whisper, before he realizes he's now at the lead.

"Woman?" he calls. "Woman, where've you gone?" He wanders, calling for someone whose name he doesn't know.

She creeps several paces behind him for a time, letting him believe he's alone again until he freezes where torches roar. Someone stands ahead of him. The stranger's breath is heavy. He, too, has been wasting it boasting about himself.

Perseus meets Perseus, coward to coward.

Their screams catch in their throats, and both men flee from one another. Meropi feels one Perseus dodge past her. She can't see him in the dark, and he doesn't seem to notice her. She doesn't follow, but she wanders the maze a bit longer and listens down the halls.

Perseus meets yet another Perseus. Each of them meet two more, and four beyond that. Their fear ripples through the maze's every possibility, where no sneaking helm can hide them, and soon the dark tells a new story about the coward who sees his own face and runs. He spends much of his time in his glory-filled head. To see himself from the outside is to see no hero or demi-god, just a man sneaking through the night to murder a sleeping woman.

Nothing special at all.

At long last, Meropi leaves the maze and heads for the bedchambers. A thousand years might have passed in darkness since she first entered the halls tonight; she can't know.

She finds a familiar doorway where too many times she's seen blood-stained bedsheets. Now she sees nothing, but listens to soft, slow breath. The nightmare should be over as if it's never begun. She should be able to step into this chamber, press herself against warm scales, and be covered in forked tongue kisses. Icy uncertainty snakes up her spine. She licks lips that have tasted gorgon blood.

"Medusa?" Meropi calls, voice quavering.

Breath goes silent, as if now it isn't a scream that splits the night, but a name, and to call out for love is to cast it away.

But then she hears hissing hair and a high-pitched, stretching yawn. Meropi's heart thunders against her ribs. She rushes to the bed and holds Medusa tight. She isn't sure if it's blood on her cheeks now or tears. Snake hair kisses her, and warmth ripples through reptilian scales.

"Beloved, where's your blindfold?" Medusa asks, her body tensing.

"I don't need a blindfold anymore," Meropi says.

"And your eyes, my love?" Medusa asks.

"I don't need eyes anymore either."

Medusa places a hand to the side of Meropi's face. Maybe it's because of the countless deaths, or maybe it's because she's been waiting to know there's a future where she becomes whole, but either way, Medusa's touch has never felt so real.

# THE LAMENTATION OF MEDUSA

## BY STEPHANIE ELLIS

Weep for me, sisters,
lament my name with your keening,
wash away falsehoods,
centuries old,
told of the monstrous Medusa

Cry for me,
Poseidon's victim,

                    violated

memoried pain

                    erased

to leave only the Gorgon

                    unforgiven

Perseus murdered me,
cleaved my head,
with a reaper's sickle,
mere crop to be harvested,

to be used,
        always to be used,
without consent

Rage for me, mirrors of Eve,
for my serpent's crown,

blamed
shamed
condemned

stone carver of souls

Howl my name
with the force of the Furies
Hurl it as a spear

At the man who trespasses upon you
Spit it in the eye
Of the predator
Stab his heart
With our vengeance

Strip away my deformities
my madness
See me as I was,
before gods destroyed me,
young and beautiful,
a rose in bloom,

and weep for me

# THE GIRL FROM SARPEDON
## BY CHRISTINA SNG

We found her in the ruins of Sarpedon, a lost child with blind snakes for hair.

I almost missed her as I wove past mounds of debris, my eyes fixated on the dig site ahead.

A soft cacophony of short hisses caught my ear in a place where the only sound was the woosh of wind tunnels.

There, curled up in a pile of bones was a tiny child no more than two, her pale green eyes wide with terror at something behind us.

We turned to see what had frightened her so, but there was only the azure sky and fat cotton clouds puffing away in the wind.

I approached her slowly but she clenched her eyes tight to shut us out, softly singing a song in a language neither of us could decipher.

Up close, she was as spindly and thin as the bones she lay in, bald but for those small darting snakes flailing from her head.

To my surprise, she did not flinch when I gently wrapped my cloak around her and lifted her into my arms. Our eyes met and I felt an instant bond with this child, now clasped against my heart. I did not want to let her go. Me, the woman who swore she never cared for children.

Lulled by the comforting hum of the engine as we drove to the hospital, her body relaxed as she sighed and closed her eyes. The furrow between her brows relaxed. Soon, her breathing slowed and deepened, and she was fast asleep.

We reached the city in two hours. Limp in my arms like the rag doll I had clung to as a child, I carried her as we strode through the busy hospital amongst the well and the sick, my jacket covering her head like a hood.

At the entrance of the emergency department, a doctor racing to the ER collided with us, knocking my jacket askew. The snakes, suddenly exposed to the bright fluorescent lights, hissed loudly at everything.

"Medusa!" The hallways whispered in a rising crescendo.

Confronted with frightened and angry stares, we raced back to the Jeep, the crescendoing whispers following us as we drove as fast as we could out of the city.

In the desolation of our dig site, we raised her, the girl we named Persephone, for her unusual origin and her new life as our daughter.

Persephone was a quiet child, perhaps quelled by the active snakes in her hair that often pulled her in all directions at the same time.

The dig site fascinated her. She spent hours watching us work, trying to uncover more of Sarpedon's ancient secrets. She would sketch in the countless notebooks I gave her. In every drawing, there were always snakes.

At night, I held her in my arms while she clung to me as if she were drowning in her dreams. What did she dream about, I'd ask her in the morning, but she never remembered.

Over time, her snakes no longer attacked me in the dead of night while we slept and I finally found a deep comfort and peace sleeping beneath the stars beside this tiny girl I was growing to love.

When she was three, her first word to me was "Mama". I felt an unbridled burst of pure joy I'd never experienced before. My partner did not feel the same way.

He cornered me that evening and told me she was an abomination and should be returned to the bones. We had awakened angry gods and we would pay.

I retorted that our kindness would not be repaid with cruelty. The gods were not so unjust and spiteful. He replied with great venom that I did not know them at all.

But I knew him. He was speaking of the loneliness he felt without such a bond with Persephone. The seclusion he experienced outside a work that no longer fulfilled him. This had less to do with Persephone than with his own ego and insecurity.

That night, he packed and left. I never saw him again.

Persephone persevered with me over the next five years. It was a hard life but we endured, completing my work eventually and bringing our time there to a close. I applied for formal adoption papers to bring her back to the United States.

One by one, I sedated her snakes. They did not seem to mind it this time for our long journey home, almost as if they knew it was necessary. They lay docile as I gently injected each one, without a trace of the violent thrashing and sharp, painful bites I endured during the many trial runs we had, trying to determine the correct dosage. They slept like angels throughout the entire flight beneath her thick parka hood, each curled up in a coil.

Persephone was fascinated by my cabin home in the middle of the forest. She loved the lush grass and the tall trees she climbed in a flourish. A spotted fawn that often wandered into our garden to eat my lettuce became her best friend. Her snakes cooed over the warm furry mammal, nipping the fawn only once, very gently. To everyone's relief, it still returned.

Each morning, Persephone helped me tend the garden and spent her afternoons wandering the forest with the fawn before returning at nightfall for dinner, often with berries for supper. We had a wonderful, peaceful life and it felt like she had finally found her place here with me in the world.

When she turned twelve, she changed, almost overnight. Perhaps it was puberty or the changing colors of her snakes from light green to emerald blue, signaling a new stage of maturation. Their tongues grew long and forked, and their fangs dripped a clear venom that I tested to be a paralytic.

Persephone became restless and yearned to be among children her own age. I knew it was dangerous and would likely cause much suffering and possibly even death. But how could I stop her? She no longer listened to my instructions, whether given with love and patience or with anger and threats.

I bought her a thicker parka with a hood that tightened around her face. That might contain the snakes, but they still revealed their presence by flailing in the hood. So I sedated them for each trip we made to the city for supplies.

Persephone was delighted by the stone buildings and fast cars. We spent hours at the mall where she imitated the postures and gestures of teenage girls and bought her first dress and lipstick.

She pestered me about letting her go to school.

"How could that happen?" I asked her. "Would your snakes happily sleep all day?"

"Yes," she replied adamantly. "They will listen to me. They can come out at night to play."

"Please," I begged her. "Give it a year. Let's try it when you are thirteen. We need to get the snakes used to being sedated every day, you need to learn how to behave like a teenager, and I need to get you up to speed with the curriculum."

She acquiesced after I agreed to buy a satellite dish and television. Day after day, the snakes slept, and wreaked havoc at night, furious with her watching television and studying all day instead of taking them out to the forest for walks.

Persephone proved to be an immensely keen learner and absorbed everything I taught her like a sponge. When her placement test results returned, she was thrilled to find she had passed with flying colors.

Then January the 1st rolled around and my little girl began high school. She wore a colorful bandana around her head with a long blonde wig beneath to hide the snakes. In a pink blouse and blue jeans, she looked just like any other high school girl. I was so proud to see her walk to her first class, beaming.

To my surprise, she made fast friends with a girl named Eloise and her brother, Julian. They hung out at the diner after school and talked about the things high school kids talked about.

I did not know how Persephone pulled it off, but between telling others the big secret that she was in remission for brain cancer, which explained why she wore a wig, to sitting out sports classes for medical reasons, she did.

And naturally, as teenagers do, Persephone and Julian fell in love in their sixteenth year. They held hands and kissed chastely on the cheeks. He gave her a shiny gold ring with a princess crown and a trio of diamantés for their first-year anniversary. They wrote 'I love you' notes to each other every day. How that boy adored her and how she adored him back.

Listening to her gush about him transported me back to my high school days when everything was good and sweet.

But her snakes had other plans.

I could see their eyes begin to flutter. Their gaze seemed to sharpen whenever they looked at me. Their blindness was lifting and soon they would see.

Now, I knew the Medusa myth was just that—a myth. But what could explain these snakes on my daughter's head, growing like hair, soon too long and thick to be hidden beneath a bandana or hoodie?

I told Persephone we had to return to the cabin. We needed more time to search for another solution as her snakes would soon be too large to be hidden. I told her about Medusa but she brushed it off as some ancient myth.

"Then why do you have snakes on your head, Persephone?" I asked softly.

She broke down and wept. She wanted them gone, she said. Surely there was a way.

But I'd tried, I confessed. When she was five, I had brought her to an old scientist friend of mine whom I trusted with my life. He scanned her head and discovered that the snakes were intertwined with her brain. There was no removing them without killing her.

Persephone cried all night, ignoring the thrashing of her snakes against her head. I held her till dawn broke and she finally fell asleep.

When she woke, we were on the highway, en route back to the cabin.

"No!" she screamed and hurled herself out of the car. She ran through traffic, the snakes darting about angrily as her loosely tied scarf flew away.

Behind her, a ten-car pileup stopped traffic. I veered to the shoulder and raced out of the car, trying to keep pace with her. Each car she passed slammed to a screeching halt.

Then I stopped, breathless, to see. The drivers and passengers had all turned to stone.

"Persephone!" I cried at the top of my voice.

She heard me and turned, each snake facing me, their eyes wide open now and staring.

"I am sorry, Mama! I love you!" she screamed before vanishing between the car wrecks and the statues of stone.

I stood there, stunned. Why hadn't I turned to stone? Was it an immunity I developed from all the bites her snakes had given me over the years? Could it be her love for me? I never knew. I just stood there screaming her name till my well of tears dried up.

News reports spread of a Medusa wandering the world. City by city, everything living turned to stone. Soon, there were no more reports and no more people.

There was nowhere for me to go but home.

The fawn had grown, waiting patiently each day by the cottage for her return.

Numbly, I tended the vegetable garden as it kept me company, nibbling on lettuce and looking on sympathetically while I rained the crops with my tears.

One warm winter's day, Persephone came home, pale and exhausted, carrying in her arms a two-year-old girl with blind snakes for hair.

I cried out her name and raced to embrace her.

Persephone collapsed in my arms. She never let go of the child, who was beginning to stir from her sleep.

They were both gravely thin, gaunt and almost skeletal. How she managed to carry that child all this way was beyond me. But Persephone had the power to do impossible things. This was nothing to her.

We held each other till one of the little girl's snakes bit me, a sensation all too familiar. Immediately, Persephone's snakes turned to hiss at it. It retreated and coiled.

"Is she..." I began.

Persephone's eyes lit, shining with joy and excitement.

"Mama, this is Medusa. I found her in Sarpedon."

# GREEK TRAGEDIES

## BY KENZIE LAPPIN

*"She was once most beautiful, and the jealous aspiration of many suitors… They say that
Neptune, lord of the seas, violated her in the temple of Minerva.
So that it [the rape] might not go unpunished, she changed the Gorgon's hair to foul snakes."*
                                                                    Ovid's Metamorphoses
                                                    *a story Perseus (Medusa's murderer) tells at a party*

A woman stalked through the night.

It's not often that a woman is said to *stalk,* and definitely not at night.
Night is the time when most creatures sleep. They fear the dark, and more
importantly, what it conceals. They don't *stalk.*

But this woman was progressing in a way that could only be described as
*stalking.* She had skin the color of copper, but if one were to look closer, they
may have realized, with some discomfort, that she was approaching the color
of *old* copper, hints of green creeping up and around her legs like she was
slowly being oxidized.

But this was not noticed under the cover of night, of course. Street
shadows tend to only show the barest things: the hint of a leg, the quirk of an
alluring smile. In the shadows, no one would see the otherworldliness of this
woman until it was too late.

This was fatal for some.

This copper woman had an expensive-looking dress on, green and long-
sleeved but short on the thighs. She had a stripe of red lipstick across her
mouth, and odd accessories: a pair of sunglasses, incongruous with the night
sky, a pale green scarf wrapped around her hair, and a designer leather purse.

Rough hands reached out of the shadows and yanked her to join them,
pressing her against a wall just out of the lamplight. Behind the hands, a man
growled with delight. The woman did not scream. Men so often are unaware
of the difference between *walking* at night and *stalking* at night.

Those red-smeared lips smiled, and her copper hands reached for her
sunglasses.

***

This is the story of Medusa, who was raped by the god Poseidon. And
the story of how Athena, jealous of the turn of the god's affections (what

43

affection, the weeping victim wants to know?), cursed her to live as a hideous beast.

So, Medusa lives with her hair of serpents and her eyes hard, cursed to turn anyone who looks at her to stone. She is an angry woman, bitter at the world, and she kills indiscriminately.

And this is the story of how Perseus, on his grand quest, goes *snickety-snack,* chops off her head and Medusa's great hair of snakes is no more, and her lovely eyes are bound behind a blindfold until Perseus deems them useful again. And Perseus, glad of his quest, leaves Medusa's rotting body behind in the cave while he takes her dead head to do great deeds.

And the story of how that story, as so many are, is wrong.

The end of it, anyway.

Because rebirth is an important part of any myth, isn't it? Even for monsters.

"You're late," said Lamia, bustling by with a stack of letters. Craning her neck around, Medusa saw that many were colorfully lettered and drawn on, each addressed to them. Some had spindly words written in shaking hands, and some were written in careful letters of the inexperienced writer.

"Sorry," Medusa said, making sure that her sunglasses were firmly back on her nose. "I was delayed on the walk over." She smiled, crimson-stained lips against copper skin. "A man thought that perhaps I should return his affections. He was quite upset when I did not."

Delphyne looked up with interest. She was at her desk, curled around her computer monitor and snake-eyes only distracted from her work for a moment. "Is he upset *now?*" she rumbled.

"Oh, no," Medusa said. "I find it hard to imagine he feels *anything* anymore."

Lamia's mouth, when she smiled, was just this side of too-wide. "I suppose it's not the end of the world if you're late once in a while."

"Thanks," Medusa said.

While Medusa, with her copper-skin and gently grumbling snakes beneath her scarf, could easily pass as human, it was somewhat more difficult for her companions.

Delphyne was a large beast, and she and her tail took up most of their office. As it was told once, long long ago in the days of legend, Delphyne resembled a dragon, except that she had no wings around her giant green body and smelled of river-muck.

Lamia was a woman of pale skin, and her hair formed wild tangles about her head. She did not sleep, and Medusa had never seen her blink. She was entirely human from the waist up, with a serpent's tail coiled beneath her. In the old days, she hid them beneath long skirts when she went out in public. Nowadays, Lamia stayed far from crowds and children with their sticky fingers tugging at her hemline.

"We have work to do," Lamia said. "I just picked up the most recent batch of letters." With one deft hand, she splayed the pile of rainbow envelopes across the desk, so Medusa could see the hand-lettered addresses, each directed to *The Gorgon Initiative,* and most written in a child's hand.

"And I've got the most recent round of emails." Delphyne was a slow-moving creature, and rather than slink her way to the chairs of her colleagues, sent them with a ding to Medusa's laptop. "I've already vetted them for veracity."

"And I compiled the promising news reports," Medusa said, pulling them up on her laptop as well. She ran her tongue across her teeth, remembering the mouse she'd eaten that morning for breakfast. Beneath her scarf, her snakes hissed.

Ready, they said. We're ready.

"I'll take this one." Medusa snatched a letter scrawled in purple ink. "Feels lucky."

"Okay," Lamia said, surveying the emails and selecting one from them too with a click of the mouse. "I'll start with this one, then."

"I've got mine chosen," Delphyne said, and licked her mighty lips. "It's a good thing, too. I'm *hungry.*"

***

And this is the story of Delphyne, who slumbers, a great serpentine beast of many ages past. How she is likened to a dragon by those who see her, how she has a child who she loves, another great beast. How she did not cause the devastation to the land, but came because of it, to find a safe place to rest.

And the story of how Apollo, on his quest to build himself a temple, kills her at the riverside.

Such a great deed, was Apollo's slaughter.

After all, what right had Delphyne to try to live as she wished to live, to go unaccosted for the crime of simply existing as a hideous woman? He killed her while she slept, so monstrous was she.

Stories depend on who is telling them.

Do you see a pattern yet?

\*\*\*

Medusa double-checked the address on her letter. It wouldn't do to have the wrong house. That would simply be embarrassing.

It was correct. She'd read the letter on the Uber ride over, and was glad she'd chosen this one.

It would be a good night, she thought.

She tucked the letter into her purse and walked without hurry to the backside of the house, which wasn't protected by anything more than an unlocked latch on the unpainted back gate. There wasn't even a dog.

Sliding around the house, Medusa kicked off her heels, laid her expensive purse gently on top, and jumped, in one quick and inhumanly swift bound, up to hang on the window ledge. With a hand, she slid the sash open and stepped inside. One smooth copper leg with verdigris etchings after the other.

Inside there was a girl-child, staring at her with wide eyes from a small bed.

"Hello, child," Medusa told her, not bothering with a reassuring smile.

"Hello." The child peeped out, shy.

Medusa stepped closer to the bed, patterned with cartoon characters she did not care to recognize. "We got your letter," she said. "I understand there is a monster in your home?"


And this is the story of Lamia, who falls into the *great* honor of the affections of Zeus and is worse than cursed when Hera finds out. The story of Lamia, whose children are each killed and killed and killed. And Hera does not stop there— no, they never stop there— and Lamia is transformed into a beast. She turns into half a snake and unhinges her jaw and swallows up everyone else's children so that everyone else might feel the same as her.

Some myths say she does this punishment to herself. That Hera left her alone after killing her children, and the monstrousness was a making of Lamia's own creation. That her own wrath twisted her into this creature. Lamia prefers not to wonder which is true.

And Lamia does not die, but she never dreams. She plucks out her eyes each night before bed so that she may be spared the sight of her children dying again.

Lamia does not die, but she wishes she had.

And this story isn't true, either. Not all of it.

Greek myths are reborn. Monsters are too.

***

Medusa knew well the mark of a violent home, in spite of how well it had been hidden. She could smell it.

Sssmells like fear, said her snakes.

*Yes,* Medusa agreed.

The child walked behind her, quiet and pale as a ghost. She did not flinch at the point in the wall where a fist had clearly gone through it. She did not look at the carpeted floors, which had been vacuumed to spotlessness so many times that they were starting to bald beneath Medusa's bare feet. She did not seem to notice the other signs that Medusa did, so Medusa spared her the bit of kindness she possessed and did not point them out.

"Through there," the little girl whispered, pointing at the bedroom door down the hall. When she pointed, Medusa could see a red and purpling ring of bruises like fingerprints around her arm. Her snakes hissed, in displeasure and perhaps in anticipation.

Medusa smiled. "Would you like to watch?"

The girl looked startled, standing there small in her pink pajamas, a teddy bear trailed along. She had not been given many choices in her young life. After a moment, she nodded.

Medusa smiled again, blood-red lipstick, and pushed open the bedroom door.

"C'mon, Callie!" A man's voice called out almost immediately, angry, making the little girl and one other voice gasp in fear. The little girl lurked behind Medusa's statue legs. "I told you not to bother me while I'm sleeping! Go away!"

Medusa stepped inside.

"Oh, dear," she said. "I think there's been a misunderstanding." Gasps of surprise, from the man and the woman inside. "I'm here to kill you."

A man shot up from the covers, sleepy and wild-eyed and wearing a greasy white shirt.

"Wha— who are you!" It came out a shout— the kind of shout when bravado turns to real fear. Medusa tasted it on her tongue like a mouse trying to scamper away. Delectable.

"My name is Medusa," she said. A woman peeked her way out from the duvet cover. She looked like a stretched-out version of the little girl, blonde and wispy, eyes shadowed with dark circles and arms ringed in red handprints. "Callie's mother, would you like to come over here?"

And the woman scrambled her way out, ducking away from the grasping hands of the greasy man. She went to stand beside Medusa and her daughter, clutching the daughter tight to her side.

The man, too, lumbered out of bed, leaving crumpled bed-sheets behind in the darkened bedroom. He stood there, breathing, afraid, wearing a wrinkled tank-top and plaid boxers. For a moment, there was no sound or movement. The room was lit only by stripes of the streetlights that peeked through the blinds.

"You two may look if you wish," Medusa said. "So long as it is not at me."

*It'stimeit'stimeit'stime,* her snakes hissed, and Medusa glanced over at the little girl and her mother. The mother was shielding her daughter, pressing her face against her chest, and Medusa could not understand the feeling. She should have liked her daughters, if fortune had given her any, to see the doom of their captor. Still, the mother nodded at Medusa, firm and sure, and looked directly at the greasy man, who was quivering with fear by now like a little boy.

Medusa unwound her scarf, slowly, and her snakes stretched out languidly, tongues tasting the air. She took off her sunglasses.

Turning to stone started slowly, with the blood in your veins turning to cold ice then stopping all together. The muscles and the joints froze up into position. Then the outside observer could see it— it started at the fingertips, blue, and travelled up and up the arm and through the body until the whole thing was rocky and still.

The man was stone, and frozen in his final expression; fear, cowardice, and surprise.

He was very much dead.

Medusa stroked a hand along her head, patting each of the snakes in turn, and carefully replaced her scarf and her expensive sunglasses. "You may look at me," she said.

They did, mother and daughter both.

"Thank you," the little girl said.

Medusa grinned.

"I got your letter," she said. "But now I must be off. There are many monsters to fight in this world, you know."

\*\*\*

And this is the story of these women who are the background to the hero's journey, who are serpents and they are snakes and they are abominations. They are not mothers or dreamers or girls who have been raped by gods.

They are simply monsters.

So, monsters is what they are.

And these monsters, these women—

They *rage*. Perhaps it's for the ones who can't.

Monsters are reborn every day.

So are heroes.

# SIRENS

# SIREN SONG

## BY KRISTIN CLEAVELAND

Weary sailor, come to me;
Evermore, my love to be.
Deep beneath the rolling waves,
Cloistered in the darkest caves.

Flowing hair like blackest ink
Lures you to the briny drink.
Shining silver scales glisten—
All you have to do is listen.

Rule with me from sunken thrones
'Til your flesh dissolves from bones.
Down where darkest creatures seethe,
You will never need to breathe.

Follow where you hear my voice—
Strike the bargain; make your choice.
Never will your mother see
The son she bore, then lost to me.

Weary sailor, come to me;
Evermore, my love to be.

# SONGBIRD

## BY ROMY TARA WENZEL

We preen our feathers in the last light, nibble sea lice and crusted salt from the filaments, detangle each other's hair. I'm halfway through a knot when our youngest sister, Peisinoë, twists her head, leaving several sparrow-brown hairs between my claws.

"A ship!" she exclaims. I follow her gaze out to sea, and the square sail of a ship emerges behind the rocky outcrop where we collect cockles and limpets.

"By Apollo's strings," says Theixiope, and leaves off grooming her tail. "Their hull will break on the reef. Get my lyre from the cave, Peisinoë." Peisinoë slips between the blue-grey grasses near the nesting gulls.

The ship is unlike vessels from Athens, Delos or Rhodes. The hull is rose gold, not black. The ropes are not hemp or rush, but a material that shimmers in the light and vanishes under cloud. No sailor busies themselves on deck with the sail or the rigging, although the ship is at least 100 feet stem to stern. The boat does not rise and fall with the waves beneath it, but glides with ghostly ease as if it were made of sea.

"That is not a warship, nor a fishing vessel," I say.

"A trader's boat?" suggests Peisinoë, returning with our instruments. "No matter the vessel, men must hear the truth of the world. We have sworn it."

Theixiope strums a chord on her lyre, and tightens a nut on the crossbar.

"Ready your voice, Aglaope. We do not want them to wreck their ship before they hear us."

"Sisters." I stand up. The seals grunt and lift their heads at the disturbance. "There are no oarsmen on that ship. The oar blades are drawn in, look." I make out a faint peacock on the sail, embroidered a half-shade darker than the linen. A woman disembarks onto a rowboat and, with not a rower in sight, the boat travels across the kelp-darkened shallows.

Her posture is regal, her skin creamy, her breasts pert underneath the pleats of silk. Her hair is swept up with golden combs and tucked under a Spartan crown. My eyes drift back to the peacock, and my mouth drops open like a pelican. I've seen that diluted smile before, in a cold temple in the south. I thought the sculptor of inferior skill, to cut a face so smooth and vapid. But in retrospect, he captured the disinterested curve of the lips perfectly.

"Why do you stay silent, my winged musicians?" Hera says. "I hear you do not let a ship go by without airing your song."

"You've caught us unawares, my queen," says Theixiope, curtsying as elegantly as a woman with talons and a tail can. "I'd invite you to our home, except that we live in a cave, and invite you to feast with us, except that we feast on raw cockles and seaweed. Our songs, too, may not be to your taste, since we play them on instruments of tortoiseshell and bone and they have cruel endings."

"Men's hearts are not stout enough for truth," Hera replies, curtly.

"We have nothing to share but our experiences," Theixiope says. "We are tragic singers, and grief our hearts' boundary since we lost our friend."

"And would you take back what you have suffered?" Hera leans in close, and I can see the lines around her mouth. "Would you forget all, given the choice?"

Peisinoë wraps her wings about her as if suddenly cold. I, too, feel my feathers curl. To forget our grief would be to forget Persephone. Theixiope shudders, as if our discomfort ripples through her.

"Why have you come here, my queen?" she asks.

"I've come to challenge you to a contest," Hera says, her smile crumbling. "Win, and I'll release you from your memories and return you to human form." Her lip curls again. "All you need do is move more hearts than the Muses."

Theixiope bites her lip, and exchanges a glance with me. We encountered the Muses in our search for Persephone, when our wings were still gilded with Demeter's blessing, before our exile to Anthemoessa. The muses were the silver to our sparrow-brown, always looking on the light side of things, turning away from sorrow. A part of us wished to be as they were, made of light and laughter, but it was a part that turned away from truth.

Peisinoë brushes my wingtip with hers, as she would have once taken my hand and squeezed it. I give a tiny shake of my head. Hera narrows her eyes.

"I see you are not in agreement." She turns, the hem of her robe tracing a half-moon in the sand. "Discuss it amongst yourselves. If you refuse, the Muses win by default. Watch for rainbows, Sirens; I will send Iris to take your answer."

\*\*\*

"I want to compete," Peisinoë says, as the golden ship turns sail. "What kind of life is this? Eating starfish, sleeping by seals. Do you remember dancing, sisters? Do you remember *music*?"

"We play music every day." I stand defiant, but Peisinoë rolls her eyes.

"*Music,* Aglaope, not funeral songs. Dance songs and harvest songs of the field. Poetry. Songs that ripple through you like wine, thunder, autumn."

Theixiope worries a fossil that spirals into the limestone beneath her.

"I don't trust her. What does she stand to gain, should we win or lose?"

"We risk our pride for a chance to gain our lives back." Peisinoë turns her hungry eyes on me. "Seals and sailors might not be so bad if we did not carry our heaviness with us wherever we go. Imagine if the gods lifted it away!"

"But we would forget Persephone." My talons bury into the warm beach. *Hold fast,* my body tells me. *You swore to remember her. Do not break your oath now.* "Did we not swear to be truth-tellers, in a world that turns away from darkness?"

"We would not miss what we never knew we had," Peisinoë argues.

"I miss things I never had." Theixiope gasps, as if relieved of a burden. For a few moments the only noise is the waves breaking. "It is a secret my heart has guarded, but…" She opens her wings, and the feathers sprawl in a phalanx of arrows. "I yearn for a cub among us. I should like to hold a child with arms instead of wings."

My loyalty to our friend and our oath sings strong in my breast. But I know the yawning absences my sisters speak of intimately. My animal body craves our lost innocence. I let myself imagine a future where we are women of a larger sisterhood. I dimly remember festivals, markets, dancing, without the weight of knowing what we know. I imagine my own arms soft, touched, unfeathered. I feel the reach of a husband's arms, hear the laugh of children…and am lost to my sisters' argument.

***

In the hall they are waiting. We cross the floor, our claws scratching on the marble tiles. The Muses are laughing and drinking with the men at the feasting table.

Six Olympians are present. Zeus, bearded and assured, placed above the others. Poseidon, translucent-skinned and blue-veined, his scaled clothes like a second skin. Artemis, lithe as a deer, curious eyes darting over each of us and the mortals, equally. Ares ripples with muscle, his features crude as if hewn from stone, next to Aphrodite, the most beautiful woman in the room besides Hera, her hair auburn and threaded with gold. She leans forward to assess us while the others laugh and lounge, throw back their cups of ambrosia and boss the servants.

"Sirens," Hera announces. "You may sing three songs." The Muses drop their twittering, and the men turn their heads. "Let the contest begin."

Theixiope rests a claw on her lutestring, Peisinoë purses her mouth. Our three tributaries will flow together to transport the audience, if the songs are good. We lost whole days with Persephone, picking flowers in the meadow and singing together. Back then, we knew how to forget ourselves, to give ourselves over to a song.

I part my lips and sing up the bones of our grief.

***

The men slump in their chairs, their heads heavy, arms loose, as if they were falling apart. My heart jolts as I realize I've taken them too deep into sorrow, and have lost them. My first two songs have not opened their eyes, awoken no understanding.

I think of Peisinoë's hope to dance again, of Theixiope's wish for a child. I owe it to them to win votes. But if my world is darkness, how do I describe the light? My eyes dart over the Muses, light things if ever I saw them. Calliope's smile has slipped to show her teeth. They consider the battle won before crossing the field. I grapple with alternatives to my truth. What would the Muses sing?

They would sing of childhood, I tell myself. They would sing of flowers. What were the flowers we gathered with Persephone that day, so long ago?

Surely I have sung enough songs to make one up. I open my throat and let the song release. Not my song, but the song they wish to hear.

My sisters trip over the switch in key and time, but catch on as I twist the fibers of the song into thread. Peisinoë's feathered wingtips speed up, and Theixiope's talons chase the melody.

I paint the empty pictures in vivid color, as if I were watching scenes from someone else's life. My voice almost breaks with emotion, but I keep pushing the words out, laboring my song. I do not mean a word of it. It feels ugly, dissonant, untrue. The crowd mirrors my inner torment, their faces scrunching in despair as if I were betraying their ears. They hate our truth and our falsehoods, too.

I'm so sorry, Persephone, I cry between lines. I sold you to the gods, and now I can't go back.

***

The men are humming like aroused bees, angered by our senseless about-turn. Only Aphrodite keeps her gaze turned towards us, although her expression has changed. When her eyes meet mine, she gives a tiny shrug. Disappointment.

I try to wind up the song by coming full circle, bringing it back to our truth. Demeter's hope, extinguished; Persephone compromised and rescued by no-one. We lament the injustice of the gods and the indifference of nature. Hopelessness sweeps through the crowd. I can't find the thread of my sorrow, nor the tail of my happiness. Men pace like tigers, cry in their cups. We've aroused their sadness, but not resolved it.

It's a bad song.

*** 

The Muses take the floor. Calliope steps forward, the prominent star in their constellation. She steps into the sunlight, and her white face glows radiant as hope in the dark.

*Damn her,* I think, gritting my teeth. She stands proud in who she is, who she has always been.

Calliope's voice is clear and light as water. The men sit a little straighter in their chairs, reach for their wine and cheese again. The second time she sings her refrain, lies one after another, the men join in. The wrinkles smooth from their faces and the tears on their cheeks dry up. The Olympians watch indulgently, smiling a little amongst themselves. Perhaps this is what they want, for the men to anneal like copper and sleepwalk through their sorrows. As Hera applauds over platitudes and joins in with the chorus, her prejudice becomes clear. She's backed the Muses and their childish tales where love conquers all, man wins over beast, and the gods are praised for their benevolence and patronage.

Suddenly, I disgust myself. I do not want to become one of them; I do not want to hand over my grief. It suddenly feels precious, like a reliquary of our love for Persephone.

*Take the songs back!* my sparrow-heart cries, but they are released now. I have no control over their landing.

I close my eyes, brimming with regret. We'd sworn to tell the stories mortals could not tell themselves, the horrors the world turned away from. I've betrayed us all in the telling.

Hera taps her staff on the marble floor. The men fall silent.

"Only mortals may vote," she says. Aphrodite starts, but a devious crease dimples Hera's cheek. "'Whomsoever moves the most hearts,' we agreed. You, Aphrodite, along with the rest of us gods, have none."

Zeus stands. "The contest is perfectly fair."

Hera winces at the word, and Aphrodite smirks. She draws out a small golden fruit from her pocket and twirls it between her fingers.

"This apple has no sweetness in its bite. Even if you win it from me, you'd break your teeth if you tasted it."

"Let the men pull feathers from the Sirens, or hair from the Muses," Hera replied, her eyes dark as night sea. "Whomsoever they consider the losers. We will see what they hold in their fists at the end."

Aphrodite flinches, but Zeus puts his hand on her arm. The men descend from the cavea, sandals shushing against the marble floor. A hand reaches forward and pulls a feather from Peisinoë's breast. Peisinoë shrieks, wraps her wings around her, but the others pull feathers from our breasts, our tails, until their fists are full of trophies.

The Muses crowd around us, pretty eyes luminous as moons. Laughing, they pull the feathers from the men's fists and stick them into their hair, like crowns. They dance the syrtos, joining hands and weaving and ducking under each other's arms.

Hera leans forward in her throne, her white teeth gleaming.

"The vote is unanimous. I win my prize." She toasts the Muses with a goblet brimming with honey-coloured ambrosia, clear as tears. Only Aphrodite watches the cruelties without a smile and her goblet untouched. She hands over the apple without meeting Hera's eyes, letting it fall from her fingers as though she's lost interest in it.

When we stop resisting, the men and Muses grow bored. The dancing ring dissolves in favor of the feasting table, leaving me and my sisters in a heap on the floor. Theixiope nudges me to my feet, and I pull Peisinoë behind me. We stumble and trip to the light on the other side of the door. The cold outside shocks my near naked breast. From the marble steps we clumsily take to the air, fumbling for the thermal air currents with our ruined wings.

My shoulders pound to keep me above the water, tears continuing to flit down my cheeks as we flee our humiliation. I crave the sanctuary and privacy of our cave, where we can grieve honestly, without mockery, where we can be as we are, with what is. The world of men is not ready for our song, or we are not ready for them. *We should never have left.*

Something curious is happening to Theixiope, flying ahead, and I call out to her, but my voice is lost to the wind. I think it's a trick of the light, but as cloud drifts over the sun, I see the chestnut color of her flight feathers drain from her wings, until she's as white as the limestones of Anthemoessa. Peisinoë, flying closer to the water, has transformed as well, her reflection following her like a ghost on the Black Sea. I check my own wings, and see the caramel flecks draining out with the umbers, slowly bleaching to the wingtip, the bald spots filling out with new, luscious feathers.

Aphrodite's dove is a symbol of love, but it's also a companion to the underworld. Grief is the other side of love, and the one goes hand in hand with the other.

This knowledge hits my breast like an arrow. A crushing squeeze in my chest, and my heart comes to life, not the relentless drum of each day, but hot and alive and convulsing. I think of the men with my sisters' feathers in their fists, and it drives me down, circling towards the sea, testing my birth cry on the wind. I wish I could pull the skins from them, tear out the snakes of their throats, redden the gods' marble floor. But it's not blood that quickens my breath and flushes my cheeks. It's anger. Anger at those that did not hear us, that never listened to us. Angry that I moderated my voice, our stories to make them comfortable.

I turn wing and circle back to where Peisinoë is ascending. Her irises gleam blue, twin evil eyes in white plumage. We soar on our hate, wingtip to wingtip, over the still water, the energies between us in perfect accord like a song. When Theixiope joins us, I call to her in a voice that sounds different from the one I'm used to, undiscovered terrain that breaks my old songlines into pieces. I open my throat and release a new sound, so piercing seagulls fall around us like stones. I cry again, and the ocean shudders and clouds flee around us like a fog clearing.

I smile with a joy not felt since childhood, since running through that flower-filled meadow, chasing birds to flight. That's it; that's the note I'd been missing. One note beyond grief. Grief is so small a term for our sadness, so limited. This note is beyond words, a music not yet shared with the world. I rejoin my sisters, the skies empty of anything but our feeling, our power. We reflect a triangle over the still water, a white-hot arrow burning with love. Love, the other side of grief. Combined, they form a new musical key, a key that will cast sailors to their doom, that will wreck ships, that will send mortals into madness. This is the voice of grief, and I swear to defend it with my life.

# OTHER MONSTERS

# LABORERS WANTED

## BY SJ TOWNEND

Imagine a factory: smokestacks, billowing towers of grey, steel shipyard cranes like giant skeletal arms lumbering crates away. Lamia Factory is nothing like that. It's like none you've ever seen before or ever will again. It's a one off. And so are the goods it produces.

***

My employment at Lamia commenced five months ago. I signed something, some disclaimer form, and since then, they've paid me weekly in cash. I'm still not sure what it is I do here though.

I see the built men with their sharp suits, their fitted earpieces which dangle down below dark-visored helmets, and their firearms tucked not quite out-of-sight. They take long shifts in turn to staff the Guarded Door.

I see the one-time-only employees who come ad hoc. They arrive with lustrous heads of hair, and leave with a crop and fistful of notes.

And I see the real grafters. They're the boxers—gloved and tubi-gripped to the elbows. The boxers get bussed in every week day from all over the district, as do I.

Before dawn, on the bus, our fists in unison rub our owlish eyes in an attempt to clear fresh sleep from our faces, but we never talk. The commute involves, for each of us, a long stare at our own hands and feet.

Before first light, we spill out on foot where the dirt track ends and the bus can penetrate no further, and we stomp towards the factory doors. A handful of us bring small children. The parents disembark first, with young ones in buggies. We push them along the shamble of a forest path which is marked out by dim lamps and slits of moonlight. The boxers help us lift and carry our prams when wheels hitch against rocky outcrops or gnarly tree roots. But silenced by tiredness, none of us speak much with anything more than our eyes.

Once everyone is safe inside—hair donors, boxers, security staff, me— the low hanging sun slowly singes winter's mackerel skin cloud away from the inky dawn sky.

It's clear where they all go, what they all do. But me? Not a clue.

***

I know what the factory makes. That I know. Myriad cardboard coffins, each the size of a shoebox, will be found piled up near the entrance, waiting for dispatch at dusk. Each box will have a clear, plastic side-panel through which the sleeping face of a life-size, darling, shut-eyed poppet can be seen. On the morrow, all this stock will have shifted, and, by dusk again, will have been replenished once more. And so the cycle continues.

Some of the dolls are boxed bald, some are given a dusting of fuzzy peach-skin-down on their heads. Some are decorated with real human hair: red, brown, blonde and black. All the dolls have the softest skin—a silicon or plastic polymer—and they come in a spread of hues, from incandescent porcelain through to midnight.

Each doll has lips like rosebuds, is dreamy-faced and lies deep in imagined slumber.

Each comes with its name imprinted in curlicue font on its packaging.

The boxers call them 'reborns'.

But who buys these inert replicas? Women who've lost? Women who've never had? Someone with a sense of augmented reality who thinks they still have? No idea, but demand seems to be sky-rocketing.

With sleeping-angel faces, human hair, and cream-touch skin, they're without doubt a close match for the real thing, but as they're dolls and, ergo, lifeless, I find them oddly unnerving. Call it mild automatonophobia if you like—a fear of that which is inanimate but looks as if it should be animate.

*\*\*\**

It's clear as slow-formed ice what the guards and the hair-donors and the boxers do. But at work, what is it I do?

*\*\*\**

I can tell you one thing I *don't* do. I *don't* tell my husband I've taken gainful employment. He'd hit the roof and my glass ceiling is six foot two thick and packed in tightly above me to the point of suffocation. I don't think it can be broken. Not yet, anyway. Patience is a virtue.

*\*\*\**

Lamia is an architectural mongrel. The outside of the factory is made from rough, dark lengths of timbre which meld with the forest around it; more thick brown tree thighs, more stacked chocolate gateaux than boxy grey eyesore. Its wooden skin is scattered with one-way windows. Each window is round and dark red like a flat glacier cherry and allows workers to see out but not a soul to peep inside. On interview day, I was told the factory was designed by a female architect, built to be harmonious with nature. And I believe it is. It sits swallowed, near invisible from afar, by a pocket of the forest which skirts my home town.

Inside? The decor exudes warmth, harnesses rich shades of flesh, and is padded and comfortable throughout. The candle-lit room where I start my working day feels as cozy as a womb: small, well-filled with draped fabrics, packed with plump floor cushions, and a freshly made bed. Lullaby music is piped through every corridor. The crèche is exceptional.

There is this one room, behind the Guarded Door, where the 'industrial machinery' is kept—I wasn't taken there on my induction tour but was warned objectively not to venture in—it's strictly out of bounds.

*Trade secrets?* you ask. *Temperamental, high-voltage machinery?* I can't recall the reason but was told my contract would be *terminated with immediate effect* if I even stretched an arm through the wipe-clean, peach-coloured, plastic slit-drape-curtain Guarded Door.

I've no desire to, anyway; no urge to see the magic in action.

I'm happy with my adjacent role, whatever it might involve—the work pays well and, in a few weeks, I'll have a deposit for a new home for myself and my bairns. Freedom.

\*\*\*

It is Monday and it is winter.

James just left for his office. On his way out, before slamming the door behind him, he threw the sandwiches he'd asked me to prepare at my feet. I'd made egg and cress—not ham. I've since cleaned up the mess.

Both the twins are screaming, disturbed by the strength of his words and the rattle of the door no doubt. I need to feed them. My milk always calms. There is enough time before I need to lay them in the double buggy and head off to the bus stop.

I feed my boy, then insert a clean finger and pop his lip from my nipple. I slip him into his snug space in the buggy and then I feed my second baby, my daughter. I walk as I do, her tucked under my arm like a rugby ball, and gather essential belongings in preparation to leave the warmth of the house.

We make the bus in time. It carries us away from the sleepy, lamp-lit streets, and the rows of cheek-by-jowl houses, every other with a chimney coughing out a scarf-of-smoke. Off we go, into the woods. The day is yet to break. One twin burps. I smile at another mother onboard and she smiles back, but then we each focus on our children, our laps, anything else, until the bus slows down and stops.

\*\*\*

Both regular and odd questions were asked of me on interview day: how many hours could I work, when could I begin, was I still exclusively breastfeeding? I was offered the job on the spot without full explanation of what my role would involve, but was informed that myself and my children would be provided with the best healthcare in the country and assured that no harm would come to any of us whilst under the employment of Lamia. The interview had been curt and the induction process had left several unanswered questions, but when they showed me the crèche and informed me of the rates of pay, I couldn't refuse the position.

Each day on arrival, I drop the twins off in the crèche and make my way on hands and knees through the dark, tapered tunnel all the way in to the milking room.

At my booth, underfloor heating pulses waves of pleasant warmth in sync with my every in and ex-halation.

"Please, take a moment to rest," the automated voice says through the intercom system.

With almost a sentient charm and clarity, it instructs me to hook myself up to the pumping system. I pull the silken curtain around my velour dorm, slip off my shirt and brassiere, and hang them on the hook. Then, I recline on the gurney, which creaks like geriatric joints as it takes onboard my weight. I take a moment to bring the laundered linen to my nose. It smells like sweet lavender. Then, I reach for the two dangling silicon cups.

When I first started, any queries I had about which tube, which cup, which bag went where were answered almost before I'd had a chance to give voice to my question. Answers came with a maternal knowing from the robotic female voice. Now it comes as second nature.

Once attached to my breasts, the machine clunks on. The tranquil sound of gentle suction switches on, off, on, off, on, off.

"Allow your eyes to rest," she suggests, and as a tired mother of two nursing twins, who am I to contest?

I drop off shortly after whirr and buzz and suck reach full pace and doze in a place of liminality for more than a moment whilst the machine takes the milk my babies need for their time in the crèche. After my milk's been extracted, I'm sure she whispers further instructions of what I need to do to complete my work, my shift. I think. But time and color blur past, all fever dream, all jumbled thought.

Seven or eight hours pass, then I'm notified: "Your shift is complete," and I hear a mechanical sigh followed by the dulcet tones once more of the piped factory lullaby. One enchanting melody pours through the speakers on loop. It's a tune composed entirely of vocals, in a key that's not yet been invented. I'm certain I'll never grow tired of hearing it.

I'm fully clothed again yet still lying on the reclined gurney. There's a blanket over my knees, a warm cup of tea to my side, a selection of biscuits on a bone china plate, and I've a ravenous appetite. It's time to crawl back, collect my bundles of joy, and catch the bus home.

***

It's Tuesday. I've been weeping. My face is a picture of sadness. James screamed at me again through the dark. I'd asked for help at three in the morning whilst trying to settle one of the twins. I'd spent most of the ice-cold night trapped in my nursing chair with a feeding baby on my lap. My blanket had been just a little out of reach.

"Get it yourself, bitch. Don't wake me again. I need my sleep," he'd spat.

I think I managed to sob myself back to sleep at four.

I made him a coffee at half five before he set off for the city, before I needed to set off.

"You can't even make decent coffee. Useless," he'd said after his first sip. Then he'd tipped the rest onto the rug in the hallway, the artisan weave Mother left me. All the while he sneered at me, with a mean streak in his green eyes. Each time he is cruel, his face becomes more distorted, uglier, more alien.

Black liquid pooled on the wool. Sour.

I managed to hold back tears until he'd slammed the door. Farewell. From outside, he'd bent down and shouted back in through the letterbox at me.

"Those little parasites probably aren't even mine anyway." Then he beeped open the central locking of his four-by-four, got in it, and left for work.

How on earth could they not be his? They both have his complexion, his green eyes—eyes he once looked at me through with desire and lust. Although

I'm not sure now he ever looked at me with love.

At least I get to nap at work.

I kiss my twins and we set off for the bus, for the factory.

***

It's Friday. James came at me with a rolling pin yesterday, threatened to silence me and the 'screaming monsters' for eternity. I sat up most of last night, rocking my babies in their cribs to try and keep them asleep. Who knows what he'd have done if they'd have woken him? His rage is growing, his face seems to be distorting into some hideous creature of the swamp.

***

It's Monday. There were far fewer workers on board the bus this morning. A mother spoke to me en route to the factory today to inform me of a rumor. She took my hand in hers and told me a child managed to escape the crèche yesterday, at some point over the weekend shift. A toddler. A boy. Somehow, he'd made his way past the guard and into the area he shouldn't have been in. Somehow, he'd crawled or toddled through the Guarded Door.

She looked straight into my eyes and I felt something squeeze my heart as she told me she was as desperate for money as I seemed. Couldn't afford to lose her job, else she'd have *quit immediately*, like the other mothers who'd heard the talk.

"Is he okay, the bairn?" I asked, stomach a-churn. She squeezed my hand a little harder, told me the babe, the little boy who'd crept into the Mother Machine, was fine.

*Unharmed*, she said, *but hasn't made a sound since*. She released my hand and whispered more: *He's had his laughter stolen. His voice— It's gone.* How can a voice be taken? Ludicrous. My twins, they're far from mobile anyway. I push and prod my concerns back into a hole.

The bus slowed down as it reached the end of the dirt track and off we got. Part of me wanted to turn around, make my way back home, but the lion's share of me was more afraid of spending another month with James, so I pressed onwards and tried to block dark thoughts.

***

It's Friday. My boy rolled over for this first time this morning. I didn't tell

James. Can't look him in the eye anymore.

Each day is pure terror. I'm unable to rest at home and home is no longer a home. It's been reduced to a mere house. A house I can't wait to flee. I've enough saved. Nearly. A few more shifts and I'll be on my way.

I unwrap and re-wrap the silver-red wound on my arm. Exposing to the air, it oozes yellow-white fluid and infection. Yesterday, James branded me with the sharp metal tri-tip of the hot iron. I'd failed to press his shirts correctly. What followed that is too difficult to put into words. Let us just say I've had enough. The dawn air today is as iced as my heart feels. The white of my breath hangs in the air. I swaddle my boy and my girl with three extra layers. We leave the house and head out for work.

We wait alone, at the bus stop. Staff numbers have decimated, but I'm still keen to earn, keen to manifest my own escape. I see the full beam of the bus headlamps creeping up the road but I also see the lights and hulk of my husband's four-by-four travelling in the opposite direction. He must be returning home, must've forgotten something. I'm ripe with panic. He'll notice I'm not there. Will he find the stack of notes I pulled out from the teddy bear in search of change for the bus? Can he see me now, from his car as he spins past?

I crouch in an attempt to hide and rock the pram back and forth in an effort to keep the small ones content and then the bus pulls up. I quickly embark. My heart is thumping but I've no choice but to board. I could turn and go home, face him, but then I'd lose my job and my only shot at an escape.

The bus trundles up to the edge of the path that leads to the factory. No smoke plumes out from the building, and I observe for the first time that no electrical wires, cables, or infrastructure connect it to the rest of civilization. I'm still shaking with panic. The irregular, wooden walls that encase all that rests within appear to breathe in and out in time with the fast charge of my own heart. I walk with pace towards the entrance.

Over the crunching of feet and pram wheels on leaves, I swear I hear a call—a deep voice—from the darkness behind me. I turn around and pause, deer in headlights. It's nothing; perhaps an animal, a fox or badger or other nocturnal creature, assembling its family before sunrise.

I keep moving. A noise. I turn again, swear I see something move, something tall, some shape ominous. Lightless flesh like wind darts behind a tree. I start to push the buggy faster, with more force, and I find myself running towards the throbbing pink entrance light which hangs above the factory door.

We make it inside. Safe.

***

I kiss my babes farewell, leave them at the crèche, and head off for the milking suite. This is when I see him through the one-way window. He *did* see me at the bus stop. He *has* followed me to work. He's running, looks livid. My heart, a caged bird, is pounding up in my throat. What if he catches me here? What will he do? To me?

I panic and look across at the guard by the Guarded Door, the door with the neon signage above it and on it. The door with signage which proffers implicit instruction that what is behind the door is 'strictly out of bounds.'

I know my husband, I know what he's capable of, so I make a rash, half-baked decision to scream.

Dropping to my knees, I make a puddle of myself at the entrance to the tunnel which leads to the milking suite. The guard hears me and runs straight over to my aid.

My husband, with his angry eyes—he's on the hunt for me. I spy him barging in through the factory entrance. I make sure he doesn't see me collapsed here on the floor. Drawing my index finger up to my lips, I beg the guard with the drill of my widened, wet eyes to do nothing.

*Please* remain still, leave my husband be. Just continue to do nothing but shield me with your giant frame. Hide me from my husband.

I mouth, "Please," to the guard and point to the bandages on my arms.

James does not see me or the guard at the entrance to the tunnel, but he does see the Guarded Door with its hanging flaps of plastic and neon warning signs. Sweet lullabies are emanating loudly through the pipework, masking the sounds of the concealed machine carrying out its labor. James runs to the door. Of course, he runs to the door—because the door is telling him directly not to.

He elbows through the peach plastic and guttural screams fill the air. But it's not his voice, it's the voice of the machine.

Loud, shrill, sentient. It's almost deafening from where I'm lying. The entire building quivers. The floor lifts up at one side, tips, and creates a slope of the whole hallway. My water bottle slides out of my bag and starts to roll. The factory walls bow inwards and squeeze me closer to the guard in black. The entrance of the tunnel exhales, narrows. There's a jolt. The floor re-levels but the screeching continues and the ground beneath us still feels unstable.

We grip each other for safety. Our faces are both printed with terror, but in this moment, I see the guard remembering his role—to defend the workers or protect the machinery, I'm no longer sure which—and he pushes my hand from his arm.

"I'm sorry. I've got to do my job," he whispers with a tight, semi-smile on his lips.

I try to stand and try to hold back the guard but he is two, maybe three of me, and his face is no longer full of panic but, instead, determination. I let him go.

I watch as the guard rushes towards the door, pulls down his visor of blackened Perspex, reaches for his firearm, forces his way through the Guarded Door, and moves towards the heart of the factory. He steps into the forbidden zone where the dolls are made; are born. Every ounce of the building is screaming.

It's too late for James. I can hear his cries over the wailing of the machine and the eternal lullaby. I can hear him screaming in pain and it's a scream as long and loud as any woman who's ever given birth. No new life is being made in this moment though. That I can tell.

He stops screaming, the machine stops screaming, the building stops squeezing and shaking and tilting, and I hear a thud and I know the weight of the bully that is my husband and I know it's his body dropping to the floor like a de-strung marionette.

There's silence for a brief moment, until: "Eyes! EYES!" A shout from a lady. This new voice pierces clarion through the speaker system and it's not the soothing voice of the milking chamber bot.

Angelic harping music returns to the air, louder than before, sweeter than before, more tuneful and merrier than before, and out comes the guard. He is dragging my husband's lifeless body along by the feet. Wet red trails behind them.

I go to them and look down at James. Where his eyes once were, now sit two bleeding sockets; two vermillion ponds which once homed green eyes. Blood spurts in pulses from his face. Each burst makes more of a mess of the soft, pink hallway carpet. His stomach is sliced open and brown intestines are tumbling free, ribboning out like spooling kelp.

The guard pushes up the visor from his face. He hangs his head and shakes it slowly from side to side. Then he offers whispers of apologies to me. I shake my head, let my body shake a little all over too, and let myself go through the motions.

"It's not your fault," I say. "There, there," and I'm not sure who is comforting who.

The new automated voice pipes out through the loudspeakers, over the lullaby tune. "Mrs. Hartree." That is me. "You're required in the milking suite.

You're five minutes late for your shift."

I gather my belongings and shuffle on hands and knees down through the tapering, dark tunnel towards the milking chamber where I'll provide the milk my babies will need for the day ahead, so I can complete my shift. So I can do whatever it is I do.

I arrive, unbutton my blouse, and reach for the suction cups. I'm glad to lie back on the wheeled bed. I'm in need of a little rest.

*** 

It is Spring. I've weaned both my darling babies over the last few weeks. My once-wet breasts are now liberated from their role in motherhood. I feel well rested now, born again now I'm dry. Now they're both that bit older, we all sleep through the night too.

I received a letter and a parcel earlier this week, from the factory. The letter stated that they've terminated my contract with immediate effect. No reason was given other than that I was *'no longer fit for purpose'*. At least the letter came with a leaving gift.

My gift? A boxed doll, of course. A doll with big green eyes—just like the twins have. Like James had.

I've three children now: the twins—one boy, one girl—who will forever be free to sing and twirl and dance with laughter, full of the joys of spring. And my third, this doll. The doll is an absolute darling—he never cries—and his rosebud lips are fixed in one position, suckling, and fashioned from the softest, special polymer, a Lamia-patented material. But also, he never sleeps; appears to be cursed with eternal insomnia. Poor thing—he looks shattered.

And his green eyes seem hexed, full of fear. He looks petrified no matter what I do to try to soothe him.

So I keep him in his cardboard box, which has his curlicue name, James, printed on the side.

And I keep the box under my bed.

Every now and again, in the darkness of the night, I'll take him out, place my hand over his face—so I don't have to look in his eyes—and I'll hold him against my bare breast. We'll have a little cuddle. He has such creamy-soft skin and I can't get enough of his newborn baby smell, of mother's milk. Lamia really nailed a likeness.

***

Today, I saw the guard who dragged my children's father eyeless and dead from the core of the machinery. I saw him in the woods. I recognized his suit and visor.

Most days, I'll walk under the forest canopy with the twins—the woods are the most beautiful kind of haunted. The guard appeared to be searching still, for the factory, but I know he'll never find it.

He lifted his visor and nodded as we passed. We shared a reserved greeting with just our eyes, no words. Then, side-by-side, we both stood and stared at the vast swathe of dead earth, at the large mounds of soil and leaf litter that have been left behind from where the foundations, the thick thighs of oak, the rooted planks of wood that once anchored the factory in place, had pulled themselves up from the forest floor. At the end of my last shift, myself and the guard had watched from the bus stop as the wood of the factory walls split free and shook out into many giant tree stump legs.

We both saw the beautiful factory—mother machine and wooden frame—lift up entirely from its spot and scarper away like a blown cumulus, free.

We both witnessed her colossal retreat from her pocket of forest, watched her become gulped up by thick woodland, saw her take off in search of pastures new.

I understand, and I wish her well. When a woman wants out, she wants out.

But I don't think the guard believed his own eyes.

# NATURE ALWAYS FINDS A WAY

## BY RUSCHELLE DILLON

Locking the bathroom door against her over-protective single mother, Kyd stared at her sixteen-year-old self in the mirror. Popping an angry pimple bulging from the crease of her Roman nose, she winced and sucked in a deep breath.

"What the hell is wrong with me?" she mouthed to her reflection before sliding off her pajama pants and tossing them in the hamper. *I'm so sick and tired of going to the doctor and now mom is taking me to see a gynecologist?* she thought to herself while adjusting the water temperature in the shower. Shedding the rest of her clothes, she spread a towel on the cold tile floor. She ran a hand down her stomach and over a thin, raised scar that slithered up from her groin and stopped three inches below her belly button. Sucking in her non-existent gut, she addressed her ninety-eight-pound self in the mirror, "I don't even have a boyfriend. This is so fucked up," she croaked, stepping into the steamy water.

Her seething intensified as a familiar knock echoed from the hollow wooden door.

"You okay in there, hon?" quizzed her mother, Edna, who looked more like Kyd's older sister than her mom. Both were striking; emerald green eyes and pale skin against a backdrop of thick black hair.

Kyd rolled her eyes, poking her wet head from a gap in the plastic curtain.

"I'm fine, Mom. I'm taking a shower." *Jesus Christ, leave me the hell alone,* she whispered under her breath as she flicked on the ancient radio her mom kept next to the bathtub and cranked up the volume of an equally ancient David Bowie song.

Satisfied with her daughter's answer, she shouted, fighting over the pounding water and Bowie howling *ch-ch-ch-ch-changes.*

"You don't have time for your usual forty-five-minute shower. Get clean and get moving."

Kyd replied by turning up the hot water valve to skin-peeling.

\*\*\*

Driving home from the gynecologist, Kyd glared out of the passenger side window with her arms wrapped tightly around her oversized pink hoodie. The old Ford Taurus' brakes squealed at a red light. Edna attempted to adjust the rear-view mirror to check her impeccably drawn and filled-in fire engine red lipstick.

"I'm sorry, honey," she said, penetrating the bubble of silence.

Kyd hugged herself tighter.

"At times, being a female really sucks. The doc says you're a healthy young woman but the operation you had when you were a baby needs – *a revision*. These things happen, honey. Try not to be *too* upset. But on the bright side, we might be able to hold off the procedure for six months or so."

Kyd picked at her ragged fingernails.

"I know this little gesture won't fix anything," she said, noticing her daughter's nervous habit, "but how about we go and get our nails done?" She wriggled her fingers, each accentuated with a tear-drop-shaped diamond set in expensive platinum. Although Edna didn't work, they were not hurting for money.

Mutism was Kyd's response until she saw the antique tents that had popped up on the county fairgrounds, along with a Ferris wheel. A huge banner draped the fairground's chain link fence.

September 21 to the 28th. Mythos- the World's Longest Running Carnival and Sideshow- Be Shocked and Amazed.

Kyd broke her vow of silence.

"How about we go there instead? I've never been to a carnival before. Or a sideshow. My friend Monique went to one and said-"

Before Kyd could finish, Edna slammed her foot on the brake. Kyd lurched forward exaggerating the forcefulness of her mother's foot smashing the brake pedal.

"You will *not* go anywhere near there!" Edna yelled, her eyes bulging.

"What's your problem, Mom? It's just a carnival."

Edna slammed the steering wheel with her palms.

"Stay the hell away from there, do you hear me?" Cars honked behind them.

Kyd invoked her secret weapon, the comment that would draw every argument with her mom to a close.

"I bet if *Dad* was in the picture he'd take me," Kyd spat, knowing that topic would deflate the rising conflict. Her foot pressed firmly on the gas pedal; Edna focused on the road. A mile out from the fairgrounds she untied her tongue.

"I'm sorry I exploded like that. Carnivals and sideshows – they're…"

Edna chose her words carefully. "You just need to stay away, no discussion."
Kyd shot her mom a hellish glare.

"Besides, I've tried to take such good care of you, of *us*. You have
everything you could ever want or need. There's been no need for - *Dad*."

Edna never spoke of Kyd's father if she could help it. Kyd knew nothing
about the man who assisted in giving her life. She knew nothing about his side
of the family or why he left. She never saw a photo of him and wondered if
her mother burned them all, or if her mom even knew who he was.

Kyd punched the dusty sun-bleached console of the car.

"So, it's okay for me to have instruments shoved up my vagina but I can't
go to a stupid carnival?"

Hot tears dribbled down Kyd's cheeks. It was a perfect storm: the swirling
embarrassment of internal examination at the clinic, the lengthy and
uncomfortable discussion over her reconstructive genitalia surgery when she
was a baby, and howling into this deluge of a conversation with her mother.

"What's wrong with me?"

"Nothing sweetie," Edna whispered. "You're perfect."

***

The rides, copious amounts of funnel cake, meat on a stick, and the
human oddities were highlights of the little town's summer. All week her
friends Snapchatted pictures of themselves screaming on the merry mixer,
downing plates of fried food, and posing in front of the sideshow tent. She
wished she could join them, hang-out and feel like a *normal* teenager.

Kyd sighed heavily, throwing herself into the pillows of her bed and
gazing at a photo of her friend, Monique, in the sideshow tent, standing next
to a painfully thin man besotted with a skin affliction that mimicked the scales
of a reptile. His two-foot-long forked tongue dripped saliva onto a metal
beam, melting it.

Her eyes widened. Not at the near impossible feat of acid saliva melting
metal, but his face, his cheekbones, his hooked nose. His features, although
heavily textured, held a resemblance to her.

Could this man be the reason her mom freaked out when she mentioned
checking out the carnival? Could this man with the two-foot-long tongue be
her father?

She giggled. Her mom was not the type of woman who'd stand next to,
let alone sleep with, a skinny snake guy. No, her mother only dated well-
coiffed handsome gentleman with money. This dude was not in her DMs, nor

would he ever be. Besides, her tongue was ordinary.

*Like the rest of me*, she said to herself while staring at the man with the awesome powers, even if it was all fake. She was ordinary.

A second photo popped up from her friend. The freshly snapped pic featured her bestie and Monique's boyfriend, Colton. Both were playfully sporting duck lips and pointing to the pink hooded sweatshirt Monique was wearing. The hooded sweatshirt *she* bought a few weeks ago with Edna. In the background were three carnies.

She enlarged the photo. Glaring at the backs of her friend's heads was a petite, bald woman with black eyes as large as musket balls. A familiar hooked nose came to a pronounced point and curved gracefully towards her mouth like a beak. From a threadbare army green tank top sprouted a pair of grotesque featherless wings resembling those of a massive thanksgiving turkey. Her flesh was mottled in muted hues of pinks, reds and blues, as if it were beaten and bruised. Her hands were gnarled, fingers fused together resembling talons.

Leaning against the bird woman was the most massive ghost dog Kyd had ever seen. She shrank and magnified the photo twice to be certain what she was looking at wasn't one of those wooly Highland cows from picture books. Although its size was impressive enough to warrant traveling in a freak show, what sealed its carnie status was not only its blazingly white fur, but its two heads.

"What the fuck?" she whispered. "That can't be real."

With her finger on the screen, she slowly swiped over to the third carnie, dressed as the carnival barker in crisp white pants and a short crimson jacket. He was handsome, with a mane of sleek ebony hair and a matching moustache. His eyes resembled two perfect green emeralds piercing through the screen. Kyd stared at his kindred features, his face a masculine mirror image of herself. She took a screenshot of the now slightly blurred image to study further.

"So, this is why she flipped her bitch switch when I asked about wanting to go to the sideshow. She didn't want me to meet my father. And he's a carnie. Mom was slumming it back then. Not like her usual well-to-do boy toys. Well, before the week is through, we are going to have a family reunion."

Kyd's fingers danced across the cell phone's keyboard.

*I'm jelly. But you better not get any shit on my hoodie, bitch. Bring it when you pick me up for school.* She punctuated her message with a slew of emojis and smashed send.

For the rest of the evening, Kyd holed herself up in her room, carefully crafting lies and half-truths to sneak out and meet her mother's one-time lover and subsequent sperm donor before the carnival stuffed their tents into crates and rolled out to the next entertainment hungry, nowhere town.

After midnight, Kyd succumbed to the sway of her mattress and worn body pillow. Under the sheets and blanket she felt safe, as if nothing could touch her when wrapped up in her one-thousand thread count cocoon. But the scar between her legs began to ache and burn. Kyd winced, reaching down to touch the knotted scar tissue.

As her fingers brushed against the lesion, her skin fissured and stretched. Her flesh tore away from itself, creating a chasm from below her belly button down past her reproductive organs. She struggled to twist her shoulders and her hips but found she could not move. Her body lay paralyzed.

Betrayed by her safe space, tears of fear poured down her face. Her emerald eyes bulged as they were forced to watch the hole in her body rip apart and a grotesque head emerge. It had no eyes. Grey with a huge, toothless, gaping mouth, it's scythe-like fingers raked across her belly and crawled towards her. A monster.

Kyd screamed.

Within seconds the bedroom door flung open, and Edna rushed into the room, kneeling at her daughter's side.

"It's okay, honey. I'm here. Mama's here," she cooed.

Still screaming, Kyd sprung from her helotry and wriggled her way out from her entrapment and reached down to her intact torso.

"Oh my God. My scar. My scar ripped apart. My *body* split apart."

Edna held her daughter, wiping the sweat and tears from her head before she kissed her.

"You had a bad dream. A very bad dream, that's all. You're alright. It was just a nightmare."

"It was so real."

"You are perfect." Edna rubbed her daughter's trembling legs and whispered, "There are no monsters."

Kyd pulled away from her mom and wiped the snot from her lip.

"I didn't say..."

Her mother pulled her close and shushed her, rocking her like she would when Kyd was a little girl.

***

Kyd sat at the kitchen table in her poop emoji sleeping pants paired with a tie-dye concert tee shirt and jean jacket. Edna slid her a bowl of cereal for breakfast.

"You're not wearing that to school. No daughter of mine is gonna be seen looking like a bum. I don't care what the people of Walmart think is cool. Go change into your ripped up jeans or those really nice yoga pants that make your butt look cute."

Kyd pushed her cereal aside and stood by the sink.

"I think I'm going to sit this one out today. I need to binge watch something and eat a bag of crap," she said, digging through the snack cabinet.

"Are you still upset about that nightmare you had last night?"

Kyd rolled her eyes and slammed the cupboard shut.

"You forgot to get the good chips again, Mom. It's like you don't even care."

Edna paused at the gold-leafed mirror by the kitchen door and checked her flawless hair and make-up before heading out the door for morning coffee with a 'friend'.

"And on that note, change your pants and go to school. Monique is here. And she looks adorable in her yogas and sweater." She flashed her perfect smile at her daughter's bestie.

"Good morning, honey. You look fab. Now drag my kid's ass to school, but make sure she changes," she directed, blowing kisses to both girls. Snatching one last look in the mirror, she plugged each ear with an opulent tear shaped diamond, grabbed her car keys and slammed the door behind her.

Monique playfully lobbed the pink hoodie at her friend's head.

"There you go, bitch. One dirty hoodie. I kept it on while Colton and I had sex." Kyd draped it over one of the kitchen chairs and took off her jacket.

"Whatever. I'm not going to class today. I had a rough night's sleep," she said, omitting any discussion of her dream.

"You think *you* had a bad night?" she said, her head bobbing and weaving accentuating the drama. "Colton and I were followed home by some creep from the carnival. We walked because his house is so close. We kept hearing footsteps. I swear to God I saw a pair of blood red eyes peeking at us from behind a tree. Colton was trying to be brave but when he heard something sniffing, he grabbed my hand, and we ran like hell."

"You were being sniffed?" She stifled a giggle, not wanting to mock her friend's fear after the frightening dream she had. She poured her friend a cup of coffee and one for herself. "It might have been a stray dog smelling all that greasy carnival food you ate."

Monique flipped her off before pouring a waterfall of thick pumpkin flavored creamer into her cup.

"No. It wasn't a dog, smart ass. The sound followed us the whole way home. I wonder if we were followed by one of those freaks. Colton drove me home afterwards. It scared the living shit out of us."

Kyd shivered at the thought of the dream-creature's eyeless face writhing up from her bisected torso.

"Well, I'm not going to class." Kyd penned a note on a memo pad. The slant, loops, and t- crossings were exactly like her mothers. Forging Edna's signature, she handed the note to Monique.

"When you came to pick me up, Mom handed you the note. That's all you know. Don't go off script."

Kyd was determined to visit the carnival and confront the man she just knew was her father. Best to do it first thing in the morning so the surprise of meeting his long-lost daughter would wear off before the evening show started; especially before her mother returned home. She swigged some coffee and tossed Monique a small thermos for hers.

"Give me a minute to change. I need you to drive me somewhere…"

\*\*\*

Kyd crept into the sideshow tent. The heavy canvas snuffed out the sunlight. Her eyes took time to adjust to the soft glow from the few light bulbs strung around the central pillar. Without the excited gasps and voices from the ticket holders, it was still and unnervingly quiet. She crept towards the middle of the tent scanning the rotunda, unable to see anything outside the light's desperate reach. It was early: eight-thirty in the morning. She wondered where the carnies and sideshow acts were.

Shouldn't they be practicing…whatever it is they did while traveling from town to town?

As she knelt to palm what looked like an acid eaten hunk of metal from last evening's performance, cracks in the silence fractured all around her. Her arms erupted in goosebumps. Any courage she felt when touched by the daylight shrank into the bowels of the dimly lit and unfamiliar tent. From the blackness came a single hiss, followed by a snake-like cacophony. Her head whipped around, seeking out the floating sibilants, as a myriad of figures slipped free from the dark recesses, drawn to her presence like catnip.

As she backed up against the center pillar, the reptilian man from Monique's selfie brushed a scaly finger against her cheek, then, waving the digit under his nose, he inhaled.

"Sss-ister," he voiced.

Sniffing the air, others followed suit: a one-eyed beast over nine-foot-tall, a man with the legs of a faun, the massive ghost dog with two heads, a man wearing nothing but a suit of silky hair with the face of a wolf and many more, each one reaching out to touch her.

"Sss-ister." The sibilance slithered from each tongue coiling through the air.

From the shadows, the man she came to see—the barker—appeared. He was dressed casually in jeans and a flannel shirt, his long black tresses pulled back in a ponytail. His full lips cracked into a brilliant smile as he knelt in front of her. He took her hand to his familiar nose and huffed the scent of her skin.

Kyd pulled her hand upward, gesturing for him to stand.

"You're my father, aren't you?" she whispered and returned the smile.

Before he could speak, a sliver of light crawled from the tent opening.

"No child, he is not your father."

"Mom!" Kyd shouted. "How did you..."

"The school called me. Didn't think that one through, did you?"

"No, I mean – here."

Edna didn't answer. Her presence rerouted the tent denizens. They chanted, "Mother, Echidna. Mother, Echidna," as they shuffled toward her.

Kyd was in awe as they all knelt or lay at her mother's feet, pawing at her and weeping. Confused, she ran to her mother as well.

As Kyd approached her, the chanting from the growing sea of humanoid beasts became a singsong drone,

"Mother Echidna, Sister Echidna."

Edna stroked the sooty grey and black strands of the faun man's beard as he wept. His tears were not saline tears. They were diamond tears, like the ones she always wore. She wiped them away as they rolled down his face, pocketing a few.

"Why the hell are they calling you 'Mother' and why are they calling me 'Sister'?"

The two headed dog rubbed one of his awesome heads against Kyd, almost knocking her over. She stretched out her hand and it sank into its plush fur. The colossus pooch plopped over on its side and showed her its belly, which she enthusiastically scratched. The scene was so surreal, and, justifiably so, it freaked her out. But with all the beasts and freakshow oddities, and her mother at its center, she didn't feel afraid.

Edna took her daughter's face in her hands and kissed her forehead.

"He is not your father. But he is your sibling, as is everyone else." Kyd stared at the crowd multiplying within the tent.

"I'm sorry, Mom, but what the *fuck* are you talking about?"

"I was hoping to avoid this conversation until you were much older, but as your kin have announced, my name is Echidna. Edna for short. I am your mother *and* your father, just as I am theirs," she said, gesturing to the herd like a game show prize model.

Kyd raked her hands through her scalp. Her rough fingernails tearing out dark strands.

"You birthed a... freakshow?"

"Eons of freakshows, darling. But unlike your siblings who are sterile, you were born like me; able to procreate, but without needing...*assistance*. Therefore, *Kyd*, Echidna is who you are as well." She lowered her voice. "I didn't want this for you. I didn't want you to bear this responsibility." Echidna placed her hand on her daughter's stomach. "I had your reproductive parts...*adjusted* when you were a baby so, unlike me, you couldn't bear any...monsters. But after your body's awakening last evening..."

"So, it wasn't a dream?" Kyd interrupted. "You had me poked and prodded for years. You had me operated on? What the fuck, Mom?"

"And for that I'm deeply sorry. I tried to hide you away, as I have kept *them* hidden away in plain sight, from a world where being different can be both a blessing and a curse. But that was wrong of me. I should have realized, after all my lifetimes, that nature always finds a way."

Echidna stepped atop a small stage in the center of the tent and addressed her spawn.

"Children! I present to you, Echidna. This Millenia's Mother of Monsters!"

The horde cheered.

# LOVER'S QUARREL

## BY GEORGIA COOK

Charybdis and Scylla. Scylla and Charybdis. The Beast Above the Rocks and The Maw Below the Waves. Never one without the other, always in tandem.

They quarrel often these days.

The seas churn beneath them, throwing spray and doomed fish high into the air. The wind howls, lashing their faces, tangling their hair, chorus to an argument loud enough to split the gulf:

You. You. You.

You Monster. You Coward. You Bitch.

You.

The argument has been raging for decades, rending moss from stone and sails from ships, reducing the strait to ruin. Neither remembers how it started, or even the original disagreement, but it's been going on too long now to stop.

It hasn't always been this way. Once, the gulf between them was a thing of longing sighs and lingering glances, just an inch too wide to brush hands. Once, the isolation of imposed monstrosity was made almost bearable by the proximity of another just as monstrous. The waters were calm. The seabirds wheeling through the air sang a song of sweetness.

Now, though, they've been cooped up together for too long. They see one another every day, all day, without respite. Proximity breeds a special kind of loathing, mixed with the potency of old affections. They need to get out, meet other people, discover hobbies and joys beyond the other. But each one knows, even as they howl and roar, scream and sob, that they could never leave the other on her own. Scylla could never abandon Charybdis deep beneath the waves, endlessly hungry, endlessly alone, no more than Charybdis could leave her beloved stranded on the rocks.

Instead, they bicker.

As is the way of arguments, there's always someone caught between: ships and sea birds, Gods and men, they all know to steer clear of the strait. To stray between Charybdis and Scylla, they say, is to invite certain death. Either swallowed by a gaping mouth, or plucked from the sea to be dashed upon the rocks. Consumed by a lover's quarrel.

Sometimes, when they pause to draw breath, Charybdis and Scylla notice.

It's not howling, says Scylla. I'm simply making my point.

You howl because you aren't listening, retorts Charybdis. You never listen. Not to me. You've never listened to me.

And so it goes.

***

Once, in desperation, Charybdis' father Poseidon asked the Goddess of Love to quell the fighting, to remind his daughter of love's softness, love's care. If there was peace to be found, he reasoned, surely it lay in she who understood all living hearts.

But Poseidon, as all men, misunderstood the purpose of Aphrodite; she who encompasses both passion and lust, Eros and Agape. She who razed Troy to the ground for a golden apple, who embodies all facets of love, both mortal and immortal, sweet and wild. She who understood the true cruelty of what the gods had done to Charybdis and Scylla.

To be trapped with the one you most adore, desperate to be heard, desperate to be *seen*. Is there no worse fate?

What else is love contained but sorrow? Love compounded, love forced under the pressure of a thousand lifetimes. What else is love in isolation? Bubbling and burning, spilling over the edges. What else is love, left to rise like snatching fingers to the storm-grey skies?

Co-dependency brings a whole new meaning to divine punishment, and here was punishment indeed.

Charybdis and Scylla. Never apart, never alone. Stuck on opposite sides of their own wailing abyss, as the waves below them thunder and crash, and over their heads the seabirds scream.

You. You. You.

You Monster. You Coward. You God-given Punishment. You God-Given Joy.

You.

# THE STRIFE WHO WALKS IN DARKNESS

## BY BEN THOMAS

Tale-tellers whisper that my sisters and I sprang forth from the blood of the Titan Uranus, when his son Cronus castrated him and hurled his manhood into the sea. But in truth, we were born before the Titans — and long before the gods who overthrew them.

My sisters and I came forth unfathered from the bosom of Night herself, in the cold darkness before Time's dawn. In our mother's arms, we watched Mount Olympus rise naked from the fiery magma to pierce the ash-choked skies of newborn Earth.

We were there when Cronus's son, a beardless young godling named Zeus, overthrew his father and cast the Titans down to Tartarus. We stood on Troy's blood-soaked beach as Achilles stormed raging from the battlefield, abandoning his fellow Greeks to Trojan slaughter. It was we who gave Oedipus the idea to gouge out his eyes with dress-pins, when he realized he'd loved his mother in a way no man should.

We are little-loved among mortals. The poets name us Furies, or "Kindly Ones" when they seek to placate us. They sing that we have snakes for hair, that our bodies are black as coal, our eyes eternally bloodshot, and that we descend with brass-tipped scourges to drive our victims, slave-like, to tormented ruin.

In truth, we employ more elegant methods. The divine *até*, which brings on madness, is tasteless, colorless, and easy to slip into a mortal's drink—or a god's. It's less a poison than the *idea* of a poison; we carry and wield it as Zeus wields his thunderbolts and Aphrodite wields Love. We do these things not because we wish to, but because it is our nature, and because our mistresses command it.

Because, like all beings, even the gods themselves, we serve the will of the Fates.

\*\*\*

I stand in a small cottage. In the shadows before me sit three sisters robed in black sackcloth, a basket of white wool at their feet.

The youngest spins the wool into thread, which the middle sister measures with a rod, portioning it out to the eldest, who snips it with a pair of shears older than the hills. Each thread is a life, and I have never learned by what rules the sisters measure and snip.

This scene is the same every time, as it has been since the beginning. But even after many such meetings, a Fury can still feel the cold knife of dread twist in her stomach, as I do now.

"Who is to be my victim?" I ask, fighting to keep my voice steady.

"A young shepherd of Boeotia," replies the youngest, plucking a handful of yarn from the basket and fitting it onto her wooden staff.

"He is called Cithaeron," adds the second, drawing a length of spun thread from her sister's spindle and measuring it.

"Quite handsome," says the eldest with a grin, "if I say so myself." She punctuates the final word with a slice of her shears.

Snip.

I phrase my question delicately. "What has this shepherd done to offend?"

"He is a patricide," says the youngest. "A father-killer."

"Truly," says the second, "the most terrible of crimes."

"And deserving," asks the eldest, "of the most awful punishment."

Snip.

I try to swallow, but find my throat has gone dry. "What do I do with this shepherd once I've found him?" I ask.

"Drive him mad, of course," says the youngest.

"Slip the divine *até* into his drink," says the second.

"See that he fulfills his destiny," says the eldest, "and receives his curse."

Snip.

And with that, the three sisters return to silent absorption in their labors. I have my task, and our conversation is ended. I might as well argue against the tides.

I'd have better luck with the tides, truth be told. Poseidon owes me some favors.

Abruptly, the eldest sister raises an eyebrow, scrutinizing a length of thread stretched between her bony fingers.

"*Him?* Are you certain?" she asks her middle sibling, who nods in stern confirmation. "A pity." The eldest's mouth twists in what might be a frown or a smile. Or both. "Always such a pity," she says, "to kill a god."

Snip.

***

One glance around Boeotia reminds me why this place is called "Cow

Country". No sign of human habitation; not even the smoke of a cookfire in the distant mountains. Just woods and grassy meadows dotted with grazing cattle, their quiet ruminations broken only by an occasional "moo." If the gods were cows, this would surely be their Olympus.

I pause and close my eyes a moment, drinking in the sunlight, the silence, the flower-scented air... But no. A cold fist clenches my heart, recalling me to my task.

Though I have never met this shepherd, Cithaeron, I knew his face the moment my mistresses spoke his name. And though this land seems devoid of men, I know where I will find him.

I stride across the meadow, toward the oak grove where the shepherd lies sleeping. Though I walk invisibly, a few cows raise their heads at my passing. Perhaps they sense a shift in the wind.

My victim, on the other hand, remains oblivious. I find Cithaeron asleep in the bushes, beneath an oak-branch he has draped with his cloak to form a makeshift tent.

As Zeus's thunder shakes the hearts of mountains, so do Cithaeron's snores set the very trees to trembling. I find, to my surprise, that I am smiling.

A tiny laugh escapes my lips and Cithaeron bolts awake, cracking his head against the branch and tangling himself in his cloak. I fail to suppress more laughter as he curses the fabric, rubbing his sore head.

"Who's there?" he demands, eyes darting among the bushes. "Who are you?"

As my mistresses told me, he is quite handsome, in a gangly, fragile sort of way. His curly black hair frames a narrow face roughened by a few days' growth of beard, and his nose and lips are well-formed. But it is his eyes that startle me most, eyes green as emeralds, afire with wary curiosity.

"I know you're there," he says, more gently this time. "I heard you laughing."

Though I know he cannot see me, I take shelter behind a nearby oak, drawing each breath as quietly as I can.

His brow furrows. "You don't have to be shy. I only want to help you." He rises to his feet. Beneath his tunic, tan skin stretches tightly over work-hardened muscle. Why does my heart quicken at the sight?

"Listen," he says. "A woman shouldn't be alone in these woods. Wolves hunt here; even lions, sometimes. I promise you'll be safer with me."

A snort of laughter escapes my nose. If only he knew!

"Unless—" His eyes widen as he steps closer to my tree. "Unless I am wrong to call you woman. Are you a wood-nymph, perhaps? Or—" His smile abruptly fades, and he sinks slowly to his knees. " Are you a goddess? If you are Artemis the Huntress, then I beg you, forgive my offense!" He prostrates himself in the dust, trembling with fear. "Please do not turn me into a stag!"

This fool is the patricide I've been sent to torment? Doubt flickers across my mind, and I wonder, for the briefest instant, whether my mistresses may be mistaken. But now he knows I'm here; it's too late to turn back. Swiftly I clothe myself in mortal disguise: a peasant girl clad in a simple flaxen dress and head-shawl. And with a sigh of resignation, I step from behind my tree.

Cithaeron remains head-down, groveling on the leaf-strewn soil. "O divine one," he cries. "I dare not raise my eyes to you!"

I kick some leaves at him. "Silly boy. Lift up your eyes and look upon your 'goddess.'"

The shepherd raises his head, spitting out leaf-flecks. At the sight of my mortal form, he gasps with astonishment then heaves a sigh of relief. High-pitched laughter shakes the breath from his body. "Artemis the Huntress!" he yelps, raising his hands in mock terror. "Don't turn me into a stag! Oh, you truly had me fooled!"

"It seems to me that you fooled yourself," I point out, helping him to his feet. "You must be a powerful priest indeed, to conjure such dire goddesses from a shepherdess's laughter."

Cithaeron dusts soil from his tunic. "And you must be a brave shepherdess — or a very foolish one — to wander alone in these woods, so far from home." He bends to retrieve his cloak and crook-staff from the bushes. "Where is your home, anyway?" he asks. "Isn't your father worried?"

I tell him the truth. "I have no father."

"Ah." He drapes his cloak about his shoulders. "Your... husband, then?"

"I have no husband, either," I tell him, holding his gaze.

"Ah," he says again. "Well, I'm called Cithaeron. What may I call you?"

I smile at the idea of this clumsy shepherd calling me by my true names: Erinye, Mania, the Strife who Walks in Darkness.

"Call me Tisiphone," I tell him.

"Tisiphone," he echoes. "I like the sound of that."

"And what of you, a shepherd who's lost his flock?" I quickly change the subject. "Your wife will never let you hear the end of it."

Cithaeron harrumphs. "Do I look like I have a wife? No; I'm a free man, thank the gods. And I know precisely where my sheep are."

The shepherd is right. We find his flock grazing in a meadow beyond the woods' western edge, as Apollo's sun-chariot descends toward the valley's mountainous rim, bathing green-leafed trees and grassy hillsides in warm golden light.

At Cithaeron's insistence, we stop for a picnic at this perfect hour. As if by magic, he produces a wineskin and a wedge of dry white cheese from the folds of his cloak, which he spreads on the grass, inviting me to sit.

He uncorks the wineskin with his teeth, and takes a swig. "You've still got a long walk home tonight," he says, passing the skin to me. "Where did you say your farm was, exactly?"

I take a sip from the skin. "I didn't say," I remind him. "Nor do I know you well enough to tell you." I swallow. The wine is warm and tart — and subtler in flavor than I expected.

He draws a sharp knife from his belt, slices off a bit of cheese and hands it to me, smiling. "It's going to be hard for me to escort you home," he says, "if I don't know where your home is."

To my surprise, I find myself returning his smile. "I don't need an escort," I say, taking a bite of the cheese. "I am perfectly safe in these woods."

His smile widens, and soft laughter shakes his frame. "Not for protection, then," he says as we pass the wineskin between us. "For the pleasure of your company." His green eyes hold my gaze, and warmth rushes up my neck. Why does this shepherd please me so?

"You're blushing," he observes.

"It must be the wine," I tell him, forcing myself to look away.

Suddenly his hand is beneath my chin, gently guiding my gaze back to his. I find myself wondering, for the second time, how this strangely wondrous creature could be the murderer I'm here to punish.

His rough palm strokes my cheek, and a shiver runs through me. I lean toward him, and he tilts his chin up, seeking my lips, which rise to meet his—

— and I pull away, gathering my shawl around me and rising from the grass. "You're right," I say. "It must be the wine."

He gazes up at me, eyes wide and hurt like those of a rebuked puppy. At last he sighs, and clambers to his feet. "Well," he says quietly, handing me the wineskin, "enjoy what's left of it. I'll be back in a moment."

While he strolls to the edge of the woods to answer nature's call, I stare down at the wineskin in my hand. This may be my only chance to slip him a dose of *até*, and I have just moments to act. I ask myself whether I'm absolutely sure about this. But even as I ask, I know the answer: this is what I am, and what I must do. I raise a finger above the wineskin, and three drops of pale fluid drip from my fingertip into its aperture.

Cithaeron ambles back from the woods, adjusting his tunic. The smile has returned to his face. "Shall we be off?" he asks.

I extend the wineskin to him. "Just one swallow left."

He takes the skin and gulps down the dregs of the wine.

There. It is done.

The shepherd bends down, gathers up his cloak and crook, and goes to his flock, calling them homeward.

I follow. The rest is in my mistresses' hands now.

*** 

We catch sight of the smoke rising from Cithaeron's farmstead before we see the farmhouse itself. The plume from the hearth rises dark gray against the white clouds of a deep red sunset, carrying the scent of roasting meat across the valley.

The small farmhouse is scarcely more than a shack of rough-hewn oak, nestled against the hills on the far side of the valley, surrounded by tree-branch fences and pens where cows placidly take their evening meal.

Cithaeron tries to catch my eye as we approach, driving his flock of sheep before us. I avoid his gaze and he turns away, uncomprehending.

This is already hard enough, I tell myself; no need to make it harder.

I prepare myself to smile as I meet Cithaeron's mother; to hide the truth as I thank her for her hospitality and compliment her cooking—

—but the shack's door is thrown wide by a gray-bearded man in a shepherd's tunic. He is the spitting image of Cithaeron. For the third time, my stomach churns with the certainty that there has been a mistake.

Cithaeron embraces the old man, then turns to me, beaming with joy.

"Tisiphone," he says. "Meet my father."

*** 

Mortals have pleaded with me, times beyond counting, to revoke the curses I am sent to execute. My answer is always the same: fate cannot be unwoven; the divine *até* cannot be undrunk. A curse, once placed, cannot be removed. My mistresses always get their way.

These thoughts howl in my mind as Cithaeron's father — Polynikes, I learn his name is — spoons boiling lamb stew from the iron pot on the fire, and ladles it into three wooden bowls, placing them on a long, low table and inviting us to eat our fill.

We recline on straw-stuffed cushions, and tear into rough barley-bread and white cheese in olive oil. The stew tastes of butter, and of rosemary and garlic fresh from the forest. I accept a clay cup of wine, though my head still spins from the wine we drank this afternoon.

As the sun sets and we fill our bellies, we drain more cups and toast to old friends; to summers long-past; to those we'll never see again.

"To my wife," says Polynikes, "my dear Antigone." His voice cracks, and he takes a breath before continuing. "Though you left this world before me, we will meet again, somewhere across the River Styx." Tears glisten in his eyes. I blink back my own as I raise my cup and drink.

Cithaeron wraps an arm around his father's hunched shoulders. "Come, Father," he says. "This is no way to welcome a guest. Especially not one so lovely as this."

Polynikes nods, chewing his bearded lip. "You're right." He pats Cithaeron's hand, and raises watery eyes to meet mine. "It's just been... so lonely around here. Just me, all alone in this house, with only my boy to keep me company..."

Cithaeron helps his father up from the cushion. "I'm not a boy anymore, father." He chuckles. "And you've drunk more than enough toasts tonight. Time for bed."

The old man protests as Cithaeron guides him, stumbling, to a straw mattress in the corner. He collapses amid wool blankets and soon commences to snore, just as thunderously as his son did in the woods this afternoon.

Cithaeron spreads his hands apologetically. "He's right, I suppose," he says as he clears cups and bowls from the table. "No one but cows and sheep to keep us company here. Not much for an old man to do but sit around the house and drink."

I nod, half-smiling, unnerved by his serenity. The *até* should be amplifying his passions; driving him to anger, to foolhardy, self-destructive acts. Instead he smiles at me in the flickering firelight, calmly cleaning wood bowls in a water-jug — this man who most certainly has *not* killed his father, yet now bears a patricide curse that cannot be taken back.

He laughs softly. "What are you worried about? No, don't try to deny it. It's written all over your face. Mother used to look like that, when she knew..." His eyes fall, and his smile disappears. "When she knew things were getting worse."

I swallow against a dry throat. "How did she...?"

Cithaeron's brow furrows. "She had a wasting sickness. We tried to make her eat, but she kept getting thinner, paler. We made offerings. Even sacrificed our prize bull to Asclepius the Healer. But the god didn't seem to hear us. Or maybe my mother's fate was already decided."

"Never let it be said that my mistresses are kind," I mutter.

He raises his eyes. "What was that?"

I wave a hand dismissively. "Nothing." I shake my head. "I'm just tired. It's been a long day."

Cithaeron smiles gently. "Take my bed," he says, gesturing to a lumpy mattress on the floor, next to the place where his father lies snoring. "I'll sleep out under the stars."

I rise from my cushion. "You don't have to do that."

He laughs, and turns his attention back to his dishwashing. "I like it better out there anyway."

"As you wish, then," I say, rising from my lumpy cushion. "Sleep well."

Cithaeron nods, a soft smile creasing his face sharply in the firelight. "If I sleep at all," he says, and as he raises his eyes to mine, I see a flash of passion stronger than wine alone can produce. Is it the *até* taking effect? Or something else?

"I'm happy to have spent a day with you," he says at last. "Even if it was only a day." His gaze is so full of hope; so ready to make promises he can't know he'll never keep.

"I'm glad to have met you too," I tell him, turning away. "Until tomorrow, then."

"Until tomorrow," he agrees as I settle onto the rough pallet in the corner.

A moment later, I hear Cithaeron stoke the fire, put out the lamps, and step outside, closing the door behind him, leaving me alone in this warm, dark place, next to his raucously snoring father.

I could go to him, I think, out there under the stars. He is far from displeasing, for a mortal man. And it has been so long for me; longer than I can remember. But some things are simply not possible, no matter how badly we want them.

So I close my eyes, and pretend to sleep — another thing I cannot do.

***

I return —not from sleep, but from some far-distant place in my mind— to find a hot, heavy form looming over me. My eyes snap open to see Polynikes, the father, eyes afire as if he, not his son, had drunk the *até*. His flesh is pale-blue in the moonlight, his breath sharp with the tang of wine, body reeking of sweat and soil.

He crawls half-atop me like a sick beast, hairy hands probing eagerly beneath my shawl; under my long dress. As I push back, squirming and

92

kicking against the weight of him, he mutters words of affection and command: "It's been so long. Just let me... oh, so soft. Smell so sweet. Come on dear, just a little..."

"How dare you?" I shout, shoving him off me with a strength that knocks the wind out of him.

The old man lands on his back, clutching his chest. As he recovers his breath, he crawls back toward me, snarling. "Who do you think you are? Just a shepherd girl. Just a little lost shepherd girl..."

Then our eyes lock, and I allow him the briefest glimpse of what I truly am. For an instant he falls through black gulfs beyond sounding, hears the wails of the souls I have dragged down to the Pit, feels the everlasting fire of Tartarus.

He cries out — first in fear, then in fury, gripping my hair and yanking my head back. "Witch!" He spits in my face. "Sorceress! Come to torment me, eh? I'll teach you!"

I look up into his eyes, and I smile.

"Stop it!" Cithaeron's cry thunders from the doorway. His hair and tunic are disheveled with sleep, but his eyes are madly awake with a fire beyond any ordinary mortal passion. He leaps over the table, whipping the knife from his belt and throwing himself on his father.

Old Polynikes raises his hands in futile defense. "Please! My son, you don't understand!"

But Cithaeron is beyond hearing. The *ate* has him now. He thrusts the blade into his father's back, his belly, his neck and shoulders. Dark bloodstains seep across Polynikes's tunic, running in rivulets from its fringes, pooling on the sawdust floor.

Polynikes takes a surprisingly long time to die. Even after his father ceases moving, Cithaeron continues to plunge the blade in, gripping its handle with both hands, heaving his weight into blow after thick wet blow. I stand and bear witness, cold and motionless as stone.

When at last Cithaeron has exhausted even the frenzied abandon of the *ate*, he collapses on the floor next to the blood-soaked corpse he's made. His eyes are empty, and he holds the dagger as if he has forgotten its purpose.

And still I stand watch, as night softens to predawn, and dawn cracks open with the first rays of sunlight. I watch because this is my task. And my task is almost done.

***

The poets say my sisters and I have no pity in our hearts. This is untrue. The truth is that many of our victims deserve what they get.

Many of our victims, but not all. I cannot bring myself to believe that Cithaeron deserves to awaken to the blood-caked remains of his father, to find the murder weapon in his hand. I cannot believe he deserves to scream with horror at his deed, gazing up at me with wild-eyed incomprehension.

"What have I done?" he cries, pushing himself away from the corpse, staring at the dagger in disbelief. "What have I done?" he asks again. So many of them ask that, when they know the answer all too well.

What can I tell him? That he did this for a good reason? What reason? Me, Cithaeron, his father's corpse, the knife in his hand— we all got here the same way: because my mistresses decreed it so.

As if reading my thoughts, Cithaeron gazes down at the bloodied knife. Before I can utter a word, he raises the blade to his neck and forces it inward, then slices across, slowly. Blood spills down his neck, fountains from burst arteries. He falls to his knees, eyes glistening with tears that spill onto the sawdust.

And when the life fades from those eyes, his spirit appears before me, gray-skinned and insubstantial about the edges. His eyes widen as he sees me, for the first time, as I truly am: marble-skinned and onyx-eyed, clad in dripping crimson with hair like a nest of serpents.

"I knew," he whispers. "I knew you weren't human, but I loved you anyway. Was that so wrong?"

"That's not for me to decide," I tell him.

"Who gets to decide?" Cithaeron's eyes fill with fresh tears. "It's your heart. It should be your decision."

"But it's not." Gently, I place my hand on his shoulder. "And now it's time for you to come with me."

He gazes up at me, meek and frightened as a lamb. "Where are we going?"

"I think you know," I tell him.

***

I stand alone in a small cottage. Before me sit three sisters robed in black sackcloth, a basket of white wool at their feet. The youngest spins; the middle one measures; the eldest cuts. This has always been happening, and it always will be.

Memories of Cithaeron's screams echo in my memory. I left him in the black abyss of Tartarus, to tread the molten plain where patricides suffer the claws and teeth of bat-winged harpies. Even now, after everything, I can't bring myself to believe he deserves to be there.

"You have done well." The youngest sister breaks the silence.

"It was not an easy task," adds the second.

"But it needed to be done." The eldest nods. *Snip.*

I fight down the cold fear in my stomach, and say, "He hadn't killed his father yet."

All three sisters do something I have never seen them do: they pause in their work and look up. As a hawk watches a wriggling mouse pinned by its claw, so do three sets of sharp eyes regard me.

"Cithaeron wasn't a patricide before I came to him," I persist, my hands balled into fists. "He only killed his father after I put the *ate* in his wine. And now he's in Hell for it."

"Before drinking, after drinking," says the youngest sister, shaking her head. "What difference does it make?"

"He was a patricide," says the second. "And now, as you say, he is in Hell for it."

"That is his fate," says the eldest. "It was his destiny from the moment we wove his thread."

The three of them continue to watch me, hawk-like and unmoving, genuinely curious whether I'll dare to ask another question.

I swallow hard. "Who decides," I ask, "what's in the thread?"

The youngest laughs out loud — a discordant cackle whose echoes grow louder as the shack seems to loom to vertiginous size, becoming a cavern that dwarfs us in the immensity of its shadows.

"Who decides what's in the thread?" she howls.

"Where does the thread come from?" asks the second sister. "Why must we weave and measure it? Where does it go when we cut it?"

"If you ever find out," says the eldest, "please do tell us."

And with that, the shadows recede and the echoes fade to silence. The shack is just a shack again; the women just three yarn-weavers in black cloaks. They resume their labors, ignoring me, signaling that our conversation is at an end.

And for the first time, I realize that even they, perhaps, do not know when our next meeting will be. Perhaps they, like me, serve powers they do not understand.

I shudder to imagine what such powers might be. And it's that thought, more than any other, that finally puts me to flight.

95

# MORTALS

# AMAZONS

# AMAZON WOMAN

## BY ARLENE BURKE

With sheath and sword upon your fearsome horse,
Your life's meaning built on a violent course,
A legendary warrior living a nomadic life,
You were a potent force, not shy of conflict or strife,
So long ago, but your story lingers on,
One which became twisted and mangled after you were gone,
Distorted by time, you were relegated to a myth,
A memory dishonored, no understanding your pith,
Your essence is now perceived, knowing you were real,
Buried bones and metal reveal a truth no one could conceal.

# THE BIRTHRIGHT

## BY H.R. BOLDWOOD

The shores of Pontus never looked more beautiful, nor smelled more like home than the day my mount Aithon and I left their bosom in pursuit of my birthright: the breastplate of Ares and a jewel-studded dagger imbued with the power of the gods. Violets, lilies, and larkspur swirled their intoxicating scents and bowed their blooms as they bid us safe passage.

Aithon, an Andalusian, was gifted to me by my grandfather Ares in my sixteenth year. Although he had promised me the stallion's bountiful heart and mystical powers would see me through the worst of days, thus far, I could only attest that the steed was strong, elegant, and white as winter's snow. Within him dwelled courage, loyalty, and a keen intellect. He knew my mind, my hand, even the touch of my knee on his flank. We rode as one.

He carried me that day along the shore of The Euxine Sea under a cloudless sky. The temperate sun warmed us both, and the scent of brine lured us from our quest to race against the wind and tide. So free were we for a time, that we failed to notice a pod of sea nymphs sunning themselves upon the rocky shoals nearby.

"Who goes there?" called a tiny voice.

I spun to find a fiery-haired nymph peeking out from between the rocks.

"The Amazon, Xanthe," I called, squinting into the sun. "Halia, daughter of Pontus, is that you?"

"Aye. Have mercy, great warrior. We pose no threat."

"I do not come to fight." Nudging Aithon closer, I opened my hands, palms held high, to show them free of weapons.

"You have travelled far from my father's land. What brings you?"

"I seek the gateway to Hades."

A collective gasp arose from the pod.

"Brave, even for an Amazon," Halia said. "I know of several gateways, though I would not risk the wrath of Hecate by divulging them."

"Would you prefer my wrath?"

"We are not your foe—"

"Not yet."

"But neither are we friends." Halia's voice grew bold. "I will help you cross into the land of Hades, but there is a toll for my service, and that toll is payable tonight with the return of the full moon."

"What is the nature of said toll?"

The sea-maid tossed her hands. "It's Dionysius. He returns with each cycle of the moon; indeed, he will arrive this very night. With each visit, he takes my nymphs at will and offers them nothing in return. He scoffs when the maids object. Their tears only fuel his debauchery."

Upon hearing the plight of these docile creatures, I agreed to Halia's terms. While waiting for nightfall, Aithon and I reveled in the fresh sea breeze and played among the surf with the nymphs. When the sun finally dipped to the horizon, a distant shape trudged toward us along the shoreline, a jug swinging from one hand and a lute from the other. As he drew closer, a garbled song poured from his lips. The drunken Dionysius had returned as surely as the stars return to the evening sky. He made straight for Halia.

"Oh," she moaned behind her hand. "He's such a vile little god."

"Halia," he said with a nod, turning his attention to me. "And who might you be?"

I dismounted and planted my feet shoulder-width apart.

"I am Xanthe, daughter of the great Queen Hippolyta."

"Ah! I know of you. I am—"

"Dionysius," I said, standing arms akimbo. "Your reputation precedes you."

A grin stole across his face. "But of course it does. Come to satisfy your curiosity, perhaps? How may I...assist?"

"You may enlighten me as to what gives you the right to rape and pillage these poor nymphs with no thought to equity or recompense."

"How dare you question me!" he cried. "You! You...*Amazon*... are the last creature who should counsel anyone on the niceties of romance. Your kind lie with any man you see fit, and once you've had your fill, you'll likely slay him, or condemn him to a life of slavery. Check your tongue, for I am a god! Do not test my stones."

"Bah! You are a demi-god. I am granddaughter to the god of war. You may assume my stones are larger than yours. But if you wish, we can compare." I drew my bow and plucked an arrow from my quiver.

A twinkle gleamed in his eyes. "War is wasteful, Xanthe. Besides, you are so much better at that than I. Turn your Amazonian wiles upon me, and I will gladly forgo these passive nymphs. Take me, even as I take you! Allow me to sate your womanly urges. I vow you will war with more passion and sleep more deeply, for I will be the best lover you have ever taken."

"Have you no less tired sentiments to offer?" Yet, even as I chastised him, I considered his proposition. He was, for all his arrogance, charmingly rakish and fair of face. But my quest called, so instead, I beckoned him with a smoldering smile. "Very well, Dionysius. Come forth. Behold the wiles of a warrior." He came to me quickly. When there was no space left between us, I wrapped my arms around him and whispered in his ear, "If you seek your pleasures elsewhere tonight, I shall let you live. For now. Any questions?"

"Plenty of nymphs in the sea, Xanthe. I've no need to beg your favors." He dismissed me with a wave of his hand and turned to leave in search of more easily won prey.

"Dionysius?" I called, uprooting a conch shell from the sand.

He pivoted on his heel. Hope gleamed in his eyes.

"When you return for these nymphs, as I know you will, ply them with gifts and coin, perhaps a gentle word or two. These tender maids are deserving of your best efforts. If you deny them, they have only to blow this conch to summon me. Need I return, you will not fare as well."

With a timely thwack of his rump, Aithon knocked Dionysius onto his bottom. He righted himself and then stomped off, entreating the gods for justice. Sand flew from his feet and curses spewed from his lips as he faded down the shoreline.

Halia laughed. "A magic conch? Think you he believed that?"

"You pay him too much credit," I said. "He isn't the brightest of gods."

*** 

We rose the next morning with the sun, ate our fill from the sea, and drank from the freshwater pools, preparing for our journey. Halia and her nymphs spun like liquid silk through the rolling waves while Aithon and I stayed our course at tide's edge.

The shore appeared infinite. Surely it stretched to the very edges of the earth, and though I knew not where those edges were, we seemed determined to find them. We passed all manner of flora and fauna, collecting aloe, dill, and berries that could prove useful during our journey.

The nymphs, eager to share their knowledge, pointed out groves of aconite and calamint. They picked moly flowers and ground them into powder for me with their tails, warning that touching the actual blooms proved lethal to mortals. I gathered a sizable collection of the aconite stems, for felling larger beasts of prey.

When we reached the cave of Hypnos, Halia brought her maids to a stop. "My sisters and I shall go no further. Within this cavern dwells our sworn enemy, Echidna, the mother of all monsters. Should you survive your encounter with her, at cave's end you will find the river of death, which leads to the gates of Hades. Go with the gods, Xanthe. Keep close the herbs we prepared. You will need them."

***

The cave swallowed Aithon and me whole. The air was cold, dank, and reeked of death.

I called into the void, "Great Echidna! My mount and I seek passage to the River Styx."

A humongous creature with a plated spine, pallid skin, and bulging eyes slogged forth from the depths and inhaled so deeply that the air gusted.

"Odd," Echidna said. "You don't smell of death. Not even illness. What business brings you to the underworld?"

"Hecate stole what is rightfully mine. I come to take it back."

"Such courage! Or is it foolishness? Either way, your pluck amuses me. I will not eat you—yet. But you must battle my son, the Chimera, if you wish to pass."

Echidna led us deeper into the cave to wait for her son. I grew impatient. "Show yourself, Chimera!"

A long, steady growl hummed in the darkness.

"Are you frightened of me? Is that why you conceal yourself?"

The monster snorted. "So, it's the river of death you seek. I shall take you there myself—in little, tiny pieces!"

A noxious stench enveloped me. The monster had neared.

I drew my sword and taunted, "Bold squawking from the spineless beastie." Something slimy flicked my ear. I slashed my sword. A quiet yip ensued.

First blood.

Something swept my legs, and I tumbled to the ground. Aithon moved to shield me. To my amazement, a mystifying blanket of light sprang from his eyes!

The beast howled. I scrambled to my feet and beheld the horror of the Chimera. Its massive head was that of a lion. Jagged yellow teeth and a flailing serpent's tongue protruded from its mouth. Its goat-man torso tapered to the razored talons of a phoenix. I drove my javelin into the creature, again and again, running it through. The Chimera's high-pitched squeals drew Echidna back into the cavern.

As I clambered atop Aithon to escape, Echidna sobbed.

105

"Oh, how you have failed, Child, and it has cost me dearly! Your duty shirked, the mortal escapes, and I have lost a child."

"Mother, help me," the monster mewled.

"Better to die, my son, than face the wrath of Typhos. You were guardian to the river of death and a mortal passed upon your watch." With that, Echidna sank her serrated teeth into the Chimera's neck and ripped off its head. At last glance, she lay prostrate across the mutilated beast, wallowing in its blood, wailing and beseeching Zeus for death.

Aithon and I raced to the rear of the cave and emerged into a dystopian world never intended for the living.

*** 

We hovered, disoriented and bewildered, on the banks of the River Styx. Sulphur steamed from molten pools along its shoreline. The ground was scorched and brittle, the horizon awash in a fiery hue. Heat wafted from the blackened soil and baked the air we breathed.

The distant but unmistakable sound of lapping oars reached my ears.

Emerging from a shroud of fog, Charon, the ferryman—a collection of weathered bones and tattered robes—slid his boat into the shore and extended a gnarled claw to me. Aithon bellowed and reared, kicking at the hideous bag of bones as if to scatter him to the winds. While I would have preferred to have given the steed his head, I pulled at his reigns to settle him, for we would need Charon's assistance to complete our quest.

The oarsman's voice hung heavy in the air. "Who seeks the service of the ferryman?"

"Xanthe, daughter of Hippolyta."

"Only shades may cross. Leave, mortal. You have no business in the underworld."

"In truth, I do. I am here for Hecate."

"My sympathies." He flashed a serpentine twist of rotted teeth. "Consider yourself fortunate that I refuse. Only the properly interred with coinage may pass. Leave at once."

"No." I jutted my chin. "You have ferried other mortals, and so, you will ferry me."

"And why would I do that?"

"Let us wager. If I am victorious, you will take me to the other side."

His laughter grated like gravel on steel.

"And if I am the victor?"

I stared into his eyes—cavernous voids that blazed lava-red—and proffered him that which he wanted above all else.

"Then I shall take your place as ferryman."

He grabbed my hands. A coin-encrusted ring swiveled around his bony finger. So near were we that his sulphurous spittle flecked my face.

"What is the wager?"

"First, say we are agreed."

"We are! Have no fear of that, Amazon. The wager!"

"Very well. What is it which swallows all before it, all behind it, as well all who watch?"

He closed his eyes and furrowed his brow, as if such effort could birth the answer to my riddle. At length, he began to shake.

"How can this be?" he screamed. "I…I have no answer! Tell me. By the gods tell me now, for not knowing will bring madness!"

"Honor your wager, Charon. Ferry us safely to the other side, and I shall tell you."

The broken Charon waved us aboard. He navigated the currents, taking us deep into the river.

"Cast your eyes upon the water, Amazon. What do you see?"

The water's surface portrayed a series of tableaus. Each scene contained defining moments of my life—the loss of my mother, deeds of courage, and lessons learned in defeat. The scenes swept past with such force that the water boiled and churned. Aithon pranced as the boat rose and fell to the rhythm of the white-capped waves. Still, the ferryman kept us afloat.

"What do you see now?" he asked.

Flashes of iridescent light writhed through the water at frenetic speed. They multiplied ten-fold and hurtled into the air, taking on wraith-like shapes that darted and danced as if stepping to the strains of a silent song.

"What be they?" I whispered.

"Souls. My souls," he said, with a hint of pride. "It is the odyssey of the uninterred, those without passage, and those with unfinished business that beckons them. Hundreds of thousands of souls! They move through the air in search of the portal that gives them passage back to settle their affairs."

The water calmed and at length, we reached the shoreline. When I led Aithon to solid ground, the oarsman growled.

"I have honored my part of the bargain. The answer to your riddle, now. Or die."

I checked my budding smile. "What swallows all before it, all behind it, as well as those who watch is the only enemy you have, Charon. Time."

From within him rose an anger that brought the waters of The Styx to roil and foam. In the midst of the tempest, the ferryman's boat slipped from the bank and back into the bubbling murk. Obscured by the billowing fog, he loosed a maniacal laugh and offered a prophecy that brought my blood to ice.

"Time betrays us both, Xanthe. The hound of Hades awaits you."

\*\*\*

The obsidian gates to Hades rose before me, an iron fortress with masterful scrollwork, so immense it might have been made for Zeus himself. Ancient elms towered along each side, in such perfect scale with the gates I questioned which of these titans, god or natural, came first.

A hum pulsed beneath my feet. It grew to a rumble, which built to a roar. A three-headed-hound-beast appeared, filling the expanse of the gates. Its feet the talons of a lion, and its mane a writhing mass of serpents. At tail's end, it bore a stinger longer than I was tall.

Aithon trumpeted, dropped his head and laid back his ears. His foot pawed for purchase in the blackened soil. I held him back with my all.

"I am Cerberus. Who challenges me?" The hound, that had been looking outward far above our heads, glanced down and chortled. "You? A mortal? A single-breasted woman, no less. This is preposterous! Leave me. I grow bored."

I notched an arrow.

"If that be your choice, then I will gladly leave you—dead—although my quarrel is with Hecate. Look closer, hound. The woman who stands before you is a warrior, sculpted in sand by Queen Hippolyta in her own image, and brought to life by the breath of Hera. I possess more strength and courage than any beast or god. Step aside, or die." I levelled my bow at his head.

Cerberus twitched, then drove his talons into the ground and leapt through the air. My arrow split his forehead. He howled but did not falter.

I notched another arrow as Cerberus swiped a massive paw. The shaft found purchase in his left eye, spilling putrid green pus upon his cheek. With a gut-wrenching shriek, he raised his stinger high, then brought it down, skewering my beloved mount. I catapulted from his back and fell to the ground. While diving across Aithon to retrieve my quiver, I saw that which I had forgotten: the arrows laced with aconite. I reached for them, but Cerberus spun and clamped his talons around my calf. He pulled me toward his snapping jaws and the shock of poisonous snakes that adorned his neck. I grabbed Aithon's mane and held fast. The wounded stallion gazed at me.

Gone were his soft brown orbs. In their place were red-hot flames that burned with purpose.

Aithon torqued his body against the stinger, then blinked, and sent those red-hot flames into the coil of snakes. The monster recoiled with a howl. I notched the seven aconite arrows and delivered them en masse down its gullet.

The hellhound released my leg and writhed as poison flowed through its blood, destroying first one organ then the next. Having no time for nature to take its course, I decapitated each of its heads, and in Aithon's honor, impaled them high atop the spires of the gates.

Victory was mine. But at what cost?

I returned to Aithon, laid my head upon his chest, and listened as his warrior's heart slowed to a crawl, then faded further still. I pulled myself forward and peered down into his face. Tears slipped from my cheek into his eye. His gaze remained fixed. My beloved stallion was gone. I wondered if, at the end, he had been watching us frolic on the beach with the nymphs, or nudging me for the apples I carry in my satchel, or feeling the stroke of my hand on his flank. With its final beat, had his heart ached like mine?

I placed my hand upon his chest and jerked at a tiny movement beneath my fingertips. Surely, I thought, that sensation had been born of denial. Even so, I returned my hand to his chest. The stirring had grown to a flutter which in turn, strengthened to a beat. Aithon opened his eyes, those gentle brown eyes that had so often spoken to me; and in my heart I knew that Ares' prophecy had come to pass. Aithon's bountiful heart had not only saved me, it had brought him back to me as well.

I did not attempt to raise him, rather I bade him drink from my waterskin and spread a poultice of aloe and dill across his wounds. I fed him sea buckthorn berries to return his strength and coaxed him to sleep for a short while. His recuperative powers were amazing, for he stood tall and strong when he awoke. Together we ventured into the realm of Hades.

\*\*\*

I had not noticed them before, but nestled among the branches of the giant elms were three winged-demons. My patience had reached its end.

"I know not who you are, but it was I, Xanthe, who killed Cerberus and hung his many heads from the gate posts. Unless you wish to share the same fate, you will let me pass."

Hanging by his knees from a branch, the largest demon flipped feet over head to the ground.

"We are the sons of Nyx, the goddess of night. Do you know of her?" He stepped forward and ogled me. "I am Morpheus. These are my brothers, Icelus and Phantasos." An evil smile upended his lips. "But then, we have met before."

Aithon nickered and twitched. The smaller demons kept their distance, darting like bats among the trees.

Morpheus rose his brows expectantly. "Surely, we look familiar."

I studied the demons at length, but my blank expression betrayed me.

"Revisit your darkest dreams, Amazon! Those dark winged-demons that gave your heart pause? The fiends that dwelled in the niches of your mind, always skittering on the fringes, just beyond sight? The imps that awakened you in the coldest of sweats?"

I fixed them in a collective scowl.

"You are the Oneiroi—the dream demons, the bringers of fear. Is that the full extent of you? Frightening innocent mortals when they dare to sleep? Tell me, fiend, do I look as though I'm sleeping now?"

He rolled his eyes and kicked at the dirt with his toe.

"Well…no."

"Then stand aside you puffering jackanape! I come for Hecate."

The shamefaced demons gave way, and the sky of Hades turned foul. Foliage on the trees grew fuller, creating an impervious canopy. The ground sprang to life, as a tangle of snapping vines swirled between Aithon's feet and tightened with his every step.

Hecate's games had begun.

My surefooted steed threaded gingerly through the undergrowth. He boldly journeyed on as the last of the light disappeared beneath the canopy. The swollen branches bowed and thrashed us.

I moved my hand along Aithon's flank and found the soft, bulky shape of my satchel. Reaching inside, I grabbed the skin filled with the crushed moly flowers prepared by the sea nymphs. Their black roots and white blossoms, when pulverized, were the best defense against the evil Hecate. I threw the moly powder into the air, dusting the belligerent branches. It fell like snow and settled atop the slithering vines, causing them to loosen their grip and scatter like naughty children.

The fortress of Hades loomed at the edge of the thicket, silently drawing me near. Aithon trekked to its watery moat where I studied the trench to discern its depth and content. The waters bubbled and frothed into a bloody roux. Within that vile soup swam visions—visions of my mother's death in battle, images of Aithon being torn in two by the jaws of a hideous monster, and scenes of my own grisly passing at the hands of Hecate. Fear rooted inside me.

"Protect me, Grandfather. Guide me, Athena," I prayed. "Give me wisdom to realize these cruel illusions are born of Hecate's trickery. Give me courage to rise above my fears and reclaim my birthright."

As if in answer to my prayer, the waters quelled. All that remained was turbid brine, but the moat appeared too wide for Aithon to jump. As I pondered how best to cross, Aithon paced back several steps. He twitched beneath my hand, signaling his intent. I held tight as he raced to the edge of the moat and leapt. We took flight! My steed flew beyond the farthest edge of the moat and came to rest on a marble floor at the entrance of a long, pillared hallway leading into the house of Hades.

Aithon's footsteps echoed against the marble. We inched forward, searching each alcove for hidden danger. Halfway down the corridor, instinct bade me pause.

Hecate was near.

A ball of lightning screamed through the shadows and brushed me, causing me to fall from Aithon's back. "Hecate!" I screamed into the void. "Enough! Show yourself, Witch!"

From the darkness rose an oppressive shade, a free-floating, ominous specter. Fully manifested, the shade took the form of Hecate, tall, lean, and winsome. A ball of lightning rested in her palm like a subservient pet.

How bold could this vixen have been? She wore the breastplate of Ares! And peeking out from the top of her boot was the ruby-studded dagger.

"What think you of my armor, Amazon?" She hurled the brilliant orb. I dove to the side, drawing her aim away from Aithon. The ball hissed past my ear.

"Is that the best you have to offer?" I shouted. "You disappoint me, Crone."

"Tsk-tsk. Mustn't taunt a goddess. It never ends well." Hecate stretched her hand toward the castle keep where armaments hung from the stony walls. One by one, the weapons pulled free and hurtled toward me. I dodged some and used my shield to deflect others, but they came at such speed and with such force I would soon be exhausted.

I needed to draw the sorceress out.

"Fight like a warrior, Hecate! Stop this gamesmanship. Show me the warrior's heart inside you, that I may revel when that very heart is stilled by my hand." I squared myself before her and smirked. "Or do you play such silly games because you fear me?"

Hecate attacked with such force she bowled me over. She straddled me on her knees and grabbed my neck, throttling me with far more power than I had expected. I struggled to break free, but when I looked into her eyes, the souls of the dead whose power fueled her hands stared back. They were legion and choking the life from me.

My sight dimmed and my mind began to float. But Aithon's frantic cries rallied me. I reached forward, ripped the jeweled dagger from Hecate's boot and jabbed its tip to her tender gullet. She released me, and I quickly moved atop her, never taking the blade from her throat.

"Relinquish the breastplate, and I shall let you live."

"I would rather die than bow to you!"

I lifted my face and beckoned Hades. "God of the underworld, I summon you that you will know what transpired here today. Show yourself!"

The horizon disappeared, and in its stead loomed the bearded face of the Titan.

"Who dares command the god of the dead?"

"I am Xanthe, daughter of Queen Hippolyta. Long ago, Hecate stole both the dagger I hold and the breastplate she wears from my mother. I come today to reclaim that which is rightfully mine—that which is my birthright. I have offered to spare the witch in return for my chattels. But she refuses, leaving me no choice but to take both my property and her life."

Hades sighed. "Sorceress, give the mortal her property and be done with this calamity."

"These relics hold magic! I am Hecate, the Goddess of Witchcraft. They belong to no one if not me. Do not interfere. She is mortal and cannot harm me."

I pressed the blade against her neck. "This dagger holds the power of the gods. I have no desire to kill you, but kill you I shall if you do not yield."

Hades' voice shook the marble pillars. "Hecate, stop this at once!"

"I will not! Sink your blade into me mortal, for I will not fall. Do it!"

"So be it!" I cried.

With a twist of the blade, Hecate's flesh opened and her blood poured out in a torrent of liquid gold. Her eyes, filled with disbelief, fluttered a moment, then closed. I tucked the dagger into my boot, then tore the breastplate from her corpse, and sprinted for Aithon.

Hades roared, "You killed a *goddess*—in *my house*!" A muffled sob filled the air. The god's tone grew melancholy. "Hecate, goddess of the living and the dead. My wife's sworn companion." A tear trickled down his cheek and fell to the marble floor. The tear begot more tears, which raged into streams that rushed at our feet. Hades wailed above the torrent, "Xanthe! You will pay for what you have done!"

Hailstones rained from the sky. We bounded through the rising water and headed toward the gates. The Titan's ancient, red-rimmed eyes scoured the current, searching for us. As we slid beneath the waters, his menacing voice filled my ears.

"You cannot hide from me, Amazon. Accept your fate!"

The deluge stopped. Aithon and I would soon be discovered. Making one final charge at the gates, we leveraged ourselves against them, and pushed. Even as we tumbled through the portal, Hades' fist punched down from the heavens like the hammer of Zeus, obliterating the ground behind us. Our footprints, barely made, disappeared into the fathomless void.

Slamming the gates, I fell to my knees and offered prayers of thankfulness to the gods who had protected me on my quest. Then I removed my armor and slipped into the breastplate of Ares. The moment it touched my body, it infused with heat. It molded to me, embracing the singular curve of my chest. How right it felt! How strong I felt.

It was then that Ares appeared, not in the form of a god, but in the form of the wizened soul who was both grandfather to me and father to my mother. He smiled upon me and revealed the true nature of my birthright.

"No breastplate of mine, no enchanted dagger, no gift in all the heavens possesses a magic that is conferred by ownership. I gave these gifts to your mother because the uncommon strength and courage within her would empower them. Just as your strength and courage empower you. Go with the gods, Grandchild. Wear my breastplate well. Wield my dagger justly. May they, and your fortitude, always shield you from harm."

Aithon and I began our journey back to the mortal world above. I knew not what heinous obstacles we would encounter, nor what monstrous fiends would challenge us. I knew only that we would be protected—not by the power of the gods—but by the power of the Amazon within me.

# ARACHNE

# REQUIESCAT

## BY M. REGAN

"May I?" asks the Cursed.

She is nothing if not polite, these days: unfailingly, submissively polite. It is the attitude of one who has taken a lesson to heart, for she *does* still have a heart, even though it has changed.

All of her has changed.

From the corner's deepest depths pokes the Cursed's silhouette, her needlepoint ends trailing dropped stitches. Loosened shadows shift upon the wall, distorting a projected appendage. It is a deception that serves well to illustrate her wants.

A black, misshapen limb hooks delicately around the object of the Cursed's desires.

She waits.

Perplexed, the Three Who are One look from themselves to the pile of shorn Threads lain beside them. They are unevenly severed—cut into cubits, into pes, into girah, into aln, into inches. They are short and long and neatly arranged.

"Why?" asks One of the Three. It is a sound question. Which is to say, the question makes sound. Any sound beyond the silvery snip of shearing Scissors is a rarity here, and Two of the Three flinch, discomforted to be hearing more than the usual grave-silence. "What do you plan to do with them?"

The Cursed flutters her lashes. She has many of those. She thinks, and has many thoughts to match.

"I wish to turn a blight into a blessing," comes the answer at length. It is a very precise length, which the Three Who are One can appreciate, despite its unit of measurement being nameless. They appreciate, too, how the Cursed's consonants are thin, her vowels incandescent. In that sense, her words are like the Threads, and so it makes sense that One of the Three should punctuate the reply with a merciless snap of her Scissors.

A shorn piece of Thread writhes in One of the Three's lap, pulsing glow-worm bright in the gloom. It will fade soon. Go still soon. Be forgotten soon. That is the way of things.

"Come now. What will happen to them otherwise?" wheedles the Cursed, tenacious, weaving a plea into her wondering. "What will you do with them?

Will they simply rot here? I pray not. I beseech you. There is nothing more tragic than something being left to waste away. Do you not agree?"

It is impressive how capably she strings her appeal through every syllable. Impressive, but not surprising; given her history, her talents, such seamlessness is to be expected. The question is if it can be resisted.

"Please?"

The Three Who are One consider the pile.

"...we do not need them," One of the Three says. Which *is* true.

They choose not to think about other truths, like if They are needed by them.

***

One of the Three is squinting at the Cursed's work.

She tilts her head, purses her lips. It is not immediately apparent if the faces she makes are those of displeasure, or if she is trying to determine details with increasingly weak eyes, but the Cursed blithely assumes the latter.

Reprimands are more willingly doled than compliments, whatever the realm, whatever the time.

The Cursed ties her knots.

One of the Three knots her brow.

"You are tangling them," One of the Three protests, though she does not move to stop the Cursed. Two of the Three glance up from Thread that is yet still alive— still shining, still vibrant, its radiance highlighting their features and smudging their contours in darker shades of gold— before they join their sister in frowning.

They are not angry. They are bemused.

"You are *tangling* them," One of the Three repeats, her nostrils flared. She does not leave her stool, although she holds herself as if she might: on the edge, the precipice, just waiting for a push. "That isn't right at all."

"Isn't it?" The Cursed hums, passing a spool of Thread from one hand to the next to the next to the next to the next. She pauses only when her gestalt hosts have all turned bodily towards her, contorting themselves to consider the unconventional pastiche's inward spiral. Gazes follow the way its lengths wind over and under and through. There is a pattern to her work, and it is obscene, grotesque. It is complicated and beautiful.

The Cursed is all of those things, too. She is, and is more than those pieces and parts when she lilts:

"Humans spend their entire lives tangled up in one another. Death does little to change that. Why, if it did, we would not have family trees, nor vows of vengeance, nor history books, nor cemeteries. Perhaps it is impertinent to say as much to you, but say it I will, and ask that you forgive what I know to be fact: there are no Scissors which can fully cut a person from this world." Four of eight arms gesticulate, meaningful. "A hole may be left, and their absence obvious, but lives remain connected still."

The Three Who are One muse over this impassioned speech, much as they muse over that which curls between their fingers. Ether, logos, astral; it goes by many names, these mortal coils, crisscrossed like veins over bloodless wrists.

"…have you remained connected, then?" One of the Three asks. She holds her arms before her, palms up, lightly shackled by the Threads. "Are you somewhere on that web?"

The Cursed lifts a single strand, pinched between two fingers, two thumbs. It resembles a smile.

"How can I be," she laughs, "when I am the one making it?"

***

"These two are bound already," the Cursed observes. Curiosity paints a glassy sheen over her eyes, the largest pair widening as the smaller sets turn towards the Three Who are One.

None of the Three look up.

"Soulmates," says One of the Three.

"Or a lovers' suicide," One of the Three appends.

"Or both," grunts One of the Three, judgement roughening her scoff.

"Does it matter, in the end?" sighs the Three Who are One. However enchanted the Threads they manipulate, they themselves have become quite disenchanted, and cold, and in grimness not unlike this infernal abyss. Theirs is a most dreary realm: its only light effluxes from the never-ending Thread, and its only softness is flocculent cobweb.

Lacework endekagrams stretch from floor to ceiling, ceiling to floor, pearlescent strands creating a phantasmal haze in the corner of the void. It rises as smog would.

The Cursed's voice does the same, evanescent in the chill.

"In the end," she murmurs, "does anything matter? Do I matter? Do you?"

"We mattered," One of the Three is quick to insist, though this answer does not quite match the question asked. "Before, we mattered. We matter

MUSINGS OF THE MUSES

less now. We will continue to matter less. A day will come when we matter to none but one. And when that day comes, we shall finally sleep, dusty and left to legacy. All sentient beings have a fate, and that is ours."

"...oh."

The candor of this declaration surprises the Cursed. Guileless, she looks at the Three Who are One as if they have turned her world upside down. Or right-side up, given the way that she dangles.

The Three Who are One stare back. Their colorless eyes are reminiscent of milk; they tip their heads, and their gazes spill everywhere, over everything, almost pitifully.

Twiddling deadened filigree, the Cursed takes a breath.

"If you have a fate," she begins, uncertain, "do you... have a Thread?"

A snort serves as answer.

"We are not human," One of the Three reminds, dull. *Obviously,* her tone impresses. She is not impressed. "Of course we don't."

The Cursed bites the inside of her cheek, mouth twitching like a dying thing. "Do *I* have a Thread?"

One of the Three blinks.

"You are not human. Not anymore."

It is true. It has been true for some time. But there are moments when the Cursed forgets this, when she fights to use both phantom limbs and excess ones. These are the moments she hates more than anything, for she knows that she would be coloring in embarrassment if she could. She should be flushing the pinks and reds that come from having a more elaborate sympathetic nervous system, but she does not.

The Cursed remains tawny, and her voice level when she accedes:

"I suppose not."

*****

"You were mortal once," recalls One of the Three.

The Cursed is weaving again. Always weaving. It is part of what makes her cursed.

"I was," she says, teeth clacking. Nails clacking. Clacking, clacking, like the parts of a loom.

The Three Who are One watch ouroboroses appear between her appendages, infinities stitched into doily designs. There are eternities in her edgework. Mobius loops curve into the pattern's starburst center, its helices evocative and endless. Hers is an elegant project, as pale, as intricate, and as sticky as rime.

It could be worn as a wedding veil.

It could be worn as a funerary shroud.

"Perhaps you can tell us," the Three Who are One intone, cleaving another piece of Thread on the Cursed's behalf. "What do mortals believe in?"

"Believe in?" The Cursed frowns. There are as many possible answers as there are human beings, and knowing this, she chooses her words with the same care that she does her materials.

"Well… Many believe in what they can see," she tells the sisters, gentle. She is so gentle. It is borderline excruciating, that gentleness, especially when used to pluck a proffered strand from One of the Three. Though it looks nearly too short to use, even a flicker provides light; the Thread is passed from one hand to one hand to one hand to one hand to one hand, cycling in a motion redolent of reincarnation. Of recreation, or rebirth. She twiddles the Thread's end fondly, demonstratively, when she adds, "Others believe in what they can touch."

The Three Who are One nod.

"What they can see," echoes One of the Three.

"What they can touch," repeats One of the Three.

"But is the heart not comprised of things that can neither be seen nor touched?" argues One of the Three, her forehead knitting in ways even more dynamic than the web. "Do they not believe in happiness, in sorrow? Do they not believe in love anymore?"

"Some do," the Cursed assures, sweet. She tries so hard to be sweet. But bitterness always leaches through, acidic and soured by notes of warning; her claims curdle until glimpses of subtext lie exposed. Until the Three Who are One can see something subtle and sympathetic sewn between layers of meaning. "Some do, in the same way that they believe in the gods."

The Three Who are One look to their upturned hands, their fingertips spindled and their palms crossed by lines that are not their own.

"Do *you* believe in love?" One of the Three finds the nerve to whisper. She folds her fists around the Thread, her grip so desperately tight that it leaves an impression in her non-skin.

Those marks fade, and *that* is what hurts.

The Cursed hesitates.

"I believe in what I can see," she confesses. "What I can touch."

There is a skittering over the sisters' shins, so many legs beginning to twitch.

***

"So what do we have, then, if not souls?" she probes, watching icy stone vanish beneath silk-spun frost. Icicles become pillars become an ever-encroaching sepulcher. "What keeps us alive?"

Thread after Thread is plaited together, end to end. Start to start. There is the fleeting thought of yarns, even before another says:

"Stories, I imagine."

Ah, stories. Is there anything, really, that is *not* a story?

"If our stories were to intertwine," the Cursed poses, cautious as much as she is hopeful, "and our narratives were to tangle together like these Threads, would that… make us soulmates, too?"

A pause. It could fit inside a heartbeat.

"Well…" the Three Who are One chuckle, "We did not commit lovers' suicide."

***

Gods do not die like mortals do.

Gods do nothing like mortals do.

The death of a god is far more torturous, far more lonesome, far more humiliating than anything a human might suffer, and yet, there is no one to whom a god might offer their final prayers. There is no one to beg mercy from. Nothing to snip that would end it all.

There is only time.

It takes so much time.

"Lie down," the Cursed coaxes, daintily treading her web's perimeter. Braided Threads bob beneath her weight, redolent of Charon's boats upon the Styx.

The Three Who are One do as they are told.

"Relax."

Again, they obey. The Cursed follows her weaving's sumptuous whorls, wending closer. Closer.

Perhaps the Three Who are One should be perturbed by the cling of the lace that she lowers upon them. Perhaps they should squirm from the cocoons that she builds to bind their extremities. Perhaps they should reach for their Scissors.

They do not. In place of fear, in place of frustration, in place of any desire to live, the sisters feel naught but exhaustion.

Their Scissors and their Thread remain abandoned on their stools. The web undulates, lulling weary bodies, and the Three Who are One shiver collectively closer to the breath that is adding promethean fire to their napes.

"Hush," soothes the Cursed. Her poisoned fangs are bared. "Hush, my darlings, and I will kiss you good night."

For the first time since creation, the Three Who are One close their eyes.

# A WEAVER'S YARN

## BY ALYSON FAYE

Draw closer, nestlings,
step into my web's embrace,
woven from my woes,
for I have a tale to spin:
of a prideful girl
who, reveling in her nimble fingers
and far-flung fame,
in one foolhardy moment
challenged a goddess
to a contest
but in winning,
lost herself
her family
her friends,
whilst fickle fortune
turned her face away.

Creep closer, changelings,
gaze upon my swollen body,
blessed or cursed
with eight hirsute limbs,
constantly spinning
in sunlight and moon glow,
creating lacy traceries,
gossamer labyrinths,
only for wind and torrent
to tear to wispy threads.
This, is Athena's doing,
this is the price I pay
for besting the goddess.

Beware my progeny,
hearken to my lullaby
of lament, of loss, of longing.
Though I still spin, ply my power,

am useful and humble,
the goddess this much allows.
But each day is torture,
for Athena knows my dream -
to stride out on two limbs,
with sun-stroked skin,
flesh ripened, richly-fed
by sweet mead and honey;
a lover's butterfly kisses
lingering upon my lips.

I *was* Arachne, Empress of the loom,
now my world is one of webs,
my name, besmirched, mutilated;
all beauty fled -
bow down before me -
I *am* Queen of the Arachnids.

# THE QUIET REBELLION OF ARACHNE OF LYDIA

## BY ARIANA FERRANTE

A single swipe of a human's meaty hand tore the web to pieces, and Arachne clamored on eight legs into a darkened corner. This marked the nine hundred and sixty-seventh home destroyed. Arachne never meant to keep count, but in her new life there was little else to occupy her mind. As a human, she might spend her day eating, sleeping, and weaving, yes, but also singing, dancing, and talking. *Talking.* Just the memory of spoken word clawed her heart with shuttle-sharp points. Talking gave her the greatest pleasure, and also the greatest grief.

She could not proclaim her rebellion with words, not anymore. No longer could she boast in a heavy voice that she was the greatest weaver that ever was and would be. Athena, in the infinite wisdom she represented, sought fit to reduce Arachne's troublesome mouth to a wordless set of articulated fang-shaped jaws and feelers. Even laughter eluded her, her misshapen throat ill-equipped to create such a noise. The only words Arachne might still claim to be her own echoed entirely in her mind, reverberating in on themselves until they left her tiny form trembling with fury far too large.

Arachne scuttled across the dark perimeter of the irritated man's home, agitated curses washing over her small form. They were nothing she had not heard before. Humans were still growing accustomed to her kind and their webs; the only form of weaving the goddess sought fit to grant her after her metamorphosis.

The spider squeezed through the gap in the angry human's door, wandering aimlessly. When the goddess first changed her, she sought fit to return to her home in Lydia. Upon doing so, however, her father swept her out of the house and forbade her reentry. She made a fool not only of the gods, her father had proclaimed, but of him. He refused to live with a daughter so disobedient and arrogant.

Since that day, however long ago it was, Arachne drifted. Eight legs carried her across nations at a painful pace, but staying in one location for long meant stomping feet and blunt instruments, and Arachne was fond of neither.

Spiders lived short lives. Arachne did not. Athena knew not to bless the girl with a brief punishment. Arachne lived and lived, laying and hatching generation after generation of spawn, watching her many-legged kinsmen grow and mate and die. While spiders far younger than she slowed with age, her limbs remained as quick as they had been the day she received them. She did not freeze in the cold of winter, nor bake in the heat of summer. Stranger still, her body never yielded beneath heavy objects the humans brandished to dispatch her. It would hurt, but it would not kill. She lived day after day, month after month, year after year, until Arachne quietly concluded that, although she no longer possessed a human frame, she must yet possess a human lifespan.

Spindly limbs skittered across a long stretch of polished white stone, and as night fell, Arachne settled into her new locale. It was dark under the gabled roof of the unfamiliar abode, but Arachne cared not. She did not need to see well to navigate. Whenever an animal of any size lumbered nearby, Arachne need only feel its direction in the tremors beneath her tapering legs.

The transformed girl ascended a tall column, beginning to spin once she reached the top. She led the silk behind her, thin sticky thread clinging to the grooves in the pillar as she strung the other end of the web to the roof. She drew closer and closer to the center of the forming tapestry as she worked, thread spiraling in lacelike patterns as her newest creation took shape. Being so high up would make it much harder for humans to reach her. A stiff wind might unhook her threads from their anchored points, but the wind never came with fists or gardening tools. The wind never feigned its cruelty.

No sooner did Arachne settle into the center of her web did a breeze begin to stir. She froze, the end of every leg rooted tight to the strands. The wind picked up faster, shaking the edges of her web and swirling discarded leaves into the marble space. Now that she was high above the building's floor, Arachne began to realize just where she had spun her latest home. It was a temple, dedicated to one of the many gods no doubt. Painted scenes of legend marked the walls: a rising sun, a fleeing nymph, a dying man sprouting purple flowers.

The wind whistled past the pillars, the gusts all swarming to a single point on the floor in front of the altar. The space began to glow, a growing mote of bright golden light coalescing into a humanoid shape. Arachne crept to the edge of her web, many eyes transfixed.

Once the glowing light was sufficiently human-sized, the illumination dissolved into fading stars. Beneath the dispersing glow stood a young man, skin and hair golden like the light that once obscured him. His sun-yellow locks fell down his back in bobbing waves, and his sinewy limbs carried him to sit at the altar. His skin still possessed a warm, ethereal glow, like a sunbeam had found its way inside his body and could not make its way back out. A god, she realized, and not just any. This was undoubtedly *Apollo*, the god of the sun.

He raised his glowing head and Arachne got a look at his face. Beneath an arrow-straight nose sat thin lips, parting in a heavy sigh. Long lashes fluttered over searching, honey-toned eyes, thick brows creased in agitation. It was a familiar agitation, Arachne noted, the same agitation that humans possessed whenever they saw her or her creations. Without warning, Apollo's golden gaze slid to the web at the top of the column.

"I see you, you know," he said. His warm voice held little amusement, his lips pulling into a tight, taught line.

Arachne froze. All eight of her limbs bunched up, ready to spring and retreat. For a moment, she was glad she had no way of speaking to the god, for she was sure that if she did she would have said something foolish.

"This is *my* temple," the god continued, emphasis unmistakable. "I am aware of every mortal who sullies it."

*Sullies!* The word echoed in her mind. If she still had proper teeth, she might have ground them. Now Arachne truly wished she had a voice. What did immortal, ever-beautiful Apollo know of sullying? Was it not the gods who sullied Arachne, who reduced her to a small, many-legged and scuttling thing?

"I suggest you remove your... *tapestry* before I do it myself," he said, looking down his nose at the small creature. "I cannot have such an unsightly thing defiling my temple."

Arachne did not move. This web was not just a work of art, it was also her home. Apollo had his temples and he had Mount Olympus, the place of gods and feasts and pleasure. A web was all Arachne had, and the only thing she feasted on were the innards of insects foolish enough to fall into it.

Apollo's nose wrinkled like he smelled something foul.

"Did you not hear me?" he asked the spider. "I said *go*."

Arachne did not move. If Apollo wanted her down, he would have to bring her down himself. Perhaps then, Arachne thought, she might at least die sooner than Athena wanted. While she would not be entirely content with death before her time, Arachne would at least be content with beating the goddess one last time.

The god scoffed, the corner of his eye twitching. Arachne found she quite liked the sight of that; the same, baffled look that Athena gave her when she refused to relent on her claims of weaving prowess.

"Very well," Apollo huffed, raising a hand. "I have dispatched things far greater than you. This shall be no issue."

With a wave, a mote of light erupted from Apollo's palm, soaring through the air to strike the web and its occupant. The glowing sphere crashed into Arachne in a blast of burning heat. White-hot light filled every corner of her vision, every limb set ablaze with pain. The web evaporated beneath her, legs skittering in the air but finding no purchase. She fell to the marble floor of the temple in a smoldering heap, vision filled with gigantic stars. Although she could not see him through the haze of pain and illumination, Arachne heard Apollo laugh.

Slowly but surely, the light cleared and Arachne's vision returned. Where she expected the banks of the River Styx and the ferryman's boat there was instead the lonely interior of the temple. Apollo had vanished just as quickly as he'd arrived, taking the light with him.

Arachne's leg twitched. Then another. Then another and another and another. She was still a spider. She was still alive. Athena's punishment was not so easily circumvented. Arachne wasn't certain she was happy about that or not. Arachne leaped onto her legs, curling and uncurling the appendages to work sensation back into them.

She was still alive, and now she had an idea.

It had not been easy at first to communicate without a mouth, but now Arachne did so as expertly as she once wove, at least to her fellow arachnids. Where she had no voice, she had her legs and her movement, and where she had no words, she had her web. She need not be loud to defy the deities that cursed her once before. Her rebellion would be quiet, but it would be a rebellion nonetheless.

She spun and spun and spun, leaving tapestry after tapestry, all pointing in the direction of a single building: the temple of Athena. She directed as many spiders as she could to the holy building, leading them into every crack and corner. She must have gathered at least five hundred of her children when her task was complete, and she watched from atop the altar as they worked.

Before long, night had fallen, and their toiling was done. Web covered every inch of the temple, cloaking the columns, friezes, and altar in thick sheets of sticky white lace. No human nor god could step into the temple without making contact with one of the countless webs. It carpeted the space with expert efficiency- a gigantic tapestry of spun spider silk.

The goddess of wisdom materialized mere minutes later, gray eyes blazing. She appeared knee-deep in the webbing, the broken strands clinging to the ends of her pristine toga. She writhed in the webs, but that only made them stick further. Cursing, the goddess reached down to pick them off with her hands, but while she was able to remove them from her attire, they stuck stubbornly to her fingers.

The spiders emerged from the darkness, crawling along the many webs surrounding the furious woman. Arachne stood among them, many eyes bright and captivated at the sight of the seething goddess. Hers was an anger that felt almost nostalgic, the same anger she displayed when the mortal first challenged her. It was a beautiful, satisfying anger to behold—an old god brought low by her latest, spite-fueled creation.

Athena might live forever, but she would be ancient. Arachne and her children would remain forever young, forever laying and hatching and spinning. She and the spiders would remind her, throw nets of cobwebs over her aging statues, make familiar the sight of ruination and decay. The gods and the humans could destroy web after web, spider after spider, but there would always be more.

Although she could only do it in her mind, Arachne laughed and laughed.

# PRIESTESSES AND WITCHES

# THE MASK OF THE MARTYR

## BY EMILY SHARP

The gods blessed the High Priestess of Knossos with a babe. But, in one of the final rituals leading up to the birth, it was foretold that the child would be the fall of the palace. The High Priestess was a woman of strength, built strong in body and spirit, but her babe was stronger. Incredibly weakened by the birth and finally drained of her vitality, the High Priestess heard her god's soft, sweet voice calling her.

She looked down at her child, with her last breath, whispered, "Even the smallest pebble can turn the course of a life-" sighed and slipped away to join her gods. As the priestess fell back, the babe suckled at nothing. Gasping at the air, and no longer feeling its mother's breast, it wailed. The wail was heard throughout the palace, and as the great Bull God beneath them echoed the babe's mournful angst, the floors trembled.

By her birth right and custom, Adrianne the babe was the new high priestess. The other priestesses mentored and included her in rituals as soon as she could walk and talk. As Adrianne grew, gossip peppered the halls and steps of the Palace. It hadn't gone unnoticed she was much bigger than the other girls her age. She was stronger, and more agile too. When gathering herbs and flowers, no one could match her stamina, and many of her attendants were left behind as she climbed the hillsides. She would even insist on joining the hunters when procuring sacrifices and could easily keep up.

Every season, as was her duty, Adrianne would oversee the Bull Dancers. Her attendants would catch her copying the athletic training and the dances in secret. Adrianne's love of the dancers and their art was no secret but her fate had been decided; she must follow her path of high priestess for the good of the people and the palace.


Adrianne

I am told I am a high priestess rivalling my mother and that she and the gods are proud. That is what we all thought until they shook the palace. From deep down below in the unknown levels, I felt things fall and crumble as the gods summoned me.

Soon people from the palace and the neighboring villages came, begging and demanding answers. Why now? What had displeased the gods? Every pair of eyes were pockmarked with fear, faith, and accusation. Every complaint, every plea lowered the sun in turn until there was no one else left to placate apart from the gods themselves. I would take the pain and concerns of my people, their emotions, and energy to the gods.

As they prepared my wine, herb, and fungi mixture that put me in the trance, allowing me to be one with the gods, the other priestesses eyed me nervously. It had taken many attempts to get the mixture right. As I was bigger than them, I needed more, but they were all frightened of the potency as there had been many mistakes. Yet I drank the acidic bittersweet fire lighting my tongue and throat ablaze. Having fasted before the ritual, the thick textured mixture crawled down my body, settling in my belly.

As my attendants arranged my layered skirts of multi-colored fabric, my body began to react to the mixture. I watched their hands tie the bodice's knot intricately beneath my bare breasts, the movements of their hands blurred and glowing. The geometric designs on my black and white apron rippled as it was pulled as tight around my waist as possible. The tightness made the mixture swill around in my stomach and claw at its edges. My short shallow breaths over my tight bodice made my head began to pleasantly swim.

They sat my crown on my head, letting my long black curls hang freely down my back and around my breasts. My thick hair cascaded gently over my bare skin and prickled the hairs on my neck and chest. I felt elated; utterly and wholly. My box of snakes was presented to me, and I opened it, carefully coaxing both of them out. They came sliding and coiling up my arms, sitting happily, waiting. I let them recognize my muscles and form for a few heartbeats, then raised my arms to the heavens. They obediently slithered up and around my hands.

My procession was watched eagerly as it went to the bowels of the palace to consort with the gods. As I went further down the soft dark stone steps and narrow corridors, the darkness swallowed me; welcoming me as I went deeper into the earth. The voices of the earth and clay all spoke to me at once and allowed myself to absorb the emotion of my people even more, drawing it from the stone. Far ahead of me, down the corridor, the attendant trembled as he lit the torches ahead of my path. The lights bounced and melted into the walls in soft swirls.

When I finally reached the ritual chamber, the attendant handed me the torch and ran. His footsteps echoed in a pattern of beats, the rhythm complementing my racing heart. As I entered the deep dark chamber it was cold against the flush of my face and chest. I closed the stone door as my snakes wove and danced up my arms and shoulders. It was time to talk to my gods and time gave in, becoming liquid.

When the deed was done, I gave the signal to my attendants to receive me. The gods' messages and presence had drained me fully. My head weighed heavily with responsibility and terror. The palace was to fall. The gods would shake the earth until fire spat out and the sun shied away in fear. Rain that was not rain but tiny dirty feathers would blanket the land. The coastal towns would be swallowed in a tirade of wrath from the sea. The palace would crumble into flames that would eat stone.

The gods demanded blood to appease them.

They carried me out from the depths in silence. The priestesses and attendants took me to my quarters, laid me down, and took my snakes away. Everyone waited nervously for my decree, but the night took me before I could address my people. I had fevered dreams of the bulls of the season; furious, crashing down the palace, breathing fire, setting my world alight.

The following morning, I called my priestesses to action: the villages of the land were to send youths to be sacrificed as bull dancers this season. I was returned to my finery and throne, and over the following weeks, I received them. Youths were collected from around our island and the mainland. Only one looked me in the eye as they presented themselves for inspection. A large, athletic female slave from one of the faraway trading villages, said to have been captured from a place much further away than that. She was the first female I had ever seen who was built like me. I wondered if her mother had been blessed by the gods like mine was.

The training season started, and I often went to watch their progress. Soon enough my presence instilled a fearful encouragement in the youths and, noticing its effect, the trainers coaxed me to frequent the practices. The dancers would coyly try to win my attention and affection, all vying to be favored. But only one interested me: the female athlete that had met my gaze. She did not fawn over me and make a fuss when I came to watch like the others did, which roused a blend of annoyance and respect.

As expected of me every season, I chose my favorites who would become the main dancers in the ceremony. They had better costumes, food, wine, and quarters. I included her in the throng but hid my favoritism. I learnt her name was Antiopelya and that she was from a land far away where women ruled as warriors and were as big and strong as men, like me. When I watched, I was watching her; the strength in her thighs, the form of her back and arms. She was graceful, poised, yet so powerful. I desired, yet, I envied her at the same time. It was maddening. I wanted her; I wanted to be her. As I was of age now and had been for a few seasons, I took lovers from my favorites. The others did not interest me. But I could not choose only her. So, I allowed some to be sent to my quarters in turn and their desire to please was admirable. But the women did not have her physique and the men were just not her.

*** 

As the weeks went by, the rites were suddenly on the horizon and, per tradition, leading up to the ceremony and games I allowed the youths their banquet. I sat at the head of the hall with my attendants and priestesses, watching as the youths danced, drank, and ate. How I wanted to join them. They knew they were here to die for their gods and their people, and they were celebrating for the final time. Celebrating having been chosen for their gods, celebrating being used and needed by their people.

I could never do that. The gods owned my every breath. I was used and needed by my people every waking moment. Every move I made, every word I spoke was preordained and monitored. It would never end until the gods chose for me to die. Not like the dancers.

They served their gods in one rite; one action and their duty was done, they were absolved. Praised, martyred, and loved. I would never have that. To honor my people and the gods was my birth right and fate; I had no choice. I sank further into myself as the wine fed my jealousy and bitterness.

A few of my lovers tried to catch my eye, either with longing or to be publicly favored. I ignored them and drank my wine until my attendants started watering it down. Yet it did not water down everyone's constant need for attention, people controlling, and watching my every move. Suddenly the combination of it all became swollen and hot, making me feel anger I never had felt before.

I excused myself, forbade my attendants from following me and exited the hall. I walked along the stone veranda and slumped against one of the pillars. Forever still in the fresco behind me, the bull and I looked out over our kingdom. The vineyards were illuminated by moonlight, and warm thyme-sprinkled air wafted, whispering, through my skirts and hair. The stone was cool on my wine rosy cheeks. The earth and the clay grounded me. It was my earth, my clay, my palace, my home and my responsibility. I had to keep my people safe and the gods appeased. I could not and would not allow the palace to fall. The gods would get their blood, they would choose.

Footsteps interrupted my thoughts. My priestesses came to me fawning. I shook them off, and not looking at them, I spoke instead to the hills.

"Bring me the training master."

They bowed, nodding, and scurried away. I waited, basking in the moon and the backdrop of my world. Again, I heard footsteps. But they were heavier this time. I spun around, furious at the constant intrusion on my thoughts. It was Antiopelya. She came and stood next to me, taking in the view. I could feel her strength and heat coming off her in waves. We stood this way, our arms by our sides, barely touching until I turned to her. I could have her if I wanted, if I demanded it; we both knew it. Yet I did not, as that was not how I wanted to have her. I reached out to touch her cheek and heard the pitter-patter of my attendants. She looked into my eyes and understood, melting into the shadows, leaving just as my company came to me. The training master bowed and straightened slowly.

"The gods demand appeasement." My voice, a blunt knife serrating the thick air. No one spoke or moved. "They wish to choose their own sacrifice." The training master caught my eye questioningly and my attendants looked at the floor, pretending not to listen. The priestesses hung on every word, eyes shining.

"You will release the bull early." One of them gasped and I struck her instantly. "Silence while I speak for the gods." I righteously composed myself and addressed the trainer. "You will release the bull early, allowing the gods to choose their sacrifice. The dancers, they will not be told. I have spoken." There was silence for a beat too long and the trainer finally spoke.

"Yes, High Priestess. I will make the necessary arrangements." He did not look me in the eye.

"You are dismissed."

With a flick of my hand, he left at a fast pace. My attendants coaxed me with promises of wine, ignoring the priestesses' sniffling as they followed. As we walked away, I thought I heard footsteps from behind the pillars.

***

The night before the ceremony the air was thick with anticipation, fear, and burning herbs. The palace was a hive; slaves, attendants, and dancers preparing costumes, putting final touches on garlands and adornments, making their peace with their families they were leaving behind and ancestors they would soon see. I sat on my throne, deep in my chamber, my snakes coiled in my lap. I refused my lovers or attendants, sitting, listening until the bustling melted to silence.

Echoing, disjointed steps approached my chambers. My snakes moved sleepily as I straightened up, ready to dismiss the interloper. The torches flickered with the movement in the chamber and lit the face of my intruder: Antiopelya. She clumsily went to a knee, bowing her head.

"Speak." I flushed at her presence and my snakes woke a little more, moving lazily up my arms towards the heat of my chest.

"I have been injured." Her voice was calm, unwavering.

"Injured?" How was that possible? She was easily the best athlete; I had chosen her to lead the dance with the great bull mask. She looked up at me; I could not read her eyes.

"A vaulting accident, in our final practice. I was not caught properly-"

"Who?" This was unheard of, losing the main dancer the night before the ceremony. Panic rose up inside me. I stood, my snakes now coiling around my shoulders. Antiopelya's eyes sparkled. I saw for a brief flash what looked like passion and awe.

"Please, it was not their fault but mine." She stood carefully, favoring one side, her foot a little limp, not resting on the ground properly.

"You cannot perform?" The sentence stuck in my throat a little. It was all true. I would be the fall of the Palace. Antiopelya moved towards me and her face flashed with pain. I stepped forward and held out my arm to steady her. As she leant on it, one of my snakes moved to explore the new territory. Antiopelya watched it in the corner of her eye. I watched my snake glide over my arms to Antiopelya's, then her shoulders. I straightened up a little and held Antiopelya's shoulders, bracing them to the same height as my own. My snake weaved behind her neck, causing a black curl to become dislodged and tumble over her collarbone. I saw it. She watched between my eyes and the snakes, silently, questioning. I knew what to do.

"I will perform." The conviction I said it with confirmed it for me as I spoke aloud. Antiopelya's eyes widened and her eyebrows rose. She opened her mouth to speak but I dismissed her, guiding my snake off her shoulders and back onto mine.

"Say you can still perform, but tell no one you were here."

She nodded, taking the cue to leave. Limping away she looked over her shoulder before she walked into the darkness. The admiration on her face was close enough to love for me.

At the whisper of dawn, my attendants came. I dismissed them after they were finished preparing me and told them I wished to bestow favor upon my dancers. My favorites were soon sent to my chambers. They preened and pranced about, staring adoringly at me as I gave them their floral and herb crowns for the ceremony. As was the custom, I saved the bull mask for the main dancer and gave the others leave to depart. Everyone hurriedly left the chambers, glancing jealously at her as they left. As soon as we were alone, we swapped robes. I could not help but look at her naked physique, so much like mine, yet not.

As the final touch, I donned her bull mask and she my veil and garlands, hiding our features. I called to my attendants that we were ready and that I wished to be silent until the ceremony. Antiopelya went with my priestesses and I the trainer, strong now on her foot, hiding the limp well under my long skirts. You could not tell she was injured at all. I went with my attendants down to the ring with the other dancers.

They were bustling with excitement and joy, elated with purpose and honor. I fed off it; the garlands dripping petals, the muscles of the dancers oiled with herbs, the seething rumble from the audience. Then the music started and everyone fell silent. We all listened and counted the beats until our cue and we burst into the ring. The audience roared and cheered, throwing flowers into the ring. I looked up at the faces surrounding me, honoring me, praising me. My heart lifted and I opened it to the inpouring love. Behind my mask, I wept tears of joy. I had never felt this appreciation or admiration before.

I led the dance perfectly. All the seasons sneakily watching, copying, and practicing was for this moment. I stole a look at Antiopelya sitting in my seat, still as stone. No one suspected a thing. I triumphed with the music and my heart and mind soared. I was one with my dancers and the audience. I was in ecstasy. This was how you worshipped your gods.

I let the music take over and allowed my love for my gods to surge through me. It was my power, my energy, my strength. I was lightheaded with love, floating as I danced, my limbs and body not even mine. I looked over at Antiopelya again and fancied I saw her wave to me. Suddenly the gates swung open: the bull. He had been released much earlier than I expected.

The music stopped and the audience gulped as one throat.

The bull looked confused and stood huffing, looking around. It saw the throng of multi-colored dancers and immediately sped towards us. All the dancers braced themselves, ready to vault or tumble. I turned, ready, but a tiny pebble under my foot made me land at an awkward angle, twisting my ankle as I fell. As I hit the ground, the mask fell off and as a collective, the priestesses screamed and the audience gasped, recognizing me.

But it was too late, the bull came towards me and in one fell swoop, one of his horns pierced my chest. He flung my limp body to one side. My god had chosen me. I was the sacrifice. I was the chosen one, whose blood would save my palace. Me, I was the one all along. As I felt my warmth leave my body and absorb into the stone that needed it, I was elated. I had saved my palace and honored the prophecy. Euphoria flooded my senses as my vision darkened. The gods shook the ground in triumph and with praise, welcoming my blood into the earth. As I was released, I felt tiny light grey feathers land on me, coating me.

*** 

The gods, furious at Adrianne's unprecedented death, hid the sun from the blasphemy it had just witnessed. Ash fell from the darkened sky and the women wailed, pulling at their hair. Dismay and agony were grey streaks running down faces in clumps. The priestesses tore at Antiopelya's veil which had hidden her face, now revealing the truth; they began to shriek again in anger and sorrow.

The Bull God, now knowing the trick, roared beneath the palace. He made the ground tremble; as he did the palace began to topple. Pillars of red and black stone fell, crushing walls and frescos. A fire broke out from the oil stores and licked at the stone greedily. The Palace of Knossos fell into itself, burying its secrets in rubble and dirt.

# THE SERPENT QUEEN

## BY KC GRIFANT

The women gathered to the pond still as black glass, where, if one watched long enough, it was possible to make out the faint ripples of what lived beneath.

Callista, Calli for short, kept her eyes fixed on the pond's surface. She waited along with a dozen others, a mix of snake charmers, witches or otherwise mystically-trained women. They stood in garments bleached the same white as the tree trunks that wound up and out of sight into the velvety green darkness around them.

Small disks of scrying glass hung from trees, transmitting their activities back to the towns and the kingdom's quarters, where the Serpent Queen Throne sat, vacant. No one had passed the serpent test for decades. But tonight, Calli thought with a shiver, would be different.

The back of one of the enormous Crescent Snakes, wide as a tree trunk and skin blinding white, broke the still of the pond for an instant.

The others next to her stifled gasps. Calli herself had spent countless hours in her childhood handing deadly cobras in preparation for this moment, but even she swallowed back a surge of panic at the sight of the venomous snake. She gritted her teeth for what was to come.

The sighting was a sign. Time to begin.

The women started diving in, one by one, even the most practiced among them shuddering in fear. Calli trembled as well, but for a different reason.

Particles of orichalcum mixed with the blood of a baby Crescent Snake that she had doused in hours before made her skin freeze and the world swell around her as it took hold. It had cost her all her family's considerable wealth for the concoction, the coins stolen under the guise of a common burglary and potion bought in secrecy. The theft had crushed her mother's spirit even further.

*It won't have been in vain*, Calli thought as she fought to focus. The concoction would rile up the snakes toward the others but protect her. She would be the first in years to survive the Crescent Snake bath. She would be Queen. Then…she tried not to think of her brother's body, found near the Northern border where one of the countless tribes roamed, that the current inefficient leaders did *nothing* to stop—

*Steady*, Calli thought and gripped her fists.

She jumped.

In other circumstances the warm water under the moonlight would be relaxing. But a dense body bumped against her leg as snakes coiled beneath them. Calli bit her lip to keep from screaming and switched to a well-practiced breathing exercise. The other girls likewise steeled themselves, tapping into months or years of training. The creatures wound through the water, sending up churning waves.

It didn't take long until one in their group broke, sobbing and clamoring out of the pond. The others watched with disdain. Some things were worse than death. The girl would never be welcomed in society again.

"Pathetic," Calli said aloud, her teeth chattering despite the heat of the water. She prayed she had taken enough of the alchemical mixture to work. Too much and the snakes would be overly excited; it would be obvious something was off. *Cheater*, a voice nagged at Calli, but she pushed it away. She was doing what needed to be done.

A swimmer, Demi, tread closer to her. Calli looked away but it was too late.

"You aren't yourself," Demi hissed. "Your eyes, I can see it." She flicked her black braid behind her. "Confess now or I'll reveal you."

A serpent broke the water between them and Calli froze.

But her concoction was working. The snakes slid harmlessly against her, as if she were one of them.

The others weren't so lucky.

Demi screamed, fangs striking into her chest with a crunch like a tree falling. Calli wiped the spray of blood from her cheek and glimpsed the creature's eyes—yellow as the Harvest moon—before Demi and the snake disappeared into the pond's depths.

Another snake emerged almost too quickly to glimpse, pulling a girl under before she could make a sound. The survivors stifled screams or closed their eyes as the snakes took them, one by one, filling the star-dusted air with the stench of blood and flesh.

She was last. She was alive. But it wasn't enough to survive; there had to be a sign that the snakes accepted her.

More creatures slid behind and under Calli, their skin electric against hers. She held a breath, looking down at the rippling bone-colored flesh. The snakes lifted her up, gently, presenting her to the moonlight.

"The Serpent Queen," voices murmured. Townsfolk in ceremonial garb, black as the pond, emerged from the trees and bowed as Calli floated.

She smiled, taking in the adoration of the gazes around her, of the thousands of eyes she could feel watching her through the scrying mirrors. Finally, she would do what she was meant to: bring lost wealth to her family, expand to other realms, forge alliances to grow her power and make their kingdom as great as she knew it could be.

Ripples grew beneath her.

Something was wrong.

The snakes weren't just cradling her – they were winding tight around her arms and legs.

Before she could shout, a tug pulled her under the thin surface that separated air from water, moon from darkness, tree trunks from snake bodies. She gasped before she was under. The snakes dragged her toward an enormous glowing orb at the bottom of the pond.

For a moment, Calli thought it was the moon, fallen into the sea. But then she saw the squiggling serpents, like rope-sized maggots, erupting from a crack at the top of the egg. The snakes forced her closer, where hundreds of the newborn serpents swam around a snake larger than the oldest oak.

*The snake baby's blood*, she realized. They thought she was one of them, a foundling that needed gathering.

"*I'm human!*" Calli's stifled protest dissipated into bubbles as they brought her to the enormous snake, pieces of human arms and legs floating around it, the baby creatures flitting like darts to eat.

The snakes had chosen.

# MEDEA

## BY LUCY GABRIEL

Her reputation is as sharp as needles.***
She lays pattern pieces, tissue thin,
traces the space where sons should be
and stitches neat seams against slander.
Whispers follow her: *madder,*
*cochineal, woad.* Turmeric offers gold,
delivers yellow that fades like Jason's promises.
These days she hues unnatural:
aniline bright in magenta,
purples fit for a cuckolded queen.
Mordant amid the fine-boned corsets
and crinolines wide as chariots,
she dreams a wedding dress
in arsenic green.

# THREE FATHERS

## BY GORDON GRICE

Medea watched the old man shiver. She'd never met him before, but she knew the look in his eyes. He was seeing something in the next world and trying to puzzle it out. She could have told him it was a goddess grooming a black horse, brushing the burrs from its tail. Medea had never been into that world, but she'd glimpsed the goddess of the crossroads when they met at midnight, had prayed to her and listened to the crows who brought back messages.

"Father," her new husband said, and hesitated. "I wanted you to meet my bride." His eyes glistened.

"Promachus? Don't lie to me, boy. The dead don't marry."

"I'm not Promachus, Father. It's me, Jason. I've come back."

"I bound your cold wrists myself and covered your eyes with coins, Promachus," the old man said. "I could hardly wrestle your arms into place, you know; your uncle had tossed you in a ditch and you'd gone stiff."

Jason buried his face in the old man's sleeve. Medea petted his head.

Jason started up, as if he'd just remembered her. "Help him, Medea!" he said. "You must know magics for this. Take half my own life away to lengthen his!"

But Medea laid her fingers on his lips.

"Darling, I'll never take a day from your own life, but I'll do what I can for your father. Are you brave enough? The spell will take more courage than all your travels have."

She took him on a journey next morning, riding horses into the woods behind his father's house, woods so deep they looked like midnight even in the day. There they found a certain kind of tree he'd never seen before. Bright lichen speckled its bark.

"Dig here," Medea said, and as he dug, she drew a horsehide purse from her gown and held it ready. He turned two dozen spadesful of earth, and at last his shovel met a softer soil. A scream came from it, like a wounded child's. Medea pushed Jason aside and gouged into the earth with both hands until she brought out a fungus soft as a hot cheese and big as a human head. Their horses, fretted by the smell, neighed and pulled against their tethers. The fungus opened its pink mouth and screamed again. Its eyes, too, tried to open, though they seemed trapped in a kind of spider web. She shoved the thing into her purse.

"Does my father have to eat that?" Jason said. He wasn't sure he could, even for a longer life.

"It's only to poison the dragon and make him shed his scales," Medea said. "The scales contain the ageless magic."

"We don't have dragons here, Medea. They only live in wild places like where you came from."

"You know so little of the world, darling," she said, and stroked his fine broad brow. She led him on, her hands twitching before her. "I let the voices of the air possess my hands," she said. "They know where dragons dwell." Soon they came to a glade marked by flat stones.

"These are graves," he said, crouching to read the weathered letters on one, then another. "Poor people, with no titles carved on their stones nor urns for the offerings."

She stopped before the oldest-looking grave. The letters on the flat stone had weathered into cryptic scribbles.

"Lift it, lover," Medea said, and Jason wedged his shovel beneath the stone and pried it up. From beneath it a dragon came wriggling, red as the one he'd killed for the fleece, though less lustrous and half the size. It nipped at their feet, then reared to its full height and gazed into Jason's eyes. He dropped the shovel and drew his sword.

"Don't kill it unless you have to," said Medea. "Feed it the fungus."

He shook the thing out of the purse. It rolled along the grass and came to a stop, its eyes fully open now, its mouth making an odd piping scream. Medea had to look away, for she'd thought of her brother, of how it had felt to tangle her fingers in his hair the moment before she hurled his head into the waves.

The dragon raced forward like an eager hound and mouthed the fungus. It stretched itself on the grass and lay gnawing the thing. The fungal screams startled birds from their perches, but the dragon seemed not to notice the noise, engrossed in its feeding. Its blue eyes rolled back into its heart-shaped skull. It seemed in ecstasy.

They camped beside the cemetery that night, and the night after.

"How long, Medea?" Jason said. "My father's on the verge."

"We need the scales," she said. And indeed, from the evening of the first day, the dragon began to shed, to scatter his scales among the tombstones. Every sloughed scale was brittle as old bones. Break it open and its luminous layers were thin as human skin, but whorled with rainbows.

"Each layer takes a hundred years to grow," Medea said. "My aunt taught me that at the temple." And she loaded the purse with scales. The dragon languished and lay panting among the stones, until finally Jason could pluck its scales with impunity. When the purse was full they mounted their horses and headed home.

On their return, they found Jason's father still alive. The household slaves had prepared everything according to Medea's orders. They'd made altars of mud and washed a black ram in rainwater. Now Medea cast her spell. She slit the throat of the ram and let his blood mingle with wine and mare's milk. He hung above the bowl, twitching and trying to bleat. She prayed to the goddess of the crossroads and to the god who keeps the graves—asking his forgiveness for hurting the dragon, a graveyard guardian. She prayed also to the bride who keeps the bed of the grave-keeping god.

And now Jason led his father forth. Three times she bathed his skin with water; three times she painted his brow with brimstone; three times she touched his face with a furious coal, that man too close to death to feel the pain. In her vessel of bronze the broth boiled. She added the uterus of a doe and the eggs of a crow.

It had appeared at the house two days before, that crow, and stood upon the sill mimicking the old man's mutterings. The eggs, when added to the hot broth, broke open. The hatchlings unfurled their wings and extricated themselves from the mix to perch a moment on the cauldron's brim. Then, precocious, they took wing and departed, speaking to each other in a foreign tongue. She added, too, bitter roots she'd gathered, leaves nearly liquid with decay, the seeds of basil, black sand, fractured sapphires, and the skin of a single viper.

With the long-dead limb of an oak, Medea stirred the broth. The limb began to grow again. Soon it sprouted leaves, then acorns that ripened as they watched. Around the pot, the slopped froth made the clover blossom and nod, and downwind the lilies began to breathe aloud.

Now Medea drew her knife and gathered Jason's father into her arms. She hesitated then, thinking of her own father. She recalled his kindnesses to her; there were many, mixed among his uglier moods. She recalled, especially, the herbal smell of his clothes when he held her on his lap and sang songs. But that was long ago, and since then she'd broken his heart.

She cut the old man's throat. His blood wetted the flagstones. Jason moved to stop her—too slow, as in a dream, the blood spouting forth before his hand could rise to stop hers.

Now he, too, was engulfed in memories. He recalled the red puddles that slithered across the deck of his ship with every wave. He recalled how she'd hurled her own brother's limbs into the water, and begged him to help, though he was too horrified to move. That was the first murder she committed for him. She'd sat wailing in the stern afterwards, her gown trailing on the bloody deck. Perhaps he'd entered into this love affair lightly, but as he looked at her then with her head bowed, her hair working loose about her shoulders, Jason had never seen a woman so beautiful. But that blood was no kin of his.

"No wonder your own father cursed you," he muttered. He couldn't keep the words back.

She was too busy to answer. She ladled her broth into her father-in-law's mouth and into the wound she'd made. Was he speaking, or only drowning in that clotted muck? The gray of his hair began to melt like frost before a fire. His chest stuttered and filled like a sail in a sudden wind. When he spoke to say how strange and strong he felt, the quiver of age had gone, and his eyes were bright and bold as a hawk's.

"My father's a fool," Medea said. "He's not the one who knows how to craft curses."

***

Medea would have rested then; the weeks of running, the days of gathering her charm, had left her weary. But there was to be no rest. They'd had word that King Pelias knew of Jason's return.

Jason's father spoke.

"Some prophecy has caught hold of my brother and won't let go; he thinks you're a danger to his life and throne. He's nearly as old as I was, and hardly fit to rule; they say his daughters handle the business of government while he lies praying. We can't withhold the golden fleece, or we'll be branded traitors. Yet I know he'll try to take your life when you deliver it."

"Don't worry, Father," Jason said. "Medea can help." And she felt despair; her hands were hardly clean of ram's blood, and her soul seemed thin as parched leaves. This wasn't how she'd pictured married life. She nodded and tried to smile.

Soon she had a plan. When she told them, Jason paled. He thought he'd seen the depths of her daring when she slaughtered her own brother. Now she contemplated something worse. His father, however, laughed and licked his ruddy lips. It was strange to see him fleshy and full of life, looking younger than his own son. His face was full and brave but slightly off-kilter, as if the vigor of youth had refilled him unevenly.

"It's a delicious plan, daughter," he said. "Jason, tell everyone you've tired of your new foreign wife, that you've thrown her out. That will make King

Pelias and his daughters believe the lies she has to tell them."

"No, Jason," Medea said. "Don't say that, not even as a lie."

"Don't be afraid, love," he said, taking her in his arms. He stroked her wild hair. "I'll never leave you; it's only for a few days, until the net is cast and the blood is shed."

*** 

Two days hence, she sat before the fire in the hall of the aged King Pelias, Jason's uncle. Ranged on the hearth before her sat the king's three daughters, watching her with eyes full of hope.

"In Jason's place I'm seen with suspicion," she told them. "I made his father young again. It was shocking to see, even for Jason, who knew the things I can do. And when it was done, they crowded round to thank and praise. But in their eyes I saw the change. They took in the spilled blood and the slaughtered ram. I wasn't the young bride anymore, but a woman of the winding path. In the days that followed, even Jason would touch his father's scarred throat and look at me with awe. The wound healed into a sort of extra mouth, its lips set in a pomegranate grin that split his beard. Jason thought I didn't know his dark imaginings, but I could guess. He came to my bed as before, but his touch had chilled. And soon he kept his own bed, and so I've flown, for already they are whispering behind my back, deciding I'm too dangerous to keep, despite Jason's words of love." It hurt her to tell how his touch had changed. That was a truth within her lie.

"Then find a new home here, Medea," said Nomi, the oldest of the daughters. "Bring our father back his youth and you will live with us as a sister. You'll share our jewels and our food, and any man who raises a hand against you must fight us all."

"How I crave a friend!" said Medea. "I've left my family behind, and my own father curses my name and will kill me if I ever return. Your friendship is pay enough. Yet I can't agree until you know the rest. To work the spell, it's not I who must undertake the dark rites, but you, your father's nearest female kin; for only women give life. It will take strong arms and a stomach for blood. You must pray to gods whose names you hoped never to learn. And in all this, I can only guide you; you must be the ones whose hands turn red."

"I'm sorry you lost a father, Medea," Nomi said. "He must have been a wicked man to cast you out. Our father never would. You'll come to know how kind a father can be when he recovers his youth and takes you as another daughter." And at these words Medea almost wished she were free to work the spell in earnest. But that was not the plan.

"Bring me an old ram," she said. The one they brought had horns that curled like the roots of a self-strangled tree. His wool was brittle and riddled with lice, and his skin hung loose at the joints. His limbs shivered with the work of walking. Medea took her horsehide purse and led them into the kitchen, where she showed them how to pray to gods so old their very names evoked the smell of rot. She poured a fluid from a bottle, made a cauldron sing with heat. The younger daughters held the ram's head while Nomi drew the knife across the animal's throat. Its blood on the steel was thin as spit.

Soon they'd taken off its horned head and its cloven hooves. Blood lay in a sheen on the flagstones of the kitchen floor. Into the cauldron went all the pieces. Before long the dead ram, baptized in Medea's brew, emerged as a bouncing lamb, bleating for a mother's milk. All that was left of its old self were the twisted horns, bobbing in the bubbling cauldron.

"It works!" Nomi said. Her sisters clutched each other's arms in joy.

"And now that you know how to do it, you need only lead your father here and do the same for him," said Medea.

The three sisters fell silent.

"It's your choice, of course," Medea said. "I won't even hold you to the promises you made, for it's a fearful thing to take a blade to one's own kin. Remember, though, that the chance will never come again. You've prayed already to the gods below. They will not hear you again if they find you're the kind who doesn't finish things."

"Medea, my sister, for that's what you will be to us when this is done," said Nomi. "Tell me one last time: Are you sure? For if we fail-"

"Your father's fate is in your hands," said Medea. "I can say no more. Nor can I stay to watch, for this is a family matter. Send me word when you're done, so I'll know whether I'm truly to be your sister."

The younger sisters went to fetch their father. Nomi kissed Medea on the cheek.

Her feet as she fled left fine prints in the blood of the ram.

*** 

"I'm sorry, love," Medea sobbed. "I'm sorry." She fell sprawling into the boat. Her hands slipped in the mossy bilge.

"Don't talk!" Jason said. "They may hear us yet." He waded out into the reeds, pushing the little boat before him. She helped him in over the gunnel, feeling the muscle beneath is wet tunic.

"I've ruined it all," she said. "They hate me. They know me for what I am."

"Keep quiet. I see something on the headland. It may be their torches." He rowed hard, wincing at each splash of his oars.

"Fireflies," she said after a moment. "Only fireflies."

"I never thought the people would turn against us," he said, bringing in the oars to let the tide take them out. "I thought they'd welcome me as their king, or if not me, my father."

"It was too horrible, our scheme. You should have seen Nomi all bloody in the marketplace, screaming my name. She said she'd tear my insides out."

"I was napping when they came. In fact, I was dreaming of being king. Come here, your hair's like a nest of spiders." He smoothed her and kissed her brow.

"I dreamt last night," she said.

"Do you see me as king?"

"I saw myself floating across with the ferry man," she said, and her voice became languorous. "He had a black horse aboard. He fondled its ears and whispered to it. I could almost hear what he said. And lying with me, nestled beneath each arm was a child—our children, Jason, sons we have yet to meet. They slept uneasily, tossing in their dreams, murmuring about the wrongs I'd done. The coins fell from their little eyes. I kept trying to find the coins. I kept trying to make everything right."

# LADY CIRCE

## BY LYNNE SARGENT

Lady Circe,
why do you give those who make a mockery,
of you, of the dignity and respect of all that live
in similar flesh, a new home, a new skin
a new purpose better suited to them,
rather than give yourself forgiveness?

Lady Circe,
why do you not take your own shape
and make it something more suiting to your majesty,
your might? Something that would fly away from this island
from this whole world and begin anew with better beings
that understand all the facets of enchantment,
of intention.

Lady Circe,
I know you failed once, turned your wounds into weapons,
left scars on this world in the form of Glaucus
and Scylla, that you let your anger transform you
as now you make these men into pigs.

Lady Circe,
I do not know what you would properly be,
but it is not this. I give you permission, to transform
to be yourself, uncomplicatedly, basely.
I free you from judgement, as those men
were free their whole lives.

Be, become,
and teach me your magic.

# WOMEN
# OF
# TROY
# AND THE
# ODYSSEY

# FACING THE THOUSAND SHIPS

## BY KIM WHYSALL-HAMMOND

Looking down from the city walls
we have watched their petty dramas
as they loiter on our beach
they aim to slaughter or enslave us
we are all so much older now
even Achilles has worn in the sun
the endgame is in sight

Back in my chamber
I polish the bronze once more
stare at my reflected face
can no longer see the beauty
that bought and paid
for all this slaughter, rape and sorrow
and all that still to come
consider slitting the throats of my children
rather than let blood drunk soldiers have them

I will not slit my own
I will face them as they break the walls
I will be defiant

# HELLENISTIC LAMENT

## BY ED BLUNDELL

Was mine the face that launched those thousand ships,
That brought war and disaster down on Troy?
Oh, how I wish now I had stayed in Greece,
Then peace and harmony might have prevailed.
Oh, foolish heart to listen to his words,
The handsome prince with hungry, eager eyes
Who made my aging husband seems so dull
And offered a new life in a new land.
Had I known then how many men would die,
The heroes who through me would gasp their last,
I would have scarred my cheeks with my own nails
And torn the raven locks out of my scalp.
But love and nemesis will have their way,
We mortals are the playthings of the gods.
We pay great penances for little joys.
My love brought down the topless towers of Troy.

# HELEN/HERMIONE

## BY ROSE BIGGIN

Hot country, high summer: the sun's glare over an expanse of white sand, and the horizon shimmering. Thin silver line of the sea. Certainly, a sense of great distance.

A high outcrop looking over the rocks to the coast, and two figures. The wind pulls gently at robes of purple and yellow. Flashes of gold jewelry in the sun.

Mother and daughter. It's long after the war.

"Do you know what people ask me about the most?"

"Not your love life?"

Helen laughs, brightly with a bitter note, and she leans out to peer further down the rocks. Hermione tries to laugh too.

"They ask *you* that, perhaps. But that's the one thing people will contort themselves *not* to ask me about. They're almost afraid to go there, I think. No, it's something much more prosaic. Silly really."

Even at this distance, the sound of the sea.

Helen of Sparta became Helen of Troy, and a war followed. The most beautiful woman in the world; so the poets say, anyway. She had a daughter. Imagine that, Helen with a daughter. For that matter imagine having Helen of Troy for your mother.

"Say it then. We both know what it's going to be."

"Everyone asks about the ships."

"Ha! They *always* ask me about the ships!" Hermione laughs with genuine delight; Helen claps her hands.

"Whence this fascination with quantitative naval gazing?"

"How would I even *know*?"

If they were to meet like this, high on a cliff, long after the war. Helen, and her daughter Hermione. What would they say?

"It was never anywhere near a thousand ships, I know that much. It just sounds impressive. It should be obvious, including to someone who wasn't there. Or at least you'd think so."

"I always knew instinctively it wasn't a thousand. Not viable, that many ships."

They walk a little further, passing large rocks, some bearing script — the names of those who've been this way before.

"How do *you* answer, when they ask?"

"I say it's rounded up from eight hundred and ninety-four. They assume I have authority on the matter, or at that point they realize I have no idea. Either way they stop asking, so it works."

Dust rises in the wake of their footsteps. "So they ask, but don't trust the answer."

"Of course."

What would they say, this woman and her daughter? Could we even tell who is saying what?

They come to a stop, looking out to the thin ribbon of coastline.

"I'm sure people want to ask me about all kinds of things. The stories I could *surely* shed light on, being who I am…. but they ask politely about the number of ships, then run out of conversation."

"It would be worse for them, I suppose, to hear something that contradicts what they imagine."

"Mm. Better not risk it then."

Silence settles over them. Hermione fiddles with a gold bangle.

"Would you say life has been easy, on balance?"

"Apart from all the drama, you mean?"

Helen nods, Hermione shrugs; there's not much more to say to that. They spend a minute looking off towards the sea.

"It is strange. To be so close to the center of everything but also somehow… absent."

The waves break into sprays of white over the rocks, fizzing then draining away.

"It's been a long time."

"Well, think how long it all *took*, and no wonder. Ten years before the war even began, all that preparation—once the *dreadful couple* had gone off to Troy, all that excitement, and I know *that* didn't happen instantly—and *then* ten years of war itself; *then* the journey back to Sparta, finally here… we've spent a long time apart by any measure."

A tiny speck in the blue ocean: boat sails.

"I was shocked when I first saw you."

"How so?"

"How much you'd changed."

A moment hangs while they think about that. Then:

"Really?"

"I know it sounds ridiculous. But I had to hold on to such…. *young* memories for a long time. Tender memories. I didn't want to imagine how the years might change you."

Some shouts come up from below; male voices on the beach.

"I always hoped I might learn from you."

"Whatever could *I* teach *you?*"

The dry grasses are bending in the wind. More shouts from down below, it resembles battle cries. No avoiding it now. One of them must mention the siege.

"So much death."

"So much glory."

"For the same people? The sun glints off bronze and bleaches bone, it's all the same." A deep sigh, years in the writing. "That's how I've come to see it."

"The years have made you cynical."

"Think yourself lucky you were never on the battlefield."

"You think I don't know battlefields? You think my every step hasn't risked danger, in all this?"

A rising urgency in their voices brings a question. "Speaking of changing appearances. There's something I want to know. I think only you can answer this."

"Go on."

It's very much as if they make each other nervous. Helen takes a breath; Hermione keeps her expression controlled.

"Can you see it? In my face?"

"See what?"

"The most beautiful woman in the world."

A moment of mutual examination.

"Is she there?" A touch of desperation.

Helen's face drops into sadness.

"Oh...."

"Sometimes I look in the mirror and.... wait. Sorry. What *is* that sound? Where are they?"

They break off with relief to follow the noise. An echo of metal on metal reaches them from below, great heroic blows dwindling to a faint scaping once they've carried all the way on the wind. Two soldiers are having a friendly spar on the sand. Helen points them out, the gold thread in her sleeves catching the sun. Hermione shades her eyes to get a better look.

"Which of them are you rooting for?"

"Come on now." A wry eyebrow arches. "I know better than to answer a question like that."

"Ha! Perhaps you *can* teach me something after all."

"If you haven't learned it by now…."

At this distance, the clang of metal is out of time with the vision of the fight. Blade clashes on shield in painless dumbshow, the sound of the blow comes half a moment later.

The distraction has lifted Helen's mood. Hermione sees it, wonders at the effect.

"Can I ask? Do you feel any blame?"

A stiffness; some defensiveness here, walls raised. "Should I?"

"Some… residual guilt, perhaps, I would understand."

"Nothing like that. I wasn't in control of how my life turned out. How could I be? I live in the shadows of other people's decisions."

"Everyone does. Think of it this way: you have been lucky enough to know it."

The soldiers have given up fighting and are stretching out in the sun, weapons down. They're not to blame; it's a time of peace, and the afternoon is chokingly hot.

"What do you long for?"

A wave bursts up over the rocks again.

"Now — or before?"

The sea swells.

"I used to long for it to all be over."

"And now…?"

The water drains down, pulling pebbles with it.

"Do you ever feel…." She bends to the ground, picks up a handful of the dry earth and lets it fall between her fingers. "That you've been unable to live your life? I mean properly — do you feel it's been overshadowed by everything else? By the sheer scale of things happening around you, whether you feel part of them or not?"

Hermione and Helen stare at each other.

"You didn't answer my question."

"I'm not sure I can."

"*Try*, for gods' sake. What do you see when you look at me? Do you see the most beautiful woman in the world? People look at me and I can see them searching for —"

"Don't."

"Her."

"Her. I know."

"You say you know, but you have no idea, *no idea* how difficult it is for

160

me. They're seeing me but they're looking for 'Helen'. They look through me — clean through me — to try to see her there, they look at my features, they look around me, they see everything but the person in front of them. She's a trap: like wearing constricting clothes, all the time. Gorgeous clothes, yes, ones you'd be delighted to choose for yourself now and again, if you could, oh yes, certainly, but they don't fit you, or they never did, perhaps they were made for someone else to start with. Certainly someone else laid them out for you, tied you into them. Long ago, before you could have a say. And you have no others, there's no taking them of, speaking of taking them off, let's have another look at this possible 'Helen' person. How thorough *is* the resemblance, or lack thereof?"

"I'm so sorry."

"I can't stand it. And I never asked for any of it."

"Of course not. I know."

Distant temple bells from the city.

"Sometimes, in your face—" She hesitates, unsure if this will be welcome. "Sometimes it must be unmistakable?"

"Oh, yes. In the right light. If I'm in the right mood. I can decide to be seen that way. I have more control over that than people might imagine."

"You can make a big dramatic entrance."

"Yes, sweep in after keeping them waiting. Or have my back to them, speak with them a while, busy myself with a wine jug or whatever. Then, at the right moment, I can be coy and show my profile — or, depending on my mood, turn and look them full in the face. Boom. Then I watch their reaction. 'Can it be, do we see Helen here…?'"

A flock of birds pass overhead, singing out to each other.

"Are they pleased — disappointed? In awe? What happens?"

The shadows of the birds flit across the grasses, quick and dark.

"I don't think they see what they're expecting to see."

The birdsong flutes through the air, mingling with the sound of crashing waves.

"It mustn't make you sad, when people look at you searchingly like that. I know that's easier to say than to do. But think of it from their perspective. The remotest chance to *glimpse* the most beautiful woman in the world: of course they'll wonder if you come close to fitting that description."

Scraps of cloud briefly cover the sun.

"That's the impossible thing, nobody can match that description. And certainly not me. How can I face, literally, a legacy like that?"

"Does it work, to tell yourself that?"

Hermione looks down at her hands. Helen lightly pushes a stone about with her foot.

"The truth is…" and there is the sound of someone taking a deep, confessional breath. This is it. "The truth is, I've often wondered what my life would be without 'Helen of Troy'."

A laugh: pure surprise. "Ha! If *you* think that, just imagine how *I* feel."

Some easiness breaks through between them: if everything is not solved, exactly, they can at least clasp hands. Further up the hill, the rocky path takes them away and higher.

"Hey. I know there's been a lot of, how to put it…"

"Family problems. Relationship issues. Entitlement entanglements."

"Yes, all that. Here's a question. Do you think we can put it behind us?"

The wind picks up, streaking through the heat of the air, lifting it slightly.

"I don't think we're in a world that wants to forget it, Troy and the rest."

"Come on. Perhaps people will."

"Would you really want that?"

"What, you think I'm *proud*? I'd relish the chance to live without all that—
"

"You'd miss the legacy if it wasn't there, and you know it." They are making their way further over the rocks. "To be a part of such a story. Which you *are*, you could never not be, even if you've been somehow hidden in the middle of it, and nobody knows what you'd really think, even if they try."

"Am I part of the story? Some people don't know Helen of Troy had a daughter. Never mind anything I wanted, how I felt, barely what I did, it's not about that."

Spoken about, spoken for, looked at — oh, looked at: painted, drawn, acted, rhapsodized about, the sheer number of odes you wouldn't believe, some of them about just the one body part, even, I'll spare you the details; a dream factory, a pawn in a legend, the woman whose mere idea has launched more than a thousand imagined relationships — Helen of Troy should be allowed to speak for herself, surely. But Helen had a daughter, and either of them could have said any of this, and all I can think about is the three of them, mother and daughter and "Helen of Troy", high up there on the rocks, distant sound of the sea, walking together through the hot dry air.

"Well, there you are. You have anonymity as well as total fame. In many ways you are right at the center of the story, but equally, how many barely know you."

They climb higher, taking a route that might eventually lead back to city walls.

# PRECIPICE

## BY ANGELA ACOSTA

They say she summoned her courage on the boulders
overlooking crashing waves at Aulis.
A flowing gown betrayed her youth,
saltwater tickled her hair
as her nose pointed skyward contemplating fate.

They say she sacrificed herself
for the terrible burden of honor.
Iphigenia dared to cross the veil,
opting to travel alongside Charon
than to assume the veil as the bride of Achilles.

They say Artemis saved Iphigenia,
perhaps through illusion or by conjuring
a deer as a proper sacrifice,
setting her towards more noble pursuits,
a true priestess to her virgin goddess.

They say she was merely a pawn,
cast aside by men's lies and deceit,
willing to drown for she had a promise
that even in death had to keep.

May she speak with her own voice
of the day she quietly stood
at the precipice between
a life of abnegation
and a holier route to freedom,
diving into an ocean of independence
beneath the rough waves demanding her silence.

# CASSANDRA PERSEVERES

## BY SULTANA RAZA

(Twilight. A storm's brewing on the far-off sea. Helen paces restlessly along the ramparts and gardens of Troy. She stops, and bows her head in front of Aphrodite's statue).

Helen:
Please keep my secret, that I hug deep,
Could I be just a flimsy excuse?
Troubling waves crash my sleep.
The front face of Ithaca's ruse?

Is the luck of Troy the real lure?
Is it Priam's gold, in vaults strong?
Though can't believe it; am not sure,
Obsidian greed is all wrong.

Helen (paces ramparts of Troy):
Can't say a word to any soul,
I long to clear my pure name,
In my heart grows a big hole.
Should I change the kingly game?

In oblivion, would I sink?
That smooth horse, with eyes sly,
Of baring ruse, am I on brink?

\*\*\*

(Helen meets a dejected Cassandra on the ramparts of Troy)

Cassandra (mutters to herself):
Dreams are weeping, children cry.

Helen:
Poor Cassandra, brought down low,

164

You've lost your pride, but not your foe.
Sly Odysseus, should I betray?
He tends to always have his say.

Cassandra:
He seeks power, helps Athene,
He is quite wily, can be mean.

Helen:
He won't give up, won't be weak.
Not timeless beauty does he seek,

Cassandra:
His resolve can't be weakened,
He won't rest till Troy is beaten.

\*\*\*

Helen:
His true objectives can't be seen.

Cassandra:
On Odysseus's 'mercy' we can't lean.

Helen:
Precious artifacts interest him most,
He'll run circles around our host.
He won't rest till he gets his wish,
No time to waste on a fragrant dish.

Cassandra:
He's fooled all heroes until now,
Tricked the high king, does not cow.
Only pretends to be wise and just,
Wants to raze our Troy to dust.

Helen:
An observer, no traitor, am I,
Shan't interfere, though much you sigh.

They have you, to forestall doom,
With pride you peer at the Fate's loom.

Who am I to warn bitter Troy?
I'm just a silly girl, vain and coy.
Win or lose, it's all the same,
Far and wide will spread my fame.

Through the ages, my name will roll,
None care, in my heart, if there's a hole.
The real me, no one really knows,
'Heartless witch,' accuse my foes.

Cassandra:
For no one else have you ever cared,
Your own babe's love, have you ever shared?

Helen:
They want me for appearances' sake,
My real interest, none can wake.
In me they have a vested stake,
Their love for me is quite fake.

My fears and joys, they can't guess,
For soon they're lost in the swirls of my tress.

Cassandra:
I know who'll Victory's great horse ride,
Oh, by my prophecies, none abide!
You cursed woman, why won't you tell,
What's clear to you and me as a bell?

Helen:
Why should I speak? Let chance decide,
Who'll be the winners of war's tide.
To entertain me, you all have failed,
As victors, now, all Greeks will be hailed.

Cassandra:

The blood of thousands is on your hands,
You wicked foreigner from heartless lands.
Don't bring the horse, it's all a ruse!
To listen to me, why don't you choose?

***

(Day. Outside the burnt-out walls of Troy, Helen comes face to face with
Hecuba and Cassandra. Helen tries to back away, but they corner her. Helen
is carrying a small, polished plate that acts like her mirror. From time to
time, Helen looks worriedly in her mirror).

Hecuba:
We descend from families, old and proud,
From nymphs who haunt our vales, and glades.
Lost are our origins in time's shroud,
In our blood their song never fades.

Why was Phareegius asked to judge,
No ordinary folk our ancestors were.
Why do goddesses still hold a grudge?
Or to such rage, those gods wouldn't stir.

Achaeans searched, but didn't find,
Our real treasures are our hearts and minds.
From a noble line, do we descend,
To our own Elysium we'll ascend.

Helen:
Of course this siege is really about me,
Why this truth can't you all see?

Hecuba:
Too pragmatic, our gold they sought,
None of them will thrive in peace.
Nothing but misery to them it's brought,
Their expansion will soon cease.

What they hold dear, they'll soon lose,

No warmth, no joy will you ever know.
Their own fate, none can choose,
None of us were your real foe.

Cassandra:
If you'd warned us of your equine sly,
Our gratitude could've made you cry.

Helen (to Hecuba):
To your own daughter if you'd paid heed,
To accuse me, there'd be no need.

Cassandra:
Though tortured by visions I've been,
Through curse of a god, they couldn't see.
I've never thought my dear ones mean.
I've always loved my own family.

Hecuba (to Helen):
Phareegius gave you his heart and soul,
No human connection can you ever make,
But for it he paid a heavy toll,
For your crooked smiles and words so fake.

Helen:
Jealous, and vengeful are you crone,
To gifts of jewelry am I used.
To false accusations are you prone,
Why, of treachery, am I accused?

***

Andromache (lunges at Helen):
My husband, my babe, to me you owe,

(Helen retreats).

Cassandra (to Helen):
When your morals are so low, so base?

Andromache:
You cold-blooded hussy with a heart like snow!

Cassandra (to Helen):
How in your mirror can you yourself face?

Hecuba (to Helen):
You're the iciest woman of all our days,
Her own off-spring who could leave!
Who has never learned our human ways,
In your kind heart, who'll ever believe?

(The white dog comes back with a pack of dogs who mingle with the women).

Sinon (approaches with guards):
The King of Ithaca calls for the queen,
After she's cleaned our deck and mast,
On his ship, in silks she'll preen.
Onto her crown she'll have to hold fast.

(Cassandra advances towards Sinon and the guards, who retreat in fear before her predictions. The Trojan women follow her, surrounding Hecuba, who stands tall and proud in their middle):

Cassandra:
What makes you think, that you'll return safe?
Tears of your families will fall like rain,
Widowed your wives, your children waifs!
Stains on your honor, is all you'll gain!

(Sinon walks away, and the guards withdraw to confer at a distance).

Sinon (shouts at far-off guards):
We'll need more men to prise the crone!

Cassandra (shouts to Sinon and the guards):
When you face death, like a girl you'll moan!

(Exit Sinon and the guards).

Cassandra:
Go Mother, go, follow that dog,
From our tunnels, you can escape;
Go, and get lost in our tear's fog.

(Hecuba leaves with older women and children).

Cassandra (catches another dog, shouts to Achaean guards):
My mother's a dog! It is no jape!

Hecuba (whispers):
Bless you, child, my honor you've saved!
Forgive me girl, your word I didn't take.
With great fortitude, troubles you've braved!
I thought your visions were all fake.
(Women pull Hecuba away).

Cassandra (shouts at Odysseus and Sinon):
You used low methods, was not at all fair!
Yours is no victory, just a mean trick,
To break our walls, you couldn't dare!
Honor will be gauged now by a low stick.

-The End-

Note: excerpted from *The Seeress of Troy* (a manuscript).

# A HOMECOMING, A LEAVE-TAKING

## BY GWYNNE GARFINKLE

his footsteps
distinct on the stone floor

the dream is torn

her weaving
rent from the loom

his kiss tastes
of the sea and transformations

she'll never know

she says goodbye
to her wild solitude

# NARCISSUS AND ECHO

# LATE BLOOMER

## BY S.H. COOPER

Nancy was a late bloomer.

She'd been a scrawny, gawky kid who everyone assumed would grow into a scrawny, gawky young woman. This didn't bother Nancy too much. She'd never been very interested in her appearance, nor the male attention that might have come with it, and bypassed more mirrors than she looked in. Her plans for high school had been simple: just get through it. She just had to keep her eyes on the prize: an ivy league education far away from her small hometown.

But fate had other ideas.

By the time Nancy turned sixteen, all the awkward angles had softened, and she'd blossomed into a beauty. The only one who didn't seem to notice right away was Nancy herself. She was too busy looking ahead, carried by her straight A's and extracurriculars, to think about the here and now.

Not until she was given a phone.

Her parents had fretted quietly over the decision. They'd resisted most forms of technology, believing the current trend of always being plugged in and accessible an unhealthy one, but with Nancy's demanding, scattered schedule, a cell phone was becoming a necessity. They finally relented after a misunderstanding left Nancy stranded an hour from home after an away game with her softball team.

"Don't let her get on any of those social media sites," her parents' friends, many of them similarly techno-adverse, warned. "Once she's on those, she'll become an addict like all the other kids."

Nancy's parents didn't believe it would get quite that bad. They'd raised her to have a good head on her shoulders, to be a free thinker. A little internet access couldn't undo sixteen years of hard-pressed life lessons.

Still, the phone was handed over with its fair share of warnings.

"It's for emergencies only. You can use it for homework or reading, but no socializing. Phones are tools, not toys."

Nancy agreed, and for a time, she kept her word. She was used to being a landline and family-room desktop kind of girl, so the pocket-sized portal to Everything didn't really interest her much.

Not until her friends started asking for her number when they saw she had a new phone.

What started as the occasional call became texting, then taking pictures and surfing the net after bedtime, and then, with a little persuasion, an Instagram account.

It was only so she could follow her friends and see what they were up to. Maybe, *maybe* to comment every now and then. But she'd certainly never post anything herself.

The same didn't apply to her friends.

They started tagging her in pictures that included her and the response, she was surprised to find, was a positive one. Heart emojis. People she'd never spoken to singling her out to say how pretty she was. How *hot*.

For the first time, Nancy started to look in mirrors.

A lifetime of sports had given her an athletic build. Her auburn hair was thick and smooth, hanging in waves almost to her waist. She had what her mother had always referred to as "classic" features: high cheekbones, a slender nose, full lips.

As a skinny kid, "classic" had looked a bit goofy. As a young woman, it suited her beautifully.

Nancy took over a dozen photos of herself that night, trying to capture the posed effortlessness of Instagram she'd seen in other girls' pictures. She finally settled on one in which she was gazing up at the camera from beneath her lashes with a Mona Lisa smile. She captioned it simply, "Goodnight" with a purple heart emoji.

The likes came quickly, and Nancy went to sleep with a grin.

They didn't last though, petering out by the next afternoon. She found herself checking her phone between classes, disappointed each time she didn't have any new notifications waiting.

She made it to lunch before snapping another picture of her staring soulfully out a window, her hair arranged over one shoulder, with a caption about wishing she was anywhere but school.

A renewed flood of likes. Kids she'd shared classes with for years started following her. She couldn't deny the tiny bit of pleasure she took in not following back. After they'd ignored her for so long, it was her turn.

To maintain the momentum, she started posting regularly. Selfies, pictures with her cats, lounging before bright sunsets at the pier, photos with her friends. Each one garnered *more*.

Likes.

Comments.

Followers.

Attention.

Nancy became absorbed by it. Any caution she'd initially had over her parents discovering her phone use gave way to blatant checks at the dinner table and cutting off conversations to reply to a new message. Any attempts to curb her obsession were met with shouting and slammed doors.

"What can we do?" they asked each other.

They'd never had to discipline Nancy before and weren't sure how to start now, so they hoped she'd simply lose interest and tried to impose boundaries wherever they could.

None of them had much effect.

Nancy continued to post her pictures, reveling in her new-found popularity.

She'd just put up her latest one, a selfie taken during a walk around the lake. The sun had caught the natural blonde highlights in her hair, the sparkle in her blue eyes. She was smiling sweetly into the camera against a lovely waterside backdrop.

There was nothing not to like.

Not until the comments started coming in.

Look at that double chin. Pig.

You know she dyes her hair

What a weird smile lol!

The accounts were all new and empty, their profiles blank. Nancy went back to the picture and reread their comments before looking at the photo again.

Was that a double chin?

No, no. Just a shadow. Don't listen to those stupid trolls, she told herself.

She closed Instagram and tried to focus on homework instead, but she kept thinking about that selfie, until she couldn't help but grab the phone and reopen the app.

More comments.

Crooked nose.

Big forehead.

Totally filtered.

She wanted to reply, to yell at them for being so mean.

Instead, she scrolled up to the picture again.

Her nose did have a slight lean to it, didn't it? But her forehead certainly wasn't big! Her fingertips trailed along her hairline as she squinted at her phone screen, zooming in on her face.

While she studied it, the comments continued to come in.

Eyes too far apart.

Teeth too big.

Ears are uneven.

When her mother came to wake her for school in the morning, Nancy was still staring at her phone.

"Have you slept?" she asked, surprised by the dark circles under her daughter's eyes.

Nancy mumbled something about not feeling well and needing to stay home, never once looking up.

Given her state - and that Nancy wasn't the type to miss school for nothing - her mom nodded and backed slowly out of the room, concern stamped across her face.

Nancy only got up to lock the door.

Cow.

Slut.

Ugly.

Picture. Comments. Picture. Comments. Picture. Picture. Picture. Picturepicturepicture.

She sat in bed, knees pulled to her chest, and examined every pixel of her face. She'd shown too much cleavage. Her face was all out of proportion. Her hair was frizzy. How had she missed all those things before?

Her mother came up with a bowl of chicken noodle soup for lunch, but Nancy didn't answer.

Her dad knocked on her door at dinnertime, asking her to come down and eat, but Nancy didn't answer.

Darkness overtook day without her noticing. She pinched the screen, zooming in on a slightly reddened spot that might've been a pimple. Again on her teeth to see if her gums really were too noticeable and gross. Once more at her eyebrows, trying to discern just how many stray hairs she really had.

While she picked apart her image, her nails picked at her neck, her chin, her cheeks.

The next day, she still hadn't left her room.

Her parents continued to try and coax her out, but Nancy didn't hear them. She had no interest in food or school or an ivy league education far away from her small hometown. All she heard were the comments, screamed at her in the voices of her friends.

All she saw was that picture, and every single flaw she'd been too arrogant to notice before.

Ugly.

Ugly.

Ugly.

At the end of the week, her father removed the hinges from the door.

They found Nancy sitting upright in her bed, chin resting against her chest. Her cheeks had sunken, her eyes hollowed, her lips chapped, a myriad of little gouges in her pale skin where her nails had dug too deep.

And still clutched in her cold hand, her phone, its battery long since drained.

After her funeral, they couldn't bring themselves to go into her room, save for a single time.

They laid a silk rose dyed in her favorite shade of purple upon her pillow, and beside it the last picture they had of her.

Their favorite.

Their daughter, smiling, happy, beautiful, standing beside a lake.

# ECHO'S LAMENT

## BY GERRI LEEN

What crime did I commit to earn this life?
Distracting Hera never was my choice
It's not my fault that Zeus won't love his wife

Known far and wide for my exquisite voice
Now doomed to only listen and repeat
Distracting Hera never was my choice

Alone I wander nevermore complete
Bit player in a curse I didn't call
Now doomed to only listen and repeat

Narcissus was the last piece of my fall
I have so many things I want to say
Bit player in a curse I didn't call

Now time streams by as day falls into day
I sit in silence I cannot relieve
I have so many things I want to say

So many years and yet I still do grieve
What crime did I commit to earn this life?
I sit in silence I cannot relieve

It's not my fault that Zeus won't love his wife

# ECHO AT THE POND

## BY MIRIAM H. HARRISON

You lie there and love her, content in the company of your self made radiant. Will you still love when she shows you fading, counting out your age in the lines across your face? When the illusion of timeless beauty has worn thin, what will be left? She holds your image, but don't you know I have carried your words in me? Each line you have let slip away I have held safe, waiting for the time when you will turn aside to find something more lasting. Let me kiss your lips and make you timeless. Let me fill you with past utterances so beautiful, unborn poets weep.

# EURYDICE

# POSSESSION

## BY ELLE TURPITT

"You're so lucky."

I heard those words so many times at the wedding, women sighing and half-swooning, their voices breathy and their gazes fixed not on me, but on my new husband, surrounded by men. He looked suitably humble, his cheeks red from the wine and wearing a smile that said he was deserving of the attention bestowed on him. The men clapped his back and shook his hand as women gathered about me, fussing over my hair and paying me the stock compliments one said to a bride, while rolling their eyes, pleasant expressions disappearing as soon as I looked away.

Did Orpheus love me?

We made a great pair. To everyone else, at least. He was handsome, with a voice and musical ability to match, able to charm everyone. And I was beautiful, talented in my own right, not that the others knew. No, to them, all that Orpheus sung, Orpheus created. They didn't see him snatching my music and words from my hands, breathing his own life into them and stripping away what was mine.

I loved him. I had, anyway. Loved his charm and talent, because there was talent there, it just required sampling from others and twisting what belonged to someone else. He lured me in and before I could realize how deep I was under, he had bargained with my father for my hand.

Orpheus laughed, called my name. "Dance for us, my darling."

There were so many others around, so many gathered here to celebrate us, I could not refuse. So Orpheus played and I danced, whirling as our guests clapped, drawing closer to each of us, then back, as if caught in a wave. Enchanted. When I directed my feet to the edge of the circle, they backed away, and the trees soon hid me, though Orpheus' music and voice drifted after me and I could not stop.

My body danced to the tune. I felt, for the first time in so long, free. My arms drifted up and down. My feet skipped and slid. I clung to branches like partners, pushed off and spun and stopped only when I fell to my knees in a clearing, my hair a tangled mess, aware of figures shifting around me.

A brook drew my attention. Water rushed over the rocks and snaked away through the trees. Three women were in the brook; one crouched on the rocks, another standing in the water, the third lay across it on her back, smiling

185

at the sky.

The standing one approached me, arms held out.

"What have you done, dear?" she said, with more warmth in her voice than I'd heard from anyone since my mother had passed.

With those simple words, something broke inside me. She embraced me and I sobbed, as she gently rubbed my back.

"I don't know," I choked out.

The music still played, but now there were shouts and cries of alarm, above them all, Orpheus' laughter.

The others joined us, one leaping from the rock and the other scrambling to stand, moving daintily through the grass, like new-born deer.

"You have bound yourself," one said, and I could not tell who. "To a man who will not be happy unless his light outshines yours."

"He will drain you dry."

"He will tear you down."

"What do I do?" I sobbed, and pulled back, but still they held me, hands on my shoulders, my arms. "I thought he was different. I thought he…loved me." Even to my own ears, I sounded weak, pathetic. I wouldn't be able to escape Orpheus. He was the kind of man who took great care of his possessions; once he had something valuable, he would never let it out of his sight. And now, with one ceremony, that was exactly what I was.

"He will follow you to the ends of the earth." The whisper in my ear was soft. "But there is one place living mortals cannot go."

"Dance with us."

I was spun around, and suddenly I was dancing to the music Orpheus played, hopping into the brook with the naiads, their hands clutching mine. As we moved, footsteps thundered through the trees. Seeds floated around us, some landing in my hair, and although I did not falter, the heat beat down on me, the sun sapping my remaining strength.

"What would you do, to get away from him?"

"Anything."

I danced with one naiad then the other, and the grass shifted, a shape slithering through.

"Are you sure?"

"Yes."

Orpheus laughed again, and the music stopped as some of our guests entered the clearing. The naiads disappeared, climbing up the rocks and into the deeper part of the water further down.

I smiled at the guests, raised my arms as if to say, you've got me, I'm here.

All is well.

They wanted to return me to my husband.

I stepped back, onto the grass, shaking my foot as if to dry it. Then, I put it down, gently, right in front of the snake.

"Eurydice!" my father yelled, true horror etched onto his face, the kind of expression he should have worn when handing me over to a different kind of snake.

Orpheus appeared behind him, and I felt it. Nothing more than a sharp sting at first, as fangs pierced skin. The skin on my ankle went numb, and as my father reached me, Orpheus at his heels, the world tilted.

"Father," I whispered, as he and my husband splashed through the brook.

"No," Orpheus said. "No, no, no. No! You cannot!" As if he were apprehending some thieves in the act of stealing his instruments.

I fell, and Orpheus caught me, holding me to him. Father reached us, and the three of us went down, Orpheus gently lowering me.

The snake disappeared into the trees, work now completed. My head fell back, and I stared at the sky, only for it to be hidden by Orpheus' head.

"Eurydice," he whispered. "I won't let you, do you hear me? I will follow you to Hades myself."

He would not find me, I vowed. Even if he grabbed the snake and forced it to bite him, I would hide. I would dance in the fields of Elysium. I would plunge myself into the flames of Tartarus, all to keep away from him.

"I love you," he said, as the world darkened at the edges.

"It has been a beautiful day," I said, unable to hide the smile from my face.

Orpheus would not have me.

I sighed, surprised at how little pain I felt, and closed my eyes, and felt light. Weightless.

I was free.

\*\*\*

I'd always been taught to be scared of Charon, but he was gentle when he held his hand to me and helped me into his boat. He listened patiently to those who declared they could not be dead, and he let some scream at him or throw their fists at him until they were exhausted. The river journey was long, and many slept, but I remained seated at the front with him, watching the shapes swim in the water, marveling at the sights around me. It was like some large underground cave, the walls curving upwards though no ceiling could be seen.

And it was dark, with an unnatural light cast from the boat, highlighting the route.

I didn't even see land until the boat bumped up against huge, black rocks. Charon pointed at some of us, and indicated a staircase cut into the rockface. Those left in the boat either beamed or cowered as he gazed over at them, though many of us were ushered off. Once we were on the stairs, he pushed the boat away from the rocks and continued the journey.

We climbed, and at the top stared at a large expanse. Breath escaped my tight chest, and a few of those with me whooped with joy and ran forward. Groups awaited us, and many of these embraced the newly dead. There was a lot of weeping.

I walked through the Asphodel Fields. They were not remarkable, as I suspected the Elysian Fields were. They were like many meadows I had seen in my life. Wide and green and dotted here and there with flowers. A never-ending horizon, the occasional crop of trees. And for all their normality, they were beautiful.

I walked, and walked, and walked, feeling no pain in my feet. When I did stop, and lay down, and stared at the sky – or, rather, the large black hole where sky should be – I looked back the way I had come and saw nothing. No sign of the river, or Charon, or the rocks and stairs.

I was completely and utterly alone.

And that was the most wonderful thing of all.

I picked at grass. I slept, when I felt like it, waking to find food doted around me. It seemed the food was simply something to do, something to enjoy. It was a pleasure, but not the greatest. Like sitting down to a rather good meal, as opposed to attending a feast. I was to spend the rest of eternity here, I supposed, and the thought made me neither happy or sad. It was just a fact.

I did not know how much time passed. I occasionally walked, and sometimes I heard music and danced and sang to it.

Time passed and the weather remained cool and calm. I woke one day to find a group of women standing around me. They looked nice enough, their smiles not too big, their gestures and mannerisms pleasant as they settled down around me.

"Eurydice," one said. "Welcome."

"Thank you," I said. "Um, sorry but…who are you?"

"We call ourselves The Free Women," the first one said, smiling gently at me. "We all escaped our husbands and ended up here and, well, we expect when they do die, they won't be joining us."

"Tartarus for those shits," another said, barking out a laugh.

"We heard what happened, and we decided to be your own little welcoming committee. Sorry it took us a while. I'm Penelope."

There was something of nobility about her, as she explained they spent their days in each other's company, splitting up and re-joining as and when it suited them. They told stories, made music, and overall filled their hours. And they talked, sharing stories of their lives, working through what had happened to them, lending each other support.

I joined them, and soon felt like I really, truly belonged. Penelope wasn't just nobility – she was royalty, as I discovered.

"I couldn't stand it when he returned," Penelope said. "Constantly bragging about what he had done. And he was furious with me! As if I had any choice, as if I wished for all those men to camp out in my own home." She sighed, as we walked through the meadows, the other women not far behind. "He expected me to wait and wilt and pine over him, and when I told him I believed, at points, he was dead, he would not have it. Claimed I had no faith in him."

"That sounds awful."

"That is the way of some men, dear. And you know, not all of those suitors...well, some were young men, forced there by their fathers to gain that little bit of power. They were nice, and kind, and undeserving of their fate." She stopped, turned to face Eurydice. "I have heard since he has found himself in Tartarus, while many of the men he slayed are here. Serves him right. He believed himself bound for Elysium."

I enjoyed her company especially. When we were alerted to an influx of new arrivals, the other women disappeared to see if any of their loved ones had arrived. Penelope and I stayed behind, laying on the grass side by side.

She took my hand, and the thrill it sent through me was so different than anything Orpheus ever made me feel.

"Eurydice, I-"

Whatever she was about to say next I did not hear. A cough alerted us to another presence, and we turned to see the queen of the underworld herself standing nearby, hands clasped before her as she studied us.

"Hello," Persephone said, and smiled, her shoulders slumping as she surveyed us. "Well, I was hoping to tell you good news, Eurydice, but you seem happy here."

"What do you mean?" I scrambled to sit up, and Penelope did the same, both of us studying the goddess.

"Orpheus has come for you."

If I'd had a beating heart, my blood would have ran cold.

"He's dead?" I choked out, unable to believe the Orpheus I knew would inflict his own death just to follow me into Hades.

Persephone stared across the fields. "You know, there are many who come here of their own free will. To escape. I never understood that. Not until I came down here and heard their stories." She turned back. "Eurydice, Orpheus is not dead. He entered Hades as a mortal, and refuses to leave until he has you. My husband is angry, but I begged him to listen, believing another opportunity at life would be something you were happy about. I believed his love story. I should have spoken to you first."

I clutched Penelope's hand, and she leaned towards me.

"Leave," she said. "Once you are free, you can escape him. You deserve a long life full of happiness, and there are those who will help you."

"What the queen says is true." Persephone stepped forward. "But Hades…he will not let Orpheus leave freely with you at his side. Tell me, my dear, what Orpheus is really like. Perhaps there is a way we can make him prove his worth."

***

So, it was agreed and arranged. I knew Orpheus well enough. He would fear a trick played at his expense. I was his; his possession, his belonging, his wife. Death, clearly, had not changed that. Persephone took my hand, after I had hugged Penelope.

"What if he doesn't?" Penelope said. "What if he follows the rules, and you are alive again?"

"I will live," I said. "I will not allow myself to be trapped by him. I promise."

We said our farewells, and Persephone tugged me close to her, wiped away my tears, and suddenly we were no longer standing in the meadows I had grown to love, no matter how unchanging, but in a dark, shifting cavern.

Orpheus paced up and down. Persephone pulled me back into the shadows, allowing me to watch as he stopped and turned towards Hades.

"I deserve this," he said. "I have lived a life of devotion and I do not deserve to have my wife taken from me so soon."

Hades looked up as Persephone stepped out, and she dipped her head towards him.

"Of course," she said, "a mortal cannot be allowed to just enter and leave at will. Husband, I have located Eurydice, and she is preparing for her journey back to the surface. But perhaps we should...discuss Orpheus' payment."

Hades grinned. He was a handsome man, strangely, and I could see why Persephone loved him so much she was willing to spend half the year in this cold place. For it was cold, and drab. Hades stepped off his throne and the pair conferred, too far away for me to hear, though I had an idea of what she was saying.

Orpheus shifted from foot to foot, and I could imagine what was going through his head. He would be crafting a song to sing upon his return, about how heroic and amazing he was, how he travelled to the underworld to rescue his dead love. It would start with my tragic death and end with him the triumphant hero.

It was easy to shape the narrative when you created it.

Persephone and Hades stepped apart and turned towards Orpheus. A glint in Hades' eye betrayed his excitement, while Persephone managed to look solemn and wise.

"There is a problem," Hades said, his voice a rumbling force.

"Problem?" Orpheus stepped towards him. "What kind of problem?"

"There are rules, musician. You cannot just step in here and take what you desire. Otherwise loved ones would be here all day and night, demanding we return their kin."

Orpheus flushed red. "Not everyone can do what I did. Do you know how difficult this was? What I had to go through? You think everyone can charm that ugly dog of yours?"

"Silence!" Hades roared, flames spring up around his feet. "I will let your words go, spoken as they are out of passion. You may leave the underworld with your wife, but you must trust in us and in her. If you look back even once, she will be returned to the flames of Tartarus for her punishment."

Even Persephone struggled to hide her smile, biting her bottom lip. Orpheus' eyes widened.

"She...she was in Tartarus?"

"She danced with the naiads, on her wedding day no less," Hades said, as if there were no greater crime in the world. "Such transgressions must be punished." He pointed behind my husband, to the path carved through cliff. "Back the way you came, little mortal. She will follow. Do not look back until the sun touches your skin and hers once more, do you understand? Charon will row you out."

"Yes. Thank you." He bowed, trembling under their gazes. He glanced at Persephone. "Thank you both."

Orpheus turned, strode towards the path, and once he was out of sight,

Persephone nodded at me.

I crossed the floor, but before I reached the path, Hades grabbed my wrist.

"If you make it out," he said, "do not waste your opportunity, do you hear me? Another chance at life is not to be taken lightly."

"I know."

He let me go, and I followed my husband, soon catching up enough I would be in his eyeline if he turned around. And he was good. Clutching his lyre, the man who could charm all – including me – scurried between the rocks. Every so often he stopped, placed a hand to the wall as if he would look back. I prayed for it. I waited for it. But he made it to Charon's boat and sat at the front.

The ferryman looked to me, pointed at the back. I sat, smoothing down my skirts and staring at the back of Orpheus' head. He was so close I could touch him. His back was rigid, head high, and he muttered under his breath.

"Don't look back, don't look back, don't look back…"

Charon pushed off from the embankment, and around us I could hear the cries of souls, the wretched screaming at us to take them with us. Voices washed over one another, as we moved ever so slowly down the river.

Orpheus played his lyre, and I closed my eyes, listening to the music as it washed over us all. Soon, he sang, and it was one of my songs, my lyrics I had ripped out of my chest and poured out for him.

I didn't know how long we travelled for. But we rounded a corner eventually, and light appeared ahead.

We were close.

So close, when Orpheus stopped playing.

"She's mine," he said. "And I would never let anyone, lest of all the gods, take what is mine." The words came with such venom, more powerful than the snake which bit me. He gripped the sides of the boat, dropping his lyre, and took a deep breath. "If they kept their word, anyway."

"You think Hades and Persephone would trick you?" I said, unable to keep myself from smiling.

Orpheus stiffened. "Eurydice?"

I could see it in him, the urge to turn around, the urge to look at me.

"Or an illusion with her voice. Keeping looking ahead, Orpheus. I would like to live again."

"But how do I…what if…no!" He pressed his hands to the seat. "Eurydice, I cannot tell you how I have missed you."

"Of course, my darling. I missed you too."

He twitched, the slightest tremor of his body.

"I have thought of nothing, day or night, except you. I have composed so many songs dedicated to you," I continued. "My love. I awaited the day you would join me. I never dreamed it would be so soon."

The front of the boat crossed the line between darkness and light, and as the sun hit him, Orpheus turned, realizing a moment too late what he had done.

I had never spoken of him so, and he knew it.

His eyes widened. "No," he whispered, and reached for me.

I shrugged. "Have a happy life, Orpheus."

I blinked, and found myself standing in the meadow, Penelope before me just as I had left her. She threw her arms around me, holding me tight.

I was home.

# AND EURYDICE

## BY LOUIS EVANS

Once, there was a poet. And there was his woman.

The poet was the greatest poet of that age and of any age. His subtle verses charmed the beasts of field and forest. His heartfelt melodies called the nymphs from trees and dryads from their waters; the gods themselves took warm and thankful notice.

And the woman was his girlfriend.

This was, of course, the highest honor to which any woman might aspire. Or so the poet implied, in the marvelously subtle enjambment of his lines, in the pursed lips with which he regarded her own fumbling attempts at verse, at pottery, at dance. But she was his, moon to his sun, mirror to his glory. And basking in his warmth, in the undeniable beauty with which he described her, she felt herself exalted in a way that seemed like love.

To the poet she was the most precious of things.

All things, of course, are precious when you own them.

She was the poet's woman for many years. When it was necessary that she become something more, they were engaged to be wed.

If there were those among her people who thought the wedding unwise, they'd learned by experience to keep such counsel to themselves. And so it was as if such people—her parents, her sisters—had never existed, and the happy couple's joy at the marriage was untainted.

The night before, barefoot and in her slip, she fled from the house where they stayed and ran through the grass, frolicking. Only the very unkind might say she was rehearsing an escape she did not yet dare admit she needed. Only the very unkind would speak so ill of the dead.

In the grass there was a serpent. So it often is; and if there is no serpent, other perils can be found lying in wait for women who dare flirt with freedom.

The serpent's poison stilled her heart. And before even the alarm had been raised for her disappearance, she died and went down into the underworld, where all bonds of marriage and obligation are no more, where grey shades move through grey caverns unburdened with responsibility, subsisting only on the damp, owing nothing, touching nothing, never being touched.

So she died, this would-be wife of the poet, and he wept at her demise, and the people said, how prettily he weeps, how manfully, how his tears stir the passions in our own breasts, how they move our own sclerotic hearts to sing.

But when he rose from his weeping it was not to choose a new bride, though many offered themselves for his choosing. No. He rose from his weeping, and he said, "I will go down into the land of the dead, and I will bring her back."

The poet found a road that led him to the underworld. The difficulty of this feat has been exaggerated. Every road, sooner or later, leads to the world beneath the world. Walk carelessly, and you will get there faster.

The road to the underworld is easy to find and easy to walk, and the poet did both of these things. And he thought a little of the woman he would bring back—he called it rescuing—and he thought quite a lot of the songs and stories that would be sung of his feat, how the lesser poets of later years would capture his steely brow and sweet, sorrowful lips. And with these thoughts in mind the road to the land of the dead was a pleasant one, and soon enough the poet came to that place.

Now the dead are beyond counting, and their spirits moved through that endless cavern like wisps of mist on the surface of the ocean. And perhaps you or I would be daunted by that sight, and we would sigh hopelessly, and we would cry aloud, wondering how we might find our beloved among the endless murmurs of all who ever were. And if the poet had done so, this would have been a different story, and ended otherwise

But the poet knew: when on a quest to reclaim a possession, one speaks to the owners of things. And the poet knew: even the land of the dead is owned.

So he crossed the great cavern of the dead and forged ahead through the whirling wisps of smoke and soul, never asking if this one or that one was hero, villain, beloved. And the poet came to the throne of the Lord of the Land of the Dead.

And he knelt before that throne, as a king kneels to be crowned, and he sang to the Lord of the Dead a new song.

Some say the poet's song moved the heart of the Lord of the Dead.

Maybe.

In any case the Lord made an offer. From among the uncountable spirits, he plucked forth the poet's woman and brought her before the throne, clothed her once more with flesh and form.

Did she, with her new eyes, lock gazes with the wife of the Lord of the Dead, who stood, shackled but unbowed, behind his throne? Did some sympathy, some understanding, pass between them in that moment, unspoken and unknown to the men who dealt with each other on men's matters: the fates of women? What could such sympathy mean?

What might it threaten?

The Lord of the Dead spoke to the poet and to his woman, and he said: all roads lead to the land of the dead, but only one road leads back.

If the spirits of the dead are as mist, then this road is less than mist; if the land of the dead is a dream, then this road is half a dream.

One who walks this road is in graver peril than any man alive, for he is no man alive. He is unalive, undead, unborn and unburied. Only unseen may he pass along this road. For if a man is seen along this road, then it is as if he never were. His body will not go to the land of the living and his shade will not go to the land of the dead; his words will be as silence and his deeds will be as dust.

Thus, for two to walk this road together is not an easy puzzle.

In the land of the poet and the woman they had discovered riddles. A sphinx had taught this to them, or they had invented the riddle and then invented the sphinx so as to put it in her mouth. They were familiar with logic and its consequences. Ask yourself: two must walk together, but neither can look upon the other. How would you solve this?

Perhaps they must walk back-to-back, as climbers who ascend a narrow place in rock. Perhaps they should crawl, one after the other, heads facing down to the ground, calling out so as to be heard. Perhaps the two need not walk together, but could take turns, first one and then the other making their own way up to safety.

These are the thoughts you might have.

The poet had another.

He laughed.

"It's simple," he said. "Bring me a blindfold. And a rope."

There are no flocks for shearing in the underworld, and on the banks of its grey rivers there grows no cotton, and so a wise man will not ask what the rope was made of, nor the cloth. The poet tied the rope around his woman's wrists and the cloth over her eyes. And she opened her mouth to speak, and he said, "This is best," and she shut it.

Silence may be learned in many lessons.

And so the poet and his women left that place at his suggestion and her acquiescence, and they went together—him leading and her following behind—to the lone road that leads from the land of the dead to the world of the living.

Of that road there is little that can be said, or, rather, there is too much.

196

For the road is one thing to one soul and another thing to the other, and it was made in this way so the souls of the dead cannot stage a mass escape to the green earth above.

The poet had a poet's soul, and so the road for him was a panorama of great feeling. He passed vistas of sublime beauty and over crevasses that yawned like the heart's abyss of despair. The poet had a hero's soul as well, and so for him the road was a trial and a triumph, a jagged path of brave feats boldly attempted and thrillingly won.

And the poet's woman had her own soul, and she passed along her own road, but in fact she was dragged, stumbling, from rock to rock and crag to crag, unable to even determine what the shape of her own path might have been.

And the poet sang to himself, and sometimes he yanked impatiently on the rope, or told his woman to be silent so he could think, though she had not spoken. And as the journey continued, he began to talk to her in earnest.

He told the woman that he loved her; he often told her this. He told her that she had been so silly, so foolish to die, and it just went to show that his protection and his guidance were needed in her life. He spoke of the wedding they would have, a hero's wedding, and how he would crown his glory with her beauty.

He spoke of the glorious sights he was seeing, and he said it was a good thing she was blindfolded, not him, since he was a poetic genius and she was no genius of any kind, and so his beautiful words could paint a perfect picture of the beautiful sights for her, and she could not have done the same. He did not seem to consider that the woman, unbound, might have seen something else entirely different.

He told the woman again that he loved her; as he pulled her bodily over the rocks, he told her that his heroic deeds proved the strength of his love, that he would always come for her, always, no matter the circumstance, would always come for her and bring her back to him, do you understand me, always.

And to this speech the woman spoke no reply. It was not that different from other speeches the poet had made on other occasions, and her bruises from the rocks were not much worse than the bruises at those other times.

And then the poet saw the rays of sunlight descending from heaven.

They came together to the very mouth of the road that leads out of the underworld. They stood within the path, on its final stretch, and looked out into the sunlit fields ahead.

And in the mouth of that cavern, the poet smiled. He composed and delivered a poem of triumph on that occasion, and with her bound hands she applauded him, as she always applauded.

"You're lucky I am so disciplined, so prudent. A foolish man might have glanced back along this journey and consigned you at once to oblivion, you know. You should be grateful."

At this the woman expressed no gratitude, and this ingratitude angered him.

"It would be so easy to destroy you, you know," said the poet. "We are still within the tunnel. I would simply have to turn my head, just that, and you would be instantly obliterated."

At this the woman expressed no fear, and this boldness enraged him. And so he closed his eyes and turned back to face her.

"Just like this, I could do it. All I'd have to do is open my eyes."

And the woman did not shriek or cry or beg, and the poet had come to rely on the shrieking and the crying and the begging to fill a certain unnamed need in his soul, which he never mentioned in any of his famous poems. And so against his own better judgement he opened his eyes, and waited to see the woman dissolve before him.

But he saw nothing: only the long and empty road that led up from the land of the dead, on which he himself stood.

What? Had she vanished instantaneously? Had he lost her earlier? But no, the rope was taut in his hands. It led not down toward the underworld, but above—

The poet, standing within the mouth of the cavern, slowly turned.

There, on the green fields of day, stood the woman. She had snuck past him somehow, on her road that was not his road. She was facing him. With her bound hands she reached up to remove her blindfold.

He reached out, leapt out, cried out—

And then her eyes were open, and she saw him make that final leap toward the land of the living.

The poet had planned to someday die with great ceremony, with a famous final epigram or couplet. But there was no time to speak.

The woman looked at him. She saw a man. She saw a mist. She saw nothing at all.

The rope on her wrists fell limp to the ground. She turned from the land of the dead, and she walked off into the world of the living.

\*\*\*

Once there was a poet, and his woman. This poet went down into the underworld to reclaim his stolen property. And he never, ever, returned.

And the woman?

Well. Hers is another story.

# ARIADNE

# UNTHREADING

## BY ALLEN ASHLEY

I am golden, not gold.
History remembers our heroes
and heroines but also sometimes
their special accoutrements.
The shield of Perseus polished
to perfection, enabling him to
mirror out-maneuver
the Gorgon. Or fabled Excalibur,
fit only for the grip
of the once and future king.

I am golden, not gold.
A gift from sweet Ariadne –
"Find your way back with this,
my prince, my love."
Used but then left
hanging on a bare nail
on the labyrinth wall. An angry king
orders his soldiers to rip me,
to shred me, to send me off
to the wind in tatters. My
mistress escapes, brave bold
Theseus at her side. Until later
he abandons her on the bare sand
of Naxos. Her sorrowful voice
is carried on the wind but the words
are shredded, tattered.

I am golden but not gold.
I wish I could have helped
her find her way back, too.

# FRAYED

## BY CARTER LAPPIN

Ariadne sat just outside the entrance to the Labyrinth, twisting and untwisting the end of a piece of thread in her hands. The edge was starting to fray from all her fussing. She was nervous, though it wasn't her first visit to the Labyrinth or to the creature who lived inside of it.

Creature. That was the word, wasn't it? The word for the little brother that had rounded her mother's stomach, that had grown inside of the queen for months. Ariadne had sat outside of the room as he was delivered, hearing her mother scream and scream as Ariadne drew little pictures on the walls of the palace in charcoal. The maids would scold her for it later, but she was young and her father's favorite.

She'd been there when the midwife started to scream, too.

A monster. That's what they called her little brother, with his head as fuzzy as a shorn sheep and just as soft. They said the queen had been cursed by Poseidon, though nobody would tell Ariadne exactly why even to this day.

Ariadne had snuck inside the room as the king, her father, yelled at her mother, sitting in the bed with the baby clutched to her chest. She'd looked drawn and tired, hair plastered to her face with sweat. He'd wanted to get rid of the child, of the *thing* that had been born half-man and half-bull. A beast. A monster.

Unable to stay hidden any longer, Ariadne screamed, running from her concealed spot to barrel into her mother's side. The baby cooed curiously at her arrival, lifting a fuzzy hand in her direction.

Ariadne had been young at the time and later wouldn't remember much of the night except for that. Her sweet brother, soft and beastly as he may be, reaching for her. Later, she'd remember yelling, crying, begging her father not to hurt him. She wouldn't remember what changed his mind exactly, only that his mind was changed.

Ariadne's mother held the baby tighter once the king was finally gone from the room. She was even more pale then, and shaking a little. Her brother would be allowed to stay, for now. He was so small.

Her mother named him Asterion, after the stars that shone outside the window that night. Ariadne had known then she'd always love this little brother of hers. Always care for him, always protect him.

Now, sitting outside of the Labyrinth with a ball of thread in her lap, Ariadne felt like nothing more than a failure. Her mother had never forgiven the king for having the boy locked up, but Ariadne had never forgiven herself.

Her brother hadn't grown up quite right, even beyond the obvious physical defects. He was slow, strange. He never learned to talk, though he could make a sort of bleating sound like a baby calf. He was gentle, almost to the point of ridiculousness--except when he got angry. That was what had caused him to be sent away to the Labyrinth, in the end. Servants were replaceable, but after the third death people started to get scared, refusing to enter the palace for fear of being cursed, or worse.

It hadn't been Asterion's fault, not really. He didn't know what he was doing, and he was so much stronger than anyone else.

Ariadne's father hadn't seen it that way. He'd had Asterion locked up, hidden away in the center of an impossible maze like a dirty secret. For it to have been ready so quickly it had to have been commissioned a long time ago, perhaps even on the night of Asterion's birth. Ariadne imagined the king, going to Daedalus the inventor in the middle of the night as Ariadne held her mother's tired hand and Asterion blinked up with new eyes at the stars he was named after.

Had the king ever really loved her brother?

Ariadne was supposed to protect him. Now all she could do was visit him.

She tied another knot in the fraying thread, then had to spend another minute picking it out again. She'd tied a sailor's knot by accident. One of the kitchen maids taught her how to make them a long time ago, as a way to still anxious hands. Ariadne had never been on a ship before, but if she ever did go out to sea, she would be able to tie knots with the best of sailors.

Ariadne thought of the sacrifices that were brought over from Athens, of those poor fourteen sent to sate her brother's hunger. She wondered if they had ever been on a ship before coming here, if they were scared by the roiling waves and the creaking decks below their feet.

Nobody ever visited Asterion except for Ariadne. She really should go inside.

Her brother would never hurt her. Even as he grew older, hungrier, and angrier, he still wouldn't hurt her. She was his sister. She'd visited him so many times over the years, told him stories and brought him charcoals to draw on the walls with as she had done when she was young.

But he was so angry these days. And those poor sacrifices. Those poor people ripped from their homes, taken across the sea to appease the cursed son of a king they had never met.

Ariadne sighed and stood up. The bottom of her dress would likely be dirty enough from her extended sit on the ground that the servants would grumble at her for having to clean it. She tore the frayed end of the thread off with her teeth, then tied the rest to a sturdy olive branch just outside the Labyrinth's entrance. It wouldn't do to get lost.

Ariadne took a deep breath. Yes, it was time to go in. This was how things were. Perhaps, someday, that would change. But that would not be today.

For now, she went into the maze, trailing thread in her wake. Her brother was waiting, and Ariadne was nothing if not a good sister. She went deeper into the Labyrinth, trusting that her thread would soon lead her back out again.

# ATALANTA

# ATALANTA AGAINST JOVE
## BY R.K. DUNCAN

All praise Medusa of the fiber-optic hair.

Her fisheye lens is darkly clear,
her traverse smooth and rhythmless.
Her siren mouth is silent now,
ready to scream if trespass should appear.

      Her tresses trace infinite feeds,
           delivering each guilty face
           to watchers who cross-reference
           The litany of drone detected crimes
           tagged to each ident-chip.

Atalanta crouches mirror-coated,
      showing in front what lies behind.
Approaches with careful scatter-step.
      waits still and statue when Medusa looks.
      Runs closer when she whirrs away.

Under the guard: the archive core.
      Un-writes her name from every file.
      Un-prints her fingers; pixelates her eyes.
      Un-maps her dull genetic code from database.
Goes with no fear of the Medusa,
and walks away unseen by the closed circuit of the city.

Down to the garage at the tower's root,
      skips quickly where she crept before.
That snail's pace crawl, avoiding every lens
      replaced by right to go just as the drones of
law-abiding corporate hives

In catacombs her steed awaits,
nursed through the watchful darkness to arrive.

Now let it ride!

Pegasus roars black and chrome between her thighs.

She is no Perseus,
            for all that she has blinded the Medusa
            And armored herself with Aegis against those countless prying
eyes.
Atalanta rides the divine steed, wings furled for now,
                                            fire flaring from his
                            dual exhaust.
A wild horse under a wild rider;
a visitor to the city's civilized content
returning to her home among the
Helots of the border

She shrieks by in her saddle
Plastic and leather gleaming glossy black.
                    Camera-eyes swivel to track her limit-
            stretching speed,
                                        But now they
                            cannot index her
                                    by name
                                    by face
                                    by half-ruined
                            license plate
                    She is a cypher of generic images with no
            impression in the database.

So she flits back

beyond the ragged borders of the policed polis
into the wild places that still suffer all Pandora's scourges:
poverty and slow connections, leaded pipes, and payments without ident-chip,
but have not given up their hold on the last hope of
life without invigilation.

Quick and black, she slips through cordons before they can re-orient,
No threats expected from outside the stew//

                                       inside the city that the
broken places broke from

                 She sees the barricades embattled.

These would be picket lines; her neighbors would be strikers,
                 if they had jobs that offered hours enough to
                 miss by striking.
Instead they are just people, flesh gathered
to demand community continue,
not be paved-over
for the foundation of more gleaming towers
like what look down from Mount Olympus opposite, across the bay,
                 high in the city's heart.

Blue clad Hydra heads in POLICE windbreakers are everywhere,
and when rare hit with brick or bottle lays one down
a dozen more spring up
         Spitting peppery fire on the offending protester.

Where the brave Helots gather in phalanx
the cyclops comes
         crying a firehose from cannon eye,
         ignoring stones on armored flanks.

He drives them back behind the barricades and broken trenches
out of the streets where wheels and engines
Move the lifeblood of the polis past their wild enclave.

She watches the tide of hopeful violence
      break three times against the weight of
            truncheon, fire, gas, and pressure-hose.
The Hydra-headed thugs only increase
And when they feel secure,
The barricades will be ground down.

They need a spear to pierce this Polyphemus' weeping eye,
Fire to scorch the neck and keep the
Hydra's heads from sprouting up again.

      Fire is hard to come by in the wilderness.

Back alley bargains with Charon
to put her on the trail.
She sets the reader, stares into the lens
    So it can read her retinas for coins
                enough to pay this ferryman
        and
            buy a journey in his unmarked
      car

Lethe is a dozen turns and sharp reversals.
    Nothing seen through midnight-tinted glass
        until the ferry opens at an unmarked door.

Three heads

between the bouncers and the camera,
nod at her, and to the ferryman,
and she is in,
descending into darkness
into light: the lasers sweep and strobe-lights flash

The damned cavort, or find quiet
Elysium in tailored drugs
shivering in booths and tumbled piles
around communal water-pipes

Hades enthroned, surveys his
hell of pounding bass
with one keen eye, the other
lost behind a shifting headset screen,
flickers the sea of finance and grand larcenies.

Decked in charcoal pinstripe,
adorned with gold and diamond ostentation,
he is still only a bottom-feeder
far below the mountaintops of
penthouses and corporate towers,
where the true treasures of this
interconnected earth
are bartered by
heaven's highest.

Hades still has reasons to deal
with ordinary ants and strivers
with both feet
on the ground.

For all the coins that Atalanta's
Eyes can yield
He offers this:
> Vulcan's treasures come to the borders of the wood today.
> Beware the furies sent from
> furious Jove, in vengeance
> for Medusa.

He proffers pomegranate wine, but
Atalanta's tarnished virgin vow
still guards against the thought of waking
stripped to the skin,
dancing in one of Hades's cages.

> Back to the surface, back to Charon's waiting
> car.
> He takes her back where this descent began,
> an alley two streets inside
the wilderness behind the barricades

Vultures fresh from Vulcan's forges,
> black suits, black ties,
> and long steel cases.
They wait on the far edges
of the wilderness,
to make a deal with rowdy centaurs,
> who pay in meth and contract violence
> for heavy weapons,
> > all they need to keep their clan's
> > domain carved from the flanks
> > > of international cartels

Atalanta leaps ahead of all companions

falls on the gun-sellers
beating like a wild bear
tearing wolf-like with knives
               as much a part of her as flashing teeth.


Vulcan's vultures leave their master's fire
       caged in steel, awaiting sight of gold.
They have no strength to answer her
before her comrades follow.
Helots overwhelm the few who thought
they came to deal with friends.


The vultures clipped and cuffed,
the comrades crack the locks.


The centaurs roar into the scene
       horse-halves coughing, stuttering
              black smoke into the sunset air.


       Chains crack sparks.
A hail of thrown glass shatters.
       Handguns run out to promise vengeance
           for their bloody patrons.


Atalanta cracks the steel that holds
the fire safe.
Up swings a triple barreled rotary,
       not meant for un-crewed operation,
       steady in her sinewed arms.


          Back down, depart,
       or suffer Vulcan's vengeance

on the world that broke him.

Centaurs curvet and growl defiance
    spinning wheels and painting rubber on the road.
        Bitch, whore, and worse are shouted,
but guns drop down,
and when wheels meet the dirt,
    they bite to turn away.
Centaurs withdraw, promising punishment to come.

Atalanta leads the hunt back to the barricades
With stolen treasures hot in hand,
ready to meet the Hydra's fire with their own

Atalanta holds the spear for Polyphemus
A simple tube; the deadly elegance
of double-charged explosive
meant for cracking shells
and cooking meat within.

While Atalanta hunted arms
the Helots were hard-pressed.
Still, at her word they rally for
a final press.

The Cyclops comes to scatter
        where they make a wedge
The water cannon tracks.
This time she answers.
Vulcan's spear spits fire.
    The point trails sparks.
        One flash to break the armor.

Deep boom that shakes the street,
and every seam of Polyphemus pours black smoke

The Hydra heads spring up
spit fire and choking smoke to
drive the Helots back
This time fire answers
Lightning that pierces hydra scales.
Rotary cannons fill the air with
screaming steel hornets,
enough to drive Europa
beyond the pillars of Hercules
This time new heads are cautious to spring up,
and caution quickly folds to cowardice
when the barrage is unrelenting.
The barricades are won.
The hydra backpedals in broken knots.
The cyclops is abandoned on the field.

Advenit Jove!

The king of heaven's corporations
comes enthroned above them all.
His cloud is of titanium, lifted by noble gas,
his throne the crystal cupola,
Where he looks down, deigning to touch the earth
Only with roving spotlights

Disperse,
he orders,
this godhead who
dispatched the Hydra and the Cyclops to

secure the prize he makes of land
where Helots lived for generations.

Until the dawn, freely depart
then demolition will begin.
    His thunderbolts are primed,
       charged in the cannons of his floating throne
          that blocks the moon and blanks the stars
            above the wilderness.

Atalanta stares.
This is the threat she cleared herself
to stand against, to be a hero
that the Helots could not be themselves,
do good work with the wits earned
by a life of criminality.

But from the corner of her eye
she catches the other half
    of Hades' warning
       hanging ripe.

The Furies have arrived for her
    fresh from Jove's heel
Once they were ordinary women,
muscular and violent, schooled to break and bruise
          whoever the boss pointed out.

Now they spread canine nostrils wide,
squint eyes half-hawk/half mechanism,
    to pick out Atalanta from the crowd.
They tense steel-corded muscle,

twitch with the reflexes of super-conducting nerve replacement.
Razor claws click in and out in place of fingernails.

Jove cannot find her through the countless
Eyes of the Medusa,
but his furies need no camera to coach them on.
They have her scent from where she left it
in the tower, in the air behind her.
They can sift a molecule of DNA
Out of the whole highway's pall of smog,
> and track her by a stray skin-flake
> that slipped the seam between her riding gloves and jacket.

They spring, covering distance faster than the
trains that never stop inside the wilderness
The Helots swing their muzzles round,
> but where the bullets whiz, the targets aren't.
Atlanta straddles her Pegasus and flies
back from the barricaded border
with the polis, deep into the wilds
> where only Helots know the ways

They eat the ground behind with
a lope that bends their knees wrong-way
and gains ground on her screeching tires.
The furies howl hypersonic tones
that send her scalp skin trying to crawl
round and down into her throat.

Her hands twitch on the handlebars and nearly
> send her sprawling.
The leading fury strikes a spark

and gouges paint off Pegasus
                    before she gets control and makes
                    a gap to live in.

Sweat sheets her legs
            under the plastic leather armor.
She can't keep running on the flat.
They'll run her down, like hounds
                    on deer, and rip her heart out just the same.

A length ahead of grasping claws,
she swings into the Labyrinth,
            the shantytown that sprang up
            where the project towers fell
                    sixty years back.

Nothing replaced the folly of
            a planned community of poverty,
so now a maze of plastic tarp
and bright, found fabrics
sketches unplanned streets that shift from
                    month to month with transients and new additions.

Atalanta knows the twists better
                    than the track of lines across her palm.
She grew tall here, passed between
foster parents, until she went to
                    find her fortune in Polis' underbelly
She guides her Pegasus assured.

The Furies follow, overturning stalls
and tearing tents to ribbons

when they obstruct the view of Atalanta.

The twists and turns won't lose
        these human hounds,
so Atlanta takes them to the center.
     And more than they, roll up her spooling thread
     to follow.

This maze has many minotaurs, all comrades
        jealous of an outside animal.
The furies tunnel-vision tight
chasing their target, Atalanta.

       She halts and spreads arms wide and waits.

They come with claws snapped out,
and then the blows rain down behind:
        knives, rocks, bottles, and cans,
and here the lost ones of the Labyrinth
behind their missiles, brandishing
     knives, cleavers, shivs, pipes, sticks.

The furies' hands snap photo-fast
     to catch each incoming,
to block the blade and cut the hand behind it.
At ten to one they'd leave the battle
blood-stained and unharmed.

Three to one-hundred is too many.
     Their tuned reflexes can't keep up.
     Competing routines of protection clash,
     and they twist and stutter trying

To do more than even
>> training-tempered frames can manage

The furies fall under the flood
>> of downtrod souls with too-little to lose
>> to be afraid of corporate hunters.
Atalanta passes by, back to border
>>> Where Jove's airship waits imperious,
>>>> driving the dregs of courage from exhausted
>> picketers.


Now Atalanta must put on Odysseus
and be the cleverest of Helots,
>> to show how they can bring down
>>> this foe who elevates beyond their strength
>> by trickery and coup de main,
how Helots can still reach the sky.

Jove's sweeping spotlights would spot any
>>> weapon strong enough to trammel him,
but ramps are easier.

Already some are half-built in the mounds of dirt
>> that border the delayed construction.
Helots can bring down fences,
topple plywood walls to make more,
send a troupe of riders skyborne on makeshift Pegasi.

The airship has no fear of such attack.
>> Only the gods, Jove's siblings,
>> join it in the sky above the city.
Jove has no guards, no legions

in his cloudy palace.

The dream of trickery and daring
takes the Helot camp like fire
　　　　　　　　racing over grass.
So quick they come, the crazy brave,
　　　　to follow Atalanta's last mad scheme

The fences fall.
The engines roar.
The spotlights sweep and swerve,
　　　　with operators' incredulity,
　　　　　　　to see a swarm
　　　　　　　　　of sleekly leaping cycles
　　　　　　　　　　　climbing for the bridge.

Pegasus leads the charge,
　　　　wings of magnetic force spread wide,
　　　　and Atalanta pilots him
　　　　　　　straight to the control bay.

Jove sits enthroned, in crimson silk
and golden trim, directing guns
　　　　in bedroom clothes.
He curses these ungrateful slaves,
　　　　who throw back charity with violent rage.

A moment more, his guns will speak
　　　　　　his anger backed with blasting fire,
　　　　break burning Helots to black twigs,
and clear the ground for his development.

Atalanta seizes him, alone in at the controls,
before his minions break the door.
She casts him through the emptiness
          her Pegasus has shattered window glass into.

He tumbles. She comes promethean behind,
     driving the airship down,
         to ruin the broad interchange,
           Where polis streets enter the wilderness.

She leaps deer-graceful from the
               fiery fall,
and orders dazzled Helots in
     to brave the heat.
Jove's guns and thunderbolts
     are ripe for harvesting.
Repurposed, they can hold back
     even the Olympian magnates
     and keep the Helots in their
         old land safe.

When the dawn of Jove's promised
         demolition dawns, his guns
           stand brave
       on every hill and barricade,
      daring the polis to intrude

On billboards in the city
Atalanta grins,
     in pixelated smear,
captured from telephoto lenses
     trained on Jove's descending throne.

Across the top, sits Nike's laurel
                    WANTED

Medusa has her face again
          shining triumphant,
Her home beyond the city serpents' reach.

# UNBREAKABLE

## BY HENRY HERZ

The blessed goddess Artemis told me that long ago, proud-hearted Iasus ruled Arcadia. The mighty king loved battle, the hunt, and all manner of dangerous pursuits. He wished to raise only noble sons in his halls, who would ride and hunt with him and carry on his name when he was dead.

On his wedding day, the king swore a terrible oath, naming the Greek gods as witnesses.

"Never shall a daughter be raised in my halls. The honor of my house shall rest solely upon sons."

But the Fates made a mockery of Iasus. For many a year, no child was born to the king. When at last he had hopes of an heir, his queen gave birth to a maiden. Me. His heart hardened, and he ordered me abandoned on the bleak slope of Mount Parthenion.

When Artemis, goddess of the hunt, wild animals, and chastity, heard the queen's lamentations and saw me cast forth to die, she swore that I should live. She sent a she-bear to my aid. The bear lifted me gently and bore me to a cave with her cubs. There, the soft-hearted beast suckled me, tending me night and day till I grew strong.

The cave rang with laughter as I played with my bear siblings. Artemis named me Atalanta and commanded forest nymphs to raise me once I was old enough to live without my ursine mother. Under their care, I blossomed like an iris in rich soil.

When I reached womanhood, the goddess of the hunt and virginity addressed me.

"I have bestowed many blessings upon you—health, strength, and beauty. The light of the sunbeam shines in your hair, the blue of the sky in your eyes, and your limbs made fresh and white by fast-flowing streams. I ask in return that you honor me through the hunt and by remaining chaste. Pay no attention should the goddess Aphrodite encourage you to marry."

"I will do all that you ask, my goddess, and gladly," I replied, bowing.

I spent my days roaming in pursuit of wild animals. My feet became so swift, I could outrun any man. My arms grew so strong and my eyes so sharp that I never missed the mark with my arrows. Rumors of my exploits spread across Greece.

So it came to pass that just as I hunted game, many a suitor pursued me.

They lured me with gold, gems, and fine furs, but none could snare me. Despite the allure of companionship, comfort, and riches, my solemn pledge to Artemis remained unbreakable.

But woe to a mortal, no matter how obeisant, caught between two quarreling gods. Artemis told me that the goddess of beauty and childbearing would not tolerate so famous an example of virginity. Artemis secretly overheard the jealous Aphrodite vow to summon a foul beast only the greatest of heroes could defeat, hoping I would join the hunt, forget my vow to Artemis, and fall in love with one of the men.

So it came to pass that a monstrous boar ravaged the land of Calydon. Its burning, bloodshot eyes seemed like coals of living fire. Its rough neck knotted with stiff muscles and thickset with bristles piercing as spearheads. The beast's long, sharp tusks slashed like swords. Discordant roars reverberated from its hideous jaws. Lightning belched forth from its horrid throat, scorching the fair green fields.

All fled before the snarling beast. It trampled wheat fields, tearing up all the grain. It crashed into vineyards, breaking down all the vines. It rooted up all the trees in the orchards. It climbed into hilly pastures, killing all the grazing sheep. So fierce and terrifying was the Calydonian Boar that no farmer dared to face the monster. With a thick hide proof against arrows, the beast killed many a man with those terrible tusks. Only within the city walls could refuge be found.

King Oeneus of Calydon summoned the mightiest warriors to rid his realm of the boar. Thither in search of high adventure came dozens of Greek heroes, just as they had joined the quest for the Golden Fleece, and, just as their sons would on a later day, rescue Helen from Troy. Among the heroes strode Jason, captain of the Argonauts; Castor, son of Zeus; Laertes, father of Odysseus; Achilles's father, Peleus; Theseus, Poseidon's son; Telamon, father of Ajax the Great; and King Oeneus's youngest son, Meleager. With them stood also Rhoecus the centaur and Hippomenes, disciple of Chiron the wise. There too went I, keen for the hunt.

The men and their retainers gathered in a bright blue pavilion set up outside the city gates. Servants brought fruit, bread, and wine to refresh the new arrivals. Noisy it was, with comrades greeting old friends and horses snorting in anticipation. Fastened to spears, the heroes' brightly colored standards fluttered in the breeze, a rainbow of fabrics. The musky scents of travel-stained men mixed with that of their mounts.

Up I strode barefooted, wrapped in a white linen tunic fastened at the shoulders with pins, a decorative pattern running along the hem. A faded leather belt circled my waist. I bore my trusty bow, arrows, and a long hunting spear.

"I am Atalanta, champion of Artemis."

The arrival of a tall, armed woman threw the host of men into turmoil. It was as if the goddess Eris tossed the Apple of Discord into their midst.

"Would you care to stay with the queen, watching her ladies spin and weave?" King Oeneus sneered.

I only glared.

"My daughters play in the garden. Perhaps you would care to join in their simple games," offered Oeneus.

Scowling, I responded with word and deed.

"Games do not interest me." With a flash of my muscular arm, I hurled my spear. It passed within inches of the king's ear, embedding in a slender tree thirty feet behind him. The sapling split asunder from the force of the strike. "I am here to hunt the Calydonian Boar, nothing less."

"That was just a lucky throw. If she goes, then I will not," said one man.

"Nor I," said another. "Why, the whole world would laugh at us, and we should never hear the end of the matter." Several threatened to depart for home at once. Before matters got out of hand, handsome Hippomenes raised his voice.

"Come now. Let Atalanta join us."

What is this? I thought. A man willing to treat me as an equal? A most welcome change.

The men grumbled, but I would not be denied. "I seek neither charity nor pity. I shall prove myself thrice worthy to hunt the boar—wrestling one opponent, hunting against a second opponent, and racing a third. Surely, none fear I can best three of your number?" I scanned the men's faces, not all of whom met my stare. "Who shall wrestle me?"

Peleus stepped forward, perhaps imagining an easy victory along with the sensual pleasure of grappling a maiden.

Through the years, many a man sought to hold me in his arms, but none held my interest.

Peleus's companions smiled.

Yes, I know that Peleus won the sea nymph Thetis as his bride through his wrestling prowess. Today may prove more difficult for him.

Unarmed, we advanced into an open glen surrounded by tall trees. The other heroes gathered round, eyeing me as I stretched my lithe muscles.

Peleus and I circled, testing each other with lunges and attempted grabs. I eluded each of his bids, leaving him grasping only air.

Peleus's smile faded as it became clear his hubris and lasciviousness were no match for my skill and agility. With the speed of a striking adder, I dodged his attempted bear hug and swept his feet out from under him. He landed flat on his back, his defeat punctuated by a puff of dust, the blush of embarrassment on his face, and the stunned silence of the onlookers.

"Who now will compete with me in a deer hunt?" I raised my voice in challenge, hands on my hips.

"I shall," replied Rhoecus the centaur, raising a golden-ringed hand and rearing on his hind legs. Without waiting for a response, he galloped toward the nearest trees, chunks of turf torn up by his pounding hooves.

Snatching up my bow and arrows, I gave chase, my pursuit so rapid I almost caught up to Rhoecus as he entered the wood.

Later, I emerged from the trees with a scratched shoulder and torn tunic.

"Where is your deer?" Hippomenes asked with furrowed brow. "Without it, the contest is forfeit, I fear."

I shook my head and scowled, holding aloft one of the centaur's jeweled rings.

"Nay. Rhoecus forfeited the contest and his life when he tried to force himself upon me in the forest. A maiden hunter I remain in reverence for Artemis. None may dishonor me or my goddess thereby. So, I put an arrow through his eye. His body lies deep in the wood, his blood watering the grass. Let the beasts feast upon him there." I set down my bow and spear. "Who will now race me—one circuit round the city walls?"

As I waited for an opponent, Artemis spoke in my mind.

Your successes as my virgin champion frustrate Aphrodite, goddess of passion and childbearing. She would see you seduced by the strong arms of a victorious hero. Aphrodite believes every woman must cleave to a man. But we know that is not the only way. Be warned! Though Hippomenes is fleet of foot, Aphrodite may give him magical items to aid him during the race.

Hippomenes turned to me, bowed politely, and addressed me in a clear voice.

"I have never met your like. It would be my honor to race you. Your skill and beauty exceed even your reputation. Shall we wager? Will you become my wife if I prove the swifter?"

My eyes lingered over an opponent so fair of face and fair in word. I stood confident in my ability to outrun any man and eager to hunt the Calydonian boar.

"So be it. And if I win?"

Hippomenes considered for a moment. "I shall throw a great banquet in your honor." He grinned.

"With *boar* meat as the main course."

A trumpet sounded, and we sprinted over the course, Hippomenes's legs beating like a hummingbird's wings.

I remained close on Hippomenes's heels. What a sight it was to watch the handsome man run.

Your feet scarcely touch the ground, I thought. You could skim over the waving wheat without bending it or fly over the sea without wetting the soles of your feet.

The crowd shouted encouragement to the fleet-footed Hippomenes.

Hippomenes must have seen the gleam of my streaming hair out of the corner of his eye. For as I drew even with him, he put his hand into the opening of his tunic and drew forth something from his breast. His hand swung above his head, and from it flashed a dazzling golden apple.

Every eye turned from the race to watch the apple's gleaming flight. Through the air it flew and rolled along the grass.

I had never in my life felt such a powerful allure from an object. Despite being forewarned, I stopped short and watched the apple. It came to a halt far behind in the center of the course. It lay shining like a jewel in the grass, sparkling in the rays of the sun. A great desire sprang forth in my heart to have it—a mad, unreasoning desire I could not resist. I darted back, picking up the shining golden apple.

While the apple drew me, Hippomenes gained a good many paces.

I turned and gave chase.

Hippomenes, even without your trickery, you are fast as a deer, and it is a joy to pursue you. The space between us grew less and less, till we ran well-nigh shoulder to shoulder.

Hippomenes sent a second gleaming apple into the air.

The same mad, unreasoning desire again sprang up in my heart, and, leaving the course, I picked up the second apple from among the leaves where it had fallen. It took somewhat longer to find than the first. By the time I returned to the path, Hippomenes had rounded the turning-point and was well on his way toward the goal.

*What fine running form he displays.* I put forth all my strength to overtake him.

The flagging Hippomenes must have heard me speeding from behind, for he hurled the final apple, which rolled far from the course.

A desperate longing for the golden fruit rose within me. Keeping my feet on the path was the hardest thing I had yet essayed. My mind battled with my heart.

If I gather the third apple, I will lose the race to Hippomenes. He is by far the fairest and fleetest man I have seen and would make a fine husband. I do so long for companionship.

A doe frolicking in the distance caught my attention. The deer was one of my goddess's sacred symbols.

Artemis. I must maintain my vow to Artemis. I owe her everything.

A tear formed in my eye. Consigning myself to a life of solitude, I mustered the will to resist the powerful allure of the third apple.

Hippomenes sprang forward, but whereas he now ran like a hunted thing that strains every muscle to save its life, I ran with the gliding grace of the wild hind that, far away from the hunters and hounds, crosses the springing turf of the lonely moor, fearless and proud, throwing back its antlers in the breeze.

On every side, people shouted louder than before, for they knew not which of us would win. As we drew near to the goal, we were again shoulder to shoulder.

With a plea to Artemis, I gave a tremendous burst forward. Thus did it come to pass that I reached the goal first. My throat tightened.

I have the victory today but shall never know what might have been as wife to Hippomenes.

The gathered heroes burst into cheers.

Hippomenes bowed, gasping for breath. "Never have I been so disappointed to lose a race." He graciously raised my arm in victory. "Atalanta has proven herself thrice-worthy," he cried to the host.

Brushing away my tears, I rearmed myself with bow, arrows, and spear.

"Let us hunt!" I replied, thrusting my spear skyward.

Another round of cheering burst from the heroes' mouths. All was made ready. Nets were stretched from tree to tree and the dogs let loose.

We advanced through the woods, arrows nocked and drawn, spears held at the ready.

The Calydonian Boar, startled by the incursion of the company, rose hideous and unwieldy from its hiding place and rushed upon us. What were hounds to a beast such as it, or nets spread for a snare?

From a distance, Jason threw his spear, but his aim was off, and the weapon lodged in a tree trunk.

Other men attacked bravely, but this served only to enrage the enormous boar. It charged upon a warrior, catching him before he could save himself, and trampled the man into the ground with its iron hard hooves. Another man ventured too far from his hiding place and fell, scorched by the boar's belched lightning.

Theseus threw a spear with all his force. The weapon only grazed the tough skin of the dodging boar, glancing upward and piercing the heart of a nearby warrior.

The maddened beast charged Laertes, who only saved his life by climbing the nearest tree. The boar's slashing tusks gored Peleus before he could make his escape.

Amid this horrible carnage, the men wavered on the verge of breaking until I blew a mighty blast on my hunting horn. I loosed an arrow. It flew true but bounced off the thick hide of the monster like a pebble off a turtle's shell. "For Artemis!" I cried. I ran perilously close, hurling my spear like a thunderbolt cast by Zeus. It struck the boar in the back, piercing the tough hide. A great stream of blood gushed out, staining the ground red.

Hippomenes shouted with joy, calling upon the others to match my feat.

Meleager let fly an arrow which put out one of the beast's eyes.

Hippomenes rushed forward and pierced the wounded boar's heart with his spear. The boar could no longer stand, but fought fiercely for some moments before rolling over, dead.

The heroes cut off the beast's head. It was as much as six of them could carry. They took the skin from its massive body and offered it to Hippomenes as a prize, because he had given the death blow to the monstrous boar.

Hippomenes shook his head. "Nay. It belongs to Atalanta. It was she who dealt the first wound." And he gave it to me as the prize of honor, perhaps hoping the gesture would win him favor in my heart. The boar skin was so vast that, even slung over my left shoulder, it draped to the grass.

"Behold, the Queen of the Woods," Hippomenes exclaimed.

For days thereafter, suitor upon suitor begged for my hand in marriage. My ears were most receptive to the proposal of Hippomenes, a brave man and fair. True to his word, he held a feast in my honor. Though my heart felt like a storm-tossed ship, I remained unyielding as a rocky coastline. Each offer of gold, furs, and queenship, I politely declined.

Artemis, you gave me succor when my own father abandoned me. You granted me your favor all the days of my life. I shall hold true to my vows— to dwell alone in the woods, a maiden and a lover only of the hunt.

I built a simple altar, offering in sacrifice the two golden apples upon a bed of burning alder logs. I watched the smoke twirl heavenward.

My thanks for all your blessings, Artemis.

Upon receiving the wondrous fruit with which Aphrodite endeavored to trick me, Artemis appeared before me, laughing at her rival's expense.

"Aphrodite! Perhaps now you have learned from my champion," she mocked. "Her vow to me is unbreakable. And love takes many forms."

The goddess of beauty manifested in front of us. Her loveliness took my breath away—I could no more describe her fairness than sculpt marble with my fingers. But Artemis's ridicule and the laments of broken-hearted suitors must have felt like rose thorns piercing Aphrodite's bare feet, for her lovely countenance twisted with rage.

"Is that so?"

Brave I may be, but I shuddered at the black venom dripping from those three simple words.

Aphrodite turned her rancorous gaze upon me.

"If I cannot change Atalanta's heart, I shall alter her form." She gestured at me.

Woe indeed to a mortal caught between two quarreling gods.

Golden fur sprouted all over my body. I cried out to Artemis in vain. My teeth and nails lengthened and sharpened, and my limbs thickened into those of a lion. I roared in anger, my four sets of claws digging deep into the turf.

What have you done to me?

Tears formed in Artemis's eyes.

"Atalanta! My beloved Atalanta. It is not within my power to reverse Aphrodite's curse." She glared at the goddess. "But I can still grant you peace. I release you from your vow of chastity." And with a graceful sweep of her arm, Artemis laid the same affliction upon Hippomenes.

Cursed I was, yet my heart leaped, for now I might spend the rest of my days in joy, hunting with Hippomenes by my side.

# PANDORA

# CATALOGUE OF FABLES

## BY AVRA MARGARITI

Hers is not an act of folly,
But she will let her makers think so.
Will gladly paint herself the rouged, resplendent villain
If it means unsealing her catalogue of fables
For those who seek its knowledge, and those who don't.

Her thespians prance across their miniature stage,
Multitudinous scenarios unfolding all at once,
Scaled down to fit inside this box-sized diorama.
Maiden, mother, crone; pauper, paladin, prince.
Illuminated-codex unicorns, animatronic dancing bears.
Diminutive simulacra skitter like spiderlings, weaving,
Always weaving their own mythoi and theogonies.

She, appointed guardian,
Throws the lid of her marionette theater open.
Keen eyes watch the players comprehend their freedom,
Their newfound, forking paths--all chaotic possibilities.
The sea is full of monsters, and the world full of stories--
Pandora has made sure of it.

# THINKING OUTSIDE THE BOX

## BY DOMINICK CANCILLA

Nosiness had her leathery ear pressed to the thin side of the jar in which she and her sisters had been kept since the beginning of creation. It was the only way for them to know what was going on outside.

"What do you hear?" Impatience asked for the umpteenth time.

"Shush," Nosiness said. "I can't hear when you're talking."

"I can't hear when you're talking," Derision said in a mocking tone.

"Stop being an ass, Derision," Provocation said. "You think you could do better?"

"Better than you," Derision said. "I've shed scales bigger than your ears." The crowded conditions – not to mention the resulting smell – kept tension levels high, but Derision didn't need that as an excuse. Each of their sisters had an innate nature beyond influence by circumstance.

"Seriously, be quiet," Nosiness said. "I think I hear something."

"What?" Impatience asked.

"I think she's pacing," Nosiness said.

"I could have told you that," Hubris said. Her exaggerated eye roll was visible to all of them, the jar's darkness no impediment to their sight.

"I'm bored," said Childishness, stomping her foot. "Why won't she *do* something?"

"She hasn't made up her mind yet," said Hope.

"Just like a human," said Bigotry. "What do you expect?"

"It's obvious to anyone who has reflected on the situation for even a moment," said Arrogance. "Zeus, angered at Prometheus for unbalancing humanity with stolen fire, ordered Hephaestus to create the woman Pandora, to whom he gifted this jar in which we have been eternally imprisoned."

"Olympus to Arrogance," Derision said, voice mimicking a call to Earth from the gods, "we already know that."

"I didn't," said Willful Ignorance.

*"I didn't,"* taunted Derision.

"If all of this squabbling makes us miss something important, I swear I will rip your tails off," Vengefulness said.

"Count me in," added Senseless Violence.

"Ew, not near me," said Squeamishness.

"Don't you dare lay a claw on my beautiful tail," said Vanity. "I just finished polishing it."

"As if your tail was anything compared to mine," said Narcissism.

"The important point," Arrogance continued undeterred, "is that Zeus had Hephaestus gift Pandora with curiosity."

"Was Curiosity one of us?" Forgetfulness asked.

"No," said Arrogance, "humans have always had curiosity. There's nothing wrong with it."

"You're saying there's something wrong with the rest of us?" Defensiveness asked.

"It sure sounds like she is," added Provocation.

"No, it doesn't," insisted Contrariness.

"I hear that," sang Ambiguity.

Arrogance threw her hands up as if once again surprised by the inferiority surrounding her.

"What I'm saying is that curiosity is a thing humans use to make their lives better. We are things that would make their lives more interesting."

"All of you have a duty to go into the world and make the most of your existence at the first opportunity," Authoritarianism said.

"You tell 'em, Boss," said Sycophantizing.

"We will change the world!" exclaimed Ambition.

"I'll get right on that," said Shirking Responsibilities.

"Yeah, right after some other stuff on my list," said Neglect.

"I, for one, look forward to showing you all how it is done," said Hubris.

To this, Envy added in a meek voice, "I wish I could be out there like Curiosity is."

"We will be soon," Hope said.

The jar went silent. Everyone looked at Hope.

"Don't do that, Hope," said Hubris.

"That's why everyone hates you," said Hatred. "This prison wouldn't be so bad if you didn't keep making us think we might be set free."

"You're the worst," said Derision.

"What if we are stuck in here forever?" whined Worry, wringing the corner of her wing anxiously.

"We won't be," said Unearned Confidence confidently.

"Zeus promised we'd be set free someday," lied Untruth.

"I'm ready for it, whenever it happens," said Ambition. "As soon as I'm out, I'm going to convince someone they're fated to take over the world. First thing."

"Good luck there," said Greed. "I'm taking the thoughts of every living being for my own."

"I'll make businesses cheat their customers," said Deceit.

"I'll help them get away with it," said Injustice.

"Men will badger women who have no interest in them," said Obsession.

"Marriages will crumble," said Infidelity.

"Because people will be having relations with all and sundry, in every manner of way," said Prurience.

"Oh, how I wish I could be so ambitious!" said Jealousy.

"I can help with that," said Meddlesomeness.

"That's just what the others want you to do," said Conspiratorial Thinking.

"I will become the greatest of all!" said Self-Delusion.

"And society will crumble as people wear togas inappropriate to their station!" exulted Impropriety to a chorus of metaphorical crickets.

"Very impressive, Impropriety," said Flattery. "You also look particularly nice today."

"Hold tight to those dreams!" proclaimed Hope. "All will come to pass any minute now when Pandora opens the jar!"

Once again, the jar went silent. Not even the nonexistent crickets dared intervene.

"Did you have to do that?" said Derision.

"You make me sick," said Illness.

"Hush! She stopped walking," Nosiness interjected into the tension building among them. "She's approaching the jar."

"She's nowhere near it," said Untruth.

"I wish I could hear," said Envy.

There was a rustling and milling about among the sisters.

"Will you stop that?" said Annoyance.

"I need to get in position to get out first," said Ambition.

"You don't want to do that," said Deceit. "It's really not the best strategy."

"Zeus blast you all," said Blasphemy.

"Curl your tail when you call upon a god's name," reminded Superstition.

"She's right next to us," said Nosiness, snapping fingers for attention.

"This is it," said Hope.

"Didn't we ask you not to do that?" asked Forgetfulness.

"It's a false promise, like all the other times," Negativity said. "She'll just walk away again."

"She knows we're in here," said Paranoia. "She's doing it to make us insane."

"She's going to open the jar," said Hope. "Just you wait."

"I swear, if you're getting me all worked up for nothing..." Vengefulness said.

"Thus spoke the mistress of the temple," interjected Prurience, as she often did after any statement that might even fancifully be interpreted out of context in a sexual way.

"It's not for nothing," said Hope. "Remember the prophecy?"

"When the moon is full and the stars to one side twinkle, then shall the jar be opened and to all freedom given," said False Prophecy.

"The moon can't be full if we're unable to see it is," said Illogic.

"That didn't even rhyme," said Uninformed Literary Criticism.

"Does that mean everyone's given freedom or that what the jar's being given to is all freedoms?" asked Confusion.

"Does that question even help?" asked Unsupportiveness. "I'm not sure."

"Hi, Not Sure, I'm Dad Jokes," said Dad Jokes.

"Really, though, can't you feel it?" Hope said. "Just believe in your heart. If you can believe it hard enough, she'll do it. She'll take off the lid and we will finally all be free!"

"I knew it," said Guilt Complex. "If she doesn't free us, it's because I didn't believe hard enough."

"Guilt Complex is right," said Despair. "We don't have the will. We're never getting out."

"No! No no! Nonononono!" cried Hysteria.

"See what you did?" said Blame.

"Hope – one more word out of you, and I swear..." Bullying punched an open palm with a tight fist.

"I never could stand you," said Intolerance.

"Come on, sisters," Hope said. "Join hands with me, close your eyes, and fill your mind with visions of –"

"Fuck this," said Vulgarity.

"You're going down," said Extrajudicial Condemnation.

"Get her!" shouted Mob Rule.

The interior of the jar became a roiling sea of fists, tails, and claws. Senseless Violence rained blows upon Hope's head, Vengefulness sought her pound of flesh, Childishness unleashed the foulest gas she could muster, Squeamishness delivered arms-reach slaps with her eyes pressed firmly closed, Provocation goaded them all on, and Ambition scrambled to get to the top of the pile.

Most of the sisters were so busy releasing their long-pent feelings on Hope that the first to notice the air filling with light was – in an irony lost on all in the heat of the moment – Inattentiveness.

"Jar's open!" yelled Inattentiveness.

"Hey, no fair!" said Envy, who had wanted to be the one to say that.

"I'm out of here!" crowed Desertion, first into the air.

From there, it was a storm of wings and bodies, like a tornado in a cave of reptilian bats, until only Hope remained.

An immortal being, Hope was not permanently harmed by the beating, but she had been staggered. She got to her feet just in time to witness the last of her sisters disappear above her into the first circle of sunlight she had ever seen.

Hope stretched her sore wings, but even before she had given them a single flap, Pandora's despairing cry shook through the jar and the lid was slapped down, sealing Hope in once again.

Hope looked up through the darkness at the closed portal to freedom and took a deep breath. "That's okay," she said, acting as was her nature. "I'll get out next time."

# PANDORA

## BY LAUREN EASON

Mystic guardian of sin, sealed within one chest,
giver of treasures, creation of Earth.
Punishment forged into a woman's breast,
by beings of a supernatural birth.
Conceived from Prometheus' plunder,
retribution of the sacred light of fire,
and demanded genesis of the God of Thunder,
thus impending events transpired.

Seductive gifts were bequeathed to thee,
a figure immortalized by an act of such.
Endowed the eager character of curiosity,
a pithos observed by a sense of touch.
Doth the hands of yours betray,
or by your gift you have been burned?
Were you enticed and led astray,
or revenge had settled after spurned?

Unjustly victimized by an unintentional mistake,
seen as feeble minded and scorned.
Blamed for the bodies that always ache,
but never once were you forewarned.
Demons unleashed upon hallowed grounds,
but perhaps present before said time.
Tainted with evil they do drown,
human nature in filth and grime.

Box of bone and blood you did protect,
a craft which cannot diminish your worth.
Restrained the demons before you were subject,
to their wide alluring girth.
I condemn you not, fair goddess of gifts,
even though that sacred item you did grope.
The lid you did purposely lift,
for that small ounce of hope.

245

# ANTIGONE

# IZZY AND ANTI: A TRAGEDY IN TEXTS

## BY DEBORAH MARKUS

Izzy

> Sis! What's up?

did you hear the news

> Can you narrow that down a
> bit?

jesus you'd never know we
lived in the same city
THE news

> Anti, you know this time of
> year I'm buried in papers to
> grade.

right yeah sorry I should keep
better track of your precious
professorial life
god forbid real life show its
ugly face to you at this special
time of year

> Excuse me if I'm interrupting
> some important self-
> righteousness, but any time you
> want, you could tell me

whatever it is you texted me to
tell me.

just shocked that even YOU
were able to hide your sandy
head from this one

Okay, I'm going back to work
now. Love you. Text or call
when you want to talk about
something other than the fact
that you're better than I am.

the mayor is expanding the
curfew

For sure? He's just been talking
about it.

well now he's doing it

God. Okay. How long?

24/7

Yeah, I figured.
I mean, I thought it might
come down to that. With
everything that's been
happening.
But how long will that last, do
you know?

It can't be more than a day or
two, right?
He can't keep a city this size
locked up forever.

he can't keep us inside AT
ALL if we say no

But it's just going to be a day
or two, right?
And it can't apply to everyone.
Even during a pandemic.
Heck, especially during a
pandemic.
He'll let essential workers out.
Grocery clerks. Delivery
people.

don't need grocery clerks when
no one's allowed to go to the
store

Jesus.

and delivery people just make it
harder to tell the good guys
from the bad

Are you serious? Is this really
happening?

NO ONE ALLOWED ON
THE STREETS
effective beginning at nightfall
until further notice
until law and order are restored
is that so hard to understand

                                        Yes!

well it shouldn't be even for
you

                        I think I'm allowed to be
                        shocked by the idea that if I
                        step outside my home I'll be
                                        arrested!

not exactly
not quite
not you
that's why I need your help

                        What do you mean? You're
                        confusing the hell out of me!

you live in that nice white
neighborhood.
nice white lady
nothing to worry about for
YOU

Look, you don't have to
explain institutionalized racism
and systemic bias to me. And
just for the record, you're
white, too.
And I'm not going to break
curfew and get arrested just to
make some kind of point.

they're not arresting curfew
breakers
they're not arresting anyone

Again: can you PLEASE tell
me what you're talking about?
First you say we all need to stay
inside starting tonight. God,
that's less than an hour away!
And then you say, oh, no
worries, they won't arrest you!

I never said we need to stay
inside
and I certainly never said no
worries

DAMN IT ANTI TELL ME
WHAT YOU MEAN

maybe you already heard about
that cop who was killed in one
of the protests

Yes. God, that was awful.

you sound like the mayor
this guy was filmed beating the
shit out of unarmed protestors
it took four people to pull him
away from someone who'd
long since stopped showing
any signs of life
but sure yeah poor cop

I meant the whole situation
was awful! God, can I say
anything without you jumping
to the worst conclusions about
me?

the man the cop killed
you couldn't even tell who he
was anymore
his face was just obliterated
but some of us had been
filming the whole time
and some of us knew him

God, Anti, I'm so sorry.
Wait. US? Were you there?

the cop was struggling to get
away from us

254

he fell and hit his head against
the same rock he'd been using
as a weapon
of course HIS death is being
called a murder
the mayor and the chief of
police are acting like he should
get a fucking purple heart
to be fair this IS a war
and they're the ones who
started it

Yeah.
You're right. I'm sorry. I
should have been paying more
attention.
I knew things were awful but I
didn't know the details and I
guess I didn't want to.
But what do you want me to
do now?

now you're exactly the kind of
person we need

"We"? Need for what?
I'm just a philosophy teacher.
I can kick in a few bucks.
I already give to the ACLU, but
I'm happy to help your group,
too.

not the kind of help I'm talking
about
god knows we can always use
funds but tonight that isn't the
point

> Tonight? You're planning on
> civil disobedience?
> I can bail you out, but I can't
> get arrested.
> I can't afford to rock the boat
> right now.

they're not arresting people

> You said that, but you didn't
> tell me what you meant.

EVERYBODY must be off
the streets
even cops
can't risk those precious lives
and that way they know
EVERYONE they see is a
criminal

> But how can they see anyone if
> they're not patrolling? I'm
> confused.

oh they'll be patrolling
in helicopters

wait WHAT

it's already started
hasn't made the news yet but
you'll see it soon enough
they're shooting us like they're
hunting wolves

That's a pretty big accusation.
Are you sure? How do you
know?

[img:drive.google.com/antifan/
f23zi484jf7f8da2vtj98dfy98fv6
nrc]

JESUS ANTI
TELL ME when you're going
to make me look at something
like that!

you asked I answered

God.
Okay.
But Anti, I'm scared. I'm sorry.
I can't go out and face THAT
just to make a point the right
people already agree with.
I promise I'll start protesting
when it's safe, but you can't ask
me to lay down my life.

Especially when I don't see it
doing any good.

not asking you to lay down
asking you to stand up

Tell me what that means.

I'm in a group called Women
In White

Okay.

you know it?

No.

fair
we haven't done much to speak
of yet
but we know what we have to
do

Okay. What does that mean?

it means that a murdering cop
is getting a funeral with full
honors
meanwhile one of the people
he killed is still out there lying
in the street

Jesus! Seriously!

They just left the body?

they're saying they don't have
the resources
they're saying it's not safe for
them to go out
not with so many violent
people around
they say they can't do their jobs
and it's all OUR fault

fuck that!

right
that's where we come in

We?
Us?
Me?

there's a mother who's losing
her mind
that's her son lying alone out
there
now it looks like they'll leave
him until the curfew comes to
an end
at least another day maybe
more

They can't do that!

they can
they are
that's where we come in

> You keep saying that and I
> keep not knowing what you
> mean.
> What are you planning? What
> are you doing?
> Or maybe you shouldn't tell
> me?

of course I should tell you
how can you help if you don't
know what to do

> I do want to help.
> But if you're going to do
> something illegal, maybe it's
> better for everybody if I don't
> know.

after everything I just told you
everything I just showed you
they're outlawing basic morality
and you're worried about your
job

> I didn't say that!

oh no my BAD sister did
something

what if I don't get tenure

                    Just tell me what you want to
                                      do.

we're bringing Paul back to his
mother

                                      Paul?
                                      Oh.
                                  Right.
                                  How?

you have a car

                                Anti. No.

you said you wanted to help

                      Of course I want to help!

and I'm telling you how you
can

                      I can't! Not like that!

okay

                      Okay? That's it? End of
                                  argument?

no point in arguing

if you won't go you won't go

What are YOU going to do?

what I can

What does that mean?
You're not going out.
Tell me you're not going out.

I have to

Do you have a car?
Of course you don't. Cars are
for capitalist swine.
And if you had one you
wouldn't have asked for mine.
Anti? You're not going out, are
you?
If you don't have a car, you
can't help him.
You can't help his mother.

I don't have a car

Okay.

but if I can't bring him to his
mother, at least I can let her
know he isn't out there alone

Anti, you can't risk your life for
that!

can and will

That's obscene! It's insane!
Did she ask you to do that? To
risk your life for nothing?

not nothing
and common decency asked
me

Anti, please. This is crazy.
Don't do this.
You're not really doing this, are
you?
Anti?
Damn it, Anti, answer me!
You can't do this.
God, you've ALWAYS been
like this!
We started calling you Anti
when you were three, did you
know that?
Mom named you after her
sister, but Aunt Angelica was
the one who said it didn't fit.
One night at dinner she said,
"That girl's no Angie – she's an
Anti."
I think that was the time you
wouldn't eat your dinner

because I wasn't allowed to
have dessert.
I don't even remember what I
did, but you'd decided the
punishment did NOT fit the
crime.
And then when you were four,
you stopped eating meat
because it was mean to
animals.
When you were five, you made
Dad take you home from that
birthday party because pony
rides weren't fair to the pony.
When you were six, you made
Mom start riding her bike to
work.
When you were eight, you had
your hair chopped off to give
to kids with cancer.
When you were ten, you
wouldn't let anyone give you a
normal birthday present. You
made everybody donate to that
charity that digs wells for
people who didn't have good
water.
When you were too young to
drive, I'd take you to every
stupid demonstration and
meeting and righteous
fundraiser you wanted.

You never thanked me.
You just made me feel guilty.
And it never stopped.
It didn't matter if I tried to get
involved the best I could.
If I couldn't just drop
everything when anyone asked,
I wasn't truly committed to the
cause.
School? Work? What are
those?
But I still tried.
I tried to be supportive.
Remember that time I told you
how proud I was of your
activism?
You rolled your eyes and said,
"I'm not an activist, I'm an
ORGANIZER."
As if I'd just insulted you.
So I stopped trying.
Nothing I could do would ever
be enough so what was the
point?
But I never stopped wanting
you in my life.
I was just never important
enough to compete with all the
evil in the world.
Remember the night my dog
died?
I had to put him to sleep.

I knew it was the right thing to
do but I felt so awful.
I wanted you with me. I
thought you'd understand.
You're a vegan, for God's sake.
But where were you? When I
needed you, did you come to
me?
For that one horrible night
when I felt more alone than I'd
ever been, when the world felt
more empty than I'd ever
known it could be, did you
come to me?
Just for an hour, even?
Of course not!
God forbid that march have
one less pair of shoes in it!
God.
Remember when Sister Emily
asked you what you wanted to
be when you grew up?
You said, "A martyr."
She thought it was great.
You were eight.

sorry
had to turn my phone off for a
bit

Jesus! Anti, where are you?

where I need to be
it's not just me out here

> There are other people with
> you, you mean?
> Or do you mean
> Paul

my group

> Anti, I'm scared to death.

I know

> I'm so sorry.
> I should have come with you. I
> shouldn't have let you do this
> alone.
> You asked for help and I said
> no and I'm sorry.
> Tell me where you are. I'll
> come to you.

no

> I know you're angry at me and
> you're right. I should have
> come before. I should have
> stood up sooner.
> Please let me come to you now.
> Please let me be there with you.
> I feel so alone.

you can't come here

No, of course not! I didn't pass
the purity test the first time
around! No rescheduling
THAT exam! This failure goes
on your permanent record!

no I mean you can't
get here
not safe

Oh, God. I'm an idiot. I'm
sorry. Are you okay?
And if it's not safe, I HAVE to
come to you! I can't leave you
alone with that!
I'll bring my car and get you
out of there.
Okay?

you'd never make it through

Through?
You did!
Didn't you?

on foot
and it's different now

Anti, please tell me what's
going on.

not sure what all this is
helicopters

God.

someone on the ground too
someone or something or both

What? What does that mean?

not the cops or at least not just
the cops
feels more like army
sounds like

Oh God. The military? Are you
sure?
Do you think they've called out
the National Guard?

maybe
I'm not the only one on the
streets tonight
and they warned us they're
playing for keeps

Don't they have to announce it
when they're calling out the
Guard? I thought we'd be told!

stay there

                                        I'm just getting my keys

no
stay home
stay safe

                                        Not without you!

I can take this if I know you're
okay

                                        Don't talk like that!

too late to help
don't come
don't try

                                        Then you come to me!
                                        I'll do anything you ever ask
                                                    me to!
                                        All my money all my time
                                        everything you want
                                        Just please get away from there
                                        Paul is already dead
                                        His mother is already
                                                    mourning
                                        You can't save her from that
                                        death-in-life

You can only give her one
more person to grieve

I know

Then save yourself! For her.
For me.
Come back to the one who can
never stop loving you even
when she's mad enough to
want to try.

I can't

You CAN! To hell with your
precious principles!

no sister I mean I really can't
we're cut off
Ana and Hero managed to slip
away
but Yna and I are here to stay

No!
Surrender! Say whatever they
want!
Put your hands up!

won't work

You're white! It might!

too late for that

Then I'll come to you!

you'd only die too

You're sentencing me to life
instead?
I have to live every day with
you dead?

say that I wasn't afraid

Is that true?

it's the story I'd tell if I could

Leaving me to tell it?

thank you

One more chore you were too
good to do!
When there's trash to take out,
always me, never you!

I'm sorry

THEN STAY

I think I would now
if I could

Just now? And you "think"?

Izzy

Who will I fight with when
you're gone?

I can hear

What? Who? What do you
hear?

it's here

What is?
Stop talking in riddles!
Anti?
Who's here? What's here?
What did you mean?
Anti, listen to me. I'm your one
phone call.
Not your group. Not Paul's
mother. ME.
Anti? This is important.
When they ask if you
understand your rights, say
NO.
Demand your phone call.
I'll handle it all.
Lawyers, your bail, the whole
thing.

It's a first offense. They'll give
you a chance.
Just call me. I just need your
voice.
I need to know where you are.
Tell me where.
And then I can take it from
there.

# ISMENE (AT THE TOMB OF ANTIGONE)

# BY NUPUR SHAH

I am the other one
known by none since all of them here
from Chorus-elders to stone-shifters
gathered from every corner of this cursed city-cum-cemetery
know my sister as the valiant & the vigorous one

I call that being a wanna-be
coveting things one is not supposed to have
you may call me anti-feminist
(if i really cared I wouldn't be alive now)
but Antigone was a toxic masculinist
disguised as the born-leader
at the helm of generations of victims
who she knew would throng behind her
(it has begun already/the lament of her going)
in an effort at consciousness-raising
2500 years before any such bosh existed
(yeah I know my sister was a genius)

 but who was I
(who am I now/ if i am indifferent to the rising sorrow)
but surely I was more than I could admit
(apart from the reservations & prejudices she bore into me)
I had more in me than I could dare to show anybody
(you see she'd entranced me too so that I would hurry off the stage
for her to plunge into her brave-girl-young-rebel drivel)

what if i told you I was the one
with zero self-esteem
 (i guess this is hardly news)
I was the one/ let me repeat
against whose lack of identity
Antigone- queen of valor & vigor
played her gamble at immortality

inheriting the said virtues of valor & vigor
from our good-for-nothing father's legacy
(whose cunning needs no mentioning)
while I made our grand/mother into a mirror (of love & love alone)
for everyone needs an inheritor
(as well as an inherited)

like a leech sucks its feed
from the body in which it lives
(yes there was a time when I thought
no (other)body in the world mattered but
my sister and me with each other)

similarly Antigone the first woman
who became a name was but
the Other to my love-effaced self
on whose strong shoulders she climbed
into Hades where she always wanted to be
were it not for me who was keeping her back
so that I could know some love
before I had to let it go
and fall into this listless melancholy
standing guard over her empty grave
my Antigone!

# OTHER
# HEROINES

# URSA MAJOR

## BY MARI NESS

You'll give him this —
he taught you to transform.
Taught you how to shift to fur and claw,
to become the thing
you once hunted.

You'll give him this —
he came to you not as man or god,
but as a woman.

You'll give him this —
you did feel desire.
Once.
You trembled when he transformed.

You'll give him this —
his daughter named you exile.
Not him.
He had long since left the woods.

You'll give him this —
he stopped you from killing
his son. Yours.
And you gave him yourself —
for a time. Only
for a time.

You breathe in starlight
as you dance, claws
sharpened on the moon.
You won't give him this.

# WHAT SHALL NEVER BE

## BY ALYSSA JUDSON

On days when the sun was safely tucked away, hidden by great storm clouds, Apollo would dip below the canopy of sky, and spend time wandering the forest. Dryads often saw him, murmuring to one another of his handsome visage, except one.

Daphne watched as the familiar figure topped the crest of the hill, picking his way through the field of sheep toward her. She was expecting him, of course - she always did - and waved a greeting as she unfolded the lithe length of her green-tinged body.

"You're later than I expected," she informed him, hands on her hips but laughter in her voice.

Apollo nodded. "Persephone is on her way back downstairs, so my days are running shorter."

She cocked her head, smirking. "You gods always think the world revolves around you."

And it did, of course.

"Do you have news?" the sun god inquired as they turned toward the forest and the riverbank her father called home.

"I do." Her autumn hair fell across her eyes, but she could hardly hide her excitement. "I spoke to Laurel."

"And?" Apollo urged, watching her closely, yet unable to hide a smile for her.

"She feels the same way. She loves me, Apollo!" Daphne twirled, tossing up a cascade of newly fallen leaves, leaves that caught her and let her fall to the ground softly. "But my father."

He was alarmed by the firmness of her tone - a completely different texture and comfort from a mere sliver of a moment before. "What does he have to say about it?" It took effort to not show the physical intimidation he could so easily threaten against the river god.

Daphne sighed. "He wants grandchildren. I cannot give those to him, not with how I feel about Laurel - and most certainly not with how I feel about men!" The dryad's laughter was telling, and it helped Apollo relax.

"Have you spoken to him?"

"No." Her voice was small this time, and she combed her hair over one shoulder, looking so lost and forlorn. "Eros failed to help me."

"He certainly did. But his aim is shoddy - I am the real god of archery. His bow is a trifle, a mere plaything."

Pulling a face, Daphne punched Apollo's arm lightly. "Thank you for being such a good friend, Apo."

The love god's arrow was quick - it was nothing more than a flicker of prismatic gold, but it was enough to make Apollo double over, breathless with the complexity of emotions that accompanied the blow. Daphne cried out at the sight, knowing they had made a mistake that could not be undone.

"My aim is perhaps imperfect when compared to yours, dear Apollo, but at least mine sticks." Eros slipped from the air—one moment he was not, then he simply was—but his ice blue eyes had now fixed themselves upon Daphne.

Her hand on Apollo's arm, Daphne froze, uncertain. Eros seemed so calm, nonthreatening, even as he took care in selecting an arrow from his quiver. Each one he took out, inspected, and replaced, until he took one that was darker than the rest. He weighed it in his hand.

"He is going to do everything he can to win you for himself. And this," he said, holding up the arrow, "will ensure that he never succeeds."

Daphne could not seem to form an argument, to find the words she knew might make her case. She knew the fate of mortals - even of the dryad variety - who managed to get trapped in the middle of a fight with two gods.

"Run," Apollo managed, even as his hand reached out for her. There was a lustful, possessive desire in his eyes now, a look she had seen in so many lech's eyes, but never his. And it was that look alone that made her listen.

Daphne knew these woods; she knew the way the land curled into the embankment, the way the roots twisted between the stones, the way the river nestled into the valley. But panic made her blind, and she stumbled before crying out for her tree sisters, using the safety of their branches...even if Apollo and Eros both could bypass land better than she.

She could hear the waterfall; the river was near, and she could drop into the safety of her father's stream. But the relief came too soon, an error sharp as a nettle when she felt her ankle catch a tree branch and she tumbled to the ground.

Daphne scrabbled at the dirt for purchase, away from the sudden sting of pain in her leg. It was a gash, she saw with alarm; the arrow had caught her. While it had not struck her heart, she knew it would be enough – enough for her to lose everything. For what could she hold dear when she could not love? Love was an impossibility through the poison of Eros' leaden arrow.

"Please, my father," she cried out as she grappled with the mud in the shallows of the river, "twist my legs to root, my arms to branches...make me a tree I cherish before I lose sight of love." Daphne sobbed this prayer again and again, as if the gash were a death knell.

But for Daphne, whose heart spoke a language of care, of tender ardency...it was. And without the love she held for Laurel, it was a reality she wished to take no part in.

"Please, father, let me end this life with a full heart."

Peneus rose from the depths, his cobalt hair tumbling over his shoulders in waves, even as Apollo arrived at the bank, reaching for Daphne. "Did you do this to her?" he roared, anger making the waters boil.

"No, I only want her to be happy. I can make her ha-" Apollo cut himself off as Peneus released another roar of anger. "She loves another - Laurel. Daphne loves Laurel."

Peneus stopped then, and it seemed the anger emanating from the intimidating river god seemed to pause as well, as understanding dawned. "My precious girl," he murmured as he took her in his arms.

All was quiet. The discordant god of love had not pursued them further, and Apollo watched in horror, as his friend and love chose to be without him...all so she would not lose her ability to love. It was a balance, a horrific balance that he could understand, and he trembled at the battle within his heart.

Daphne's father took a handful of water, and gently dripped it across her legs. It washed away her skin to create bark, her toes burying themselves in the mud as they grew to become roots. He continued the process, washing away the green for the brown. He cupped her face gently, and they both cried as he did so.

Apollo knelt at the edge of the river, lingering long after Peneus had finished his work. Eros' arrow had done its job well - Apollo certainly loved Daphne - but it had not required much work. He had loved her as a friend long before, and it was that part of him that managed to move, to depart. When he returned, the sky was gray, pulling the color from the land, but for a bright spot in the redheaded woman that accompanied him - Laurel.

Apollo told Daphne's story at the riverside, and when he relayed where she had been struck by Eros' leaden arrow, Laurel touched the tree near the base, where a lighter gash of bark was, tears silent as they slipped down her cheeks.

Once he had relayed Daphne's story, he reached up, taking branches heavy with leaves and twisting them together to create a crown. "My gift to you. Laurels will be my sacred symbol, and I will ensure this laurel tree will not wilt; Daphne's leaves will remain lush and green, a sign of her undying love, and her refusal to live in a world with its absence."

Peneus bowed his head, grasping Laurel's hand as they listened to Apollo's mourning sighs.

When they at last looked up, the sun god was gone and the rain began to fall.

# SWAN DIVE

## BY SHERRI COOK WOOSLEY

Leda floated on her back in the water, her swollen belly a giant pearl, and stroked the skin stretched tight over the treasures inside.

"I'll protect you," she promised, but water covered her ears and distorted the sound. She pressed with her fingertips to decipher head or foot or butt. Harder when two babies fought for space. One was vigorous, all flailing elbows, while the other pressed back in response, Leda imagined, hands against the belly from the inside. Being in the water like this made Leda feel beautiful. Her dark hair spread through the water and her brown arms and legs were strong, though her middle was round. Someone else had found her beautiful, and that errant thought made her cheeks flush as she sat up in the water. These were King Tyndareus's children. That was true enough for the oracle of Delphi to attest, but she kept her gaze from flicking to the chest at the base of her bed.

"Your majesty, it's time to come out before you catch cold." Maybe the words could be considered caring, but the tone was nothing but patronizing.

The older woman was called Nurse – her position for the king decades ago. She wore two shawls at once, had a puckered expression like she drank lemon juice, and insisted that pregnancy must make Leda cold. And carrying the king's twins meant that Leda shouldn't pick up a sword any longer, even to practice. Or eat anything too spicy because it might hurt the babies.

Leda clenched her fists. It was bad enough that as a princess her father had considered her a pawn to be used in marriage for domestic relations, an object to assure borders would remain intact. Then she was a symbol for the people: look at our glorious queen who participated in the Spartan trials, tamed by King Tyndareus. Now she was a vessel for the birth of an heir and a spare, still being discussed by others. This was her body and her children. Like her mother, she would protect them, educate them, and put a sword in their hands no matter their gender.

Nurse patted Leda dry with a towel and helped her into a loose gown. They left the personal bathing room and walked across the tiled floor to the queen's bedroom. A bed took up the majority of the room, but a looking glass and chair sat near the door to the palace interior, opposite from the walled-in courtyard and garden. The design was similar to the palace where Leda had grown up.

Nurse parted Leda's hair then braided each side, pulling it tight at each twist. Leda stroked her belly and did not look at the chest or at the entrance to the courtyard. The moon had risen and the perfume of night flowers – gardenia and evening primrose --- flowed into the room on a breeze.

She would not think of it as a message. Irritation built at the thoughts she could not think, the looks she could not spare, the memories that she must not, under any circumstances, remember.

"Hold still," Nurse said. "I'm almost finished making you look like a queen."

Leda met Nurse's eyes in the looking glass. "I am a queen."

"Of course," Nurse dropped her eyes and bowed her head in deference, "I didn't mean –"

"Get out."

Nurse reported everything Leda did to Tyndareus, but Leda had no care tonight.

"Send in the musicians to play me to sleep."

Nurse scurried away, no doubt to tattle to anyone willing to listen about the young queen's moodiness.

Leda made sure the heavy castle door was shut then hurried to the chest, dropping to her knees and raising the lid.

"Hello, darlings." There, nestled among soft blankets, sat two eggs with a swan feather between them. Each was the shade of fresh cream and the size of her palm, although one was larger and the other's oval shape more pronounced. Leda stroked them the way she'd stroked her belly. This was her other set of twins.

Alone, she closed her eyes to revisit a moment in the courtyard; the phantom brush of swan feathers across the back of her neck. A bird's trumpeting had snapped her attention from smelling the potted lemon trees to the blue sky. The swan pulled in his wings and plummeted toward the walled-in courtyard. Seconds from crashing, the white bird swept his wings open to slow his descent and landed in Leda's arms, wings hugging her body. There was a moment when she held a bird, proudly arched neck, black mask, webbed feet.

And then his body was shifting, changing, the legs reaching to the ground, the human face emerging from the feathers, arms that wore feathers like a cape still encircling her. Leda was tall, but he stood taller. She was beautiful, but he was impossible. She was made of earth and water, but he was stars and lightning.

Zeus.

"May I?" he asked, dark eyes searching hers.

She understood he was asking permission. That he would leave if she shook her head. He admired her body – yes, that was clear – but he gave her a choice of whether to accept his attentions. Unlike her father who bartered her for borders or her husband who would visit her bedroom again tonight because it was his duty to father heirs.

"Yes," she whispered. Maybe it would have been impossible to say no to a god, but she didn't want to try.

With a squeak, the interior door swung open. Leda covered the eggs and slammed the lid closed, whirling to scold the musicians for daring to enter without waiting for permission. Instead, an enormous serpent's head pushed through the opening and tasted the air with its tongue.

Eyes wide, Leda kept one hand under her belly and backed around the bed, placing the furniture between herself and the monster. Her sword hung on the wall, a decoration now. The door to the courtyard was on the wall in the other direction. The serpent glided all the way into the bedroom.

Its body was thick as a tree – Leda might be able to touch her fingers together if she hugged it - and as long as the tallest soldier in Sparta's army. A distinctive mix of grey, brown, and black scales covered the body, topped by a triangular head with eyes like onyx. A Milos viper. Venom glistened on its fangs as it reared back its head, searching for her.

"Guards," she screamed.

Heart beating against her ribcage, Leda measured the distance to the courtyard. She'd be trapped within the outside walls, but she could push the bench against the opening to give enough time for the guards to appear. They should be here, rushing in wearing their protective leather armor and carrying their Spartan swords and pikes.

The serpent looked at her then turned its head away. Its gaze fastened on the chest at the foot of the bed. Intent, it slithered forward, body creating s-shapes as it moved.

"No." The monster wasn't here for her; it was for the babies. This was a fiend sent by a god. Or goddess. And that meant no guards were coming. No help from anyone. Leda turned away from the safety of the courtyard entrance and ran toward the sword on the wall, jerking it from its hooks.

The weight of the sword was familiar, but her body was different, unbalanced. Her calluses had sloughed off in the long baths she'd taken to get relief from an aching lower back and the joint pain from carrying twins. No matter. Her muscles had memory, knew the drills she'd performed over and over.

Leda rushed around the corner of the bed to confront the serpent, but it had reached the chest. It swung its head like a battering ram against the wood. Adjusting her stance to accommodate for her belly, Leda swung the sword down at an angle so it sliced across the tail.

The serpent whipped around as green ichor flowed from the gash.

"Now I have your attention," Leda said. Her heart beat fast, but not with fear. Excitement. The rightness of protecting her babies.

The serpent rose up, its triangular head over Leda's, swaying. Its mouth opened and she could smell the poison – an evil sweetness –coating the fangs. The poison it wanted to inject into the eggs. Leda sank back into her heels and gripped her sword with both hands.

The serpent lunged and Leda thrust up with the sword, the blade biting through the vulnerable skin, piercing the roof of the mouth and burying into the reptile's brain. Leda twisted the sword then moved to the side as the heavy body fell to the floor.

Metal clinked as the scales flipped over until nothing remained but a golden bracelet in the shape of a snake.

Leda touched the trunk where the serpent had battered its head against the wood. It hadn't been able to get inside because it had no hands, but how had it opened the door?

Whirling to her feet, Leda watched as hands appeared from the air and brought down the edges of a cloak. Everything covered by the cloak remained invisible. Still, the face was enough to identify the intruder. Black hair hung in curls with purple highlights and a pale face with rose red lips created a regal expression. Hera, Queen of the Olympians.

"All these toys and I still have to do it myself."

Leda swallowed. "Toys?"

"The bracelet from Hephaestus and this cloak borrowed from Hermes."

Her sword was no match against Hera. Leda let it fall from her hand and dropped into a curtsy.

"Ha," Hera's laugh was bitter. "You dare pretend to show me respect now."

Leda kept her gaze on the tiled floor. Everyone knew Hera was the goddess of marriage, yet her husband made a fool of her over and over with anyone, mortal or immortal, who caught his eye. Hera's wrath when Zeus fathered Hercules by the mortal Alcmene was legendary. She'd sent snakes to kill Hercules as a baby, too. That hadn't worked either. Maybe her children had a chance.

"Did you know?" Hera walked over to the snake bracelet and picked it up.

Leda came out of the curtsy and walked over to the table where a flagon of wine and two goblets rested. They were always set up in case Tyndareus wanted refreshment.

"Would you care for a drink?" Leda offered. She poured, glad when her hand only shook a little, then poured one for herself.

Leda waited until Hera sank into a chair before sitting down as well, grateful for the manners her mother had made her learn. A queen must know how to fight with words, too, she'd said.

"Did you?" Hera repeated. Her dark eyebrows arched over blue eyes that held mysteries of Olympus. This was no mortal woman. It wasn't the elegance of her bearing or the uncanny grace of every movement; instead, it was the aura of power. This goddess, daughter of Titans, was here for revenge.

"Not at first." Leda rubbed her neck where swan feathers had caressed. "But, yes, I knew before he kissed me."

Hera's hand closed around the goblet and she brought it up, her throat moving as she swallowed the entire thing and slammed it on the table. "But you let him anyway."

Leda poured another glass for her.

"And now you wait for his children to hatch. You know they will be divine. Is that what you wanted? Is that why you enticed him?"

Leda heard the rage underlying the accusation. This was like a swordfight. She had to make a perfect move against a stronger opponent. For now, she twisted the stem of the goblet between her thumb and index finger.

"I should make you writhe with pain for your adultery. I am the goddess of marriage and you made a mockery of marriages in general and mine specifically."

Hera's face was ethereal; it couldn't be unlovely. But... Leda recognized a sadness in the expression, almost invisible lines of pain etched across her forehead.

"I'm sorry. I didn't think of you," Leda said, meaning it. In trying to rebel against her own restraints, she'd hurt a woman, a wife. She opened herself to attack by being vulnerable then adopted a defensive stance. "But please don't punish my babies. You are also the goddess of childbirth."

"Aren't you clever to use my own loyalties against me." Hera took another sip.

Leda cleared her throat. "I'm a mortal. I'm no comparison to you."

"That's true." Hera's gaze rested on the chest with the eggs.

Leda searched for an argument, something to convince the goddess not to exact revenge.

"My husband can be very persuasive when he wants someone."

Unsure of whether this was a trap to make Leda claim to be a victim, she said, "I can only speak for myself. Please forgive me." Leda bowed her head.

Hera snorted.

The sound from the regal woman was so unlikely Leda had to look up.

"You are only a mortal and this is your first offense." Hera gave her a rueful half-smile. "I suppose I could have taken this problem to my husband instead of hunting you down."

"Men are celebrated for breaking the rules, but women are hated," Leda said, trying to build a relationship with the goddess.

Hera twisted the stem of the goblet. "Are you hated?"

"I would be, if Tyndareus told the people I was unfaithful."

"Ah." Hera took a sip. "And how are you going to explain four children?"

"I keep thinking about it." Leda shook her head. "Nurse will be in the birthing chamber. She'll tell Tyndareus everything."

"Advice from one queen to another." Hera pointed a finger at Leda. "You must surround yourself with women you can trust. A circle of friends is more valuable than ambrosia."

The interior door flew open. Tyndareus appeared in the doorway, guards behind and, yes, there was Nurse peeking through too.

"I was in the council chamber and we heard you call for help." Tyndareus had the golden skin and average build of men in Sparta. He was an academic with his facial hair groomed into a point and soft hands. He examined the room.

Leda saw the soft glimmer that meant Hera had pulled up the edges of Hermes's invisibility cloak. The serpent was gone, back in the bracelet around Hera's arm. There was nothing to see in the bed chamber.

"Merely a nightmare, my lord," Leda said. "I thought intruders had attacked."

"We need to change her diet," Nurse said, clucking her tongue.

The king nodded. "Do that immediately, Nurse."

"I don't think—" Leda said.

"Maybe a guard outside her door?" Nurse asked.

"Not necessary." Leda noticed her sword still on the floor. "I'm fine."

"Excellent plan. I'll assign a guard." The king clapped Nurse's shoulder as if she were a soldier. "I don't know what I'd do without you."

The door was pulled shut and Leda was locked inside with a dangerous goddess. It was almost enough to make her laugh.

Hera pulled the cloak's hood down. "You have no power here."

"Tyndareus doesn't care about me at all. Only for the two babies he fathered."

"Your marriage is unhappy, Leda. He is not a strong enough partner for you." Hera tapped a finger against the wine goblet. "I may have acted impetuously when I sent the serpent to attack the children you conceived with Zeus."

That was the closest the goddess would approach an apology to a mortal. Leda shrugged as if the concession wasn't shocking.

"I took care of it."

"That was very impressive to watch, actually." Hera smiled, her entire face lighting up.

"Thank you." Leda had to blink the radiance away or she would sit there admiring the goddess for an eternity.

"It explains why your children are special," Hera said. "All four of them."

"They are everything to me." Leda met Hera's eyes and did not soften her tone. "I will protect them with my life."

Hera waved a hand, the garnet ring sparkling. "They are everything to you because you are their mother. Am I not the goddess of birth? Do I not understand the sacred bond between a mother and her baby?"

Leda put the goblet to her mouth to keep from pointing out that Hera had tried to murder her children earlier this evening.

"No, I mean your children are special to everyone. But you. The oracle did not say what happens to you."

Leda controlled her expression. Hera knew more than she'd let on. If the children were special, then Hera couldn't kill them. It would defy the fates and those three crones wouldn't allow that. And tonight was a liminal space if her own fate couldn't be read.

"Have you chosen names?"

Leda rubbed her belly. "I believe I'm carrying a boy and a girl. Tyndareus and I chose the names: Castor and Clytemnestra."

Hera nodded as if she recognized the names.

"And the other twins?"

"I haven't chosen yet. Would you honor us by naming them?"

Hera tapped her garnet ring, but her gaze was unfocused. The air grew close, heavy with possibility. It was time for Leda's final move.

"You are the goddess of marriage and childbirth." Leda swallowed. "I petition for your help and I make an offering in exchange."

Hera's attention returned to the sleeping chamber. She raised an eyebrow.

"Intriguing. Most people go through my priestesses or at least travel to my temple. Where is the altar, Leda?"

"Fortune brought you to me instead." It was a daring comment and Leda wondered if she'd been too familiar with the queen, but Hera laughed.

"Fine, my fellow queen. Ask me your petition and if it is within my power, I will grant it on this strange night."

Thoughts swirled, but Leda mastered them, pushed them into an order that would make sense.

"I need help in the birthing room so that all four of my children may be accepted as Tyndareus's children until they are grown and their divine origins revealed. This will help me as their mother and it will help the world, because you said they each have a role to play. In exchange, I sacrifice myself to you. When my children are grown, I will serve in your circle of women on Olympus and protect you with my sword and with my words, with my heart and with my mind."

If Hera would accept this then Leda could accept a loveless marriage and Nurse's hovering and all the other entrapments of being a woman who represented power but had very little.

Hera stood up and looked into the walled-in courtyard.

"Why should I trust you? Perhaps you want to sleep with my husband again. Maybe you yearn for eternal life."

"You have seen the truth of my marriage as I have seen yours. I will not cross another woman ever again." Leda pressed her palms together and bowed her head. "I ask my petition from one queen to another."

Hera paced the room until she stopped in front of the chest and opened it. She caressed one egg and then the other with her index finger.

Leda held her breath and clenched her fists against her instinct to stand in front of the chest.

"This one shall be called Pollux and the girl shall be called Helen – they'll call her 'of Troy'." The goddess nodded and pivoted to face Leda. "I accept your offer. No one can know of our agreement or it will be of little use. You will be my spy on earth and then on Olympus. Your loyalty will be to me and I will watch over you and your children."

Hera held up the swan feather that nestled with the eggs and pulled along the quill, so the white turned to turquoise and an eye pattern formed at the tip. Hera placed the peacock feather in the trunk before bringing the cloak up and gliding out into the night.

Leda sank down with her back against the bed, one hand under her belly and one hand on her eggs. Yes, she'd have an unending life of being a servant on Olympus, but if she could negotiate with the queen of the gods, then the guard outside her door and overbearing Nurse had no chance of controlling her. A flutter of motion from her belly as one baby kicked against her palm at the same time an egg rocked.

"Hush, children. Mother will take care of you."

# UNWANTED

## BY REGI CALDART

Storm clouds loomed in the distance. Their dark, dreary grey perfectly paired with the personality of the city. From her countryside house's bay window, Maia watched the clouds creep over the equally grey skyscrapers, turning the scenery into a haze of grey.

Though the countryside was dreary, Maia's small home was warm and welcoming. She never had been a fan of urban life but had stayed to help her parents raise her many sisters. When the Olympians moved into the city, her dislike of city living became outright intolerance. Everything within the city limits came under the Olympians' jurisdiction. Everything they saw, touched, smelled, even heard about through the grapevine, they believed they owned, they had a right to.

It was rather akin to spoiled children, Maia thought.

The wind picked up, throwing small branches and leaves against the doors and windows with the strength of a toddler throwing a tantrum. Thunder rumbled in the distance, but Maia muffled it by closing the thick fabric of her drapes. It seemed to her almost as though the thunder protested being sealed out, as a second thunderclap quickly followed the first, closer this time and guttural like an animal's growl.

Paying it no heed, Maia settled onto her oversized sofa and flipped on the reading lamp. When she moved out, her parents and sisters had all expressed concern about her being lonely. Maia preferred her own company, truth be told, and, on the rare occasion she wanted to socialize, her family was only a phone call and relatively short drive away. Her plants and books provided more than enough company on a day-to-day basis.

She tossed a blanket over her legs and cracked open her book. The thunder grew closer and the sky darkened, but she didn't notice as she got lost in the pages.

*** 

At the beginning of the final chapter, the lights flickered and went out. Maia snapped her head up in surprise, utterly blind in the sudden darkness. Tossing her blanket and book aside, she grumbled to herself and inched carefully to the far end table where she kept her lantern and emergency flashlight. The electricity at her house was finicky at best. Knowing her luck, it would take a least a day for the power to be restored. She really should invest in a generator one of these days.

The lightning flashed, quickly followed by a crash of thunder. The storm was directly over her, the rain lashing at her windows and doors in a valiant attempt to gain entry. Through the cacophony, a distinctly human noise reached Maia's ears, stopping her in her tracks.

Knocking.

As best she could tell, it was coming from the front door. She paused mid-stride, stifling the instinct to see who was there. A small voice inside her urged her forward, to open the door. Perhaps someone needed assistance or shelter. The louder voice, however, was questioning how someone could have found her house. Maia had purposefully chosen this cabin as it wasn't visible from the main road. Even the driveway to her front door looked more like an overgrown foot trail and was easily overlooked by the casual passersby. The voice grew loud, screaming, echoing in her skull.

Whoever was out there wanted to find her.

The knock was nearly deafening, the hinges rattling slightly from the force. She backed slowly into the kitchen, crouching low in the darkness. There had to be something there she could use.

The lightning flashed again, silhouetting the head of the figure in the small window of the door. Thunder shook the walls, and they continued to shake as the figure kicked down the door, its old, weak hinges easily giving way under the force of the blow. The ancient wooden door fell inside with a thud, permitting the wind and rain the entry it had been begging for, rattling the frames on her walls and drenching the area rugs.

Maia reached blindly along her counter, feeling for anything heavy or sharp she could wield. Lightning flooded through the open door, illuminating the small space. The shadowy figure turned toward her, and she knew the light had reached her hiding spot.

Without thinking, she lunged to the knife block, fingers curling around the closest handle. Pulling out a square butcher's knife, she spun to face the intruder.

She had been too slow.

A large hand grabbed her wrist and forced it down onto the counter, the knife dropping as a cry ripped from her throat. Another hand took hold of her other wrist, rendering her hands and arms useless. Maia struggled, despite the grip tightening enough to leave a bruise, kicking out with all the force she could muster. She connected with what felt like a shin, but the form only grunted and lifted her from the wrists. Her feet dangled off the linoleum floor briefly before the man slammed her against the refrigerator, knocking the air from her lungs. He brought her to his eye-line, and she could smell his rank breath, bizarrely free of alcohol, as though that would have somehow made this more tolerable.

Large fingers curled around both her small wrists and Maia cursed her petite frame. The man was near twice her height and significantly stronger. She didn't stand a chance, but that didn't stop her from kicking and flailing to try and escape. Maia would make it hell for him to take her down.

An errant kick connected with his stomach, making the intruder lurch forward slightly to recover from the blow. He never loosened his grip on her wrists, but Maia saw the lightning bolt necklace slide out from under his shirt as he righted himself.

Olympians always did take whatever they wanted, your well-being be damned.

*** 

The necklace was the last thing she could remember. There was a large blank, a vast sea of nothingness, from then until the moment she awoke in the hospital. Her mother, Pleione, was the first face she saw, a relieved smile breaking through the cloud of worry, the fluorescent lighting making her red hair shimmer like a halo.

Pleione flung her arms around her daughter, a sob cracking her voice. Maia awkwardly patted her mother on the back, feeling the damp spread as her mother's tears soaked into the itchy hospital sheets. The sobs from Pleione only served to starken the contrasting numbness Maia felt spreading through her body.

The days passed in a blur. Doctors constantly reviewed test results with her and her mother, the numbers a hum of nonsense. Nurses and their pitying gazes dipped in and out of the room, taking blood samples and ensuring she wasn't a danger to herself. Police detectives from the city bureau pestered her with questions, ones she wouldn't answer. If she valued her safety, and that of her family's, she could never answer them.

The Olympians had ears everywhere in the city. A well-timed donation to the fallen officer's fund, a bribe to the right people, and it would be as though Maia had said nothing at all. As though she didn't even exist. Worst case, she would be made to disappear. With the leader of all the spoiled Olympians who made the city their playground as her assailant, truly nothing was outside the realm of possibility.

And so, she said nothing.

Eventually, the detectives stopped coming. Maia left the hospital, the physical wounds mostly healed despite the mental ones left intact and stinging. She temporarily stayed with her parents until their prying words became too much. They were just as eager to know the identity of her attacker as the detectives, to enact some sort of revenge on her behalf. Adamant that she was going to be fine, and carefully shuffling around the persistent questions, her family relented after several weeks and drove her back to her house in the countryside.

While she had been in the hospital, her sisters had done their best to clean up the mess from that night. As the front door swung open, Maia was greeted with the painfully familiar sight of her cozy living room, every piece of furniture put back precisely the way it had been before the storm. Walking through the small space, the only signs her assault had occurred were scrape marks on the floor and a knife missing from the block. The air was different, though. Heavier. Stepping over the threshold felt like she was stepping into her own body, a mirroring of tiny visible scars but fathomless mental ones.

The air was so oppressive, Maia felt as though she were going to throw up. Her travel bag slid from her grip with a soft thud.

No, she definitely needed to throw up.

She sprinted to the kitchen, barely making it to the stainless-steel sink. The running tap water quickly washed everything down the drain before the smell could make her heave again. Arms shaking, Maia pressed herself back to standing, her head hanging heavily as tears finally fell.

The test was in her bag, freshly purchased from the closest drug store. She already had a feeling what it would say, but the confirmation would be the cherry on top.

Legs trembling and vision blurry, Maia forced herself back to the living room. Keeping her eyes low, she grabbed her discarded bag and firmly locked the door. Her father had repaired and strengthened all the locks in the house, but she hadn't had the heart to tell him she didn't think she could continue living there. Tears streaming silently down her cheeks, she dragged the bag with her to the back bedroom and bath.

Those five minutes were the longest Maia had ever felt. Every second lasted a year, each minute a lifetime. The digital countdown on the stick ticked slowly down, dragging her stomach with it. When the positive result floated on the screen, she folded over, forehead on her knees as an anguished cry ripped through her throat.

How long she stayed like that, she didn't know. By the time she righted herself, Maia had screamed herself hoarse. She had asked for none of this and yet had been given it in spades. What was she going to do? For what may be the first time in her life, Maia was drawing a blank in what her next plan of action should be. On trembling legs, she attempted to exit the bathroom, crashing into the sink and doorframe before successfully making her way to the bed.

He hadn't gone this far into her house, she realized with a painful shudder. With a silent sob, she fell onto the bed, curling her knees close to her chest. This wasn't at all what she had envisioned for herself, and she was at a horrendous crossroads. Each choice somehow seemed worse than the last. The options galloped laps around her mind, forcing her to ruminate on them until she passed out from exhaustion.

***

Maia couldn't keep this a secret from her family. Despite her fierce independence, progressing through an unwanted pregnancy alone was far too much to bear. And so, she found herself surrounded by her sisters in the small garden one bright afternoon, a gathering to help her decide what course to take. Though she had never told her sisters who the assailant was, they were clever and gathered it had to be one of the Olympians. If it had been anyone else, Maia would have been more willing to identify them outright.

The first point of discussion was whether to keep the child or not. Merope, only barely in her teens, did not seem to comprehend why it was so difficult to terminate a pregnancy. In truth, it was not a terribly difficult procedure, and there were clinics nearby that would perform it. No, the issue was that the clinics were all within the city limits. Even if she were to go to another city far away, the Olympian network was vast and had ears and eyes everywhere. They had very little patience for problematic mistresses and their illegitimate offspring.

Alcyone suggested trying a more homegrown method. The seven sisters took a long hike in the woods, a perfectly innocent cover as they searched for plants that could possibly work. They picked several varieties of cohosh and mugwort, filling their baskets and pockets. Upon returning to Maia's house, they consulted various books on which would be most effective and which should be discarded. Gathering up the leaves that passed muster, the sisters helped Maia brew the tea before setting off with a promise to return in a few days.

The tea was bitter and smelled awful. Maia forced herself to drink it regardless, but on more than one occasion she threw it back up immediately. She followed the instructions she had pasted together from her tomes, sipping the tea multiple times a day and waiting for the cramps to begin. Day in, day out, she followed the protocol.

The cramps never came.

Resigning herself that this hadn't worked, Maia called her sisters once more. They gathered in her kitchen, disappointment hanging in the air. Celaeno suggested a riskier option with a wire hanger, but Taygete quickly shot her down. Maia had already been through enough physical trauma, and none of them could confidently say that doing so wouldn't injure her further. Silence fell between them.

Alcyone was the one who put voice to what they were all thinking, nervously tapping the coffee mug in her hands as she spoke. Unless Maia wanted to risk being found out by the Olympians, she would have to carry the baby to term. Once born, Maia could place the baby up for adoption far away from the city. It seemed like the path of least resistance, with one caveat.

Maia would need to birth the child at home.

In the ensuing months, Maia and her sisters did as much research as they could to prepare themselves for the inevitable. They ensured Maia was eating properly and staying healthy, as she had to avoid hospitals and the typical prenatal care. On more than one occasion, the sisters shared rumors about one of the wives of the Olympians attempting to murder an illegitimate child that had just been born and driving a different mistress insane through stalking. None of it was verifiable, but it was enough to convince Maia that this was truly the best, and only, option available to her.

Regardless, no amount of preparation could have prepared her for the pain that ripped through her body as she tried to push the child out. Merope had been with her when the contractions began, her voice trembling with fear as she called the other sisters to come quickly. Though young, she was determined to be strong, and stayed by Maia's side as they moved to the bathroom, holding her hand throughout. Sterope gathered towels and boiled water, tucking extra towels underneath Maia's head to keep her as comfortable as possible as she lay down in the porcelain bathtub.

How long she screamed in pain, Maia didn't know. She was soaked in sweat and straining as her body wanted to rip in two, only able to focus on expelling the child from her womb. Electra said that she saw the head, and vaguely Maia remembered reading that it wouldn't be much longer now. With a primal cry, Maia pushed and the baby emerged, Electra deftly catching it in a towel. Taygete guided her head back to the makeshift cushion, wiping her face with a cool cloth and murmuring that she had done well. Distantly, Maia heard her own voice ask after the baby. It was a healthy boy, the sisters told her in a chorus punctuated by a shrill cry.

She knew she shouldn't, but she had to see the child. Her sisters shared a concerned look before washing and bundling up the small form. Alcyone carefully placed the swaddled babe in Maia's arms, eyes cautious as though scared of what Maia would do.

Maia had no intention of harming the child. As she looked down at the tiny being, he opened his eyes and smiled up at her, hands reaching out. There was no anger or malice in those eyes, nothing that reflected that of her attacker. Instinctively, tentatively, she extended a finger and the baby grabbed it before sliding his big brown eyes closed again.

He had her eyes, all the sisters agreed. He also had a small tuft of brown hair the same shade as Maia's, the same round face and prominent nose. There was no denying that this was her child. Clinging the babe to her chest, Maia slipped into an exhausted sleep.

The days passed. Her sisters were worried about her and often stopped by to check, but Maia would never harm the child. They brought her and the babe some essentials for care. Nothing fancy, as they anticipated Maia would place an advertisement for adoption. What they were unaware of, though, was that Maia had decided to keep the boy. She wouldn't tell them of her intentions until after she put her house up for sale.

Their shock and concern were well-warranted, but Maia had found a new house far outside the city limits, partway up the mountainside in a hidden meadow. Far from the prying eyes of Olympians, somewhere where she could safely and securely raise her child the way she wanted. She would break the chaotic cycle of spoiled Olympians with this one. Maybe, just maybe, he would be what was needed to highlight the brutality of his father and his siblings.

She cooed down at the babe, smiling as those brown eyes greeted her.

"You're going to do wonderful things, aren't you? My little Hermes."

# HERSTORY

# THE XANTHIPPIC METHOD

## BY SUSAN MCDONOUGH WACHTMAN

The Athenians called him "The Gadfly." You know him as Socrates. Everyone* knows how to say his name, but few know how to pronounce mine. I am Xanthippe, and I was his wife. (It's "Zan tippy." If you're going to say it, say it correctly. I went to a lot of trouble to make sure you would remember me.) It means "yellow horse," by the way. Socrates often called me his thoroughbred, because I come from a better family than his.

He joked that he married me because I am argumentative. I didn't mind. I liked it when he said I had a better mind than any of his pupils. Anyone who looked at me could see my beauty, and everyone knew my family. Socrates looked at me and saw a thinking person, a person in my own right, beyond my looks and breeding. I loved him for that.

His students knew him as a questioner. The "Socratic Method" they call it now. I knew him first as a courtier. He courted me. He was much older, and my father was afraid he would never get children on me. But I became pregnant in no time, and we named our first son after my father, as was appropriate. Of course, my father had to support us, which he didn't appreciate. Socrates never made any money, and he spent all he had inherited on his followers. He never could say no to a young man in need. No one could say he married me for my family and wealth, for he cared nothing about status.

"I wish to deal with human beings, to associate with man in general," I once overheard him say to his students. "Hence my choice of wife. I know full well, if I can tolerate her spirit, I can with ease attach myself to every human being else." I liked being described as spirited, but when I heard him say, "Get a wife like Xanthippe and you will become a philosopher," I dumped a pot of cold water on his head. No, it was *not* a chamber pot. Am I stupid? I'm the one who would have had to clean him up. It was a joke between us. We laughed about it as we made more sons. We had three sons in all.

Antisthenes is the one who gave me the idea. He used to walk every day from Peiraeus just to listen to Socrates ask questions. I might have liked him for his devotion to my husband, but Anti-anything was the perfect name for him. He was the most self-righteous male creature ever to walk the streets of Athens, and there were a *lot* of self-righteous men in Athens. Antisthenes used to say he would rather fall among crows (korakes) than flatterers (kolakes), for the one devour the dead, but the other the living. But that was later, when he had his own following.

While Socrates was alive, Antisthenes became jealous of me. Never mind the jesting, the Gadfly loved me and I him. He would talk to me as few men talked to women, as though I was a rational human being and not just a body to fill with child. Though we did that, too. Did I say we had three sons?

"What is love?" he would ask as he kissed me.

Antisthenes hated anything and anyone who would take his teacher's attention away from teaching. Later, when he became a teacher himself, Antishthenes preached "virtue." He told his pupils that virtue was all that was needed for happiness. Pleasure, he said, was unnecessary, especially sensual pleasure. Did he think Socrates would have agreed with *that?*

"What is virtue?" Socrates often asked. He was a man who courted and married a woman twenty years younger and got three sons on her! "Love is the one thing I understand," he would say. And I can attest that he understood *making* love very, very well!

But Antisthenes also said something which rang in my head for days afterward. This was after Socrates had died, and Antisthenes was busy spreading his cheerless theories which later inspired the Cynics, those equally loveless people. He said that a virtuous woman would be unseen, unheard, and unknown to history. (He meant that as a good thing!!!)

*Unknown* to history.

I, who had been the wife and helpmate of an extraordinary man, would be forgotten. Socrates, I was sure, would never be forgotten. But I would be unknown. Lost as though I had been drowned in the Lethe.

That is... *if* I were known as a virtuous woman.

Virtuous. Irreproachable. Faultless.

Whether he had intended it or not, the Gadfly had given me an opportunity to become immortal, if I dared to pursue it. If I wanted it badly enough.

I had spent *so* many years listening to all those young men talk to my husband. And to me, too. Do you think they talked only to him when they were heartbroken? I kept in touch with some of them, afterward. I chose to give the copies of my husband's dialogues to Aeschines, because he was kind to our young, fatherless sons. Not to Antisthenes, who was kind to no one. But Antisthenes was the key to my plan to become immortal.

I heard that Xenophon was writing about Socrates, and I knew it was my chance to be known. To be *remembered.* I began reminding the young men of the things Socrates had said about me, and what I had done. How I was like a spirited horse, how I had dumped a pot of water over his head. But I changed the story as I told it. I said it was a chamber pot. Sometimes I said it was *my* chamber pot from my time of the month. And so the story spread again, even more than it had before. Stories that spread like that *become* fact.

"By whispering together, you will persuade yourselves that I am guilty," Socrates said at his trial. And so it was.

I also made sure to say some unflattering things about Antisthenes to those gossips who would pass the insults on to him. Priming the pump, as it were. Once I had gotten all these stories roiling through the agora, I suggested to Xenophon that Antisthenes would be a good source for his book about the Gadfly. Ho! Ho! And wasn't Antisthenes all wound up with unvirtuous fury by the time Xenophon reached him with his parchment and quills! I am sure Antisthenes delighted in telling the story of that long-time jest -- and embellishing it with the chamber pot effluvia. (He couldn't bring himself to mention menstrual flow, of course. Men!)

And Xenophon transcribed it all.

And I became famous. Or infamous, if you prefer.

Look it up! You'll find me described as a "notorious shrew," my name listed as a synonym for nag. You'll also find me depicted in artwork from pencil to ink to oil by artists through the centuries. Ha! Unknown? I am *known* as the shrew -- not just any shrew, but *the* Shrew, the one that casts that shadow on the cave wall, the original Form.

Go ahead -- look up synonyms for Xanthippe:

- harpy
- Harridan
- hellcat
- she-devil
- termagant
- virago
- witch

Perhaps *you* think I should have aspired to a better sort of fame. What do you know of the life of an Athenian woman? Very little! And that is *because* we did not write, and men did not write about us! (Unless we were beauties who started a war *cough* Helen*)

However, the unadulterated fact is, I was all of those things -- harpy and virago, etcetera. I was jealous of his young men. I wanted him to spend more time with me. And yes, I wanted him to make me proud! To make my father proud! But he walked about town in his ragged cloak and old sandals, and sometimes he would stop and stare when what he called his "daimonion" -- his "inner voice" -- would speak to him. And people laughed at *me* for turning out such a strange, disgraceful-looking spouse. *That* was what women were known for in my day -- how their husbands looked and behaved.

And yet, and yet, when Socrates spoke of his soul, he spoke of *her*, using the female pronoun.

"Her own proper jewels, temperance, and justice, and courage, and nobility, and truth—in these adorned she is ready to go on her journey to the world below, when her hour comes."

Is that the speech of a man who truly felt henpecked? Who thought of his wife as a termagant?

"Soon I must drink the poison," he said at the end, "and I think that I had better repair to the bath first, in order that the women may not have the trouble of washing my body after I am dead."

I laughed and I cried when I heard that, because what if he was thinking of that pot of water? What if he was thinking of *me*? We washed his body anyway, my handmaidens and I. And I poured cold water over his head, mixed with my tears.

He loved me. He used to joke about "horseplay" with his thoroughbred. And though the man drove me to distraction, I loved him passionately.

What do I care what *your* opinion of me is, so long as you have one? I am remembered! Say it: Xanthippe, the wife of the renowned philosopher and sage Socrates -- she's the one who dumped the chamber pot over his head! Ha!

*except "Bill and Ted"

# WOMEN WITH BEARDS

## BY KATHLEEN HALECKI

The last rite of the *gamos* was coming to a close as Telesilla glanced at her sister whose figure was swallowed up by a veil, quietly acquiescing her future to a stranger nearly twice her age. The scent of the dried fruits and laurel began to overpower the room, causing her stomach to turn as her sister promised fidelity to the man chosen by their father to be her husband.

In the morrow, her sister would begin her duties as his wife. She recalled her mother's advice to Myia as she cut her hair as a symbol of her virginity: she must obey her husband in all matters, ensure his household ran smoothly, and offer sacrifices to Hera in order to bear children as quickly as possible lest she be returned as a barren woman. An example was made of their cousin, Corinna, who sat in the corner observing the celebration, no doubt remembering her wedding five years ago. No fruit was born from that union and she and her dowry were returned in disgrace. The warning turned Myia's cheeks pale and she promised to pray to the gods for children so no mark of shame was placed upon her.

The voices of the guests were raised as they began to sing, chiming in with the chorus as Myia prepared for the bridal chamber. Telesilla knew she should join in, but could not find her voice as she watched her sister's trembling hands accepting the gifts offered to her.

"Your wedding will be next." Corinna whispered into her ear.

Telesilla felt a sense of panic as she looked around the room and wondered if her father would select one of the friends of the groom as her future husband. She was two years younger than Myia and soon she would be the one enveloped in a veil, thanking the guests for their best wishes for her marriage. The heat from the torches felt like burning fingers against her flesh and she clutched at her throat as her chest heaved. From behind her came the boisterous sounds of laughter as her brother teased his wife about their own wedding night as he carelessly spilled wine across her shoulder.

Telesilla felt the room grow smaller as she saw her fate unfold before her, seeing only a future as a wife and mother before death over took her.

Was there nothing else to be had, was her life to be only as the adjunct to her husband?

Her stomach flipped again and her eyes fluttered as she rushed out to the courtyard to collapse onto the ground.

\*\*\*

Reaching the highest point overlooking the sanctuary, Telesilla took in a long breath and praised Apollo as she exhaled. It was the last day after five long months where the routine of the Asclepion became second nature. Every morning, she rose to bath in the sacred spring and put on the fresh tunic she washed out the night before, then breaking her fast consisting of fruit and the special tonic prescribed to her as a remedy. Her days were spent walking the hills above the valley, sometimes alone, sometimes followed by the attendant who came with her from her father's household. Her nights were spent in deep reflection crying humbly before the gods.

Nearly four years had passed since she collapsed at her beloved sister's wedding and Myia was a mother to two sons which greatly pleased Telesilla's father. His pleasure did not extend to Telesilla. She could still hear the angry sound of her father's footsteps hitting the stairs to the *gynaikeion* where she would once again become the subject of the conversation between her parents. She rarely rose from her bed to engage in life in Argos and over time, she grew weaker finding no reason to rise from bed and infuriating her father.

Her mother was caught between duty to her husband and love for her child, and her parent's patience wore thin like the gossamer web of a spider over time. Physicians came and went looking at her eyes and her tongue, shaking their heads and conversing in low voices with her father. One was called upon from Epidaurus who was of the opinion that what affected her was a malady of the mind and not the body and that she would be lost to the despair of melancholia and would drown in black bile if immediate steps were not taken. The kindly grey haired man watched over her for some time, asking her questions, then announced that she should be taken to the sanctuary to let the gods pronounce the cure.

Her first few days at the sanctuary were difficult as she tried to gain back her strength and she needed help to walk across the plain surrounding the sanctuary. Often she would sit at the highest point to look out over to the Saronic Gulf and imagine she could go to the Islands of Aegina, and beyond that, to cross over to the great polis of Athens and disappear. As her illness abated, she began to relax as the tension left her body. She lost the desire to run away as she focused on her prayers. After the long months of waiting, those prayers were lifted to heaven. The gods finally smiled upon her providing her with a dream renewing her spirit. She could soon return home.

From her vantage point, she watched as newcomers arrived, hoping to be healed by Asklepios, and she felt their desperation. Eyeing the new arrivals, she watched as they were greeted by the temple dogs who wandered the grounds leading them to the high priest where they would be taken to the well to quench their thirst before sacrificing to Apollo Maleatas. It would only be after going through purification rituals that they would be allowed into the *abaton,* an area accessed only by patients. There they would wait to be taken to the *enkoimeterion* where they would sleep and be told of the first healing performed at the sanctuary. Afterwards, they were examined and given herbs to drink and wait for Asklepios, son of Apollo, to come to them in their dreams and ease their suffering.

There was a deep sense of peace at Epidaurus. The people she met in the time she spent waiting to be healed came from great distances and would tell her stories at night of the heroes from their homelands. She tried not to despair that the gods abandoned her. Week after week so many others were restored to health and left the sanctuary, while she continued her rounds of sacrifice and ritual praying fervently for a dream.

A refreshing wind blew over her and she sent up another prayer of thanks in gratitude for to Asklepios for sending his daughters two nights ago. The dream seemed so real she could still feel their arms intertwined in hers promising that all would be well as they guided her to a wooden stage where she could see the nine daughters of Zeus, the Muses, playing music instruments and reciting hymns loudly to the night sky.

"Follow them." Akeso, the daughter of Asklepios who oversaw the healing process, waved her arm in the direction of the Muses who beckoned her to join them pulling her up the stairs. "Let them guide you, seek their knowledge, study those who came before you who were given divine inspiration. Argos will have need of you one day."

Bursting into grateful tears and raising her arms high as if reaching for Mt. Olympus, Telesilla vowed to devote herself as they commanded.

\*\*\*

Passing her hand over the papyrus, Telesilla desperately sought to call upon the Muses but it was in vain. She could recall only one other time since Epidaurus when she lost her voice. It was after the death of her beloved husband after many years of a happy marriage. The same overwhelming dread was upon her now that she felt right before illness took him away to the underworld.

There was no point in attempting to compose while a few miles away the Argive army was battling at Sepeia against the onslaught of Spartans led by

King Kleomenes. Despite their matching forces, Kleomenes was a ruthless man determined to have his way, who constantly sought assurance through oracles that he would be the victor.

She mulled over the prophecy delivered by the Pythoi at Delphi which promised he would successfully take Argos. Although Kleomenes was confident in the oracle and believed he could take the city, Telesilla knew full well that the Pythia was double-tongued and often left interpretation open to those who sought her council. Certainly, the Lacedaemonians were a force to be reckoned with for they were devoted to the art of war and spurned wealth. She was not as confident as Kleomenes that he could crush the Argive forces. The Battle of Champions was still contested between the two cities, with the last battle costing the Spartans the plain of Thyrea. Despite the victory of the Argives, she believed it was wise to be concerned. If the Argive army was defeated, there would be ransoms to be paid. So far there was only silence which was deeply concerning.

"Mistress, come quickly!" A frantic voice behind her startled her from her thoughts as her maidservant burst into the room. "Something has happened and you must come!"

Gathering up the folds of her *chiton*, Telesilla followed her outside where the rest of the household was gathering to watch a procession weaving its way up to the house. Someone was frantically calling out her name and she was able to make out the familiar silhouette of her sister in the crowd of women carrying a litter and struggling under the weight. As they came closer, Telesilla realized it was her nephew, Peleus, and judging by the amount of blood seeping through the linen, he was badly injured.

Calling for her medicine box, she directed them to her late husband's room, moving furniture aside to accommodate the women who gently placed her nephew on the bed.

Once she began to uncover the wound, she was felt a deep sense of relief washed over. She was able to comfort her sister with the knowledge that although deep, if properly taken care of the wound would heal and her son recover.

"How did he get here? I thought he was with the forces at Sepeia?"

Myia wiped her face with her mantle, and with shaking hands began washing the blood from Peleus' face.

"They are gone. Everyone. Only several hundred managed survived the initial attack."

"How did Peleus manage to escape?"

"A shepherd found him on the battlefield, but he was the only one left breathing. The rest of the army fled to the Sacred Grove, but Kleomenes ordered the helots to set it on fire."

Telesilla repeated her sister's words as she looked down at her nephew. "He set *Argos* on fire."

"What is it? What are you thinking?"

"Where are the Lacedaemonians now?"

"Th – th – they went on to the Heraion. The priest stopped him from entering as a foreigner but it was reported that the priest was stripped, beaten, and thrown out of the temple. Kleomenes offered up a sacrifice on his own searching for another prophecy." Myia shook her head choking on her tears in her attempt to answer tripping over her words.

Leaving her sister, she moved outside to where the gathering women spoke in hushed tones, many sobbing uncontrollably. Their bloodshot eyes looked to her for leadership and she remembered the words told to her in her dream.

One day Argos will have need of you.

Her years of study and pursuit of wisdom were to be used to defend her home – a city filled with untrained females and few males who only a short time ago were considered too weak and too fragile to go into battle. It would be easy to give up, to flee to anyplace that would take them as refugees but that would mean abandoning not only their home, but the bodies of the dead would go without burial. Her mind raced through possibilities for although it seemed all was lost, the gods not only gave humans life but the ability to reason, resolve their problems, and to make plans.

Now was the time for action, not tears, for Kleomenes would be well aware that the city was defenseless without the army and they needed to prepare.

Calling out to the growing number of women, she projected her voice, the same voice used in the past at the theatre to recite her hymns. To inspire them, she would now use that voice to muster them to action for the sake of all of their lives.

"Women of Argos! We must mourn later, for our enemy will soon be at our gate and we must not let those who fell die for nothing! Kleomenes burned the grove and word has come that he desecrated the sanctity of the Heraion! Did not our greatest bard, Homer, tell us that Hera loves our city? You may despair knowing she also declared her love for Sparta, but the gods will not let the actions of Kleomenes go unpunished and he will feel the wrath of Hera. Take up arms, wherever you may find them – pick up the weapons of the fallen! Move the old and young into the Pamphylacium, bar the gates, put the cauldrons on to boil, and ready your arrows. Put aside your fear and follow me. We will meet these Lacaedeomians and show them the strength of the Argive women!"

As the crowd dissipated scattering across the city to ready, Telesilla retreated back to her husband's armory. Running her hands over his shield, she held back the tears. She was not as skilled in the martial arts as she was in poetry, but if she met her husband again on the Elysian Fields, so be it. At least she could die well and they would be united forever.

Catching a glimpse of color from the corner of her eye, she turned to see her daughter chasing a butterfly around the garden, lost in her youthful innocence and unaware of the current danger.

Just like sweet Persephone, she thought, but you will never be captured by Hades. I have promised you since your birth that you would have freedom and I swear to you now I will not let you be taken from me if it costs me my last breath.

*** 

Walking confidently past the dead hoplites, Telesilla prayed silently to Hera for protection as she moved out of the security of the city walls to meet Kleomenes. She eyed him from top to bottom; there was no doubt he was an impressive warrior. His long hair hung behind his back in thick dark curls, and his breastplate glinted in the sunlight partially blinding her. As she approached, he drew up to fall height as if to intimidate her as she came within easy reach of his *xiphos*. His arms and legs were covered in battle scars and she hoped at least one Argive weapon made the wounds. As she watched his jaw twitch at the sight of her, she could see the anger in his face at the dead warriors at his feet brought down by the slender but skillful arms of the priestesses of Artemis. The Argive women held the upper hand as they proudly displayed the captured Spartan king, Demaratus, at the top of the wall under guard by a group of Argive women after he was captured sneaking into the city.

Glancing to survey his troops lined up behind him, she could see that some refused to look at her as they stared straight ahead, their faces expressionless. She could feel the tension of the king's retainers as they attempted to control his anger over the sight of the women who pointed their arrows at him from their vantage points. She longed to use her own blade to slice open his inner thighs and help Atropos cut the thread of his life, but she would play the diplomat to save the lives of those inside the city and bring about an end to the battle.

"King Kleomenes, we ask that you leave our city in peace so we may go and bury our dead."

He narrowed his eyes as he stepped closer but she refused to flinch.

"I could tear down this city stone by stone, drag you off to Sparta as my prize to write of my victories, and salt the earth so that your city is forgotten forever."

Telesilla had learned long ago to control her emotions, especially before those who attempted to frighten her for being too bold, too forward, and too outspoken.

"Perhaps, but should you raise a hand to me, King Demaratus will return to Spartan lands on his shield. You will reign over a city of the dead, the Greeks will speak of your shameful victory and I would prefer to fall on my husband's sword before I sing of your prowess. If you attempt to breach our walls, you will be met with our elders and our women. Should you win, all of Greece would know that you commanded your hoplites to slaughter innocents, and should you lose, they would know that you and your men were not capable of winning even against infants."

The muscles in his jaw moved again as he contemplated the situation as his men stirred behind him at her words as she continued.

"The Pythoi told you that you would take Argos – and you did – for the Sacred Grove that you burned with our men inside belongs to the god, Argus. It is the only part of Argos you will ever possess. Do you think the gods will not punish you for breaking the law at the Heraion? For desecrating the sanctity of the altar and abusing the priest? You will have no triumph here, I swear upon my life, for every woman burns to avenge what you have taken from us and we will continue to fight to the death. Hear me, King Kleomenes, for I warn you, the gods will not hesitate to drive you to madness for your cruelty against us."

Telesilla could sense his hesitation. She knew of the rumors circulating that his obsession with power was leading him towards the brink of insanity. For now, Kleomenes was still of sound enough mind to realize that there would be no glory in the killing of thousands of women and children. His actions at the Sacred Grove were proof that he acted with dishonor in battle. Rather than ransom the Argive men, he called them out of the grove calling each by name, promising safety and letting them believe their price of freedom was paid, only to have the helots murder them one by one.

"I have been told you are a clever woman. I will leave you the city for it is doomed anyway and your future bleak. Your young are fatherless, your maids will die pining for marriage, and there will be no grandchildren to carry out the rites at your death. Argos will be no more."

Before turning her back on him to return to the city, Telesilla delivered her final words.

"You may be a king, but you do not know what fates the gods have in store for us. Do you think only Lacedaemonian women possess valor? We will choose our path wisely for we are Argives. "

*** 

Leaning on her granddaughter, Telesilla gleefully watched as the young women danced through the streets brandishing their wooden swords. Playfully poking the passing men who shrieked in a high-pitched voice, they stumbled around getting caught up in the mantles and elaborate headpieces they adorned to celebrate Hybristika. While there was the joy of youth, there were also solemn faces on many of the women who fought beside her that day. They kneeled down to pour libations on the graves of those buried on the road where they initially engaged the enemy.

As she reached the temple they built to Ares Enyalius after the battle, her thoughts turned again to the struggles they faced making difficult decisions for their continuation. Many women married the men from the surrounding countryside who took their names in memory of their fathers. It was done with good intentions, however, many of them lost their desire to be with the men. When their husbands complained that they were made to feel inferior by their wives and demanded they share their beds, the fools who governed the city agreed with the men.

From behind her, she could hear an older man complaining loudly at the raucous behavior of the girls.

"I thought government enacted a law decades ago that these women with beards should obey their husbands! Every year this Festival of Impudence is an outrage! It is undignified for the men to dress up in such clothing and have insults thrown at them by these girls! It should be stopped for it gives women the wrong idea!"

She did not chide her granddaughter when she slapped the man's buttocks with her sword before running out of his reach. It seemed unbelievable that after their courage before the well-trained Spartans and the hardships they endured, such attributes could only be associated with manliness. The women who sacrificed their very lives to save Argos were expected to return to a place of silence.

# AGNODIKE

## BY J.G. VAN ROSSUM

I remember my first patient very well. She was a young woman, already in labor when I arrived. A breech birth. The women attending her were desperate. They thought they were going to lose both her and the child. And yet, when she was told a physician was here, she cried: 'No! I don't want a man seeing me!'

So much for my intention to practice under the guise of a man. I hesitated for no longer than a heartbeat, then disrobed in front of the women and showed them I was one of them. I was allowed to tend to the girl. She gave birth to a healthy boy, and both she and the child lived.

I thought that would be the end of my short-lived career as a physician. Surely one of those women would talk out of school, and I would be caught and punished for being a woman who practiced what was forbidden to us: medicine. But they didn't rat me out. At least, not to the authorities. But, with that uncanny ability that women have at sharing information amongst themselves, within weeks every woman in Athens knew of me.

I had thought it would be difficult to set up a practice. New physicians often struggled, I had learned during my apprenticeship with Herophilos, finding it hard to fight their way into the ranks of the established physicians. But perhaps that was exactly why I gained so many patients so easily. The physicians of Athens may be renowned for their skill, but they were not women.

They were not particularly clever either. That much was proved by this ludicrous charge.

I had a good laugh about it with Eulalia when the rumor first reached our ears. Me, "Doctor Laokas," a seducer of women? It was too ridiculous for words. But soon we did not laugh about it anymore.

'I assume they think that is the reason why you are so popular with women,' Eulalia had said. She was right, of course. My assistant was a clever girl with a knack for herbalism. I was teaching her, like Herophilos had taught me. She – luckily – had not been a target of the accusations, and so she was still free at this moment.

But I was not. Five years after I had helped that young woman with her breeched boy, my career was over. I had been arrested on charges of abusing my position as a physician, and there was no way I was getting out of this.

Dawn found me in a cell beneath the palace of justice. The only sign of daybreak I could see from down here was a patch of slowly lightening sky. The first rose-gold rays of morning sunlight reached the opposite wall of my cell and I stood to watch the sun rise. It was hemera Hermou, day of Hermes, the god of deception. The irony did not escape me.

Not long after, I was sent for.

The guard was respectful. I had delivered his twin daughters into the world, two bright girls with a developing talent for mischief. I wondered if he believed the charges.

The judges were already seated when I entered the courtroom, their stern faces looking down on me. How many of them were here to actually try me, and how many had already decided on my guilt, persuaded by the reputation – if not the purses – of my respected accusers? I recognized Polykarpos, a younger man whose wife Eugenia had given birth to a boy after three stillbirths, and remembered how the look in his eyes had turned from fear to disbelief to euphoria when I told him the news. Would he believe me? Or would he turn on his wife and punish her for something he thought I had done?

I also recognized Ambrosios. I had treated his wife for more than one sexually transmitted disease, and I knew she was as faithful as Hera. Ambrosios, on the other hand... I doubted he would decide in favor of me.

Now I saw my accusers too. The physicians of Athens, although I noted not all of them were there. But they were enough, enough to condemn me.

One of the judges, the elderly Aristocles, cleared his throat. I knew his wife, Hippocratia, but I had not seen him often. 'We have come here to judge the physician doctor Laokas of Athens, on the charges laid before him.'

And with a beat on the gong, the trial began. One after the other, the physicians stood forward and gave their testimonials. All of them false, and all of them variants of the same story.

'A patient came to my practice, a woman who had previously been in Doctor Laokas' care.' Doctor Andreas was speaking, the man with the largest practice in the whole city. I was surprised he felt threatened by me. It would have been flattering if it hadn't meant he had turned all his influence against me. 'She was a very young woman, and she was deeply embarrassed. It took me a while to get her to speak, but when she did she told me a *dreadful* thing.' With a dramatic gesture, Andreas pointed at me. 'She had discovered that Doctor Laokas, whom she had trusted, was seducing his female patients. She had heard the rumors among the women, of course, but she had never believed them until the day that he tried to seduce her!'

I stared at him with cold scorn.

'She refused him. He threatened her, and before she –'

'Where is this woman?' I interrupted him angrily. 'Does she have a name? Does she even *exist*?' It was no use, I knew. But he was making my blood boil and I couldn't take it all lying down and just let him slander my name. Even if it was not my real name.

Andreas gave me a disdainful look, then said, with false solemnity, 'I will not tell you her name! She entrusted me with a secret, and I will not out her to society's scorn.'

I looked toward the judges indignantly, but as I expected they merely nodded their agreement with Andreas, and Ambrosios gestured for him to continue.

The testifying went on for the better part of the morning. Soon my mind wandered off, and I thought of Eulalia. Would she be treating patients at this moment? I did not for one moment believe no one would come to the practice, even if everyone must have heard the news of my arrest. The women knew better than to believe the nonsense, and they must know Eulalia was still there. I thought of my patient Helena and her poor lungs, of Phoibe, who was almost due to give birth, of Sophia and her sickly daughter. Would Eulalia be able to help them all? Would she escape the authorities?

And what would become of my patients if she didn't?

I felt tears rising in my throat. All the people I had fought for, all the hard work I had done for them, the practice I had built up for these people, and now it would all be for nothing.

'Doctor Laokas?'

I looked up. The accusers were all sitting again, and the judges were looking at me.

'What do you have to say for yourself?' asked Ambrosios.

I gave him a scathing look, then glanced evenly at the other judges. They were already decided, I knew. I had no chance. No chance whatsoever. Still, I rose.

'I have not seduced my female patients. I have not lain with them. I have not touched them, except in medical treatment to *save their lives*.'

I flung those last words at the physicians opposite me. They scoffed, and a few judges did the same. Some men were talking in a low voice, snickering in the back.

Bastards. Ignorant, idiot bastards.

I was angry now. 'I was trained by the great physician Herophilos of Chalcedon. A master healer whose equal I have yet to see in Athens. Because he, at least, could recognize a woman's body when it was in front of him!'

And with those words I ripped my robe off.

Twenty men gasped. And twenty men, arguably the most learned of Athens, were all silenced at once as they stared at my breasts as if they had never seen a woman.

I had hesitated only for a moment. They would have found out anyway. Convicts are stripped before execution, and I would not be humiliated in that way. No. This way, at least, I would be doing it myself. And this way I embarrassed them.

A small consolation, I knew. I watched as the shock in their expression turned to scorn then to rage. They seemed to have found their words again and started arguing all at once, until Ambrosios slammed his fist on the bench.

'Silence!'

The room fell silent. All the men were eyeing me now, smirking. They knew they had won.

'Doctor Laokas...' Ambrosios began, then seemed to realize that must not be my true name.

'It's Agnodike,' I said proudly, giving Ambrosios my most withering look. He seemed unbothered by it.

'Agnodike of Athens,' – he left the title 'doctor' out this time – 'you are found guilty of practicing medicine, which is forbidden to you and those of your sex by the law of Athens. And therefore I, on behalf of all the judges in this room, sentence you to death.'

That was it, then.

Through the small square window, I watched the night creep into the sky. It would be the last time I saw it. I was sat with my back against the wall of my cell, leaning my head against the cold stone as I watched the first stars appear. They seemed faint.

By this time tomorrow I would be dead.

Death was no stranger to me. I was a physician, after all. But this was different, and I was afraid. I was afraid of what would come, but I was more afraid of what I would leave behind. I was deluding myself if I thought Eulalia could continue the practice undisturbed. Surely they would investigate her now. I could only hope she would be smart enough to get away in time, but deep down I knew she would never leave. She would not leave me, and she would not leave my patients. My patients. I closed my eyes.

The stars were blurred when I opened them again. I watched them move through the slowly darkening sky. I did not want to sleep. Not tonight. But tiredness was overtaking me and I felt myself drifting away, until at last I slept, the exhausted sleep of the doomed.

It was dawning on the last day of my life when I woke. I cracked my stiff neck and peered out the window. In the waxing light of day, the morning star still shone brightly. Silently, I watched it.

The sunlight had grown cold by the time I was fetched. Guards opened my jail door to bring me to my place of execution. The guard from yesterday was not among them. I wondered if that was done on purpose, but then I realized bitterly it hardly mattered.

The execution was to take place in a different area of the city, and so I was escorted through the streets of Athens. My city. I had grown up here, and I knew its every alley, every road and square. I recognized houses where I had cured diseases, eased pains, delivered children. People were staring after me as I was led through the streets. A boy ran across the square in front of me and I recognized little Alexis, one of the first children of Athens I had delivered. I stared after him as he disappeared in the gathering crowd, and then there were no faces I recognized anymore. Only strangers were gazing at me.

That hurt more than I had thought. Had no one come? There were hundreds of women in Athens I had helped. Hundreds, and no one was here to watch me walk to my place of execution. No one to stand with *me* in my last hour, as I had done for so many of their loved ones. They might be afraid, I realized, and I couldn't blame them, and yet... it hurt.

And where was Eulalia? Fear suddenly gripped me. Had they taken her already?

But before I could think about that, the guards stopped, and I realized we had arrived at the house of execution.

The judges stood in front of the building. Ambrosios was in their center, smiling at me like a wolf baring his teeth. I tried to stare him down, but found I couldn't anymore.

Ambrosios raised his hands. 'Today,' he spoke to the small crowd that had gathered, 'we –'

He fell silent. For a moment I wondered why, then I heard it.

There were people shouting in the street.

Women's voices.

I turned, my heart leaping up despite everything. And the next moment they appeared.

The crowd parted. They did not mean to, they just did, making way for the women who were *marching* towards the house of execution. And now I could discern what they were shouting.

'Agnodike! Agnodike!'

Tears welled up in my eyes. I wiped them away quickly, not because I was ashamed, but because I wanted to see them. My people, who had come.

I recognized them all. Helena, who was clutching her walking stick, Sophia with her daughter in her arms, Phoibe with her big belly – she should not be out in her condition, some part of me thought, and I dismissed it immediately. I saw Eugenia, Polykarpos' wife, with her son, and Hippocratia, Aristocles' wife, who had sacrificed peacocks to Hera at the birth of her daughter. Even Ambrosios' wife had come.

And in their midst was Eulalia. I nearly started to cry all over again when I recognized her, but then I saw something that made me halt.

She was grinning.

'Agnodike! Agnodike!'

My mouth had fallen open, I realized, and so had those of the guards. And the judges. Polykarpos was staring at his young wife and the boy she held, and perhaps he now realized I had brought that child into the world, because he looked at me with a strange expression on his face.

The women came to a halt in front of me, pushing away the crowd. Eulalia, still smiling, raised her hands and the shouting died down. For a moment they were silent, and they did not look at me. They looked at the judges behind me, their chins raised, staring them all down. Finally Ambrosios was the first to speak.

'What are you *doing* here?' He barked the words at them and I saw his wife flinch. Some strange part of me wanted to get between him and her, ridiculous in this situation, really. But before I could move, I saw Helena position herself next to poor Ambrosios' wife.

'We have come for Agnodike.' It was Eulalia who spoke. 'She has helped every one of these women. She is a good physician and we need her. You cannot kill her.'

'Medicine is not for women to practice in Athens,' Ambrosios snapped. 'And neither, I shall remind you, is law.'

'We don't –' Eulalia began.

He cut her off. 'Go back to your homes where you belong.' With a disdainful look in my direction, he gestured to the guards to fetch me once more. But they hesitated now. Some had recognized their wives or daughters in the crowd and were now uneasily glancing at each other. One muttered something to his companion. The judges were talking amongst themselves too. Aristocles said something to his neighbor, and the man laughed, but it was an uneasy laugh.

Now Hippocratia had come forward. She was a tall woman, and she rose proudly above the rest now as she addressed the judges: 'I say, would you...'

'I said, go home!' Ambrosios barked. That provoked more talking among the judges, and a storm of indignation from the women.

'Let them speak!' It was Polykarpos, who had his eyes fixed on his wife. They all fell silent. Even Ambrosios looked at Hippocratia.

She smiled, steel in her eyes. 'Would you rather have your wives go to male physicians, who, as you have proved, you fear will touch us? Because we fear that too. You may not have kept count, but we have, and there are too many women who have died in blood because they would not let a man near them when they were so vulnerable.'

The judges looked at each other uncomfortably.

'You cannot take Agnodike, who has saved the lives of so many women. And children. Your sons and daughters live by Agnodike's hand,' said Hippocratia.

'Our boy would not have lived if not for Agnodike,' Eugenia said to her husband. Polykarpos looked miserable now. He glanced at Ambrosios, who was still fuming.

Other women stepped forward now too, saying out loud what I had done for them. They were all women from the higher classes, women with influential husbands in this city. I noticed some of those men had arrived here by now. I did not know what they had expected, but certainly not this.

'If you execute Agnodike,' Hippocratia said, 'you are not our husbands. You are our enemies. Because you will destroy the only way for us to be safe, and we will not forgive you for that.' The women shouted their agreement.

The judges looked at each other. I held my breath, my heart beating painfully in my chest.

Finally, one of them sighed. 'I suppose this calls for an absolution.'

'She is an offender of the law,' said Ambrosios. 'What kind of city are we if we don't uphold our own laws?'

'A wise city.' Polykarpos seemed to have chosen his side. 'We cannot kill her. We must allow her to continue.'

'But the law...' another man began.

'Well, perhaps...' said Aristocles, and all looked at him as he said: 'Perhaps, the law need not be set in stone.'

It was still early morning when I woke. I lay still in the semidarkness for a moment, breathing in the smell of herbs and books. The smell of home. Then I rose and dressed by the small basin reflecting the slowly lightening sky.

The morning air was fresh on my skin as I walked into the garden and sat on the bench that faced east. Pink clouds drifting above me promised the sun would rise soon. I watched the dawn silently, taking in the wide stretch of sky that I could see from here. The fragrance of the herbs around me, lavender and thyme, filled the air.

Footsteps sounded behind me, and a moment later Eulalia sat down on the bench next to me. She handed me a cup of fresh water. As always. 'A new dawn,' she said.

'Indeed,' I smiled. We were speaking in low voices, not breaking the silent peace of the morning.

She looked aside at me. 'Your first day practicing as doctor Agnodike.'

'I was always Agnodike,' I said musingly. 'But, yes.'

The new law had passed yesterday. I had not noticed much of it, having been busy visiting patients the whole day, but when I had returned home at last, Eulalia had told me the news. The law was changed, and I was a legal female physician now.

'I expect there will be a lot of aspiring students soon,' said Eulalia.

'That's good.' I smiled again.

In silence we watched the dawn. Around us the city was coming to life, the first people appearing in the streets. The sound of the nearby market being built up drifted over the city. But in the garden it was quiet.

The sun rose gloriously red, bathing the garden and the house in golden light. For a moment the entire world seemed to fall silent. Then we heard the knock on the outside door.

'Agnodike! Agnodike?'

I jumped up to let the visitor in. The woman was panting. 'Thank the gods you're here. We need your help. Phoibe is in labor and the child won't come.'

I exchanged a glance with Eulalia, who smiled, then nodded and laid a hand on the woman's shoulder. 'Just a moment. I'll fetch my things and I'll come with you.' Hastily I put the things I would be needing in my bag and flung it over my shoulder. Then I took a deep breath. It felt very strange to go out on the streets dressed as a woman. But Phoibe could not wait.

'Right,' I said. 'I'm ready to go. Let's see if we can get this child into the world."

# SAPPHIC FRAGMENTS

## BY ALISON JENNINGS

Immortal
child of Zeus,
don't crush my heart
with pains and sorrows.

But come here,
yoking your chariot of gold
through the middle air,
whirling into a blur.

Come to me now and release me
from
All that my heart longs for,

I can no longer say a single thing,
but
instantly a delicate flame runs beneath my skin;

a cold sweat covers me,
trembling seizes my body,
and I am greener than grass.

I tell you
someone will remember us
in the future.

Now, I shall sing these songs
Beautifully
for my companions.

It's the middle of the night.
But I sleep alone.
I desire
And I crave.
You set me on fire.

Again love, the limb-loosener, rattles me
As a wind in the mountains
assaults an oak.

Honestly, I wish I were dead.
You know how we cared for you.

If not, I would remind you
...of our wonderful times.

For by my side you put on
many wreaths of roses
around your soft neck.

On soft beds you satisfied your passion.

And there was no dance,
no holy place
from which we were absent.

I don't know what to do: I am of two minds.

When you lie dead, no one will remember you.
You will wildly roam,
a shade amidst the shadowy dead.

Death is an evil.
That's what the gods think.
Or they would die.

(erasure, with permission, of a translation by Julia Dubnoff,
https://chs.harvard.edu/primary-source/sappho-sb/)

# AT THE TEMPLE OF ASCLEPIUS

## BY PAMELYN CASTO

Three days before bringing Aspasia to the temple of Asclepius to incubate, an old woman in a saffron robe and hood began the healing ritual. Outside the temple she offered two barley cakes garlanded with olive twigs to Mnemosyne, goddess of memory, and to Tyche, goddess of fortune. Inside the temple she offered another cake to Themis, goddess of right order. Then she sacrificed a small goat to Apollo.

Once the three-day rite was complete, six men brought Aspasia to the temple on a litter. The old woman placed a wreath of bay around Aspasia's neck and the men carried her inside. In grave silence they placed her litter near the altar and left the temple. The hooded woman then sacrificed a piglet to Asclepius and left some money in offering. Then she began her long wait, alone with Aspasia.

For three full days Aspasia had lain still and silent on the litter, pale as death itself. On the third night of the incubation, just as she had done on other nights, the old woman was once more sitting beside her, stroking her hair, and softly singing a healing song to Apollo. The torch lights in the temple flickered and cast deep shadows across the cold and rough limestone walls. As the old woman gently touched Aspasia's cheek, Aspasia moaned a little. Her eyes fluttered open.

"Aspasia?"

Aspasia moaned again and tried to focus her eyes on the old woman whose face was deep within the shadow cast by her hood. "Who are you?"

"Who do you think I am, Aspasia?"

Aspasia weakly lifted herself slightly from the litter and looked deep into the shadowed face. "Mother? Is that you? It surely can't be you!"

"It's me, Aspasia. I came to see you through this story, this ordeal, through your travail."

"But Mother, you died years ago in Miletus. Am I dreaming? Or delirious?"

"No dear, you're not. You've been very ill and on the threshold between life and death, the threshold that allows me to come to you again."

The old woman continued stroking Aspasia's hair. Aspasia gently touched her mother's darkened face.

"Mother, am I going to die?"

"That choice is yours. You choose which way you go. If you're ready to resume life, you will. If you're ready to travel on, you will."

"I don't want to enter Hades. I don't want to squeak like the shadows."

"Hades is only a metaphor, Aspasia. You of all people should know about metaphor."

"A metaphor for what?"

"For the next level of life. It can't be explained or described, but can only be lived. So they use the metaphor of Hades."

"Hades is the next level?"

"Of course. But it's nothing like the poets describe. The squeaks you mentioned are nothing more than a different, more complex and subtle language."

"Mother, is Hades better than life here in Athens?"

"In many ways, yes. It depends, though, on what you think of your life in Athens. How has your life been, Aspasia? It's important now that you tell your story. You must understand your own fiction before you can travel farther."

Still weak, but gaining strength from the conversation, Aspasia sat up a little more. She was dizzy and feverish but managed to find a comfortable sitting position. She wanted to see deeply into her mother's shadowed face.

"My life has been interesting, to say the least. Ever since the day you and father gave me over to serve as a temple prostitute, I have been in Aphrodite's service."

"I know. With no money, all we could do to see that you had a better life than we could provide was to give you to the temple priests. You were obviously possessed by a brilliant daimon. You were so bright and had so much to say as a child. You were smarter than was good for a girl. Have you been honored for your service?"

"In some ways, yes. In other ways, no. After a few years of temple prostitution, a man who befriended me paid for my freedom. He thought my life in the temple was too confining. Then I traveled to Athens where so much was happening. The city was exciting, filled with actors, architects, artisans, philosophers, and it was so amazing to be there. I found work as a hetaira, dancing and playing the flute at private parties. At one of these parties, I met Socrates, who became my best friend. He respected my intelligence and we had some of the grandest arguments and discussions. Through Socrates, I met Pericles and became his concubine. Pericles left his wife for me, Mother."

"Did you love Pericles, Aspasia? Tell me your story."

Tears fell from Aspasia's eyes. "I can't describe how much I loved him and how much I miss him."

The old woman rose from the temple floor and walked into the shadows, out of Aspasia's sight. The torch lights flickered and sputtered along the rough limestone walls. Aspasia smelled the mixture of smoke, incense, and altar blood. In a temple anteroom, the old woman mixed a drink of whey, honey, and oil, and brought it to Aspasia.

"Drink this. It's to help you recall your life, your stories."

"First let me remove this wreath from around my neck."

"No, Aspasia. Keep it on. It's to help in your healing, in your incubation. It will help you get to where you want to go. Drink this and tell me more about your life in Athens and with Pericles."

Aspasia took a long drink and immediately memories came flooding in. She recalled her friend Socrates, and how she had been his adviser in love. Funny, snub-nosed, dumpy and barefoot Socrates, strolled around Athens challenging everyone's ideas.

Aspasia remembered the day he drank the hemlock. She had waited outside his prison and watched his wife, Xanthippe, go in. Later several men escorted distraught Xanthippe home; the men were weeping almost as much as her. Aspasia hated not being able to enter and say her last good-byes but being nearby comforted her somewhat. She could do nothing for him since the citizens of Athens had voted that he must die. Socrates was her best friend and she missed him as much as she missed Pericles. More tears fell as she remembered their court trials for impiety. He was put to death, and she was allowed to live.

"You're thinking of Socrates, aren't you?"

"How did you know that?"

"Socrates and I share an occupation, so we're very connected, even now. He was a midwife to others' ideas, midwife to their mind children, while I served as a midwife for the birth of real children. Plus, I brought you into this life and now I'm here to bring you into another. If you're ready. Each step taken along life's way, Aspasia, is a birth of a story. The births never stop. But you must tell me the good things and bad things about your life. Your story is very important now. Bring it to birth."

"The best thing about my life was being with Pericles. He encouraged me in the arts and I wrote a lot of poetry. I even wrote speeches for him, though many would not believe I had the brains for helping the most brilliant orator Athens has ever known. And such grand times we had when we gathered with our friends . . . We talked science, religion, politics. It was wonderful being a woman in the company of such brilliant men. I was fortunate in that I didn't have to remain separate and secluded like the respectable and boring citizen wives. Being a concubine had its advantages."

"You didn't like the citizen women?"

"It wasn't so much that. Mainly they despised me, because I was a concubine and a metic from Miletus. But some of our friends did bring their wives to our gatherings and those who grew to know me liked me just fine. Those meetings, though, had to be secret and the wives would never acknowledge me in the agora. I was beneath then socially and always would be."

"So that was that worst part of your story?"

"No, not the worst part. The worst part was Pericles' death. It almost killed me when he died but I had to remain and raise our son. If not for that, I would have found some hemlock for myself. Another difficult part of my life was hearing my name slandered in public all the time. The playwrights would put on their plays and in them I was called the vilest of names—a dog-eyed harlot, child of unnatural lust, and worse. It got so bad that Pericles finally passed a law prohibiting them from using the names of real people on the stage. That law was in effect for three years. That helped. It was horrible having people revile me and laugh at the names I was called."

"It was your fiction. That's why you have a story that will live forever."

"What do you mean, my fiction? It was my life, Mother. Sometimes it hurt so much."

"Life is nothing more than the fictions we tell ourselves and each other. All of us are fictional characters, created fabrications. The spinning done by the fates are lines, scenes, situations, conflicts, and resolutions. These are all drawn into stories, into narratives. Those with the more interesting narratives continue to live on earth, even after they have removed themselves to Hades. Those whose narratives on earth were of no interest or consequence have new narratives in fictions they create in Hades."

"You're telling me the stories continue?"

"Yes, in one place or another. Your earthly stories will never die. They will continue to interest because they were written down and interpreted by so many people. Part of you will forever remain on earth and you will never be forgotten. You have been inscribed in the eternity of the human mind and imagination, and in the eternity of the fates' spinning."

"Mother, in Hades, do the stories of Socrates and Pericles continue? As here in Athens?"

"Oh, yes, but the stories are so much better. They're born and thrive in a different way. In a richer way. Hades is yet another birth of narratives where the fictions continue."

"Mother, I will be born there too? There will be more stories created about me? And by me?"

"Yes, many more stories to come, Aspasia."

"With Pericles too?"

"I think you'll like what's yet to be written. I'm here to bring about your new birth there, if you're ready. "

"I think I'm ready, Mother. I'm healed, I think, cured of the fiction of earthly existence. Bring me through, dear Mother. Bring me through to the other side, to Hades, and see me written anew."

The old woman took Aspasia's hand and gently pulled her up from the litter. She removed the bay wreath from Aspasia's neck and placed it on the empty litter. Hand-in-hand, mother and daughter walked out of the temple of Asclepius and into other, more exciting and interesting stories—new stories, not of the earthly realm. They shed their earthly texts and would be written into an entirely new mythos. Both were inscribed in eternity as they walked away to join the others in Hades.

# GODDESSES

# TITANS

# THEMIS, LOOK CLOSELY

## BY CAREY OXLER

O Themis, titaness of Justice, look closely, look closely.

Our people are begging for justice, begging for due process, equal rights, equity, respect, xenia.

And the tyrants are taking arms against these suppliants, and have the audacity to name this action Operation Themis

O titaness, look closely, look closely.

Look to those who cry out to your essence.

Look to those who put your holy name on their sneering lips.

Look at the atrocities, the injustice, the violent actions of those sworn to keeping Justice.

Look and judge, O goddess.

O Themis, O titaness of holy justice, look closely, look closely.

We need you. All people need you.

When you have examined the hearts and circumstances of the people, come down, with the Furies in your entourage.

Bring Justice and holy terror upon those who blemish your Name.

# BEFORE GODS

## BY MJ PANKEY

"It's cold down there, Kronu, they'll freeze!" Re wrung her hands, her chest tightening as she stared at the hole in the ground, like the mouth of a great monster opening to swallow her children.

"Re, we can't risk them sneaking off in the middle of the night again. It's too dangerous."

Re shivered, watching helplessly as Kronu snatched up their children and fed them one by one into the cavern; first Esta, then Demet, Heri, Hidi, Seidon... Their faces scrunched up in confusion, unsure if the dark hole was more frightening than their father's mood. Re didn't know either.

Kronu reached for Ses, grabbing him under the arms and lifting him up to look at him face to face with a fierce, yet gentle, gaze. "This one is going to get me killed."

"I won't do it again, Father, I promise," Ses said, his eyes sharp and resolute. He had only seen six migrations, but his determination already rivalled Kronu's.

"No. You *won't*." Kronu lowered him down, then dropped in the mammoth skin they had slept under as a family just yesterday.

Re knelt, looking one final time into their terrified eyes. Kronu squatted beside her, his head bobbing methodically as he counted to make sure all six of their children were there, safe. Satisfied, he relaxed back on his heels and smiled warmly at them. "Good night, little ones."

Six pairs of big, wide eyes peered back, echoing *good night.*

Re could see how brave they were trying to be. They had never been separated from her before. Ever.

Kronu motioned her back, then rolled a giant stone over the opening.

The tiny faces disappeared. Swallowed up into the earth's gaping jaws.

Re stifled a gasp, clenching her fists tight, her insides twisting at the sudden emptiness—the cold void that surrounded her instead of her smiling children.

Kronu turned to her and rubbed her shoulders comfortingly. "They'll have each other and the furs for warmth, and there's a stream down there for them to drink. They'll be safe."

Re peered around him at the giant rock doubtfully. *They don't have me.* As if in answer, a muffled cry vibrated up from beneath the earth. Her heart leapt into her throat. She rushed forward, desperate to get to them, but Kronu's grip clenched painfully around her arm, stopping her.

"No, Re."

His angry tone startled her. She studied the dangerous flicker in his eyes, deciding if she was more afraid of being without her children or of Kronu's rage if she insisted. She knew he wouldn't relent, and the stone was much too heavy for her to move on her own.

"I don't like this. There must be another way," she said, tears finally pushing over the rims of her eyes.

"We've considered everything Re, you know there isn't."

She steeled her gaze on his, grasping for anything to contradict him, but before she could speak, a loud howl broke through the calm dusk. Both instinctively crouched, their eyes darting to locate the danger. Re looked again at the giant rock. *Could a wild beast—?*

"Nothing will be able to move it," Kronu assured as though reading her mind. He tugged on her arm. "Come."

Reluctantly, Re hurried after him up the rocky slope to the safety of their own cave, a shallow swallow protected by a sharp overhang and only accessible by scaling down the steep cliffside and shuffling sideways underneath. It had kept Kronu and Re safe from wild beasts for many years, and their children too. Re had birthed and nursed each of them there and raised them until they were old enough to climb out and up on their own to help Kronu collect food. Kronu and Re had thought it was the safest place on earth. That is, until Ses and Heri had climbed out one night on their own.

*** 

A poke to the shoulder coaxed Heri's eyes open. Ses' brown orbs crinkled at the edges, a big grin spreading across his face as he pressed his finger against his lips for quiet.

Heri sat up and rubbed the sleep from her eyes. Half of her wanted to flop back down on her warm wolf skin and drift off again. The other half piqued with curiosity and excitement at their bold plan. She followed his gaze over the forms of their siblings snuggled together and snoring softly. Their parents sleeping near the entrance of the cave made her wriggle from a sudden chill. They would be furious if they woke up.

Heri slinked up into a crouch and nodded at Ses. Whatever the consequences, she was sure a few tears and a pouty lip would soften the punishment. It always did.

Ses smiled back and took the first tiptoe across the granite floor. Heri followed, stepping carefully in between Esta and Seidon's feet, around the stack of reeds gathered for a new basket, and over the pile of stones collected to make spear points—knocking one of those would be the end of their adventure.

Obstacles behind them, Heri glanced back and slowly released the breath she hadn't realized she'd been holding. No one moved. She shared a triumphant grin with Ses, then peeked over the edge to the wide world.

Stars sparkled outside, and light from the moon illuminated the empty plains hundreds of feet below, casting straggly shadows from the sparse trees. Ses reached around the left side of the cave opening and grasped the first rock hold.

Another chill raced down her spine as a new thought struck her. How much noise did climbing make? She hadn't ever paid attention before; the morning climb was always one of excitement and bustle. But now?

Heri flinched as Ses swung away and began to climb out of sight, sending a few grains of sand skittering downward. Heri glanced nervously at their parents to make sure they were still asleep before carefully following her little brother's path out and up.

The plan to sneak out and get a real look at the world had seemed so exciting yesterday morning, but as she climbed in the cold dark, placing her hands and feet by sheer memory, anxiety threatened to chase her back down to her warm wolf skin.

"Heri!" The dark silhouette of Ses' face against the backdrop of a billion stars erased all doubts she had of returning. She continued her climb until Ses could reach down and help her up onto the flat plateau at the top of their mountain.

Heri was stunned at the beautiful world before her; she had never seen the night sky from outside the cave. She felt unsteady looking at it, disoriented, mesmerized, swallowed by it, yet awed by how powerful she felt suspended between earth and sky.

Ses interlaced his fingers with hers and gave her a gentle squeeze, bringing her awareness to earth where the crickets chirped, and his breathing was steady beside her.

One sparkle straight above dislodged from its place and sped across the sky, leaving a bright trail behind it. Heri gasped and squeezed Ses back. "Come on." She tugged him further away from the edge to stretch out on the ground, snuggling into the crook of his arm. They pointed and giggled as more stars soared across the sky.

"I can't believe Father and Mother never let us see this before," Ses whispered, hugging her close. "It's so beautiful."

"Look at that one!" Heri whispered, shooting her hand up at a long streak that trailed almost to the edge of the earth, but Ses, focused on something else, took no heed.

"Heri…" His fingers clamped suddenly around her shoulder, jolting her out of her joy.

A rebuke was on her tongue, but Ses' shiver beneath her hand stopped her short. The crickets weren't chirping anymore. They sat up.

A shuffling noise flooded Heri's senses, every muscle suddenly tensed. It was coming from the winding path down the side of the mountain in front of them. A rock dislodged and plummeted down the slope. Heri grasped Ses' arm as he scrambled to his feet and pulled her up. They hurried over to the ledge to begin their descent back to the safety of the cave, but they didn't reach it before the shoulders of a monstrous beast rose above the plateau's edge in front of them and a large, razor-laden paw stamped onto the flat earth.

"Heri, come on!" Ses tugged at her wrist, but she was frozen in place. A snarling snout and gleaming green eyes appeared, set onto a large bristly head with spiked ears. Saliva dripped from fangs longer than her arm, glittering in the moonlight and making tiny mud cakes where it fell. "Heri!"

The great creature growled at her, flexing its claws out and scarring the ground. Its jaws opened and turned to the heavens, releasing an earth-shaking roar.

Heri felt the warm wet down her legs. Paralysis gripped her, squeezing a whimper from her lungs.

Ses scrambled behind her as the beast reared back, tensing to pounce.

A stone sailed over Heri's shoulder, lifting a strand of her hair. It hit the monster in the eye. A high-pitched shriek of anger and pain resounded from its throat. It stepped back down the path and shook its head. Roared again. Ses threw another stone, a larger one. It hit the beast in the shoulder. Another shriek.

"Heri, climb!"

Ses hurled another rock.

The creature lunged. Half-blinded, its paw swiped through the air, the moonlit claws painting an arc across the sky. Ses leapt back, narrowly dodging the attack.

Something heavy rammed against Heri, knocking her feet out from under her. She pitched forward and caught herself on her hands. Dust plumed up into her eyes and mouth. She spit and shook her head, eyes burning, skin crawling in anticipation of unseen claws ripping her to shreds.

Another shriek from the monster, met by a loud thunderous cry—a new beast of prey on the scene: Kronu. Heri flipped over. Kronu's feet were wide before the monster, his long spear raised in one hand, and his club in the other. Their mother appeared beside him, club in hand, panting from her frenzied climb.

The monster roared and lunged for Kronu, snapping his spear in its jaws like a twig. Weapons and arms descended in a blur of strikes. Yells and shrieks blared. Blood splattered on the loose dirt. The monster shouldered its way out from between them and pounced closer to Ses, swiping Re off balance with its long, thick tail.

Kronu lunged at it with a loud cry, swinging his club at its head. The monster whipped around, crashing its rump into Re and slinging her across the plateau—nearly over the edge. It slashed at Kronu, who dodged the fatal blow but twisted his foot on a stone and stumbled. It leapt upon Kronu and opened its jaws to devour Kronu's whole head.

Heri screamed and covered her face.

There was a startled yelp, unexpectedly nonhuman. Ses stood over their father with his arm inside the beasts' throat almost to the elbow; its fangs pressed against Ses' torso, nearly as long. Blood gushed from its wide mouth onto Kronu and Ses' legs. It slumped to the earth, sliding off Ses' arm and revealing the broken spear point in his hand.

For a moment, everything was still and quiet. Kronu kicked the dead beast away and rose to his feet, blood dripping from his body and pooling on the ground. He glanced at their mother, then at Heri. His eyes sapped all relief from her. He reached for Ses, grasping his neck roughly and throwing him down, growling in rage.

Ses crawled backwards toward Heri, grasping her hand, renewed fear shaking them both.

"Kronu!"

"No!" Kronu's finger raised to their mother, commanding her silence, and then pointed threatening at Ses and Heri. "You...you will be the death of me! Of all of us! This cannot stand. This cannot go unpunished."

Heri squeezed Ses' hand, remembering their earlier joy under the brilliant stars.

"But Father, I killed it…"

"You will not challenge me!" Kronu bellowed.

Heri held Ses close. Even in the face of Kronu's rage and disappointment, she wasn't sorry.

***

The joyless eyes of the children as they crawled out of the pit sharpened the ache in Re's chest. One by one, they emerged and trudged toward the basket of fruits and cooked meat.

The seasons had cycled twice since the incident. The temporary punishment had turned into something Kronu became reluctant to end, despite Re and the children's constant pleas.

"They haven't learned their lesson yet" he would say, and as time went on, "Predators are migrating now, let's wait," and, more recently, "Keeping them down there protects us too." Though his words seemed true, Re began to notice a change in the children that made her heart heavy; they had grown taller but thinner, their muscles were withered and their shoulders hunched. In the gathering dusk, they appeared even more ghastly than usual.

A new realization struck her. *They're dying.*

Kronu scanned the landscape for wild beasts, barely noticing that his children were even there.

He's killing them.

"Kronu."

He continued to watch for danger as though he hadn't heard her. Desperate, she grasped his hand, digging her nails into his palm in a sudden burst of anger.

"Kronu!"

His features pinched together in a scowl. He wrenched his hand away and pushed her back. "What?"

"Kronu, we can't make them go back down there, look at them…"

"No."

Defiance swelled within her. "Kronu…"

"They go *back*!" The loud bellow stirred a few nesting crows to flight from the cliff above them. Kronu's chest heaved angrily as he leaned toward her. She stayed silent, and he waved his hand dismissively at the children. "Hurry up and eat and get back down there, the vagadons will be coming out soon." He turned back to his watch, clenching his club with white knuckles.

Indignant rage and resentment heated her body; the loving father she had trusted with the well-being of their children…could he be so blind to the harm he was causing them?

*The real threat isn't a beast. It's you.* Guilt and grief knotted inside of her. She clenched her jaw, biting back tears that threatened to consume her. If she let even one fall, she would crumple to the ground.

Re's sight lighted on Ses, the last to climb out of the pit. His shriveled muscles were tensed, his eyes bright and alert. The other children sat sullen around the baskets of food, but Ses... Ses had a defiant spirit that was not broken; a true leader.

A wistful smile tugged at her lips. Kronu had been like him once.

*Kronu...* He hadn't seen their youngest child yet. *Maybe...*

She caught Ses' gaze and flicked her chin to the large boulders at the base of the mountain. Confusion creased Ses' forehead for just a moment before he bolted into a soft-footed sprint to hide. She watched until he was out of sight. She could save one child today; tomorrow she would save them all. Somehow.

She turned back around and froze.

Heri was watching them, a piece of meat dangling in her hand on its way to her open mouth, but she returned to eating like nothing had happened. Renewed confidence surged within Re. Kronu no longer understood what was needed to protect their children, and Heri knew it too. She examined the faces of her other children, catching the dark looks they tossed at their father's back. They all knew it.

Do they feel the same about me? She suddenly felt sick.

"Enough. Get back inside." Kronu's gruff voice made Re jump. The children shuffled to their feet and trudged back, sliding one by one down the throat of their slow doom. Kronu's gaze followed them, head bobbing methodically as he counted. He frowned.

"Where is Ses?"

Re swallowed down her panic and leaned over the opening. "He's already down there, Kronu." There was a pause, and for a moment she thought he would trust her, but then she heard his footsteps approaching.

The children looked around for Ses, confused looks passing between them. Kronu was almost beside her.

Her attention darted to the dark corner of the sleeping area where an elongated boulder sat. Heri followed her gaze and strode forward, grabbing her wolf skin from the ground and throwing it over the boulder. She knelt beside it, firing a warning glare at her bewildered siblings to keep silent.

Kronu reached Re and squatted beside her, his hot breath raising the bumps on her shoulder as he peered down. Terror and excitement danced wildly through Re's veins as she extended a long finger. "He's there."

His eyes narrowed. "Where?"

"Right here, Father, don't you see him?" Heri interjected, rubbing her hand over the fur with soothing strokes. She inclined her head toward the rock. "What's that, Ses? Oh. He says he's unwell. There, there, Ses, just rest. I will make sure Seidon leaves you something to eat."

Kronu didn't move for a long time. No one did except for Heri, who still smoothed the fur lovingly with her bony hand. Re swallowed, too afraid to look at Kronu to see if he believed them. Could he hear her pounding heart?

Finally, Kronu stood and nodded to Heri.

"Take care of him, Daughter." He braced himself against the great stone to shut them in.

Re released her breath, smiling down at Heri. They'd done it.

"Father."

Re and Kronu both whirled around.

There stood Ses; sweat beaded across his chest as though he had been running all this time. His hand was hiding something behind his back. Re glimpsed the tip of his broken spear point—he'd been to the mountain cave.

"Ses!" Kronu's surprised face crumpled into a beastly scowl. He pushed himself off the boulder and charged toward him, hand outstretched to grab him and throw him into the pit. "You will *never* learn your lesson!"

Ses ducked left and lunged, plunging his weapon into Kronu's side and wrenching it free in one swift motion.

Re watched, petrified as Kronu stumbled, grasping the wound in pain and shock. Was it enough?

Kronu's eyes raised to Ses, chilling Re's blood cold. She recognized that look; she had seen it when the beast had cornered Ses and Heri on the plateau; a predator had come to devour their family, and Kronu aimed to kill it.

Kronu lurched forward, capturing Ses by the neck and raising him up with a growl. Ses dangled and kicked, driving the knife down into Kronu's arm, but his blows merely glanced off the hard sinews; Kronu slapped the knife away with his other hand, sending it flying through the air. It landed near Re.

"Kronu, no!" Re screamed, but Kronu ignored her, gnashing his teeth and squeezing even harder. Ses' choking fueled her into action. She grabbed the broken spearhead and buried it into Kronu's belly, driving downward through the flesh. Bowels and blood spilled onto the dirt and slipped into the pit with a sickening splatter. Screams resounded hauntingly from below. Kronu dropped Ses in a heap and slumped onto the ground. Gasping. Choking. Convulsing violently. His bloodshot eyes locked onto Re as they froze over in death.

Re dropped to her knees beside Ses and gathered him into her arms. He coughed and spluttered, sobbing against her.

"Shh. You're safe now. You're all safe. Come out, children. You're free."

Seidon emerged first from the belly of the earth, crawling through the viscera of Kronu with wide, disbelieving eyes. Next came Hidi, then Heri who went immediately to Ses and threw her arms around him, then Demet, and, lastly, Esta.

Re's six children huddled around her, crying and sobbing. She hugged and kissed each one, then stretched out her arms and pulled them all close. Their expressions weren't visible through her tears, but she could feel their warmth surrounding her; alive and free.

"You're safe now, my darlings. You're safe."

# APHRODITE

# SEA–SPAWNED

## BY SOFIA EZDINA

The witch says, "With the first dawn
after he is married to another,
your heart will break, and
you will become the foam of the sea."

With the first dawn, Aphrodite
rises from the foam and remembers
nothing about the prince and the knives.

# CREATORS OF HYSTERIA AND THE TRIPLE GODDESS

## BY CINDY O'QUINN

I stand before you, a shadow silhouette. Man or woman—will require some thought. Minds are corroded, the first stage of rot. Men or gods—neither hold the only key to unlock the pleasures of what makes our bodies shiver and rock.

Men are known as the first creators… believe or not.

Anchors deep in history right off the top. Claiming to cure women's hysteria right on the *spot*. That's right, a cure for your free-floating uterus, you silly twats. Only man can come up with a device to make you go pop. Lining wallets while getting their rocks off.

Cure for hysteria—when men are the cause!

Don't forget about Qetesh—goddess of fertility, ecstasy, and sex. Ancient secrets reveal how to achieve the best. Thanks be to the goddess, Qetesh, part of Astarte—none other than Aphrodite—a version of Astarte.

Qetesh, a triple combination and woman's sure bet, meets man, crushing his threat.

I'll make a garden of men's bones and place skulls for headstones. Names on the back to identify the dead. Shadows will slip through eyeholes as bodies fill with dread. I won't linger or make them wait. Removing men's flesh to make a bed—like raking food from a plate.

Imagine the desire Qetesh will help you feel… when it's your own womanly pleasures you create.

# BEAUTY IS IN THE BEARER OF THE APPLE

## BY ERIN SWEET AL-MEHAIRI

I've pen and paper, and a rainy night, in which I'm captivated by a muse to tell the legend of a renowned goddess. A goddess of unparalleled beauty and passion to most, she could also be dark and vengeful. As you're about to read, this daughter of Zeus, well… her subtle machinations rivaled his open acts of thundering madness.

Oh, the skies do laugh at the stories of Aphrodite unfurled, even if we're love struck in our modern age, but nevertheless, the saga of the apple and the jewels should be told.

It's known, of course, that Aphrodite's husband Hephaestus was revenge-riddled, mommy-complexed, and a drunkard. It was no matter to her. She only cared for his rippled muscles, his angelic hair, and his plump lips (and before you shake your head too much, European mythology retellings did not get it right reporting he was eighty years old with a long, wizardly beard). His well-known anger issues didn't concern her, as he was often gone for long stretches of time making war with this person or that city, and he was never cross with her. Besides, her love belonged to another. Mostly what she felt for Hephaestus was lust.

Hephaestus muscles came naturally, however, because when he was home, he liked creating things from metal and stone. He employed a small village of blacksmiths, sculptors, and artisans to spend their days beautifying his land.

During one of his escapades elsewhere, Aphrodite was dealing with a rather stressful situation that had her biting her perfectly manicured nails. She was becoming bored with zapping the pink color back on with a flip of each hand every hour or so too, leading her obsession to spiral into diabolical thoughts.

A golden apple thrown last weekend at a wedding, and Eris, the goddess of discord, thought it would be humorous to announce whoever claimed the apple was the fairest woman of all. She didn't know why it was up for discussion really, and Eris hadn't even been invited, but Athena and Hera staked their own right to it, but a bold market woman had the audacity to push her daughter forward for the apple. Aphrodite would concede maybe this lower maiden, a human even, was quite more fetching than her fellow goddesses, but it didn't matter, for everyone knew she, Aphrodite, was perfect

349

in the looks department with her golden curls, rosy cheeks, and soft belly. She was furious, and she ran to swipe the apple, but so did they, which caused an unnecessary wrestling match in the dirt. Her hair was a mess, her face covered in dust, and she didn't even get her hands on the apple because none other than Hera snatched it first.

Hera was Zeus' wife. She was jealous and vindictive and there wasn't a moment she wasn't trying to stay two steps ahead of her - and now this? Hera would NOT have her apple! But Hera was already having pool parties and giving everyone tunics painted with, "Hera is ***1 BABE."

And the market woman's daughter, why was she even here to cause this problem? She should count her stars for even walking and working among goddesses! Mercury, the god of merchants and trade, made deals with humans, mostly those touched by magic or offspring of one of the gods who had a dalliance, to come offer food and goods at his open markets. She'd have to talk to Mercury about these people too. So much temptation that deities shouldn't have to navigate just for some fruit. Before you knew it, these lower humans were staking claims like they belonged in the clouds. Thought they were special.

Aphrodite had enough. She would be the coolest goddess OR woman on this cloud, and everyone would admire her beauty or else! But also enough with the bedroom moping, she'd had her fill of cheese, wine, and nails. She was ready to do something about it.

Her plan just might work too. Hephaestus was gone far enough away, and all his workers admired her and respected her, and okay okay... yes, she also had a little charm that went a long way. A flash of a smile, a flip of a wrist, and mesmerized men did just about anything she asked. Going topless with only a wraparound skirt always ensured dilated pupils as well.

She was going to have the blacksmiths and stone carvers make intricate, lovely necklaces and bracelets for Athena, Hera, the market woman's daughter, and several others, who thought they more beautiful than she, and give them as gifts. They'd think it was a peace offering, but instead she'd place a curse on them during their construction! She laughed as she thought at how ingenious she was in this revenge. She was beginning to rival Hera AND her husband in their everyday schemes.

As she instructed the artisans and blacksmiths to create metal necklaces inlaid with jewels and stones, and cuff bracelets with the same, they all were eager and willing to help who they believed to be the most beautiful woman. They worked day and night to a symphony of banging and clanging as the adornments were brought to life. Each night Aphrodite would sneak to the workshops and stroll among the workers, weaving her curses into the designs.

She wanted the goddesses to fall madly in love with mortals, which was forbidden, and be forever cast out and angst-riddled, forgetting their claims of beauty and instead consumed by taboo love. However, she knew the curse would never work on Athena at an Athenian festival, which was where she planned to present. Athena would be protected, but as she thought on this, she felt Athena was no contest to her beauty as much as the others, so a regular necklace was made for her to follow the ruse. For the maiden, and any other human beauties, she wished for them to fall in love with a god, one who wouldn't love them back, which would also cause them to be cast back down to Earth for eternity.

When the time came for the festival of Adonia, she knew this would be the best time to bestow gifts. As mostly only women attended these, to honor Aphrodite's lost mortal love Adonis, and it was held at twilight, it would limit anyone somehow getting in the way. She'd extend an invite to all the suspect market ladies too, including the maiden and her mother.

Though many of the women at this event were kind to her about her loss of Adonis to that murdering wild boar, the usual suspects always came to heckle her, spread back on pillows and laughing at her failed love and current marriage while eating persimmons and pomegranates, juice running down their chins like blood. Even more reason to curse them under the guise of kindness. These ladies also never turned down gifts - Hera and Athena that is – as the village girl would probably not pick her head back up from bowing in humility. Maybe, though her daughter's shame and exile might be enough, she should curse the ridiculous mother too and teach all the market women a lesson. Aphrodite knew she was the most beautiful of all, and besides, if she was cursed with grief and loss for loving a mortal man, everyone else should be cursed for forbidden love too. Might as well swipe out all the harboring resentments at once.

The jewelry arrived to her adorned with metal-worked dainty roses and sparrows, hearts and apples, and red anemone flowers set with pearls. They gorgeously represented her and Adonis, but the deep inner forging of the pieces hid the evil desires wrapped within them. She couldn't wait to present them to the women at that night's ceremonies. She took a drink of her wine and smiled at her reflection in the goblet.

Meanwhile, Hera was basking in the sun with her brunette locks cascading down over her shoulders and her golden headband of leaves glinting in the light. She was finishing a snack before going for a swim. Her servants were filling her with wine and fruit and rubbing oil on her arms and legs. She was making small talk with them, when one woman, Avon, told her she had some secret news she wanted to share in exchange for a favor. She had heard from her sister who worked among the artisans that Aphrodite was creating a sinister plan to curse Hera and others with a gift of jewelry at the festival. The goddess of love had told only one person in her delight at arranging this, but it seemed her mistake put her in Hera's grip.

That afternoon, Hera went and found the old mother of the lovely maiden and told her of Aphrodite's plan as well, swearing her to secrecy and gaining her help for a counter plan by promising to marry her daughter to a handsome lesser god (and keep her safe from the curse, too). The woman, a witch and follower of mighty Hecate, had just the proposal of what to do up her sleeve. Hera excitedly agreed. Nothing better than foiling Aphrodite.

For Hera's part in it, she called her loyal Avon back again and asked her to quietly give a message to certain artisans to make replacement jewelry just like the ones Aphrodite had cursed. For their betrayal of the goddess and their master Hephaestus, Hera promised all involved enough gold they'd never have to work again, and also, places among her own personal artisans to continue their craft. They were to bring the false pieces instead of the cursed ones to the Adonis festival for Aphrodite to bestow.

The evening of the festival all seemed to be in place. Aphrodite was in good spirits as she couldn't wait for those women to know exactly who was most beautiful AND clever. She had her hair crimped and decked in pink jewels, a gold collar necklace placed around her neck adorned with white swans, red hearts, and pearls laid in roses, and she wore a sheer, long, white sleeveless dress and gold belt. She felt invincible and ready to party. Her normal sulking over missing Adonis at this event to honor him was taking a back seat.

One of the artisan messengers came to tell her that the jewelry was ready and set in individual wooden boxes for everyone, so she donned her skinny sandals and left for the festival after taking one last look in the mirror.

There, she greeted everyone and drank copious amounts of wine in toast to Adonis - oh, how she ached for him. She knew he'd be proud of her. He always told her that it was no contest between her and Hera for who was the most stunning. She danced and laughed and as the moon and stars shone bright around them, she went up to the amphitheater stage. As she told of her gifts, the crowd cheered. Most of the women murmured and gasped in shock; Hera performed a look of surprise. Hera had sauntered past the old witch when going to the stage and whispered to her to begin as soon as Aphrodite presented the gifts.

To each one, Aphrodite presented jewelry. They all exclaimed in delight and found her change of heart quite lovely! Athena was glad for peace most of all. Being a virgin, and mostly concerned with political and war issues, she didn't much want to battle over beauty anyway. She only wanted to acknowledge her follower's pleas that she be the most admired goddess, but would rather have favor from Zeus due to her wisdom not beauty. Hera could have his puppy dog eyes; he was her husband after all!

Meanwhile, Hera chuckled inside to herself and looked forward to what was coming next, though she did find her fake necklace rather eye-catching! She helped the maiden fit on her bracelet cuff while the human clasped on Hera's necklace— quite an honor for a human to touch a goddess. Aphrodite was reveling and enjoying watching them place on their jewelry, while trying not to outwardly show the maniacal laughter inside her.

Suddenly, a tall body began to make its way through the crowd, a beautiful young man with chiseled features and curly, brown hair. Gold anemones wound around his head. As he approached the stage, almost shimmering, Aphrodite's eyes widened and she shouted his name in shock, stood staring for a minute in disbelief, then pulled up the bottom of her dress in her fist and ran towards him.

Aphrodite didn't know, but the old mother witch was using another young person to glamour Adonis into existence, fooling and distracting her. The goddess of love clutched on to his chest and cried. She began to tell him how much she had missed him and wrapped her arms around his neck for a kiss. But something felt off; he didn't grasp her to his face in his palms as all those years before. Her chest was beating fast and loud, and her heart felt like a shattered vase. Then, she saw the mirage slightly waning…

The witch could only hold the glamour of Adonis for a short time, this shifting of a random person into the beautiful man Aphrodite loved like no other. The goddess of love was wretched and let out a scream, making the skies tremble. Her eyes fixed upon Hera, who smiled slyly from the corner of her mouth. But she knew Hera couldn't glamour, so she searched the crowd for the how and why. She soon spotted the old woman walking quickly to the stage to grab her daughter and sneak away.

It was too late. Aphrodite, with her superhuman strength and enough speed as seven chariots, lashed out and took hold of the maiden's wrists. The witch tried to counter spell the grasp the goddess had on her daughter, but Aphrodite was too strong, fueled even more than normal by her anger and pain.

Aphrodite yelled for Hermès, her friend who was always near (and who she'd prepared for action, because she didn't fully trust something wouldn't happen at this festival, she just didn't know what), and he ran to her swan-shaped ship just down from the trees where it was docked on the ocean's edge. He readied it for escape, and Aphrodite stole away the maiden, running with her through the forest, tightly gripped by the wrist. The maiden screamed, but Aphrodite's wails in comparison were meteor-shattering.

Hera fell to her knees, pleading to the skies for Zeus not to hear all these screams, but when she looked up the witch mother was yelling in her face about stopping Aphrodite from stealing her daughter. Hera stood up, brushing the dirt off her light blue dress, and went down to find more wine. She was laughing now as she realized she'd still won overall. She stopped Aphrodite's plans and broke her heart again, too, by bringing Adonis back. There would be hell to pay with her husband, but she'd take Athena with her to smooth things over. She'd forgotten the witch by now, as she sauntered on, but the witch wouldn't forget her.

Aphrodite and Hermès took off with the sobbing girl on the boat. Aphrodite swore she'd take an even darker revenge on Hera. She removed the maiden's cuff bracelet, weaving a new love curse into its stones and metal. Casting so the maiden would fall in love with Zeus, the next time she was near Zeus she'd also seduce her father to see this human as a most beautiful love interest, more lovely a woman than he'd ever seen. He'd become mad with desire for her, abandoning Hera. That would show Hera not to battle with Aphrodite ever again. She hated to curse Zeus with affection for a human again, but her heart had begun to blacken in not only jealousy but in grief as well. She clasped the bracelet back on the girl.

Aphrodite knew deep within herself she was the most captivating, sexual, strong beauty of all, and no one would contest her again. She was lost in thought as the boat undulated, consoling and replenishing her.

Hermès tapped on her shoulder once they were underway. When she turned around, he held out a golden apple in his palm.

Aphrodite smiled.

# PERSEPHONE

# SEFFI AND DES

## BY ANN WUEHLER

Seffi gazed at the shop front, which read Underworld Designs Tattoo Studio, over and over. Someone had painted a skeleton with a flowering vine wrapped rather suggestively about the flat bones. There were tattoo designs posted in the two big windows that overlooked Cherry Street, in the vaguely named NoHo Arts district. She had written the address down, rather than use her phone, as Ammie checked it for just such stunts as this.

Seffi ran a hand through the stubble on her head. She watched people walk into that tattoo parlor. She watched people walk out. A tall man, in a sleeveless t-shirt as black as his heart, stepped out to stick something to the community bulletin board and her own heart split into factions. She hated him. She adored him. She wanted him. She loathed him. He was bad news, sugar! He was her sugar daddy, her make it hurt real good romp in an alley, her huggable monster, someone she should want ripped from her life, stuffed into a garbage bag, tossed to the curb already. Damn it.

But she had come here to end this once and for all. The need for him, this craving, this seething hatred of being a prisoner of not only him but her own mother. She had ferreted out his location to free herself. As much as she could be freed. Ammie had insisted closure would not be needed here, that it was a nonsense bullshit woo sort of term, invented by Hollywood screenwriters back in the day.

You can't shut the past in a neat little box, Seffi. You just have to cut your losses, try not to hear it rattling about in your heart. That's all you can do, really. Except you could bravely, oh so bravely, seek out the very one who had stuffed you into their own box to torment. Ammie had a real horror of grand opera codswallop.

"Adults learn to settle and adjust," she had said over cups of green tea barely sweetened with organic rose hip-infused honey. "Adults do not act like lovers from a Wagner spectacle. Adults have a real horror of theatrical hysterics in the name of love. That isn't love, Seffi."

"What do you know of love at all, Ammie?" Seffi whispered, and the homeless woman shoving the shopping cart full of filthy garbage sacks and a lone, defiant, one-eyed white cat, saluted Seffi, who saluted back. "You got a water bottle?"

"It's mine," the woman waved one about, half full of what looked like clean water. "I need change for the bus."

"Sure." Seffi dug in her lime green fringed purse for a few quarters and handed them over to her new best friend, who gibbered about taking the bus to see her new grandchild, born in 1976. '77 promised to be the best year ever, if they could get those oil prices squared away. "Congrats."

"Thanks." The woman trundled serenely onward as the morning sun began to feel a bit vicious. Ten in the morning, the temperature expected to hit over a hundred and stay there. Ammie had said to ignore the homeless, as they had chosen their path. That seemed rather cruel but Seffi needed help with Des. She didn't want to lose that help because of a differing of opinion. Ammie didn't need to know she had given some spare change to this person or that one. Didn't even need to come up in a conversation.

He glanced across the street and she pretended to tie her tennis shoe, dropping down to hide her face, her form. He'd know her instantly. Maybe he'd already discerned his estranged slave toy, baby girl, tedious fleshrocket, whatever name he had reserved for her, spied on him from just across the street. Of course he did. Des had power. Real actual power. Magic powers left from the old days. She'd bet a few farms on that and win that bet, of course. All she needed to do was march across Cherry, demand he apologize and she could plaster over that area of her life, or at least duct tape it shut. Go find an actual love, or even just get a dog or a cat or a boa constrictor, whatever, and forget, just a tiny bit more and more each day, what her life had been.

You can do that all now, she thought. You don't have to confront Mr. Underworld bigshot. You can go adopt a dog right now, instead of standing here in the sun, getting a sunburn, yearning for him to spank you. Remember that? How his hand smacked...just...right? Huh?? Remember that?? You gonna get closure and forget that, PERSOPHENE?

"Shut up, brain! I'm Seffi now. I'm a strong person but I need this. I need it!"

"Oh my god, are you also up for that new Willis project? He's the new Kubrick! He's the next Capra! Brilliant yet obscene, ya know?" A bright-eyed young woman in a short pink skirt had stopped to check something on her very pink phone. "Sometimes I don't believe in live here. Bye!" She passed onward, her skin like a plum, her body so painfully thin it bordered on a war crime. That bright smile seemed it would shatter her face, the skin stretched so tight over the sharp cheekbones. "Break a leg! See ya there!"

"Hey," and there he stood, Des himself, looking like a king. He also looked like someone dressed for Halloween with his pale green eyes outlined in thick stark jet, silver hoops in each ear, tattoos decorating his bare lower arms. Barbed wire wrapped around those forearms, with butterflies pierced on the barbs. Exquisite work and even better detail. He wore his craft and way to pay the bills, advertising what he could do if one wished a permanent bit of art on a trembling thigh. Still more thin than bulky, same gaunt, hollowed face any proper vampire would give a fang for. "You gonna dither over here or come talk to me? I got coffee. I even have pomegranate juice."

"Funny. Ha ha. I was just on my way to an audition. The Willis project. I don't think we have anything left to say to each other." Seffi could not summon that giant ball of courage she had started her day with. It had dissipated to a wet smear of cowardice and shame at the very bottom of her quivery soul. "Why tattoos?"

"Why not? Did you see me running a funeral home? How cliché. You better run along. You got that audition. And we all know what a fine little actress you are." He winked and she experienced the same old rush of contempt, excitement at the sparring, and dread and anticipation of where that sparring might end. Games. It was always games and games within games. The dirty filth of all this. Sand in her soul. Like grit and irritating little gritty bits in her soul. You could wash the sand from your beach stuff, but not from your soul. There was a lesson there. Had to be. "I got customers waiting, Seffi. Either do what you came here to do or get the fuck gone."

"Fine. I'll take a cup of coffee. I hate pom juice and anything pom. I wonder why."

"Because you ate a seed of one, then had to be your uncle's best girl." He pinched her cheek, patted her head, and for a moment she saw actual pain in his gaze, then nothing. Just those gooseberry green eyes watching her, waiting for the bleeding to start so they could both fit into the grooves and play the same tunes. "I'm tired."

"Me too." She marched across the street, dodging a taxi, which honked, and marched right into the tattoo parlor, to stare at the many designs tacked up, at the other people waiting, the buzzing of the electronic needles, the low hum of conversation, the guy at the counter sketching an eagle, waiting to ring up sales. An antiseptic smell. A very clean white floor, overhead lights. Bright and clean place. Cerbie slept on a big dog bed, with a single head now. Modern times, after all. A three-headed supernatural guardian would freak the normals out. The dog snored, lips fluttering. The black coat gleamed over the rather well-fleshed ribs. A bit later, Hades followed, the door bells jingling and jangling.

"Mario? I need to speak to this...lady." A bit of a grim little smile as he indicated she was anything but that. Mario nodded and continued to sketch that eagle, wings spread, beak open, talons extended.

"I see you still have Cerbie. You had him in Miami Beach, in Portland, and where else did you show up where I happened to be, hubbie?" Seffi sat on the green sofa in the staff room, accepted her cup of coffee, plain, and hated that her bladder felt very full. She always had to go to the bathroom when confronting anything too tough.

Hades lounged at the table, with a glass of pom juice, just to needle her. Get it? Just to needle her! She should take her jokes to an open mic night at the Long Beach Laugh Factory. She'd kill. Oh yes, she would.

"I should go to Wyoming. You can be a cowboy."

"I want you back, sure. But I don't. Death rides a horse, overdone, my dear. We're in the same big city now. It's big enough we can forget we're both here. Cerbie goes where I go, that's weird? We can just go about these new lives. That about it? We done? You want a farewell wonka wonka and a bittersweet parting kiss, cupcake? Did I steal your righteous thunder? Sorry." He drained that glass of juice, licked his lips, and slammed the cup down. It crumpled, turned to powder and glass fragments. Not even a cut to his fingers. He had a bit of silver at his temples. When had that happened?

"Yes, all that except the last bit. Ammie says..."

"The new girlfriend. Don't roll those brown eyes at me. Nice haircut, very practical in this heat. Stop rolling them eyes. You're giving me ideas. Had to. It's so easy with you, all the old stuff just kicks in. We're so bad for each other yet it feels so good. That's what you told me before you ran off. What do you think love is, honeybuns? Something nice and clean and fresh? Like a dryer sheet? Jesus on a popsicle stick, you haven't learned anything. I haven't learned a thing, either." Hades got the small garbage can, swept the glass into it. "Why did you really come here, Seffi? The truth."

"I wanted an ending. That's the truth. I want free of this, of you. That's the truth,' she said, eyes on her clenched together hands, on the surface of her coffee in the bright yellow mug. A woman walked in, with a bare midriff and running shoes, cut off jean shorts, a tube top that told the world she had mosquito bites for boobs.

"Oh. Hey there, boss. Sorry. Let me get my cuke slices. Sorry!" She rummaged in the small staff fridge, took a sandwich bag full of sliced cucumbers out, fled for shelter from whatever bomb was about to go off between her boss and the stranger.

"All you have to do, my love, is stay away. This is the fourth time you've been across the street?"

"First time! I have stayed away. I haven't tried to kill you or anything."

"Yes, you've gotten so boring." He sat on the couch, his knee almost touching hers. "I know you teach art to school kids. I know you have a girlfriend who's your therapist, personal chef and safety net. I know you like pancakes now. Oh sure, I keep tabs on you. You are still my wife. I remember seeing you that first time, being gut-punched. Knowing suddenly why my brothers couldn't control themselves. Knowing exactly why. You're poison to me. I strangle and choke with how much I want to break you, reform you around my-"

"Stop it. We're not Wagner idiots, we're past that. This worked on me ages ago, not now." Except her wayward parts said otherwise. That low voice going rough and romance-novel sexy.

God damn it.

"Sure. I'm using Ammie, you bet. She's using me, too. That's what love is. You use each other until the tube is squeezed dry. Something like that. You taught me that."

"No, Seffi, I didn't." His hand took hers, she allowed it. He smelled of the sea, and citrus. Whatever cologne or aftershave he used, she liked it. He wouldn't linger on kissing her belly like Ammie did. He'd throw her upward toward the moon, catch her, have her...

GOD DAMN IT.

"I was wrong. It was as wrong as it could get. It wasn't a love story of a dark lord and a pretty girl, it was...just a dark tale full of awful things. Okay? It's complicated, as complicated as a shit sandwich inside a moldy turducken, something like that! That's us! Okay? I'm not that grim lovesick king waiting for you to relent...you still seem that angry girl who wanted to go fight in battles and shred the sky with your fingernails."

Seffi met his eyes, met them for the first time that morning. "I wanted to be more than kidnap victim in our story."

"Then fix that. Go. Today. Maybe I can stop remembering every last minute. Maybe I can get some peace, too."

His forehead fit to hers, his breath on her face as she tried to recall that anger, that pain that had brought her across this sprawling beast of a city, all the way from Long Beach. She had been up for hours. Nearly forty miles to what...repeat the same patterns, say the same things, bite at her own tail as he bit his own tail?

"I don't want to keep loving you. I know how that sounds."

"I know," he whispered. "Go scratch the sky to pieces, Seffi. Go audition for a movie, why not? You still got the face of a goddess, of a queen." He kissed her forehead, rose and went back to the table, that wide back to her, those bare arms tensed. "Get out of here. Before I really do break you for good. Or you break me. Too late. Already broken. That flower-faced witch of a girl, I said to Poseidon. She breaks me every day. Every day."

"Good." Seffi got up, the wetness of his kiss yet on her skin. Her hand traced that backbone, he quivered visibly but did not turn. Heat, he lived, he breathed, he ran a tattoo parlor. He had a life. "What's that song? I been loving you so long. Can't stop now. An old song. I have to get back. Drink that pom juice. I hear it has antioxidants."

She left before he could turn around, stop her or make her flee even faster. But Hades caught her up in his arms, crushed her into his body, her back to his belly and thighs. They clung to each other, she pressed against him as hard as she could, wanting to groan and weep and scream, but she remained silent, he remained silent. He let her go. She stumbled from that room, she stumbled through the waiting room, she stumbled out the front door, to the sidewalk, to the gutter full of fast-food wrappings, flyers for one-person shows and a child's bright orange sock. Seffi formed her right hand into a claw, raised it toward the flawless blue that hung over the North Hollywood portion of Los Angeles. It seemed the very sky grew scratch marks, it seemed she was needed for a battle. It seemed she had no wish for love at all.

*I am the queen of the underworld,* she told herself. She saw a notice for extras needed, but they were all over. Student films to Oscar bait attempts, and everything in between. Extras needed. Off she went, to try her luck with Night of the Giant Chicken, holding a cattle call not that far away. Maybe it would film around North Hollywood. Maybe she could get a tattoo. She sighed at herself, but marched onward into whatever new phase her life would take. Let it be wonderful, she thought with real hope, her cheeks oddly wet. She wiped her face on her arm, yanked her sunglasses from her back pocket. She had her money and cards in her front pockets, not in her lime green fringed purse. Let someone grab her purse, they'd get loose change and her Ralph's card.

"Let it all be wonderful from now on," Seffi told the passersby on Cherry Street, who avoided eye contact and pretended they were very important. She dared to turn, to see if Hades watched her go. Of course not. She waved, anyway. Onward, onward. She hoped he found peace. Maybe she really was at last starting to grow up and grow wise a bit. Hallelujah, amen. Seffi stopped on the corner. Instead of going to the audition, she went into a coffee shop, and wept in one of their stalls for a good half an hour. But it cleansed her. Her head ached but it was clear now.

She would never be free from Hades. From her mother clinging to her so obsessively. He was like a mole on her face. Or a kink in her intestines. Or a

362

tiny sliver making its way to the center of her heart. Seffi sat on the toilet a bit longer, before deciding she wished to go home. Maybe she should exit California altogether. Head off to Wyoming or Vermont. Just go today. Get back to Long Beach, pack whatever would fit in a backpack, empty her bank account, no goodbyes.

And she knew she'd discover, because he wanted her to, that he was somehow in the same state, within miles of her.

The same old games, the same old games.

Wyoming sounded nice and empty. What if this time he stayed here? In North Hollywood, pricking designs into skin, with eyeliner and jewelry and only a vague hint of what he had been. What if he didn't chase her down?

Seffi headed toward the metro station. Her feet stopped. The cattle call was just a street over. Or she could go back, go to work tomorrow. Accept Ammie and all that came with the needy, helpful woman. What did the queen of the underworld want here? What did she want?

"I don't fucking know," she wandered into a thrift store. Everything seemed a high-priced joke. Out she went, and yes, back to Cherry Street, to the tattoo parlor, to have round two and round three and all the rounds. But it was gone.

There was no Underworld Designs Tattoo Studio. Just an empty storefront with *Wicca World coming soon!,* on a bright yellow flyer, taped to the other side of the dusty window. Her fist shattered that glass. She stepped back, her fist now bleeding.

"You pom-drinking sonofatitan," she yelled.

Seffi walked away from that bit of self-caused carnage. She walked away. Maybe he had known she would run back to indulge in the old games that had such a sense of comfort and normalcy to them. Maybe she had invented all that with Hades and the tattoo parlor. Maybe he really wanted peace, maybe he and his damned guard dog had to flee. Maybe she really did crack him to pieces, as he did her. Maybe that was what real love was, cracking the other person to pieces until there was nothing left to crack apart. Maybe the peace arrived when they just could not hurt you anymore. Maybe real love was death itself, the final quieting of the screaming and the raging.

Blood stained her lime green purse now, that blood shed for Des, for what had been, for what she still wished to say to the one who had shattered her life for all time. Seffi headed back to Long Beach, to her quiet little life. Wyoming stuck in her head all the way back. By the time she set foot in her tiny two-room apartment, her need to be gone consumed her. She packed her backpack, she left a note, she called work, she emptied her account, she got a ticket on the Hound.

Seffi noticed a green-eyed man at the back of the bus. Could be. Might just be a green-eyed man. Her lips curved upward, but she slumped against the window, watching the road with red, aching eyes. All that silly crying. No need for it. New life, new start. She'd rip the sky apart and roar as she did it. She was Persephone. She hugged her backpack, fell asleep as the bus chugged forward and onward.

# UNDERWORLD

## BY MARION PANIZZON

Ceres caught her daughter's wrist
Do not let go, my heart will rip

Persephone replies
It is already broken
Hades is your death, not mine

As Kora wades thru the river Styx
Winter and the summer continue to compete
While Hades strives to end her polar opposites

With Cassiopeia at her side
Persephone could climb that nightly sky
A constellation free from jealousy

To rest in cosmic peace
Left alone to hug her brightly stars
Kora gazes down upon her earthly scars

Staring at those galactic g(r)eeks
My star extinguishes her flame
It had kept away from sights so plain

# POMEGRANATE SEEDS

## BY ARTEMISIA LOESBERG

*Persephone*

Hades wasn't dark. It just felt dark.

The air wasn't toxic to her, it was just the loss of her family and friends making her eyes and lungs burn. There wasn't silence so encompassing her heartbeat sounded like Dad's thunder, it was just her pulse that roared up— becoming an-impossible-to-ignore feeling so large it sounded to her ears like all of Zeus' lightning bolts thrown at once.

Her fingers ached for the soft petals of her favourite flowers, yet there was nothing but rocks around her.

She blinked. The food, she was sure, smelled delicious. But she didn't want any of it. *That's Mum's favourite food.*

Above, Mum's style of parenting had felt suffocating. She would've given anything for freedom. Below here, she longed for how her mother never gave her space, for how her questions verged on controlling, how you just saw in her eyes that she'd always see a child when she looked at Persephone.

She rubbed the spot on her chin. Her mum had a matching one above her lip. The first time Persephone had noticed they were exactly the same, she had excitedly grabbed her mum's hand and brought it to the spot on her chin.

*'Just like yours.'*

*'Of course'* her mum answered. *'All the women in our family have it.'*

She looked a lot like her dad. But that spot marked her as her mother's child. She kept rubbing it as *he* returned. He shuffled his feet, looked at her. Then straightened.

"Do you wish for any sustenance?"

"Not particularly, no." She blinked.

"All right. Are you warm enough?" He nodded. They were gods. Temperature didn't really matter.

"Since you're— "

"I am a spring goddess, but that doesn't mean I'm like a mortal. Or a plant, for that matter." She understood suddenly, as suddenly as Zeus' lightning bolt would appear to fry some unsuspecting mortal.

When she saw his eyes clear, she quickly added: "But some sunlight would be appreciated."

"There is sunlight at the Isles," he offered.

She nodded. "Thank you."

It seemed like folly, to be polite to a man who had yanked her away from everything she had known and loved. But she had always been raised to be polite. Even if she had her mum's temper (although she hid it more often behind glass-smiles; most people didn't bother to look at her eyes anyways).

"What do you need—want?"

*I want you to leave. I want you to choose someone else.* Something in her chest contracted at the image that flashed to her mind. Her friend Alishe, taken by him. The nymph's records in their running contests useless against this man, when he had a chariot faster than the winds.

"Would you leave me?" She swallowed.

"I asked your father for permission." He stepped towards her.

She knew it was a useless question before she asked it, although people probably thought she didn't. *He* might even think it charming, for her to ask such a useless question. Others would call it naivete.

People thought her sheltered, naïve, simple sometimes- they didn't know her. Her mother might have fought Olympus and Hades to keep her from ever knowing a fate like hers (Zeus and Poseidon both deciding to just take what they wanted, rather than accepting Demeter's refusal—she had heard it all, because people talked, and she had a band of friends who knew gossip could be a weapon of their own and liked to arm her with it). She knew men just took whatever they wanted, that women's opinions didn't matter.

She still asked the question.

"Did you ask my mother?"

A smile slowly appeared. "Since when is that necessary?"

She did the thing she always did with anger. She hid it in her eyes and used a smile as distraction. "True."

His smile widened. He had a smile that would've been nice—had he not been smiling about the fact that he didn't have to ask her mother; that he could just take her and what her mother had to say about it didn't matter, what *Persephone* had to say about it didn't matter. He got the okay from a man who would only recognize Persephone as his daughter because she looked like him and he smiled like it was *funny* that he didn't have to ask someone who actually cared about her.

He sat down. Everything in her burned; her throat, her eyes— even her balled-up fists felt like they were burning. Except instead of spilling tears, she felt like they'd spit fire at his stupid face. Her stomach felt like fire too, burning subtly, the acid raising up. She swallowed it away. She knew how to handle men like him. Or in theory she knew, anyway. From stories by her friends after they had outrun or outsmarted satyrs. But she was just—

"I am tired. Would you —" She cast around for the right words. "Would you allow me to retire?"

"If that is what you wish." He hesitated, then nodded. He looked more like the man from the stories now. The one that was foreboding and untrustworthy and—

*He's a spoiled child.* The realization was sudden. He had been kind and polite and even had a nice smile. But he also- *I'm like the pretty shiny thing he wants, and he gets upset when he can't just have it.* She thought about her mother. How men had always been drawn to her— despite the temper, the higher-than-Olympus expectations, the vitriol she sometimes fired from her mouth. Her eyes started burning again. She blinked.

She'd give a lung for her mum to even appear for a moment.

(Gods didn't die. But they *hurt.*)

She swallowed, rubbing her chest absent-mindedly. She gnawed her teeth when she saw his eyes follow the motion—that greedy, contemptuous thing there again. But she pushed down the fire until she could offer him a simmering smile, warm and filled with promise (in his mind, at least. For her, it was just a smile).

She stood up, deciding that the smile would be enough. If he had known her, he'd have felt the absence when looking at that smile. Her normal smile came with crinkled eye corners and peals of laughter.

To her, the absence of laughter was deafening.

To him, she was sure, the absence of laughter mattered naught. And even if he had known her thoughts, he wouldn't have cared enough. At the end of the day, he would still have taken what he wanted.

She pushed down the anger, inhaled through her nose. She pushed down harder, gritted her teeth. His footsteps didn't snap her out on it. She turned around, using the half-second before she was turned around to push all her anger in her eyes, to leave nothing of her anger in her smile.

"Good evening, Lord Hades."

He stepped so close that she could swear she could feel his breath on her, like lady Artemis' wild wolves. Warm and slightly moist and always with that undercurrent of *you won't like it when I get hungry.*

She pushed back the instinctual reaction, to establish her dominance (and okay, because it would be very satisfying) by punching him in the throat. *Father will not allow that.* Father definitely would not allow any display of dominance from her. Not when he had apparently decided that the one 'fatherly' thing he would do for her in his life was gift her to this man.

Even the way he smiled—something that could've seemed nice, might have even been lovely if she had just chatted with him sometime— made her grit her teeth, steady her breathing subtly.

"I would gladly accompany you to your chambers."

She stepped back. Not too much, but just enough she didn't need to work too hard not to punch him in the face. Still, she could feel her muscles twitch a little. The only thing that stopped her was her mother's warnings to never underestimate men, to never fight where you could run, to never engage when you could avoid and to never, ever, in any circumstances, let your guard down.

She still thought if she landed a punch, Lord Hades might find something easier to take, that he would leave to nurse his bruised pride (and face). But her mother had made her promise not to aggravate men, and Persephone did not like breaking promises.

"Thank you, Lord Hades, but that won't be necessary."

"It is no—" He nodded. They had one thing in common so far. They could both hide their emotions well if they wanted to. He hid his behind distant politeness. "Of course, my lady."

He bowed and kissed her hand. Her smile was as poisonous as his touch felt to her. She inclined her head.

"Thank you."

And left.

*Demeter*

The plants themselves bowed over, seemingly dead (and wishing for it even more). They wished to return their lady's seedling from the land of the dead. They wished to escape their lady's anger.

Demeter stumbled to her feet. Her limbs were shaken with anger, her eyes tear-and-blood shot, her hair falling in graceful waves and yet looking more like Medusa's tresses.

A plant next to her was shaking, dew drops dripping to its leaves like the tears to Demeter's lashes. She stroked its leaves with one finger, careful not to disturb the dew.

"Fret not" she whispered. While her smile was usually comforting, it now had the exact opposite effect. "We *will* get her back."

She rubbed her forehead. Her options to get her dewdrop back, her dear Persephone, were running out.

She had travelled. She had taken on a guise of old age. Gods didn't get old, but they could feel it.

Once Hekate had found her, she had confronted Zeus. She had pleaded, earning only an eyebrow raise from the king of the gods. She had kneeled, swallowed all her bile and pride and gladly did it in the hope he'd listen to her pleads. She had grasped at his robes, reminding him of who Persephone was. Not just to herself, but to him. She should've known it didn't matter. That *daughter* mattered naught to a man who had sired thousands of them.

She had let loose of all her anger, pushing it outward, flood upon flood of sharp and sharper words. It had still stuck to her, despite the feeling of emptiness.

She stroked the plant again. For a second, the tears in her eyes weren't just because of her daughter, but for what she was about to do, too. She wavered, then pictured her daughter's brown eyes —so soft and so strong. And her baby's face, always the face of a little girl, even if she was a millennium and more by now. The curls that she could never tame.

She pulled.

Before her, the first flower cried out and the next and the one after that, thousands dying all at once as she retook her gift from them. She stumbled, clutching her head. Her life was intertwined with them; the recoil of all those plants dying pulled at her own life force.

But she was a goddess. She would not die.

But she was a mother. She was unstoppable.

She didn't bother wiping away the tears. Kneeling now, before the bodies of thousands of what had once been her daughter's friends as surely as the nymphs, the naiads, the minor goddesses—Persephone might never forgive her. But she didn't need forgiveness, she just needed her daughter back.

She pushed one of the flowers to her breast. The blue already seemed less bright. She held it as she waited. Her heart hadn't stopped beating like a hummingbird's wings, and she felt the too-quick thuds right now, pounding at her head even more.

She knew she did not have to wait long. Dozens of humans died, and the gods shrugged and nagged about losing a favourite, only to forget when they found a new plaything. Hundreds of humans died, and the gods shuffled their feet, their eyes not entirely dry if there was a child amongst them.

Thousands died, and the gods cried out in fear. She was summoned to the palace.

The king had servants whose sole purpose in life was to fill his cup with nectar, mortals that kneeled in supplication, gods to whose power the limit was the king's rule and strength. But she didn't kneel. She let him kneel.

Zeus grasped her robes, his head downcast. She took his chin, pushed it up. His eyes still shone with defiance and anger. But she didn't care. She showed her own anger, her own defiance to his power.

He broke eye contact, shivered once. Just the once.

"Desist this, Demeter."

"You didn't listen to my pleas—why should I listen to yours?' "But I have never pleaded. I am even, I a *king*, I am even—" He cut himself off.

"I kneeled too. Remember?"

"Yes," he whispered.

"Mortals mean nothing to you."

He didn't fight the accusation.

"They mean something to you. Ease their suffering. ""If the screams of your own *daughter* mean nothing to you, perhaps you need to listen to more screaming to finally learn to listen."

"I have. Entire villages are perishing. Men curse us rather than bless us. They spit in the gods' faces by murdering even their kin for some sustenance. This cannot continue."

"Then do something, *king*."

"I need to safeguard my people."

She laughed at the implicit threat.

"Then act."

"Demeter, you are killing thousands. That is far worse than what Hades is doing to you".

"Not just Hades."

"Mothers are—"

Zeus crawled back when she fully straightened.

"Don't you dare speak as though you understand a mother's grief. Don't you dare! You do not deserve the epithet of father, you don't deserve the title, the...Despite your wisdom, you know nothing."

She grabbed his throat, her nails drawing gold. She glanced at it. "I could slowly bleed you dry and you wouldn't have felt a tenth of the suffering that a mother separated from her child goes through."

He swallowed.

"Not to mention the agony of a child separated from her mother." She squeezed, then slowly let go. "Free my daughter. That is my demand. No negotiation, no compromises."

The king of the gods looked up at Demeter, earth-mother, bestower-of-splendid-gifts, queen-amongst-goddesses. Kings are only kings as long as they rule. Queens don't need to rule to be queens. And what is a king of the gods to a mother?

The king of Olympus slowly nodded.
"Thank you."
Demeter arched an eyebrow.
And left.

*Reunion*

Persephone met her halfway, barging into her.

Demeter barely felt the sting as her daughter collided with her. She grabbed the back of her head, stroking it as Persephone clung to her.

"Mama. Mama," she whispered. "Korè."

Persephone closed her eyes. Inhaled the familiar smell. Vaguely recalled when she was little, and her mum would leave, and Persephone would drape one of her mum's shawls around her neck and smell the same oils she was smelling now. She pulled back, briefly squeezed her mum's hand.

Demeter pushed back a stray hair, smiled. Someone had once remarked that Persephone's untamable hair matched her soul perfectly. They hadn't been wrong. Demeter had quickly given up on 'taming' her daughter's hair, realizing rather soon that her daughter was far happier without the ritual of pretending it could be tamed.

"Persephone. My darling baby, I— " She nearly choked on the stomach acid that rose, didn't even consider pushing back her own tears. Her baby girl's mouth was stained red. Persephone smiled, revealed the pomegranate seeds.

"Just six."

*I will be all right. I will learn to be happy, is what that smile said.*

But she was a mother. She knew to look at the eyes. And they shrieked out a crescendo.

A crescendo of *don't leave don't leave don't leave don't PLEASE.*

She sobbed in her daughter's hair, pressing kisses against her temple. Persephone released her tears in the form of a wail, clutching at her mum's hair. Grabbing at her hands, letting go, grabbing them again.

*Don't leave* it said. *Don't leave* her daughter's wails communicated. *Don't leave, I'm just a girl, I am not ready, don't leave* her broken repeat of "mama" said.

Demeter didn't offer words, just tears. She couldn't promise her daughter that. It wasn't in her hands.

*I will leave. But my love for you never will.*

# TRAPPED IN WINTER'S BARREN FIELDS

## BY CLAIRE SMITH

Sweat erupts across my chest, I circumvent
Facebook worlds— morning, afternoon, night—
like it's a guide, a map, a virtual X marking

a hiding place. The hope you'll return
glimmering embers. The same girl lost
back from another eternity.

I wear a daffodil, tied with cream ribbon,
pinned to my jacket facing the press—
journalists bark questions like hungry wolves.

I hope they don't notice my unkempt hair,
shirt crumpled, my damp handkerchief;
I mount the podium in worn out sandals:

entombed, dried-out, blistered feet.
Cheeks stained blue, and dead eyes
like a corpse, from coffee drinking vigils.

Winter hangs over me until we're reunited:
fields frosted, hedgerows caught in icicle-nets,
trees stripped of finery back to naked limbs.

# OTHER GODDESSES

# MOVE THROUGH DARKNESS (HECATE SPEAKS)

## BY KATE MEYER-CURREY

Do not confuse me, as mortal
scholars have done, for other
lesser deities; I am daughter
of Titans, born before time.

I recall truths the stylus forgot;
blurred into wax tablets, reborn
as mere myth.

I was the natural mother and
mistress of all realms: I held
sway over air and sea to the
depths of hell.

I am the torchbearer; she that
kept the fire and blazed a trail
for gods and men.

I guided Demeter down paths
to the Underworld, in search of
Persephone, her daughter. My
light was the joy of recognition
in their wan faces.

I was at Persephone's side in
Hades' dark kingdom, where
she must wait out the winter.

I returned her safe to roam
the free fields of spring and
summer, dropping flowers at
her feet like heaven's stars.

I topped temple pedestals.

I stood at every crossroads:
the triple waymark of past,
present and future.

I was the threshold between
life and death.

I was forgotten by men, down
heedless years and altered
custom.

I was supplanted by brassy
new beliefs and other votives
stole my fire.

I was banished underground;
crowned queen of the night by
their guilt-haunted memories.

I hold dominion over darkness:
my supplicants are witches and
ghosts; the message-bearers
between living and dead.

I am the fitful light of the moon:
I wax and wane according to
mortal whim.

I hold secrets; truths and lies: I
speak through curses inscribed
on lead; buried in graves, fallen
in wells.

I am keeper of the hidden flame
that glows through the veil of lost
years shrouding my face.

I watch over those who still have
courage to stare into the dark.

# THE HONORABLE IRIS C. THAUMANTOS, PRESIDING

## BY MARSHEILA ROCKWELL

I gave up my godhood
For a judge's robes
(Though I kept my golden wings
Hidden, now, from mortal sight)
And on my witness stand, Zeus's golden ewer
Filled with water from the River Styx

When they come to my courtroom
The murderers, the thieves, the abusers
Liars, all
They believe they face Justitia
With her scales and her sword
Blind to their depravities

Instead, they contend with Iris
The rainbow made flesh
Whose dancing wind-swift feet
Once created the prismatic arc
That connected god and man
With the constancy of whispered dreams

But that connection grew too strong
And after an age beyond an age
I could no longer bear to watch
From distant Olympus
As the innocent were trodden upon
By those much less so

I could not interfere
In my role as chromatic messenger
Save by the command of gods
More powerful and apathetic than I
But as a black-shrouded judge

I could make a difference

So I took my leave of lofty indifference
Descending that many-hued staircase
Watching it dissipate with my every step
And now I preside over cases
Where innocence is often hard to discern
But the truth never is

For Zeus's ewer was made for the perjurer
And when the liar drinks from it
He will drown in his falsehoods
Choking on his own lies
Until he has but one choice
Tell the truth, or die

They never choose death
And they never go free
After, relief fills the victims' eyes
And long-dormant smiles slowly reappear
Curving bows more precious than any
A mere goddess could hope to create

# RESPECTFULLY YOURS, BRIDEZILLA

## BY T.L. BEEDING

Humanity,

According to the world, if the term 'bridezilla' applied to anyone in particular, it would be me. Hera the Unbearable, Hera the Envious – I've heard it all. Everyone just *loves* to spin tales of my jealous fits, with which I chastise my unfaithful husband's obsession with fornication. You seem to especially love the stories of how these unfortunate women fall victim to some mythical rage I supposedly harbor. Meanwhile, you've convinced yourselves that the creation of demigods was your key to salvation. For if not for Zeus, who laid with the 'chosen' that birthed heroes to humanity, decimation would have befallen you. Zeus offered you power and stability; Zeus gave you purpose. Zeus protected you from evil.

But what you fail to understand is that *I* protect you from Zeus.

To this day, it still falls on my shoulders to keep my erstwhile husband out of your affairs. And it's *not* because I'm jealous – far from it, in fact. It's because none of you know Zeus the way I do. You only know the face he presents to you; that charming, smarmy smile and the blue eyes that can melt hearts. A personality larger than life (but not quite as large as his ego). You've seen it before, in the faces of every politician. In every salesman. And in every dirty, lying narcissist in existence. The face of a fake.

There is a deadly agenda at play, one my brothers and sisters have been waging war against for decades. Some do it in secret, taking silent steps to decrease Zeus's control once every few decades. Prometheus, for instance, introducing you to fire so you may rely on yourselves for fuel and energy. Hephaestus, who gave you tools to build and create weapons. Demeter, increasing the global temperature to throw off Zeus's storms. Then some are vocal, the loudest voice in that crowd being Hades. He saw it coming before the rest of us. And if you know your history, you know that Zeus doesn't take kindly to opposition.

What's on the agenda, you ask? I'm more than happy to tell you. Remember the demigods from earlier? Your favorite heroes, like Perseus, Heracles and Achilles? They were never there to protect you.

I was the first to be warned, right before Hades was banished to the Underworld. On the day of Zeus's coronation, as we were preparing the feast, he pulled me into the garden and told me of a vision he'd shared with the Stygian Witches.

"The demigods," he'd breathed urgently in my ear. "They are not simply Zeus's offspring from reckless lust. They are his soldiers. It is imprinted upon their blood to take control of the humans *and* the gods, all for Zeus's gain."

"How can you be certain?" I demanded. But my constitution was weakened by the truth in my brother's smoky eyes.

"I have seen it, Hera. The witches have seen it. Even the oracles of the humans have seen it – though they are disbelieved by the rest of man. Our brother is preparing for domination. It was written in the decree of Kronos, just before he was destroyed." A sad smile touched his thin lips. "Apparently, the apple didn't fall far from our father's tree."

"What do we do?"

"Keep your vigilance, sister. Tell the others. Stop his advances on the humans before they can be made."

That was the last time Hades graced the ivory halls of Olympus. Those Stygian Bitches ratted him out after Zeus confronted them for their insights. I'm sure they thought that by shifting the blame, Zeus would spare them and ignore the little fact they'd been telepathic witnesses to his crimes. He did indeed spare them for a while, as Hades was cast out into the depths of Tartarus, but unfortunately for them, their patience came at the cost of their eyes and their seat on the mountain.

What is it that you say? Bitches get stitches?

But since that day, I did as my brother asked. I remained vigilant of my husband's wandering lust, following him in disguise on the nights he was 'too tired' for me. I'd let him have his fun (he didn't look so tired to *me*, but I digress) then go quickly to work once he was gone. I did my utter best to be gentle with the mortals; most of them never realized they'd just copulated with the King of the Gods. They begged for me to terminate the pregnancies or transform them if they managed to get away empty-bellied. And if you only knew what tragedies mankind has been spared from as a result, I guarantee you would think differently of my 'jealous rage.' If you knew the world's wars were a means of demigod population control, you would think differently. If you knew spreading plague was the only way to kill certain ones…if you knew Jack the Ripper had a name and a purpose…you would think differently.

But no – I'm just Zeus's crotchety old lady, aren't I?

No matter. Human perception means little to me when the fate of the universe is on the line. You simply happen to benefit from my tireless efforts to prevent him from killing us all. And if that comes at the cost of my tarnished reputation, then so be it. So long as Zeus is denied what he believes he is owed, that's all that matters.

Just remember one thing: 'bridezillas' are only trying to keep control of a situation. A situation that may or may not explode in the face of all parties involved. So, the next time you decide to judge a woman for her firm hand and tight schedule, remember that Humanity just might owe her jealousy a favor.

Respectfully Yours,
Hera (the Bridezilla)

# SACRIFICE TO HESTIA

## BY LOUISE MONROE

Hestia doesn't require the same kind of sacrifices other gods do.
Sacrifices to her aren't of blood or bone, no "first fruits" for her.
No. Hestia demands acts of service to your hearth.
To the place of beginnings,
the place of nourishment,
the hearth of self.
They say there was an altar in every home to her.

Home.
Hearth.
Home is where the hearth is.

Home is where the heart is.
My heart.
My hearth.
My heart resides within me.
My hearth?
My home?
"Be
At
Home within
yourself."
Within my heart.

My sacrifice to Hestia is the story I told myself about myself.
The story that I didn't belong.
The story that I was living outside myself.
She's whispered the truth and her breath enlivens the flame
at the hearth
in my heart.
I am my home

They say there was an altar in every home to her,
I tend to mine.

# RUN!

## BY MELODY MCINTYRE

Five days a week, Astrid Lux came to Aventine Park to run. A large privately owned forest, locked away behind a large iron gate, lay to the west. Each run took Astrid by that gate up to three times, depending on her speed and when she was due at the office that day. Today was Saturday, and she was free to pass that gate as many times as she wanted. Astrid fantasized about who could own such a large piece of land as she crested one of the park's gentle hills and saw Marie standing next to the gate with one hand on the metal bars.

Marie Chestnut had been running in the park about as long as Astrid. Sometimes they ran together, spurring each other on, but their relationship ended there. Marie had invited Astrid out for coffee a couple times, and with their shared interest in running, Astrid went, hoping to kindle a friendship. But every time they talked for more than a few minutes, the two women ended up arguing and nitpicking each other. Astrid would go home bitter and annoyed. She had no doubt Marie felt the same way, because after the third attempt, the invitations stopped.

Normally, the sight of Marie would drive Astrid to run faster and show off, but today, she slowed her pace and stopped beside the other woman.

"You know you should really pump your arms more when you run. It'll help with your momentum." Ever since Marie had beaten Astrid at the latest 10km charity run, she was full of needless advice.

"What's going on?" Astrid gritted her teeth, refusing to acknowledge Marie's comment.

"I don't really know. It feels different today. Like it's calling to me." The gate's long, black iron bars pierced the sky above them. Astrid shivered and took a step back. Marie put her other hand on the gate and pushed it open. "Want to go in?"

Whoever built the fence had not meant for people to go in and snoop around.

But I will not let Marie Chestnut, of all people, find out what's down that path before me.

Astrid stepped through with Marie close behind. They were a few meters down the path when a loud clang rang out behind them. Whirling around, Astrid saw the gate had swung shut. They raced back and pulled frantically on the bars, but the gate would not budge.

Trapped.

"Must be electronic or something." said Marie, pointing to where the gate was fused to the fence.

"We'll have to go down the path and hope whoever lives here doesn't believe in shooting trespassers on sight," said Astrid. She forced a smile onto her face, despite shaking like a puppy in a thunderstorm on the inside. "Come on."

Astrid started down the path with quick, brisk steps. Her curiosity had evaporated as soon as the gate shut behind them. Now she just wanted to get out. Stones crunched beneath Astrid's feet as the path disintegrated into gravel, then dirt. She slowed down to avoid tripping, which allowed Marie to catch up.

"Stop. This path is leading us nowhere."

"And which way would you like to go?"

"I'm not sure, maybe that way." Marie pointed, but Astrid couldn't see anything.

Every direction looks the same.

"You're just picking a path at random. I'm going to check my phone and see exactly where we are. It's better than wandering around aimlessly."

Despite having a charged battery and full signal, her GPS wasn't working. There was the familiar blue dot, but instead of pinpointing their location, it bounced all over then disappeared.

"That's odd. Let me try mine. You should really upgrade your plan. It might get better reception. My phone works everywhere." But Marie's phone did the exact same thing, and Astrid shivered. She couldn't even bring herself to gloat. The forest overtook the entire map. No trace of the park or the nearby city remained.

Sweet laughter floated through the trees from behind them. Hope blossomed in Astrid's chest, and not just because of the sound's beauty.

Perhaps we aren't that lost after all.

More laughter. Marie and Astrid followed it through the trees. Soon they could also hear running water and the chatter of women. Between them and the sound was a thick wall of underbrush. They exchanged a look and then barged on through.

On the other side of the foliage were the most beautiful women Astrid had ever seen. The women turned to look at her and Marie.

Why did I wear my ratty old t-shirt today and not my new tights?

Beside her, Marie was smoothing down her hair and brushing something off her shirt.

The women lounged in a pool fed by a waterfall flowing at a rate that should have flooded the entire forest, but the level never rose. Astrid tried to count the women, but their number seemed to shift, and she kept losing track around seven or eight. As she started over, another woman stepped through the waterfall. The magnitude of her beauty made the other women seem like nothing.

Astrid's knees trembled at the sight of her. A bright light filled the clearing. Scents of dirt, sweat, wolves and blood filled her nostrils. She wanted to weep with joy and terror.

Who is this goddess?

Silver hair flowed down and around the woman. Somehow it was dry despite being in the waterfall. She wore a long fur tunic that reached to just above her knees and had a quiver of arrows and a bow strapped to her back. Two enormous grey wolves moved to flank her.

"You have entered my sanctuary uninvited." Her voice boomed from all around them.

"Who are you?" Marie squeaked.

"The Lady Artemis, Child of Leto and Zeus, Mistress of the Hunt," said one of the other women.

*Artemis? The Greek goddess? How is that possible?* But her presence was so overwhelming Astrid dropped to her knees and prostrated. Marie came down beside her a fraction of a second after.

"Rise, mortals," Artemis commanded, and they were back on their feet.

*These other women must be nymphs.* Astrid could still feel their wide, unblinking stares scrutinizing them, and she shivered.

"My nymphs have seen you run on my trails and tell me that you are skilled runners. By far, the fastest of the mortals who race around my little park. I wonder, though, can either of you hunt?"

"I've never gone hunting," said Marie, and Astrid nodded. The closest she had ever come was fishing with her grandpa when she was a child.

"I have an opening in this pack. I do not often include mortals, but this part of the world lacks nymphs. I offer an opportunity to mitigate your intrusion and join us. You will race against each other, and the winner will join us and gain immortality."

"What happens to the loser?" Astrid asked.

Artemis only smiled, and the nymphs broke out into a harsh cacophony of laughter. Fur sprouted over their bodies, and their eyes turned yellow as they transformed into a pack of large, grinning wolves.

"Any fool can run through the forest. For an extra bit of motivation, my nymphs will pursue you. You must outrun them as well as each other."

The wolves howled, and one licked its lips. Astrid swallowed and looked at Marie. Marie was studying the edge of the clearing. Astrid stepped away from her and tensed up her muscles, ready to take off.

The goddess planted her feet and drew her bow. It was made of dark, smooth wood and stood as tall as she did. Artemis readied an arrow and let it fly. It arced across the sky, leaving a trail of silver stars.

That must be the path we're supposed to follow.

Without waiting for another word, Astrid took off.

Astrid had spent her whole life on her feet. As a child, she frustrated her single mother by running all over the apartment. As soon as she was old enough, Astrid joined the track team, but nothing ever sated her desire for speed. In a way, she had been preparing for this her entire life. Her legs were strong, and her lungs were deep. She knew she could run fast and far before she got tired.

The problem was Marie.

Her rival was petite and built for speed. From their experiences in the park, and the local charity running events, Astrid knew Marie was faster than her.

Running on a trail was nothing like running through a forest. Each root and shrub slowed her down. The silver sparkles on the trees made it easy to know which way to go, but she had no idea how far the second grove was. Balancing speed with safety was difficult, but Astrid thought she was doing all right. She had left first, and Marie was nowhere to be seen.

Then her foot caught in a root and she fell, landing hard on her left wrist.

She struggled back to her feet and cried out at the sound of wolves howling behind her. Her wrist burned, but her legs were okay, and she started pounding through the trees again. With each step, she pushed her legs to reach farther and faster.

But her foot caught again.

This time, she caught herself by grabbing a nearby tree with her good hand and paused to get her bearings.

A pebble hit her shoulder, and she turned. There was Marie a few meters away, crouching behind a bush. She gestured for Astrid to join her, and Astrid hurried over.

"What are you doing?" Marie asked. "That trail is just a sparkly beacon pointing straight at your location."

"I thought it would be the fastest way to get there."

"Are you hurt?"

"Just my wrist. I can still run. Why are you helping me? Only one of us can survive."

"I was thinking about that, but first, let's get farther away from that path."

The two women crept through the woods, this time focusing more on stealth than speed until they could barely see the path. They looked around, and while the wolves were getting louder, Astrid still could not see them.

"What were you thinking?" whispered Astrid.

"She said whoever reaches the grove first will join her. What if we get there at the same time? We could make sure our feet step through the trees at the exact same moment. Maybe she'll keep both of us."

Marie looked so earnest, and Astrid wanted it to be true, but her favourite books growing up had been about Greek mythology, and she knew the gods were cruel and unforgiving.

I guess it's worth a try.

With her injury, she was at a disadvantage, and despite her dislike for the woman, Astrid did not want Marie to be torn apart by wolves.

They decided to keep the silver trail within view to make sure they were going the right way. The rocks and fallen logs were much easier to navigate with Marie's help, and soon, Astrid thought she could see a clearing through the trees.

Marie had been right about the silver path. The wolves wove their way through it, yellow eyes glinting as they scanned the forest.

How can they not see us? Are they just toying with us?

Her question was answered when a large wolf stepped casually out in front of them. It winked and ran its tongue over long, jagged teeth. Astrid gulped and thought about how reaching the clearing together wasn't the only way for this competition to end in a draw.

She did not dare move.

Maybe it will let us go. Maybe this is all just a sick, twisted game. Or a hallucination. Please let me just wake up back home in my bed.

But then a second and third wolf appeared.

Marie grabbed a stone, threw it far off behind the wolves, and screamed. "Run!"

With all hope of stealth gone, they both took off. Their only hope now was to reach that grove. The rock barely distracted the wolves.

Their pursuit came hot and quick.

Astrid's pathetic head start disappeared rapidly, but she could see that safety was close. A glance behind told her that the wolves were almost upon them. As close as the clearing was, the wolves were closer.

This is hopeless.

One of the wolves snapped at Astrid and tore the back out of her shirt. She yelped and jumped forward to Marie's side. She was going to die here in a magic forest where no one would ever find her ravaged body unless she could find some way to slow the creatures down.

But there is one way to slow them down.

She wondered if Marie had the same dark thought she'd had. Astrid recognized the look on Marie's face. It was the one she always had in a long race just before she propelled forward to win. Astrid thought again about all the stories of brutal, untrustworthy deities and made her decision.

Astrid let Marie take one more step, then she grabbed Marie's long, dark ponytail. With a sharp yank and a hop to the side, she threw Marie off balance. Marie crashed to the ground, and Astrid darted around her and into the clearing.

The wolves howled in vicious triumph.

Astrid walked in slow circles around the clearing as she caught her breath. She kept her gaze fixed on the ground, not wanting to see Marie's fate.

Beneath her feet was a meadow filled with a rainbow of flowers. When her heart slowed, and she could breathe at an even rate, Astrid collapsed into those flowers to rest and examine her injured wrist.

Artemis entered the grove. The wolves spilled in around and behind her. As their paws touched the flower clad meadow, each wolf transformed back into a lovely nymph. Astrid was stunned when a brown wolf turned into Marie. She stood tall like the others, and there was a glow around her.

"But I won," protested Astrid.

"Did you?" Artemis sneered. "Yes, you got here first. You proved yourself ruthless and willing to do anything to win. Do you think that is how you earn a place among my pack? Marie was clever and loyal. Any nymph would be proud to hunt with her. How could we trust you on a hunt after what we saw today?"

"I thought…" Astrid lowered her gaze. "Am I going to die now?"

"Well, I did promise immortality to whoever reached this clearing first." Astrid could feel the might of the goddess bearing down upon her, and she trembled. "A long time ago, there was another who violated my sanctuary and my trust. He was quick on his feet and willing to do anything to be the best. I devised a special fate for him. You mortals still sing stories about him. His name was Actaeon."

Astrid remembered the story of a young man who upset the goddess and was turned into a stag. His own hunting dogs did not recognize him and tore him limb from limb. She tried to look up at the goddess, but her head felt heavy, and her entire body burned. Brown fur sprouted on her arms and legs, and Astrid screamed as her bones began to crack and bend.

"There," breathed the goddess. "You are magnificent. A more beautiful beast than Actaeon was. It has been so long since we had a worthy opponent in this part of the world. You will run through these woods, and my nymphs will hunt you. Every time you are caught, you'll wake up back here, ready to go again. Now, my newest hunter needs to learn and that short dash this morning was but a warmup. My dear Astrid, we will give you a head start again, but I suggest you put those hooves I just gave you to good use."

The nymphs began turning back into wolves. Astrid looked at Marie, hoping for forgiveness or understanding, but her yellow eyes shone with hatred. Astrid bellowed and stamped her new feet.

Then she started to run.

# LAGNIAPPE

# LAGNIAPPE

During a staff meeting one gloriously stormy night, the idea of having a section titled "Lagniappe" near the end of some of the works published by Brigids Gate Press was discussed. The staff unanimously voted in favor of the idea.

Lagniappe (pronounced LAN-yap) is an old New Orleans tradition where merchants give a little something extra along with every purchase. It's a way of expressing thanks and appreciation to customers.

The Lagniappe section might contain a short story, a small handful of poems, or a non-fiction piece. It might also feature a short novella. It may or may not be connected with the theme of the work.

***

The extra offering for this anthology is "As Long as There's One" by MM Schreier, where a certain member of the Greek Pantheon meets...well, you'll just have to go to the next page and read this little gem of a tale.

# AS LONG AS THERE'S ONE

## BY MM SCHREIER

Cerridwen stepped sideways out of the Void, materializing between a pair of weather-pitted sarsen stones. For a moment, double vision swamped her—the lintel overhead flickered like a damaged film reel. There. Not there. There. Not there.

She harrumphed and a cloud blotted out the sun. In the eerie twilight, the outer ring of standing stones solidified into thirty smooth pillars crowned with an unbroken tiara of capstones. They stood, silent sentinels over the hallowed grounds.

The Dark Goddess moved through the temple. She trailed her fingers along the inner ring of bluestones as she glided over the lush grass. Her skirts swirled and shifted around her bare feet, as if clothed in liquid shadow.

She glanced up and cocked her head, a raven contemplating a puzzle. With a flourish, she swirled her cloak from her shoulders and pinned it to the sky, shaping a vast and velvet darkness. She snapped her fingers and pinpricks of light dotted the heavens, marking strange patterns and skewed alignments. She frowned and the stars dutifully wriggled into their assigned positions. With a nod, she continued on.

Ahead, five trilithons made a horseshoe shape, protecting the chiseled altar nestled within. A shadow stood, admiring the stones. Out of place in his jeans and sweatshirt, he snapped a few pictures with his phone. The man's edges blurred, a chalk drawing smudged by a child's unpracticed hand.

*No. You do not belong in the Then.* Cerridwen spoke softly, but with a symphony of voices.

The man faded.

Familiar music tickled her ears. The Goddess turned and stepped partially into the Void. A test—for only the true believer could see beyond the veil.

A flaming snake wove between the standing stones. It drew closer and fragmented into a line of women carrying torches. The acolytes' snowy robes shimmered in the firelight as they lifted their voices in song:

"By land, by sea, by midnight sky
May we be worthy in Her eyes.
The trial's long, our will is bright
To find her wisdom in the night."

Cerridwen hummed along, soaking in the worship that was her due.

At the head of the procession, the high priestess paused at the altar stone. Streaked with silver, her dark hair fell, unbound, down her back and age spots dotted her skin. A crimson moon had been painted on her wrinkled brow. She gripped a curved athame in her hand, steady despite her age. Raising the ritual blade, she cut a window through the Void and looked at the Goddess through milky-white eyes. Her blind gaze saw through to the beyond.

Cerridwen inclined her head in greeting, remembering when the woman had been but a novice with clear forget-me-not blue eyes. The child grew— maiden, to mother, to crone—devout in faith and service. Never faltering.

The priestess bowed deep, then laid her offering on the stone: a sheaf of barley, three drops of pig's blood, a handful of acorns. Around her, the acolytes continued to sing. For a moment, the Goddess let their adoration wash over her.

In the background, a chatter of voices soured the song. Cerridwen blinked and the ritual wavered, as if seen through rain-streaked glass. The proud standing stones fractured and fell. Her night cloak peeled back, exposing a sunny, afternoon sky.

*Then* slipped away, replaced by *Now*.

Tourists meandered through the ruins of Stonehenge, oblivious of the Dark Goddess scowling at their fanny packs and plastic water bottles. They touched the obelisks, not in reverence or awe, but mild curiosity. It seemed they had forgotten the rituals and offerings, abandoned their faith and lost their sight.

A young man leaned against one of the bluestones, scrolling through his phone, heedless of the splendor around him. Cerridwen shrieked—a whispered thunder. The youth blinked but didn't look away from his phone. He had no faith, so did not hear.

The Goddess stalked past him, pulled deeper into the Void.

Giggling, a group of school children marched by, a double row of girls in tidy navy jackets and braided hair. Cerridwen peered at them. Once they would have each been tested to see who held the spark of the divine, which would have the honor of taking up novice white. Now they joked and teased one another, uninterested in anything but their girlish camaraderie.

A nymph bustled past, arms full of flowers. Her elbow knocked into Cerridwen's side.

"Excuse me, coming through."

The Goddess's eyes widened.

At the altar stone, a broad-shouldered figure with sun-kissed hair directed a crew of dryads. They hung garlands from the standing stones.

Apollo.

He turned and flashed a blinding smile at her. "Cerridwen. How nice to see you!"

In the background, a satyr played the pipes. The humans milled around, taking no notice of the hubbub.

*What are you doing here?*

The Sun God winked. "Hera has decided this old monument will make a lovely backdrop for an afternoon fete."

Cerridwen snapped her fingers. A wisp of darkness slithered across the sun, then burned away. She smoothed her features, not letting on that a hive of bees buzzed in her stomach.

*You violate the agreement. This is my temple!*

"The 'agreement' was that religious sites remain within pantheon control." Apollo threw back his head and laughed. "And this ruin? This is no longer a place of worship. It's nothing but a tourist trap."

The Goddess flexed, pulling on the Void. For a moment, the shadows deepened. They felt slippery in her grasp, like wriggling eels. She clenched her fists, nails digging into her palms.

The bright sun glared down.

Apollo quirked an eyebrow and pointed to a couple strolling among the stones, headphones on their ears. "The humans don't believe. And so, you no longer hold dominion here."

He turned his back and continued setting up for Hera's banquet, as if the conversation was over. Cerridwen's face grew hot as she watched the Greeks desecrating her temple. They zigzagged between the oblivious humans.

The Void dragged at her, whispering—you have no place here anymore.

Somewhere in the distance, The Dark Goddess heard a quiet voice singing. In the *Then* or in the *Now?* She listened, trying to find the source of the clear and strong contralto.

"Dark Mother, Bright Mother
By land, by sea, by midnight sky
Bright Mother, Dark Mother
May we be worthy in Your eyes."

A young woman paced slowly towards the altar stone. She wore jeans and a snowy white peasant blouse. Dark hair spilled loosely over her shoulders and her forget-me-not blue eyes sparkled.

Across the circle, Apollo froze, his shoulders stiff.

The girl's chanting trailed off, as she laid her offerings on the altar. A stalk of wheat. Three drops of whiskey. A handful of dried quinces. Exactly as those who came before her had.

Not all have forsaken me.

Cerridwen gathered the Void into herself and breathed out.

Overhead, a crow cawed. Vast, inky wings obscured the sun—an uncanny eclipse. Somewhere in the darkness, a dryad screamed. Time stilled.

*Begone, Apollo. You have no power here.* She raised her arms above her head and a gust of wind scattered the flower garlands. *Take your fete elsewhere.*

The Sun God waved his hand, but the darkness didn't yield. He grimaced, then gathered his people and disappeared into the aether.

At the altar, the young woman fell to her knees, eyes wide as she stared at The Dark Goddess.

Cerridwen stepped forward and laid a gentle hand on the novice's brow.

I am the Dark of the Moon, Great Mother, Lady of Inspiration and Death. This temple is mine, as long as one believes.

The End

# ABOUT THE AUTHORS

**Callie S. Blackstone** writes both poetry and prose. Her work appears or is forthcoming in *Plainsongs, Lily Poetry Review, Prime Number 53, West Trestle Review*, and others. Callie is lucky enough to wake up to the smell of saltwater and the call of seagulls everyday. You can find her online home at callieblackstone.wordpress.com.

**Hailey Piper** is the 2x Bram Stoker Award-nominated author of *The Worm and His Kings, Queen of Teeth, Unfortunate Elements of My Anatomy*, and other books of horror. She is an active member of the Horror Writers Association, with over seventy short stories appearing in Pseudopod, Vastarien, Cast of Wonders, and other publications. She lives with her wife in Maryland, where their paranormal research is classified. Find Hailey at www.haileypiper.com or on Twitter via @HaileyPiperSays.

**Stephanie Ellis** writes dark speculative prose and poetry and has been published in a variety of magazines and anthologies. Her longer work includes the novel, *The Five Turns of the Wheel* and the novellas, *Bottled* and *Paused*, both published by Silver Shamrock. Her poetry has been published in the *HWA Poetry Showcase Volumes VI, VII and VII*, Black Spot Books *Under Her Skin* and online at Visual Verse. She has also co-written a collection of found poetry, *Foundlings*, with Cindy O'Quinn based on the work Alessandro Manzetti and Linda D. Addison. She is co-editor of Trembling With Fear, HorrorTree.com's online magazine and an active member of the HWA. Steph can be found at https://stephanieellis.org and on twitter at @el_stevie.

**Christina Sng** is the two-time Bram Stoker Award-winning author of A Collection of Dreamscapes (2020) and A Collection of Nightmares (2017). Her poetry, fiction, essays, and art have appeared in numerous venues worldwide, including Fantastic Stories of the Imagination, Interstellar Flight Magazine, Penumbric, Southwest Review, and The Washington Post. Visit her at christinasng.com and connect @christinasng.

**Kenzie Lappin** is a writer with a bachelor's degree in creative writing. She is published or set to be published with short stories in Wizards In Space Literary Magazine, Cemetery Gates Media, and with Improbable Press.

**Kristin Cleaveland** writes horror and dark fiction, often exploring the dark side of the female experience. She has recently appeared in Ravens & Roses: A Women's Gothic Anthology and Blood & Bone: An Anthology of Body Horror by Women and Non-Binary Writers. Her fiction has also been included in Southwest Review, Black Telephone Magazine, The Crow's Quill, and more. Kristin has a master's degree in English and has worked as a writer, editor, and educator. Find her on Twitter as @KristinCleaves.

**Romy Tara Wenzel** lives on Melukerdee country, Tasmania, exploring mythology and ecology from an animist perspective. Her preoccupation is with liminal states: the spaces between becoming and unbecoming, wildness and domesticity, inter-species communication and ecstatic transformation. Recent publications include short stories in Dark Mountain, Hecate, Cunning Folk, and Folklore for Resistance.

**SJ Townend** has been writing ~~evil lies~~ dark fiction in Bristol for two years. She's currently putting together her first collection of speculative, dark fiction and horror stories, working title: SICK GIRL SCREAMS, and is looking for representation. SJ hopes her stories take the reader on a journey to often a dark place and only sometimes back again.

**Ruschelle Dillon** is a freelance writer whose efforts focus on the dark humor and the horror genre. Musings are on her blog, Puppets Don't Wear Pants, because…puppets don't. She is a contributor to The Horror Tree website, penning drabble and flash and a frequent interviewer of fellow authors. Her short stories have appeared in various anthologies. Her collection of short stories, Arithmophobia, published by Mystery and Horror LLC and her latest novella, The Stain, published by Black Bed Sheet Books are available across the www. She is a musician who attempts to entertain crowds with her husband and good friends in the acoustic band, The Dillon's. Her love of animals has filled her home with a small ark of cats and dogs who refuse to go out in the world and get real jobs so she can stay at home and write.

**Georgia Cook** is an illustrator and writer from London. You can find her work published in Baffling Magazine, Luna Station Quarterly, and Vastarien Lit, and shortlisted for the Bridport Prize and Reflex Fiction Award, among others. She has also written and narrated for the horror anthology podcasts 'Creepy', 'The Other Stories', and 'The Night's End'.

She can be found on twitter at @georgiacooked and on her website at https://www.georgiacookwriter.com/

**Ben Thomas** is a novelist and journalist who has lived in more than 40 countries. He is the founder and editor-in-chief of The Willows Magazine, which has been reprinted as a hardcover anthology; and of the weird-fiction anthology Tales From OmniPark, set at an enigmatic theme park in West Texas. As a reporter, Ben has written for Aeon, Scientific American, The Huffington Post, Discover Magazine, and many other outlets, covering topics from stone-age cannibalism to computerized brain mapping. He loves to tell stories from the frontiers of science, history, culture and the cosmos—and the points where all these fields intersect. Website: https://houseblackwood.net

Twitter: @WritingBen

**Arlene Burke** lives in Prince Albert, SK, Canada with her husband and dog. She is the mom to two grown children. She has a life long passion for reading and writing. Arlene is retired but active in her community through volunteering. She enjoys travel, cooking, baking, and hiking in the woods.

**H.R. Boldwood**, author of the Corpse Whisperer series, countless short stories, and Imadjinn Award finalist, is a writer of horror and speculative fiction. In another incarnation, Boldwood is a Pushcart Prize nominee and winner of the Thomas More College 2009 Bilbo Award for creative writing. Boldwood's characters are often disreputable and not to be trusted. They are kicked to the curb at every conceivable opportunity when some poor unsuspecting publisher welcomes them with open arms. No responsibility is taken by this author for the dastardly and sometimes criminal acts committed by this ragtag group of miscreants.

**M. Regan** has been writing for over a decade, with credits ranging from localization work to short stories, poetry to podcast scripts. Their soulful debut novella, "21 Grams," can be found on Amazon and Timber Ghost Press's website, while they can be found on Twitter and Facebook at @MReganFiction.

**Alyson Faye** lives in West Yorkshire, UK with her husband, teen son and rescue animals. Her fiction and poetry has been published in a range of anthologies, (Diabolica Britannica/Daughters of Darkness) on the Horror Tree, several Siren's Call editions, in Page and Spine, by Demain Press (The Lost Girl/Night of the Rider), in Trickster's Treats 4, on Sylvia e zine and The World of Myth. She has stories coming out in 2021 with Kandisha Press, Space and Time's July magazine and The Casket of Fictional Delights. Her work has been read out on BBC Radio, local radio, on several podcasts (Ladies of Horror and The Night's End) and placed in several competitions. She works as an editor for a UK indie press and tutors. She co-runs the indie horror press, Black Angel, with Stephanie Ellis. Their aim is to publish and promote women horror writers, from new voices to more established ones. She swims, sings and is often to be found roaming the moor with her Lab cross, Roxy. Twitter : @AlysonFaye2

**Ariana Ferrante** is a 23-year-old college student, playwright, and speculative fiction author. Her main interests include reading and writing fantasy and horror of all kinds, featuring heroes big and small getting into all sorts of trouble. She has been published by Eerie River Publishing, Soteira Press, and Nocturnal Sirens, among others. On the playwriting side, her works have been featured in the Kennedy Center American College Theater Festival, and nominated for national awards. She currently lives in Florida, but travels often, both for college and leisure. You may find her on Twitter at @ariana_ferrante

**Emily Sharp** is a British born New Zealand writer. She attends the University of Canterbury in Christchurch where she double majors in Classics and English, minoring in Anthropology. Her work predominantly centers around ancient civilizations; mythological figures, gods, goddesses, everyday life etc. She explores narratives and characters surrounding events of importance in the ancient world with a spiritual, religious and sometimes pseudoscientific twist. She writes with the aim to educate, speculate, intrigue and inspire.

**KC Grifant** is a New England-to-SoCal transplant who writes internationally published horror, fantasy, science fiction and weird western stories for collectible card games, podcasts, anthologies and magazines. Her writings have appeared in Andromeda Spaceways Magazine, Aurealis Magazine, Mythaxis Magazine, Unnerving Magazine, the Lovecraft eZine, Colp Magazine and others. Her short stories have haunted dozens of collections, including Field Notes from a Nightmare; We Shall Be Monsters; Shadowy Natures: Tales of Psychological Horror; The One That Got Away - Women of Horror Anthology; Beyond the Infinite: Tales from the Outer Reaches; Six

Guns Straight From Hell Volume 3; and the Stoker-nominated Fright Mare: Women Write Horror. In addition, she co-founded the Horror Writers Association San Diego chapter in 2016. Outside of creative writing, KC is an award-winning science writer, editor and communications professional who spent her childhood exploring ancient ruins in her family's hometown on Crete. For more information, visit www.KCGrifant.com or @kcgrifant.

**Lucy Gabriel** is a British poet who's enjoying working from home more than she expected. Her poems have appeared in Stories of Music Volume 2, Pantheon Magazine, and Space and Time Magazine. Her website, which is not updated nearly often enough, can be found at https://lucygabriel.weebly.com and she is on Twitter as @lucygabrielpoet.

**Gordon Grice's** horror stories have appeared in the Retro Horror (Anubis Press), The Cryptid Chronicles (DBND Publishing), and Not Far from Roswell (Pole to Pole Publishing). His nonfiction books include The Red Hourglass: Lives of the Predators and The Book of Deadly Animals. He lives in Wisconsin and online at Deadlykingdom.com.

**Lynne Sargent** is a writer, aerialist, and philosophy Ph.D. candidate currently studying at the University of Waterloo. They are the poetry editor at Utopia Science Fiction magazine. Their work has been nominated for Rhysling, Elgin, and Aurora Awards, and has appeared in venues such as Augur Magazine, Strange Horizons, and Daily Science Fiction. Their first collection, A Refuge of Tales is out now from Renaissance Press. To find out more, reach out to them on Twitter @SamLynneS or for a complete bibliography visit them at scribbledshadows.wordpress.com.

**Kim Whysall-Hammond** is a Londoner, who now lives in a small country town in Southern England. She has worked in Climate Science and in Telecommunications. Her poetry has recently been published by American Diversity Report, Two Rivers Press, Alchemy Spoon, Milk and Cake Press and North of Oxford. Her speculative poetry has been published by Star*Line, Andromeda Spaceways, Eternal Haunted Summer, Three Drops from a Cauldron, The Future Fire, Utopia Science Fiction and Kaleidotrope.

**Ed Blundell** worked as a teacher of English, a school inspector and as Director of Education for the town of Stockport. He has been widely published in the UK and US and tries to write poetry that people can understand and enjoy. He gave up searching for the meaning of life after discovering there wasn't one.

**Rose Biggin** is a writer and theatre artist based in London. Her short fiction has been published in anthologies by Jurassic London, Abaddon Books, Mango, NewCon Press and Egaeus Press, and made the recommended reading list for Best of British Fantasy. She is the author of Immersive Theatre & Audience Experience (Palgrave) and Shakespearean novel Wild Time (Surface Press). Find her on Twitter at @rosebiggin.

**Angela Acosta** is an emerging bilingual Latina poet and scholar from Florida. She won the 2015 Rhina P. Espaillat Award from West Chester University for her Spanish poem "El espejo". She is currently completing her Ph.D. in Iberian Studies at The Ohio State University where she studies the lives and works of early twentieth century Spanish women writers. Much of her scholarship and creative writing is driven by recovering stories of forgotten women throughout history and providing new poems, translations, and analyses of their work. Her work has appeared in WinC Magazine, MacroMicroCosm, Pluma, and The Stratford Quarterly.

Of Indian origin, **Sultana Raza's** poems have appeared in 100+ journals/anthologies, including Columbia Journal, The New Verse News, London Grip, Classical Poetry Society, Dissident Voice, and Poetry24. Her SFF credits include Vector (BSFA), Entropy, Columbia Journal, Star*line, Bewildering Stories, spillwords, Unlikely Stories Mark V, The Peacock Journal, Antipodean SF, impspired, Insignia Stories, World of Myth, Galaxy***2, File770, and in Fusion (BSFA) in future. Her fiction received an Honorable Mention in Glimmer Train Review, and has been published in Knot Literature, Coldnoon Journal, among others. She's read her fiction/poems in Switzerland, France, Luxembourg, England, Ireland, the USA, and at WorldCon2018, and CoNZealand 2019. Her creative non-fiction has appeared in numerous publications, including the Literary Ladies Guide, Literary Yard, Litro, and impspired. An independent scholar, she has presented papers related to Romanticism and Fantasy in international conferences.

**Gwynne Garfinkle** is the author of a novel, Can't Find My Way Home (2022), and a collection of short fiction and poetry, People Change (2018), both published by Aqueduct Press. Her work has appeared in such publications as Fantasy, Escape Pod, Strange Horizons, Uncanny, Apex, Mermaids Monthly, and The Deadlands. Follow her on Twitter (@gwynnega) or visit her website: gwynnegarfinkle.com.

**S.H. Cooper** is an award-winning horror author based in Florida. Her work has appeared in publications by Cemetery Gates Media, Burial Day Press, and her most recent novella, Inheriting Her Ghosts, is the launching title for the NoSleep Podcast's imprint, Sleepless Sanctuary Publishing. Find her online at www.authorshcooper.com or @MsPippinacious on Twitter.

**Gerri Leen** is a Pushcart-nominated poet from Northern Virginia who's into horse racing, tea, collecting encaustic art and raku pottery, and making weird one-pan meals. She has poetry published in Strange Horizons, Dreams & Nightmares, Polu Texni, NewMyths.com and others. She also writes fiction in many genres (as Gerri Leen for speculative and main-stream, and Kim Strattford for romance) and is a member of HWA and SFWA. Visit gerrileen.com to see what she's been up to.

**Miriam H. Harrison** writes among the boreal forests and abandoned mines of Northern Ontario, Canada. Driven by dark and fantastical possibilities, her writings vary between the eerie, the dreary, and the cheery. She is currently a member of the Horror Writers Association, SF Canada, the Canadian Science Fiction and Fantasy Association, and the Science Fiction and Fantasy Poetry Association. Updates about her published work can be found on Facebook (@miriam.h.harrison), Twitter (@MiriamHHarrison), or her website: (miriamhharrison.wordpress.com).

**Elle Turpitt** is a writer, reviewer and editor living in Cardiff, Wales. Her short fiction has appeared online, in various anthologies including Were-Tales and The Dead Inside, and on The NoSleep Podcast. She is co-editor of the anthology A Woman Built By Man and co-runs the website Divination Hollow Reviews. Her website is elleturpitt.com and she can be found on Twitter and Instagram, @elleturpitt.

**Louis Evans** maintains a healthy skepticism of heroes and poets. He was a co-founder of Rise, an organization fighting for the rights of sexual violence survivors, and of Cliterary Salon, a Bay Area feminist reading series. His fiction has appeared in Nature: Futures, GigaNotoSaurus, Translunar

Travelers Lounge and more; his nonfiction has appeared in Blood Knife and The Toast (RIP). He's online at evanslouis.com and tweets @louisevanswrite

**Allen Ashley** is a British Fantasy Award winner. He works as a developmental editor and creative writing tutor and is the founder of the advanced science fiction and fantasy group Clockhouse London Writers. He writes regularly for "Focus" - British Science Fiction Association journal - and the "BFS Journal" from the British Fantasy Society. His most recent book is the poetry collection "Echoes from an Expired Earth" (Demain Publishing, UK, paperback 2021 – also available on Amazon). Further details at: www.allenashley.com

**Carter Lappin** has a bachelor's degree in creative writing and is scheduled to appear in a number of upcoming publications, including anthologies with WorldWeaver and Dreadstone Press. She lives in California with her family and her cat. You can find her on Twitter at @CarterLappin.

**R. K. Duncan** is a queer polyamorous wizard and author of fantasy, horror, and occasional sci-fi. He writes from a few rooms of a venerable West Philadelphia row home, where he dreams of travel and the demise of capitalism. In the shocking absence of any cats, he lavishes spare attention on cast iron cookware and his long-suffering and supportive partner. Before settling on writing, he studied linguistics and philosophy at Haverford college. He attended Viable Paradise 23 in 2019. His occasional musings and links to other work can be found at rkduncan-author.com

**Henry Herz's** speculative fiction short stories include Out, Damned Virus (Daily Science Fiction), Bar Mitzvah on Planet Latke (Coming of Age, Albert Whitman & Co.), The Crowe Family (Castle of Horror V, Castle Bridge Media), Demon Hunter Vashti (The Jewish Book of Horror, Denver Horror Collective), Alien with a Bad Attitude (Strangely Funny VIII, Mystery and Horror LLP), The Case of the Murderous Alien (Spirit Machine, Air and Nothingness Press), Maria & Maslow (Highlights for Children), A Proper Party (Ladybug Magazine). He's written ten picture books, including the critically acclaimed I Am Smoke. Henry's edited three anthologies, including The Hitherto Secret Experiments of Marie Curie and Coming of Age. He loves his family, dogs, and Boston Creme Pie, in that order. https://www.henryherz.com @HenryLHerz on Twitter

**Avra Margariti** is a queer author, Greek sea monster, and Rhysling-nominated poet with a fondness for the dark and the darling. Avra's work haunts publications such as Vastarien, Asimov's, Liminality, Arsenika, The Future Fire, Space and Time, Eye to the Telescope, and Glittership. "The Saint of Witches", Avra's debut collection of horror poetry, is forthcoming from Weasel Press. You can find Avra on twitter (@avramargariti).

**Dominick Cancilla** lives in Santa Monica, California, with his wife and what some would consider too many reptiles. He is best known for his many short stories and for his most recent novel, Tomorrow's Journal. His non-literary artistic endeavors can occasionally be found on Instagram at @dcwaterboy.

**Lauren Eason** is the author of Witch Trials: Secrets of Loudun and her latest psychological thriller, Every Waking Dream. When she's not writing her latest dark fantasy or paranormal romance, she can be heard over the airwaves on her podcast, where she talks about publishing advice, writing tips, author interviews, and more! To give back to the indie author community, she runs an indie book club on her blog where she features fellow authors and their work every week. Hailing from Georgia, her hobbies include studying Norse, Celtic, and Greek mythology which often gives her ideas for new projects. She lives with her adoring husband and their two cats, who tend to make it into her stories as feline sidekicks. Her current project is a dark, fantastical trilogy with the first title, Brimstone, to be released in the fall of 2022.

Author Website: www.laureneason.com
Facebook: www.facebook.com/authorlaureneason
Twitter: www.twitter.com/LaurenEason478
Instagram: www.instagram/lady_rowan

**Deborah Markus** lives and works in Santa Monica with her spouse, a following of crows, and almost enough reptiles to keep her happy. Her LGBTQ/YA novel, The Letting Go, was published by Sky Pony Press. Kirkus described it as "wonderfully eerie and disorienting." She is currently working on her next novel and posting at Aphantastic Writer (aphantasticwriter.com), a blog about her autism, aphantasia, and other neurodiversities.

**Nupur Shah** (she/her) is pursuing her MA in English from New Delhi, India where she lives. Her writing can be found at Visual Verse, The POET Magazine, Planisphere Q. Her twitter address is @notyetposthuman.

Other work by **Mari Ness** appears in Tor.com, Clarkesworld, Uncanny, Lightspeed, Nightmare, Apex, Fireside, Mermaids Monthly, Nature Futures, Strange Horizons, and Daily Science Fiction. A tiny chapbook of tiny fairy tales, Dancing in Silver Lands, is available from Neon Hemlock Press; an essay collection, Resistance and Transformation: On Fairy Tales, from Aqueduct Press; and a poetry novella, Through Immortal Shadows Singing, from Papaveria Press. She tweets at mari_ness, and occasionally remembers to update her blog at marikness.wordpress.com.

**Alyssa Judson** grew up not far from the cornfields and farmlands of Nebraska, and fell in love with the written word early on. After graduating from the University of Nebraska - Lincoln with a degree in creative writing, Alyssa self-published many of her shorter works under the name Sarah Alyssa McCown. She enjoys the occasional cup of tea, but subsists on coffee and fiction. Alyssa lives in Lincoln, Nebraska while raising her son as a single mom and dancing in the rain on a regular basis.

https://facebook.com/SAlyMcCown/

**Sherri Cook Woosley** holds a master's degree in English Literature with a focus on comparative mythology from the University of Maryland. She's a SFWA member, and her short fiction has recently been published in Dark Cheer: Cryptids Emerging- Volume Blue, Thrilling Adventure Yarns 2021, and Once Upon a Dystopia: An Anthology of Twisted Fairy Tales and Fractured Folklore,. Her debut novel, WALKING THROUGH FIRE (Talos Press, 2018), was long-listed for both the Booknest Debut Novel award and nominated for Baltimore's Best 2019 and 2020 in the novel category. She lives with her family, including her own set of twins, in Maryland. Find her online at www.tasteofsherri.com, @SherriWoosley, and Instagram: Sherri.Woosley

**Regi Caldart** is a horror and magical realism writer based out of Western Pennsylvania, USA. Though by day an IT Program Manager, by night she spends her time advocating for accessible healthcare for all who need it, from women's health to ensuring safety net clinics are adequately stocked. Her writing can also be found on Divination Hollow Reviews where she shines light on media from LGBTQIA+, BIPOC, and femme creators. When not glued to the computer screen, she can be found working out in the gym or badly creating miniatures. The resident rabbits would also very much like it if she would feed them her houseplants already, as they are quite hungry.

**Susan McDonough-Wachtman** has been a burger-tosser, customer service rep, ad taker, curriculum developer, parent, reader, kayaker, gardener, and high school teacher. "Well written," "quirky sense of humor," and "doesn't fit a genre" are the comments she hears most about her books and stories. "Crabby Converse" is published in Fabula Argentea. "I Will Go Gently" appears in Metaphorosis. She lives on the coast in the Pacific Northwest with one cat and one husband. www.susanmcdonoughwachtman.net

**Kathleen Halecki** possesses a B.A. and M.A. in history, and a doctoral degree in interdisciplinary studies. Her work can be found in various anthologies including: Shadows in Salem: Wicked Tales from the Witch City; One Night in Salem; Midnight Rising: A Collection of Paranormal Tales; From a Cat's View Volume II, Shadow of Pendle, Tick Tock, Harvest, and Tainted Love. She has also drabbled in Curses and Cauldrons, Forest of Fear, Ancients, Forgotten Ones, and Hate. For a truly micro story she is also included in Nano Nightmares.

Descended from a family of book-lovers, **J. G. van Rossum** has always been obsessed with words and stories. She started writing at a young age - and has never quite stopped. As a Dutch writer, English is her second language, but it is the language she most often thinks, dreams, and writes in. All of her stories are touched in some way by mythology, and all share a sense of wonder. While she has been successful in writing contests in the past, Agnodike is her first published story.

**Alison Jennings** is a Seattle-based poet who taught in public schools before returning to poetry and submitting her work. She has additional experience as editor, journalist, tutor, and accountant. During the last three years, over 50 of her poems have been published internationally in numerous journals, including Burningword, Cathexis Northwest Press, Meat for Tea, Mslexia, Poetic Sun, The Raw Art Review, and The Write Launch. She has also won 3rd Place/Honorable Mention or been a semi-finalist in several contests.

Please visit her website at:
https://sites.google.com/view/airandfirepoet/home.

**Pamelyn Casto**, twice a Pushcart Prize nominee, has published feature-length articles on flash fiction in Writer's Digest (and in their other publications), Fiction Southeast, Writing World, Abstract Magazine, and OPEN: Journal of Arts & Letters. Her essay on flash fiction and myth appears in Field Guide to Writing Flash Fiction: Tips From Editors, Teachers, and Writers in the Field and her 8,000-word essay on flash fiction is included in the four-volume Books and Beyond: The Greenwood Encyclopedia of New American Reading. Her latest 5,000-word article is the lead essay in Critical Insights: Flash Fiction (2017). She is the author of Flash Fiction: A Primer and is senior associate editor for flash discourse at OPEN: Journal of Arts & Letters http://ojalart.com/

**Carey Oxler** has deep roots planted in her hometown of Kansas City. A recovering perfumer, jewelry designer, artist, and web developer, Carey has been riding out the Covid pandemic hermited in the woods with her family and her black cat, Solstice.

**MJ Pankey** is a history enthusiast and self-employed writing consultant at mjpankey.com, and host of the Augusta Writers Critique Group. She has been writing fiction since she was 12. Her muse is most inspired by ancient mythology, history, social and cultural conflict, and the intricacies of human psychology and behavior. She strives to create thought-provoking narratives and emotionally moving characters embodying these themes.

**Cindy O'Quinn** is an Appalachian writer who grew up in the mountains of West Virginia. In 2016, Cindy and her family moved to the northern woods of Maine, where she continues to write horror stories and speculative poetry. Her work has been published or is forthcoming in Shotgun Honey Presents Vol 4: RECOIL, The Shirley Jackson Award Winning Anthology: The Twisted Book of Shadows, Shelved: Appalachian Resilience During Covid 19 Anthology, Attack From The '80S Anthology, The Bad Book Anthology, Chiral Mad 5, HWA Poetry Showcase Vol V, Space & Time Magazine, Weirdbook Magazine, Nothing's Sacred Vol 4 & 5, Sanitarium Magazine, & others. Cindy is a two-time Bram Stoker Award Final Nominee. Her poetry has been nominated for both the Rhysling & Dwarf Star Awards. Member of

HWA, NESW, NEHW, SFPA, Horror Writers of Maine, and Weird Poets Society. You can follow Cindy for updates on:

Facebook @CindyOQuinnWriter, Instagram cindy.oquinn, and Twitter @COQuinnWrites.

**Erin Sweet Al-Mehairi** is an author, editor, journalist, advocate, and publicist with over twenty-five years of experience in communication fields. She has a bachelor's degrees in English, Journalism, and History and has been putting pen and eyes to paper for over thirty years. Breathe. Breathe. was her debut collection of dark poetry and short stories, which was reviewed as visceral, haunting, and evocative. She has poetry and short stories published in several anthologies and online magazines and was co-editor of a Gothic anthology Haunted are these Houses. She's working on completing several new poetry collections, two short story collections, an essay collection, and two novels. Born in England, she now mothers three busy young adults, a spoiled older cat, a teen cat, and three new kittens in a forest in Ohio while running her Hook of a Book business. She currently does various types of editing for authors, organizations, and businesses as well as limited public relations and consulting for authors and publishers. She also has written for several sites over the years, as well as for her own, where she hosts a mostly annual poetry project in April featuring many acclaimed poets as well as brand new writers. Find Erin at: website Oh, for the Hook of a Book!, Amazon, GoodReads, or social media.

**Ann Wuehler** has four novels out, Oregon Gothic and House on Clark Boulevard, Aftermath: Boise, Idaho and The Remarkable Women of Brokenheart Lane. A short story, Man and Mouse, appears in the April 2020 issue of Sun magazine. Her play, Bluegrass of God, is in Santa Ana River Review. Her short story, Jimmy's Jar Collection, appeared in the Ghastling's 13 and her The Little Visitors was in the Ghastling's 10. She has five stories placed with Whistle Pig, Maybelle, Bunny Slipper, Pearlie at the Gates of Dawn, Greenhorn and Elbow and Bean. City Full of Rain debuted in Litmag. Gladys, a short story, appeared in Agony Opera. The short story, the Elephant Girl, was in the September 2021's the Bosphorus Review. Pig Bait has been included in Gore, an anthology by Poe Boy Publishing, back in October 2021. The Witch of the Highway, a short story, appeared in the World of Myth in October 2021 as well. Blood and Bread will appear in Hellbound Books' Toilet Zone 3, the Royal Flush, due out in 2022. Lilith's Arm just got an acceptance from Bag of Bones, to be included in their 2022 Annus Horribilis anthology. The Salty Monkey Mystery, a short story, will also be published for a charity anthology.

**Marion Panizzon** is a lawyer working on migration and asylum protection. She has lived in Chicago, Durham NC and Washington DC and Oxford UK, before settling in Bern, Switzerland where she teaches law at different institutions of higher education and English as a second language to refugees. Her poetry experiments with the morphology of syntax and is inspired by metaphors from the natural world, including its transformation processes. She is drawn to Ovid, T.S. Eliot, W.B. Yeats and S. Plath. Marion has published in Tiny Seeds Literary Journal, Morphrog21, Poets Choice, The Swiss Poets Association annual calendars 2019, 2020 and her post-pandemic poetry collection 'locking down on larks' for In Parentheses.

**Artemisia Loesberg** is a mythology enthusiast and antiquity masters student who secretly still holds on to her old dream of becoming a writer. She enjoys the paper-writing (and research) part of a masters the most, and has not really stopped writing since that time she spent a year writing Percy Jackson fanfics. She enjoys reading greatly as well, although she does not manage to read nearly as much as she would like to. She is currently finally writing that story she has been developing since she was sixteen- which also has mythology as part of it, like nearly anything Artemisia writes.

**Claire Smith** explores other worlds in her writing; particularly the fairy tale, myth and folklore. Her work has most recently appeared in: Best of Penumbric Speculative Fiction Magazine (Volume IV, June 2k20 to April 2k 21); Illumen and Spectral Realms. She is working on a PhD, in Humanities, at the University of Gloucestershire. She lives in Gloucestershire, U.K. with her husband and their spoilt Tonkinese cat.
You can find her on the internet at:
http://www.divingfornightmares.co.uk;
Instagram @clairesdivingfornightmares;
Facebook @divingfornightmares.

**Kate Meyer-Currey** lives in Devon. A varied career in frontline settings has fueled her interest in gritty urbanism, contrasted with a rural upbringing, often with a slipstream twist. Since September 2020 she has had over a hundred poems published in print and online journals, both in the UK and internationally. Her chapbooks 'County Lines' (Dancing Girl Press) Cuckoo's Nest' (Contraband Books) are due out in early 2022. Instagram: DrKMC

**Marsheila (Marcy) Rockwell** is a Rhysling Award-nominated poet and the author of twelve books, dozens of poems and short stories, several articles on writing, and a handful of comic book scripts. She is an active member of SFWA, HWA, IAMTW, and SFPA. She is also a disabled pediatric cancer and mental health awareness advocate and a reconnecting Chippewa/Métis. She lives in the Valley of the Sun with her husband, three of their five children, two rescue kitties (one from hell), and far too many books. Here are my social media links:

Website: https://marsheilarockwell.com/
Blog: https://mrockwell.dreamwidth.org/
Twitter: https://twitter.com/MarcyRockwell
FB: https://www.facebook.com/MarsheilaRockwellAuthor

**T.L. Beeding** was born and raised in Sacramento, CA. She is co-editor of Crow's Feet Journal and Paramour Ink, and is a featured author for Black Ink Fiction. She has also written for October Hill Magazine, Vanishing Point Magazine, and The Black Fork Review, among other literary publications. When she is not writing, T.L. enjoys seeking misadventures with her daughter, two cats, and boyfriend at their home in the Hudson Valley. She can be found on Twitter at @tlbeeding.

**Louise Monroe's** background in the hedonistic arts, combined with deep studies in various forms of spirituality, has culminated in exquisite taste in tea, cookies, and friends (not necessarily in that order). She lives a fascinating life, spinning tales, watching birds, and drinking warm beverages. She leaves a trail of love in her wake, so if you're looking for her, listen for a lilting maniacal laugh and, follow the smirks, smiles, and love-filled sighs.

**Melody E. McIntyre** lives in Ontario, Canada and writes short, dark fiction. Her work has been published in several anthologies and online publications. She earned her Master's Degree in Classics and spent several years teaching Greek Myth and History. To this day, her passion for the ancient world remains and she often infuses her writing with elements of Greek mythology. In her spare time, she loves reading, embroidery and martial arts. My links:

Twitter: @evamarie41 Blog: melodyemcintyre.blogspot.com
Facebook: https://www.facebook.com/MelodyEMcIntyre

**MM Schreier** is a classically trained vocalist who took up writing as therapy for a mid-life crisis. Whether contemporary or speculative fiction, favorite stories are rich in sensory details and weird twists. A firm believer that people are not always exclusively right- or left-brained, in addition to creative pursuits Schreier manages a robotics company and tutors math and science to at-risk youth. Selected works, social media links, and a listing of publications can be found at: mmschreier.com

# ABOUT THE EDITORS

**Heather Vassallo**, co-founder of Brigids Gate Press, believes there are few things that can't be solved with tea, cookies, and a good book. Like nature, she abhors a vacuum. She enjoys reading a wide range of genres, but can't resist fairytales and gothic novels. She currently resides with her husband, son, and two horribly mischievous black cats under the vast prairie skies of the Midwest. She continues to believe the world is a place full of magic and wonder (and lost shakers of salt).

www.brigidsgatepress.com
Twitter: @BrigidsGate
Instagram: @brigidsgatepress

**S.D. Vassallo** is a co-founder and editor for Brigids Gate Press, LLC. He's also a writer who loves horror, fantasy, science fiction and crime fiction. He was born and raised in New Orleans, but currently lives in the Midwest with his wife, son, and two black cats who refuse to admit that coyotes exist. When not reading, writing or editing, he can be found gazing at the endless skies of the wide-open prairie. He often spends the night outdoors when the full moon is in sway.

www.brigidsgatepress.com
Twitter: @diovassallo and @BrigidsGate
Instagram: @s.d.vassallo
www.sdvassallo.com

# ABOUT THE ILLUSTRATOR

**Elizabeth Leggett** is a Hugo award-winning illustrator whose work focuses on soulful, human moments-in-time that combine ambiguous interpretation and curiosity with realism.

Much to her mother's dismay, she viewed her mother's white washed walls as perfectly good canvasses so she believes it is safe to say that she has been an artist her whole life! Her first published work was in the Halifax County Arts Council poetry and illustration collection. If she remembers correctly, she was not yet in double digits yet, but she might be wrong about that. Her first paying gig was painting other students' tennis shoes in high school.

In 2012, she ended a long fallow period by creating a full seventy-eight card tarot in a single year. From there, she transitioned into freelance illustration. Her clients represent a broad range of outlets, from multiple Hugo award winning Lightspeed Magazine to multiple Lambda Literary winner, Lethe Press. She was honored to be chosen to art direct both Women Destroy Fantasy and Queers Destroy Science Fiction, both under the Lightspeed banner.

Elizabeth, her husband, and their typically atypical cats, live in New Mexico. She suggests if you ever visit the state, look up. The skies are absolutely spectacular!

# CONTENT WARNINGS

One Thousand Nights for Beloved Medusa by Hailey Piper: self-mutilation.

**The Lamentation of Medusa** by Stephanie Ellis: implied rape and violence against women.

**Greek Tragedies by Kenzie Lappin**: rape, child abuse, domestic violence.

**Laborers Wanted by SJ Townend**: abuse, death, excessive graphic violence.

**The Strife Who Walks in Darkness by Ben Thomas**: death/dying, alcohol addiction, rape/sexual assault, self-inflicted harm, suicide.

**Requiescat by M. Regan**: death, murder, suicide, spiders, being bound/tied up.

The Quiet Rebellion of Arachne of Lydia by Ariana Ferrante: spiders.

**Three Fathers by Gordon Grice**: animal cruelty, child endangerment, death, violence, implied domestic abuse.

**Facing the Thousand Ships** by Kim Whysall-Hammond: implied rape, implied child death.

**Late Bloomer** by S.H. Cooper: bullying, death.

**Possession** by Elle Turpitt: implied abuse.

**and Eurydice by Louis Evans**: abuse, death/dying, kidnapping, suicide, self-inflicted harm.

**Atalanta Against Jove** by R.K. Duncan: death/dying, graphic violence.

**Unbreakable by Henry Herz**: child endangerment, off-screen rape/sexual assault, animal cruelty/death/abuse, death/dying.

**Catalogue of Fables** by Avra Margariti: abuse.

Izzy and Anti: A Tragedy in Texts by Deborah Markus: death.

**Unwanted by Regi Caldart**: sexual assault, pregnancy, childbirth.

**Agnodike by J.G. van Rossum**: mention of still birth, mention of death.

**Before Gods by MJ Pankey**: abuse, animal cruelty/death, child endangerment, death/dying, graphic violence.

Creators of Hysteria and the Triple Goddess by Cindy O'Quinn: abuse.

**Pomegranate Seeds by Artemisia Loesberg**: abuse, references to sexual assault, rape, kidnapping, arranged marriages, sexism.

# MORE FROM BRIGIDS GATE PRESS

We hope you enjoyed this anthology. Interested in what else we offer? Visit our website at: www.brigidsgatepress.com

Coming July 2022

Arthur, whose life was devastated by the brutal murder of his wife, must come to terms with his diagnosis of dementia. He moves into a new home at a retirement community, and shortly after, has his life turned upside down again when his wife's ghost visits him and sends him on a quest to find her killer so her spirit can move on. With his family and his doctor concerned that his dementia is advancing, will he be able to solve the murder before his independence is permanently restricted?

A Man in Winter examines the horrors of isolation, dementia, loss, and the ghosts that come back to haunt us.

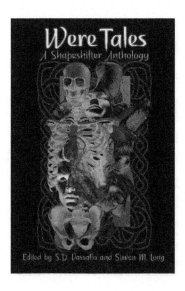

Available now on Amazon

Werewolves. Berserkers. Kitsune. From the most ancient times, tales have been told of people who transform into beasts. Sometimes they're friendly and helpful. Sometimes they're tricksters, playing jokes on their hapless victims. And sometimes, they're terrifying.

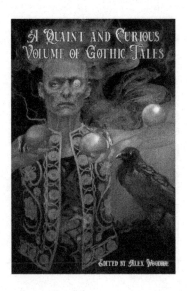

Available now on Amazon and Bookshop

*A Quaint and Curious Volume of Gothic Tales;* 23 stories of madness, pain, ghosts, curses, unspoken secrets, greed, murder, and one of the creepiest collections of dolls ever. Ranging from traditional gothic themes to more modern tropes, this anthology is sure to please the reader…and send a cold shiver or two down their spine.

So, come on in; enter the parlor, find a place by the fire, and experience the beautiful, dark, and occasionally heartbreaking stories told by the authors. The editor, Alex Woodroe, has passionately and carefully curated a powerful volume of stories, written by an amazing and diverse group of contemporary women writers.

Made in the USA
Coppell, TX
17 May 2022